THE GIRLS ACROSS THE BAY

EMERALD O'BRIEN

For Eileen
Kindred spirit, story-teller, poet, and great aunt.
And of course, for Brian too.
You bet your pretty neck I do.

CHAPTER ONE

"Strike two, Knox," Ornella Roth said, crossing her thin arms over her chest and leaning back in the chair behind her desk. "There's always something going on in Tall Pines to report on. When it seems like there's no news, you dig deeper. Thane's working under the same conditions you are, and his story about the boat thief down at the Marina made the front page."

"This is a *good* story." Madigan jabbed her finger onto the article on the desk. "I stand behind it one-hundred percent. Lower-income families can't afford the cost of school lunches, and the students of Tall Pines Elementary shouldn't have to feel ashamed of the fact they can't be served a hot lunch. There has to be some sort of subsidizing. This story needs to be told, Ornella, and it needs to be seen."

"I told you, I need *front page news*," Ornella said. "If you want to keep writing these human-interest stories, I'll put you back in the entertainment section."

Madigan clenched her jaw and stared down at her boss.

I need to keep my job. I need to keep my job, Madigan reminded herself.

Ornella pushed the article further away from her.

"Your writing could use some improvement as well, mind you. You need to keep your personal voice out of it. The media needs to be unbiased. How many times do I need to remind you of that? I can't have another article of yours where allegations are made and only one side of the story is considered—like that one about Tall Pines Nursing Home. You didn't even contact them for a comment."

Madigan's cheeks flushed, knowing Ornella had a point about her writing. The sting of criticism hit her hard, bringing back memories of the critiques on her last article. She had barely graduated from her journalism program at the local college, and if Ornella had bothered to check her marks, she might not have gotten the job at all.

She shifted her weight from one foot to the other and avoided eye contact.

The media is biased. Everyone is.

Don't say it. Don't say it.

"You show me front page news and I'll give you another chance," Ornella sighed. "But for now, you're back to the local entertainment section. Help Thane out when he asks. Got it?"

She didn't want to believe she'd been demoted purely based on her writing skills, or lack thereof. She found it easier to be angry at the politics of the *Tall Pines Gazette* and more specifically, Ornella Roth. She played to the politicians of Amherst, the neighbouring city, and ruffled the least amount of feathers while pushing their agenda.

"Fine." Madigan frowned. "But I'm taking my story to Cindy, right?"

Madigan had already promised her contact at Tall Pines Elementary she would bring the issue to light. The look on the lunch woman's face had almost brought tears to her eyes.

When she'd lived in her first foster home during the

worst years of her life, she'd often gone to school hungry. At the age of seven, she'd been more embarrassed than hungry. She pretended her foster mom had forgotten to pack her a lunch, opting to hide in the washroom, which kept her under the radar of both students and teachers more often than not.

"Ornella," Madigan said, "please?"

"Why bother?" Ornella asked, wiggling her mouse. The white glare of the computer screen illuminated her face, revealing the shadows of fine lines across her cheeks. "It's hardly news at all. It's a throw-away."

Ornella slid the papers Madigan had printed over the side of the desk, letting them fall into her trash can.

Madigan clenched her fists into balls, her heart pounding faster by the second while Ornella kept her eyes on the computer screen.

Those kids need help.

You need this job. You need this job.

Screw it.

"You've *got* to be kidding me." Madigan shook her head and walked backwards toward the door. "So much for bringing attention to what's *actually important* in this town. We wouldn't want to change anything, now, would we?"

"I sell papers people will actually read," Ornella said. "Not sad stories for the sake of depressing people or embarrassing the mayor."

An embarrassment. That's what she thinks it is. Like I'm airing dirty laundry.

"This isn't *an embarrassment*," Madigan said. "This is bringing some hard facts to light. This is a story the parents of Tall Pines will want to hear. I promised the lunch staff I would report on this."

"You know not to make promises when you haven't run something past me first. This whole story came out of left field. You were told to get me front page news."

There it was. She's upset it was something she had no control over. No guiding voice before the story had been written.

I shouldn't have made a promise.

But I did.

"What do I have to do?" Madigan asked.

Find the flaw, Madigan.

Her first foster father's words echoed in her mind through all the years after she and her sister had been taken from their house and split into different ones.

Find their weakness and use it to your advantage—one of the first things he'd taught them about manipulating people into doing whatever you wanted. He took advantage of their naivety and made it into a game at first, but when he brought them into their first cons, he expected them to use the tricks he had taught them.

It wasn't until her last year in the house that she realized he had done the same to them, and since, with each weakness she found, almost without trying, she'd note a strength, too.

"What do I have to do to make sure the story's included in Monday's issue?" Madigan asked. "It's important to those kids. No child should have to hide in the bathroom because they don't have a lunch."

Her cheeks burned as she folded her arms in front of her.

Maybe that'll tug on her heart strings as a mother.

Madigan had found motherhood to be Ornella's strength and weakness as soon as she found out she had a son.

"Get me something good." Her manicured nails clicked away at the keyboard. "Something that will keep our readers turning the pages. You've got until Sunday at midnight."

"I can do that."

What will make Ornella sit up and take notice?

A crime, maybe?

Something big. It has to be big.

"Go on, then," Ornella said.

"Thank you, Ornella."

"Make it good, Knox. This is your last chance."

"I will." Madigan walked backwards out the door.

"And fix the attitude," Ornella called, not bothering to look away from her computer screen. "And for Pete's sake, close the door behind you."

Madigan closed the door and marched down the hall as Cindy poked her head up from her cubicle.

"I think it's a good story," Cindy said in her mousy voice.

Madigan stopped in front of her. "You heard all that?"

Cindy shook her head, but Madigan raised her eyebrow with a smile, cocking her head to the side, and Cindy nodded, glancing in the direction of Ornella's office.

"Don't be afraid of her, Cin."

"I'm not," Cindy whispered.

"Those kids deserve better," Madigan said. "I made a promise. I'm going to do whatever it takes. Do you know of anything going on this weekend?"

Cindy shook her head. "I bet if Thane handed in that same story, it'd already be on my desk for edits for the front page."

"Probably." Madigan tapped her fingers along the cubicle divider. "I'll make sure she runs this story, then I'm back to covering craft fairs and store openings. It's just as well. Nothing ever happens around here anyway."

"Don't give up—on the kids *or* the front page. It might take some time, but she'll come around. You've got a great eye for detail, and you bring heart to this paper."

Madigan's cheeks flushed and the compliments made her even less comfortable than the criticism of her writing she'd just received. It would take days, maybe weeks, to put Ornella's words out of her mind.

Another writing class might do the trick.

"Okay, enough with the flattery," Madigan said. "It's tough to get to the story first when Thane's got the scoop."

"He has connections," Cindy said.

So will I, she thought, wondering how her sister's first day on the job was going.

Grace just needs to gain her confidence back.

"By the way, you actually picked a winner." Cindy smiled. "Roy was a gentleman, just like you said. A little rough around the edges, what with the cursing and all, but I'm letting him take me on a second date."

"I knew you'd like him."

"Thanks for setting us up," Cindy said, sliding her glasses on. "You were right, I just needed to get back out there."

"Ladies," Thane said in his deep voice as he strode past them toward Ornella's office. "Beat you for the cover again, Knox. Man, you make it too easy."

A tall black man, always dressed in one of three suits, Thane had ruled the front page for two decades. Probably longer.

"Some real hard-hitting journalism with that boat scandal," Madigan said, smirking.

Thane straightened his tie and ran his fingers over his smooth chin. "And yet it's good enough to beat whatever story you conjured up last minute."

He strode past them into Ornella's office and shut the door behind him.

If it had been a last-minute story, she wouldn't have felt so offended, but it had been her only focus that week.

"He's so smug." Cindy shook her head. "Ignore him. You'll get the front page, Madigan, and when you do, we'll have to stick it to him."

Madigan nodded and sauntered down the short hall toward her cubicle.

Does she really believe that?

"Hey, tell Roy he owes me some drinks for finding him a catch, alright?" Madigan said over her shoulder.

"Will do!"

As she plopped down in her chair, she stared at her cell phone on the desk.

I'm dying to know how it's going, but she won't be able to respond anyway.

She grabbed her phone and hit Grace's name, running her left finger along the chain of her necklace that matched Grace's.

Meet me at our spot when you're off she typed and sent the text.

Despite the short distance between them for more than a year when Grace went undercover in the city of Amherst, they had only spoken twice. Grace had told her the minimal contact was necessary, but Madigan always wondered if it had been her choice—if she couldn't keep her personal and professional lives separated without going all the way dark.

Madigan hoped Grace's new home and position would give her a fresh start in Tall Pines and a chance for them to reconnect.

For things to be like they used to be.

After what Grace had been through, she worried it wouldn't be possible, but she would try just the same.

CHAPTER TWO

G race took her first sip of coffee, flipping through the binder to the page that always made her heart skip a beat: the report her sergeant had completed on her.

As she skimmed the lines by the first light of morning, a shadowy crevice near the spine of the binder hid the first few words of each sentence.

It made no difference.

She could almost recite the report by heart.

She pushed her pillows behind her head, leaning back in bed.

Order for Detective Inspector Grace Sheppard to come back in disobeyed.

Special Detective Grace Sheppard accompanied Leah Culper to her apartment building on Bishop Street at 10:20 p.m. while Conrad Burke and his men were awaiting their large shipment.

Conrad Burke had exacted the order to kill his girlfriend, Leah Culper.

Special Detective Grace Sheppard dropped her off at St. Michael's hospital, stayed with her during her exam, and brought her back to her apartment to gather select belongings with the intention of bringing her into protective custody or getting her to a safe place that had not been authorized.

Nick Hill and Alex Parish attacked Leah Culper, chasing her toward Special Detective Grace Sheppard's vehicle. Three shots were fired by Hill before Sheppard left the vehicle and Parish aimed his gun at Leah Culper again.

The memory flashed before Grace's eyes. She set her coffee mug down on her nightstand before continuing.

Special Detective Grace Sheppard opened fire on Parish, killing him. Hill proceeded to fire one round, killing Leah Culper before Sheppard subdued Hill until authorities arrived.

Nick Hill later died in hospital.

Acting supervisor and lead investigator, Sgt. Bruno Colette, was not called by Special Detective Grace Sheppard, and his orders to come in were ignored. Sheppard knowingly ignored orders from her superior and endangered the case.

It is recommended that Special Detective Grace Sheppard be put on a mandatory, unpaid leave of absence for a period of no less than three months. During this period, she is ordered to attend therapy until written consent to return to work is granted by her therapist, whereby she be demoted to Deerhorn County upon her return.

Grace closed the binder and sighed before pushing herself off the bed. She crouched beside it and tucked the worn binder back under her spare throw blanket.

The report had been fairly accurate, and variations or excerpts had been passed on to any member of the law willing to listen—eager to know what happened the night they arrested Conrad Burke on more charges than she could remember—but the report didn't include everything that had happened.

Grace had lost so much of what she worked for all her life: a well-respected position on the force in the city and a reputation for being an intelligent and reliable detective.

She would work as hard as she needed to gain it all back, and she'd play by the book no matter what.

But nothing will bring Leah back, Grace thought.

Reading the report reminded her that regardless of the effort she put forth, the most heartbreaking loss could never be reversed or changed.

As she entered the small police department of Tall Pines, an officer at the front desk escorted her to the chief's office.

"Detective Sheppard, pleased to have you with us," he said, extending his meaty hand to her. "Police Chief Paul Banning. You can call me Chief or Banning, like most do around here."

Grace shook his hand, appreciating his firm grip, and he gestured for her to take a seat. She sat down and he sat behind his desk after her.

She'd never once seen her first foster father, the one she shared with Madigan, shake a man's hand, or woman's, for that matter. Her second and final foster parents had taught her the importance of a good one.

"How are you liking Tall Pines?" he asked. "You moved back about a month ago, right?"

"I've found it peaceful," she said, lying. "Big difference from Amherst."

The town had always seemed idyllic to her since childhood, but the mature trees, beautiful coast, and smaller population had yet to bring her their promising sense of calm.

Banning released a hearty chuckle and nodded. "If that's a nice way of saying you're in the boonies, you don't have to be polite here. You'll find all the surrounding towns in Deerhorn just the same if you haven't already. It's a slower pace out here, but that can be a good thing."

For someone like me, right?

"I look forward to learning the ropes."

"You'll catch on quickly, I have no doubt. Now I don't want to pretend there isn't an elephant in the room, because there is, but once we address it, I'm happy to move on."

Here we go.

She clenched her jaw and nodded, giving him the permission he didn't need to air her shame.

"I've been filled in on the details of your last case," Banning said, clearing his throat. "I've been told the whole take down wouldn't have been possible without you, but I understand there was an issue with procedure at the end of your time undercover. I need to know you'll follow procedure here working with the Tall Pines department in co-ordination with the others in the county."

"Of course," Grace nodded.

I'll never make the same mistake.

"I have a good feeling about you, but I run a tight ship here. It's nothing fancy like what you're used to, but we do things by the book, and we don't have any issues. Can I count on you to follow my orders, Sheppard?"

"Yes, sir."

Maybe he's willing to give me a clean slate.

"Good," he said. "Well, you've been cleared for duty, and I'd like you to start right away by meeting my right-hand man, Officer Adam MacIntyre. He'll let you know about the current ongoing investigation he's working on and fill you in on anything else you'll need to know about the Tall Pines PD. He must be running late. Traffic."

In Tall Pines? Doubt it.

Grace nodded and folded her hands in her lap, keeping perfect posture, as Banning leaned back in his chair.

"So," Banning started, and Grace tried not to wince.

Not small talk...

"You live up on Rosebank Drive. Right by the ocean there?"

"Yes, sir," she smiled, lifting her chin. "My property backs onto the coast."

That particular spot had held special meaning since she was a child living in Amherst and dreaming with her sister of living across the bay in the quiet town of Tall Pines.

"And you live alone, then?"

"Yes, sir."

Why was he asking when he already knew?

"Well, it's a great spot." Banning nodded and shifted in his seat as an uncomfortable silence grew between them. "You should help yourself to a cup of coffee."

A knock on the door gave them reprieve, and without waiting for a reply, it wooshed open. A man with warm brown hair and a wrinkled uniform stopped just inside the doorway.

"Ah, shit. Right," he muttered, his gruff voice filling the room as he glanced from Grace to Banning.

"This is Officer Adam MacIntyre." Banning stood and Grace followed. "This is DI Grace Sheppard."

"Right." He nodded, switching his Styrofoam coffee cup to his left hand and extending his right. "Just call me Mac."

His warm hand barely held hers. She went in with a firm grip and shook his once before he let go.

Not a good sign.

"I heard from Brooks," Banning said. "That's the Chief up in Torrance. He says we've got her 'til they need her. I've told Sheppard you'll fill her in on your current investigation and answer any questions she has."

"Sure thing, Chief." He smiled and took a sip of his coffee. "Hey, are you up for a round this Sunday?"

"You know it," Banning said, before returning to his seat. "Seven good for you, Mac?"

"See you there." He pointed to him and strutted out of the office without giving Grace a second look.

She followed Mac out into the hallway.

"Rhonda," he called to the officer at the front desk, "I'll be back for lunch. Could you get a fresh pot on before then?"

"Put your own on, Mac," Rhonda called to him as he passed her on his way to the door. "Get *me a cup* while you're at it."

As Grace caught up, she nodded to Rhonda, who smiled watching Mac leave.

"He's a handful," Rhonda laughed. "Good luck."

I should introduce myself, but I don't have time. I have to keep up.

Grace jogged to the front door before it swung shut, and took long strides to catch up to him.

"So you have an investigation in the works?" Grace asked, as he unlocked his patrol car.

"Two low-lifes going door to door posing as firemen," he said before getting in.

She strode to the passenger side and joined him.

"They're casing homes, using the guise of inspecting folks' fire detectors." He started the car. "Two white males, aged twenty-five to thirty-five."

"So we're tracking possible routes they may be taking? I assume you've spoken to the people who called in the suspicious behavior?"

He pulled out of his spot and waved to an officer walking toward the station. Grace waited for an answer as he turned left and drove out of the parking lot.

"Where are we headed?" she asked.

"I'm taking you to interview a witness," he said, turning up his radio.

Not a talker. Got it.

He turned onto the main strip of town, and not long after, they turned into the small parking lot of a diner.

The Big Spoon. He's getting breakfast.

Jerking me around.

He parked and opened his door, but she stayed in her seat.

"Not joining me on the investigation?" he asked.

Don't fall for it.

"I already ate," she said without looking at him.

Play it cool.

"Suit yourself, Sheppard."

He slammed the door shut and jogged to the diner door. He left the foam coffee cup in his holder between them—a cup with a spoon logo that matched the diner's.

He's been here already this morning. What's he up to?

Don't get on his bad side. Get in there.

She spotted him through the large glass window, sitting at the counter and speaking with the man behind it. After yanking open the heavy front door, the greasy smell from the grill and fryers filled her nose. Saliva formed in her mouth, and she took smaller breaths.

As a vegetarian, she found meat disgusting, but the old familiar smells still made her mouth water.

"Who's this?" the man behind the counter asked as she took a seat beside Mac.

Mac shrugged and shook his head, chuckling. "No, I'm just fooling with you. Terry, this is Detective Grace Sheppard."

"Ooh," the man laughed. "*Detective.*"

"I'm his new partner," Grace smiled. "Cup of tea, please?"

"Terry knows I work alone," Mac said, tapping the counter with his palm.

"Bagels." Terry slid a brown bag toward Mac. "Her favourite. I got one in there for you too."

"You remembered to let her know I'm bringing her breakfast, right?"

Terry nodded. "Those buggers practically pushed right by

her, Mac. Went into every room and she followed them helplessly."

"We'll get 'em. I need you to make that call about the alarm system, alright?"

"Used to be we could leave our doors unlocked." Terry shook his head and grabbed a foam cup from the stack behind the counter.

"I know. But this is for Martha, alright?"

"Thanks for lookin' out, Mac," Terry said, tossing a tea bag into the foam cup. "She'll feel better after talking to you."

"Don't mention it," Mac said, standing. "See you tomorrow."

He strode away, and Grace stood from her seat.

"You coming?" Mac called, just before the door swung shut.

"I'll take a rain check on that tea," Grace said.

Terry chuckled and shook his head.

She dashed out the door and got in the car as Mac turned the key in the ignition.

"We're not partners," Mac said before pulling out of the spot.

"For now, we're working together."

"I know what happened in Amherst."

Throw it in my face. Go ahead. You can't say anything I haven't heard.

Grace shook her head. "You don't know everything."

"I know enough not to trust you," he said.

Maybe you shouldn't.

She sat in silence, running her tongue along the inside of her bottom teeth.

Rebutting only made it worse in Amherst. There would be no difference here.

"I've never been to a shrink," he said, "but I bet they tried to make you feel like it wasn't your fault."

"I don't want to talk about it."

"I mean, your contact was killed right in front of you. You disregarded orders," he said. "It was almost over, and you couldn't stay out of the way."

Grace felt her cellphone vibrate in her pocket and checked it, pretending not to listen to him.

Meet me at our spot when you're off.

Grace sighed and started to type an excuse.

She had been able to keep Madigan at a safe distance during her therapy in Amherst, but since moving to Tall Pines, her sister had been more insistent on getting together, on figuring out what happened while Grace was away.

Looks like it'll be a long one, she typed.

"I'm taking you along here as a favour, but tomorrow you're on your own. Do some paperwork or something," Mac said. "Don't know why Banning agreed to bring you in. Guess he didn't have a choice."

Grace kept her head down, wanting to tell him off. To tell him he didn't know jack about her assignment, but making enemies right away wasn't smart.

A little voice of doubt always found a way to creep inside her thoughts.

Give up on the fresh start. It's impossible. Do the best with what you have.

Do better.

So far, from what she'd gathered, Mac's weakness was that he saw things in black and white. Right and wrong. Not to mention his cocky demeanor.

See you at eight. Bring alcohol, she typed and sent the text to Madigan.

Mac was quiet for the rest of the drive.

Just for you, Madigan, I'll come up with a strength, too. Mac's strength is that he knows how to shut up.

She tried not to look at him and stared out her window.

Be professional. Focus on the job. Show him he can't break you.

After her shift, she'd need a drink with the only person in the world who still thought she was a good person.

She grabbed the pendant of her necklace that matched Madigan's and twisted it back and forth.

That's because she doesn't know.

And Grace would keep it that way.

She couldn't lose Madigan.

CHAPTER THREE

Madigan squeezed the folded lawn chairs under her arm, dragging her small cooler through the sand toward the large rock nestled into the face of a short cliff.

They had claimed the spot as their own the year they met, both seven. The year they became sisters—not by blood—but by the bond they shared as misfits. Two innocent children, forced into a new life filled with manipulation, abuse, and desperation.

So desperate that on Grace's eighth birthday, Madigan hatched a plan to run away together.

Their foster mom, Evette, promised Grace they would take the ferry across the bay into the small town of Tall Pines and spend the night riding all the rides and eating all the treats they wanted at the summer fair.

The plan almost fell through after they'd disappointed Eli, their foster father, by failing one of his missions, but after he left for the night, no doubt on one of his benders, Evette kept her promise and brought them to the fair.

Without a destination in mind, only knowing they wanted to get as far away from home as possible, they slipped away from Evette through the metal gate. Following the long row of tall pines toward the coast, the hum of the crowds faded as they reached the water's edge and settled on the rocky shore that summer night.

It had been their first time seeing the ocean up close, and Madigan often compared the crashing waves and bubbling water along the shoreline to her own feelings about that night.

They were lost and scared.

Finally, free.

And together.

Madigan dragged the cooler closer to the flat rock, squinting to focus on the port for the ferry in the far-off distance across Bones Bay. Little lights sparkled further up the coast along the shore-line from tiny houses they'd seen from their bedroom window in Amherst, looking out across Bones Bay, while dreaming of living in Tall Pines with a family who loved them, or at least didn't hurt them.

They dreamed of living the lives of the other little girls at the fair who sat on their father's shoulders or tugged at their mom's leg, pointing to what they wanted next.

The little girls from Tall Pines had everything they wanted.

When Grace told Madigan she'd been relocated to Deerhorn County, Madigan was thrilled to learn they would be living in the same place again. To have her close. To have the ability to see each other anytime they wanted. But there had been a sadness in Grace's voice that day and ever since, so it still came as a beautiful surprise when Grace announced she'd purchased a place on Rosebank Drive, less than half a kilometer away from their spot.

She had chosen a small white beach house on the corner of the street with a beautiful rose garden along the L-shaped walkway leading to a blue front door. With a backyard that overlooked the ocean, a short walk away from their special spot, she'd made their dream come true in her own way.

Madigan wanted to make it a special kind of homecoming.

She spun around in a circle, finding the exact spot they'd taken refuge that summer night, and unfolded the two chairs beside it. She pushed the small cooler in front of them, opened it up, and plunked an icy beer bottle down into each of the chair's drink holders.

A shadowy figure stumbled down the short rocky footpath from Rosebank Drive toward her.

Grace's long strides would have given her away had Madigan not expected her. Her long raven-black hair blew in the breeze across her face, and as she kicked sand up behind her with each step, she tucked her hands in her dress pant pockets.

"I knew you'd do something like this." Grace smiled as Madigan dropped into her chair and cracked open a beer.

"You said bring alcohol." Madigan held the beer up high before pressing it to her lips and taking a sip.

"I know, but we could have just sat on the rock like we always do."

Grace sat beside her and pulled her bottle from the holder. As she leaned back, her hair blew across her face, and she pulled it away, sighing.

"Rough first day?" Madigan asked.

"Nothing I didn't expect." Grace cracked open the beer and took a sip, sighing afterwards. "It's beautiful."

"The water?"

"Everything," Grace said, and her eyes glazed over.

"Grace? You okay?"

Graced nodded and took another sip.

Madigan wanted to prod further, but in the weeks since

Grace had moved back, she'd learned not to pry. It only made her withdraw into herself more.

She'd managed to figure out the relocation had been a demotion, and that whatever had happened to Grace while she was undercover in Amherst rivaled the trauma they'd faced together as children.

Or maybe it was worse.

Shivers crept up Madigan's spine, sending chills across her arms. Waves rocked up the shore and rolled back toward the ocean again several times before Grace spoke.

"It reminds me of you," she said.

"The ocean?" Madigan asked, pulling her sweater on, zipping it up.

Grace nodded.

"It reminds me of you, too." Madigan took another sip. "I was remembering the night we found this place."

"I was crazy to let you drag me out here," Grace laughed, the sound drowned out by the crashing waves.

Even without makeup, Madigan thought Grace was one of the most beautiful women she had ever known. Naturally beautiful—something Madigan had never felt.

As much as she never felt like she fit in, Grace's appearance—part aboriginal and part Caucasian, both of unknown lineage—set her apart before anyone could even get to know her. Teachers in school would ask Grace questions like what are you, or why did you leave the reserve?

At least I can blend in. Go unnoticed.

"You didn't even know where we were going."

Madigan shrugged. "It was a good night. The perfect night."

"It was my favourite birthday," Grace said, staring out at the waves.

Madigan turned to her with a grin, ready to make a joke

about how mushy she'd been but decided to let the moment linger.

She looks peaceful.

"Cheers to being back," Madigan said.

They clinked their bottles together and drank.

"I was remembering how we fell asleep," Grace said. "You remember when we woke up and heard them calling, we thought we were going to jail?"

Madigan nodded. "Eli always warned us if we didn't do as he said, we'd go to jail. That's terrifying for a kid."

"The police came right down there." Grace pointed to the rocky pathway she'd walked down.

"And Evette was waiting up there for us with open arms, you remember?" Madigan pointed to the ledge they'd both come from, by Rosebank Drive.

"She was crying. She was faking it." Grace leaned back in her chair.

"I don't think she was."

Grace shrugged. "I think she knew if she didn't find us, Eli would know she took us out against his wishes. She wasn't even mad at us when we returned home. Do you remember that?"

"I remember she told us never to leave her again." Madigan clenched her jaw remembering the beating they'd each gotten the night before. They'd been given a mission to collect money from one of the richest neighbourhoods in Amherst for their supposed girl scout troupe, or some organization young girls collected money for. Eli changed the charity each time.

They'd both gotten tired, and Madigan pitched a fit in front of one of the houses.

When they returned back to the house, they each received their first bad beating from Eli, because they hadn't followed through or hadn't collected enough money.

They were too young to remember, but whatever the reason, they both had trouble sitting for the week after. Madigan had tried to fight him off, ending up with an extra beating too.

"She knew if she was caught bringing us the to the fair, she'd get a beating worse than ours," Madigan said.

"Eli knew the police wouldn't follow up with us," Grace sighed. "No matter how many marks or bruises, they really bought the whole kids-will-be-kids line."

"When he beat us the night before the fair—"

"Can we talk about something else?" Grace asked, putting her feet up on the cooler, knocking sand from the bottom of her shoes onto the top of it. "Damn."

"Like?"

"How was *your day*?" Grace asked. "Anything exciting going on in this town I don't know about?"

"Business as usual. Unless you know of anything?"

Grace shook her head.

She'd been careful not to burden Grace with any of her own problems since she came back, and after the rough day she guessed Grace had, she wanted to lighten the mood.

"I set up our chief editor, Cindy, with the owner of Roy's Tavern."

"Roy?"

"Right, and looks like I might have a talent for matchmaking."

"Oh yeah?" Grace asked. "And speaking of, how's *your match*?"

After Grace came back from her undercover job, she seemed shocked to hear Madigan not only had a boyfriend, but that they'd moved in together. After hearing about him, she'd run his name through whatever system they had at the department, disappointed to report back that he was clean. According to her, that meant trouble—until she met Will soon after she moved in. He could win over even the toughest critics.

"He's good," Madigan nodded. "At the hospital a lot."

"I know what it's like to work crazy hours." Grace set her beer back in the holder. "Do you two see each other a lot?"

Madigan nodded. "It's nice. He does his whole trauma surgery thing, and I have time to do my *investigative reporting*. Then, when we're together, we get to relax a bit or do something fun."

"Like English horseback riding?" Grace asked and stifled a chuckle.

Madigan shot her a look. "It's good to try new things, and it was Will's turn to pick."

"I know. You're more of a western girl though. I'm surprised he didn't choose that style."

"His parents are members of the country club, and they get free lessons. Plus, Will doesn't know me as well as you do. We've only been together... six months. Or is it eight?"

"Okay, okay. Any progress on getting closer to that front page?" Grace asked.

In other words, why haven't I made the front page yet? Change the subject.

"Oh, actually, about Will. He texted to tell me he has some good news for me, so we'll see what that is. I bet he got a promotion."

"Another one?"

"Everyone at the hospital loves him," Madigan said. "I bet they're trying to hold on to a good thing."

"And how about you?" Grace asked, turning to her. "Are you finally doing the same?"

Madigan sighed and took a swig from her bottle. She wondered if Grace was alluding to the fact she'd never been with any guy for long or any job for too long.

Probably both.

But she'd seen better days at the paper when she'd first started, and ever since Grace had implied there must be something wrong with Will, Madigan had tried to find his imperfections, as she always inevitably did.

"You're doing good," Grace said. "I'm proud of you. You really seem like you have it together, you know?"

Madigan had never done a good job of fooling Grace. They had both been trained with the same manipulation techniques, and they knew each other better than anyone.

Or they used to.

Grace hadn't paid attention to the way Madigan's smile faltered when she asked how her day was. How Madigan drank to avoid answering whether or not she was really trying to hang on to the life she'd built since Grace left to go undercover for over a year.

"Better than my usual hot mess, huh?" Madigan smiled.

"Well, I just meant—since Drew, you know?"

The smile slipped from her lips as she nodded, pretending to agree, and losing focus as she glanced out at the ocean.

It's been ten years. No, eleven. How? How could you be gone for that long?

Tears filled her eyes as the wind swept her hair across her face.

I miss ya, Drew.

"I'm sorry I brought it up," Grace whispered, and Madigan shook her head, although she was sorry too. "He was a great guy."

Madigan nodded, pressing her lips together to keep them from trembling.

"Have you heard from your parents?" Grace asked.

Madigan shook her head.

Her adoptive parents, the Knoxes, had bought a summer home in Florida a year after their son—her brother—Drew's death. They needed to get away from the things that

reminded them of him—that was what they told Madigan—
but she knew the truth.

They wanted to get away from her.

After she and Grace had been taken from Eli and Evette
and split apart, she felt so lucky to have been sent to the
Knox family. To become one of them and feel like she
belonged—even if something had always and would always
be missing.

The Knoxes weren't perfect, but she didn't know a family
who was.

Grace's next foster parents never adopted her or showed
her much affection. Nothing like the bond Madigan
developed with her new brother, Drew.

You're lucky, she would remind herself every day—until
the accident.

They had gone on a family camping trip, and while out
on their kayaks, away from their parents, Drew's had flipped
over. The current had carried him away, drowning him
before Madigan could reach him.

"It kind of felt like I had a brother, too," Grace whispered.
"I loved coming to stay with you guys. He'd be proud of you."

Grace's phone rang, the bleeping notes faint over the
crashing waves.

"I have to take this," she said, bringing the phone to her
ear. "Sheppard."

Madigan played with the loose material hanging from the
arm of her chair as she sniffled back her tears.

*How could he be proud of me? If he saw me now and knew
what Mom and Dad thought of me...*

She tucked her hair behind her ear and turned to her
sister. Grace frowned and stared down at the rocks.

Something's wrong.

* * *

"We've got a possible homicide down near the subdivision by Thornhill," Banning said, and Grace pressed the phone against her ear. "I'm sending you the address now. Get down here."

"Yes, sir," Grace said. "I'm on my way."

As she turned to Madigan, her long highlighted hair blowing in the wind across her face, her heart sank a little, wishing they could have sat together a while longer.

"This town's not as quiet as it seems," Grace said, standing from her chair.

"What is it?" Madigan asked.

Grace shook her head. "Can't say. I'm sorry, I have to go."

Her heart thudded harder. Faster.

I have to go now. I have to show them I'm reliable.

"I totally understand," Madigan nodded, her blue eyes staring up at her as she pulled on her faux leather jacket. "We'll catch up later."

"Thanks for this," Grace said, zipping her jacket up.

"Anytime." Madigan nodded and stood.

She never wore much colour, and her rocker chic style hadn't changed much since high school. While she had sometimes swapped out her black combat boots for sexy black ankle boots, rocker t-shirts and black nail polish had remained fashion staples for Madigan.

Grace waved goodbye and jogged back up the beach toward the small rocky pathway.

"It's not a real first day on the job unless there's a murder," Grace muttered to herself as she backed out of her driveway.

It was just as well. She hadn't sat beside her sister for more than a minute before the beautiful moment had been filled with guilt, the guilt she felt that Leah would never get to see the ocean again, or spend time with her own sister, or any of her family.

Why didn't I leave it alone?

The question seemed simple, but the answer proved to be complicated. She had spoken to her therapist about it on multiple occasions, and she must have given the right answer, because she was approved for work again.

Leah Culper had been the contact chosen for Grace by the undercover unit, and they made fast friends right away—not only because Grace had the advantage of knowing an incredible amount of information about her—but because Leah surprised her.

Leah hadn't just been the girlfriend of the Drug King of Amherst. She was an artist. A friend. A doting daughter. Most of all, a protective sister who'd do anything for her sibling.

The thing that connected them from the beginning had been something Leah never knew they had in common. Leah's strength and weakness had been doing everything with all her heart.

The trick Eli had taught Grace at a young age was something she'd later been trained to use as a detective. The most important part of her undercover assignment had been to exploit Leah, but her boyfriend, Conrad Burke, had been doing a better job of it before Grace came along. He'd abused her emotionally in front of everyone and physically behind closed doors. After more than a year of watching them together, Grace knew Leah would never leave him on her own.

And that's why she'd done what she did.

Leah's death rested on Grace's shoulders, and although the weight had been almost too difficult to bear at times, she carried it because she needed to carry it.

Simple as that.

Every time something good happened, she reminded herself what a terrible person she was for what she'd done and that she didn't deserve anything good.

It made it easier to take the painful remarks from her colleagues after she came back in, the intense glares, and finally, the demotion she'd received to move from the city to Tall Pines.

I got what was coming to me.

The only thing left to do was work her way up again. It was the only way she could think of to atone for her mistake.

As she turned down the short country road with only three houses, an ambulance and two police cars sat in front of the first house on the right. She knew who the first car belonged to before she could even read the plate. Chief Banning must have called her after realizing Mac was on the scene and hadn't followed his orders to fill her in.

As she parked behind Mac's car, some movement across the street caught her eye: a neighbour peeking through her curtains.

What have you seen tonight?

As she walked up the long driveway, she passed an officer with a roll of yellow caution tape.

"Mac inside?" she asked.

"Sheppard?" the officer asked. "He said you'd be late. Young woman in her mid-twenties. Head injury and she bled out. Mac's waiting for you in the kitchen with the vic's fiancé. He's the one who found her."

"Thanks," Grace said, and strode along the path toward the front door.

No distinguishable marks along the path, and no visible signs of forced entry at the front window or door.

She stepped inside, and a bright red puddle on the taupe living room carpet caught her eye. Deep voices carried down the hallway, and she pulled on a pair of gloves before taking a step from the hardwood hallway onto the plush carpet in the living room.

Red roses and petals lay scattered around a blonde

woman, her hair dyed red by the blood, and her body sprawled out like she'd fallen, or been pushed down.

As she crouched, light from the lamp reflected off a piece of glass. The rest of the broken glass vase had rolled under the living room table. Another glint caught her eye: a diamond engagement ring.

The floral perfume of the roses mixed with the metallic smell of blood turned her stomach.

The cycle of abuse. Apologies made. Promises broken.

After Eli beat Evette bad enough to make her bleed, red roses were sure to follow the next day. She'd put them in her painted vase and sit them on the windowsill, admiring them as she did the dishes each night.

She'd cry when he beat her and again when he brought the roses.

Before they could wilt, they'd be at it again.

"Sheppard?" Mac called from down the hall, shaking her out of her daze, and she stood.

No ripped clothing. No blood on the vase.

Where's the M.E.?

She stepped back into the hallway, her heels clicking against the hardwood, and walked toward a bright light in the kitchen. No picture frames hung on the walls, but a wooden sign hung above the entry to the small country-style kitchen.

Home is where the heart is.

The clichéd quote had always resonated with her.

She entered the kitchen where a man at least a few years older than herself sat at the small round table. His button-up shirt hung loose over his front and tight around his toned upper arms. His sleeves had been rolled up and tattoos covered his forearms, stopping at his watch. A hint of grey hair through the dark locks at the sides of his head made her reconsider his age.

Mac leaned back against the marble island with his arms crossed over his chest.

"I'm Detective Inspector Sheppard." She turned to the man.

"John Talbot," he said, leaning back in his chair.

"Mr. Talbot," Mac said, "please tell us what happened tonight."

Grace pulled a wooden chair out from the table and sat opposite John before taking out her phone and hitting record.

"I just—" John started, resting his hands on the table, and turning to Mac. "Could you *please* just look into him?"

"I'll be having a word with everyone who might be able to shed some light on what happened here tonight."

"I told you, I just got here, and she ..." Tears slid down John's tanned cheeks, and he shook his head.

"Before then," Grace said.

"I came home from work tonight at about seven."

He stared down at his dry hands, small cuts along his forefingers.

He works with those hands.

"John," she said. "I understand this must be very difficult for you, but if you want to help us find out who did this, we need you to cooperate."

He frowned, staring at the table. "I brought Lily those flowers. I was late coming home because I stopped to get her flowers. She put them in that vase from her mother. I know that because the vase was supposed to be some kind of peace offering. I watched her. She put them in the vase before we had supper."

A peace offering?

"So you ate," Mac said and glanced over his shoulder toward the sink.

Grace had already noted it was empty. If they'd eaten, their dinner had been cleaned up.

"Yes. Then I went to Amherst."

"Why?" Mac asked.

"To see a friend," he said, frowning. "I met a friend I know through work for coffee."

The front door creaked open, and Mac leaned backward to see through the doorway.

"Lockwood," Mac said, nodding to someone down the hall, and stood up straight again. "You met a friend?"

"Yes, and then I drove back along Bones Bay instead of the highway."

"And what happened when you came back?" Grace asked.

"I walked in and found her like that. The vase smashed. Flowers..." He shook his head again and pressed his hands over his face. "I—I called the cops as soon as I could—could catch my breath."

"Where do you work?" Mac asked.

"Thom's Tackle Shop." He choked out the words, wiping at his red face and clearing his throat. "Bait and tackle shop on Bones Drive, right at the end by the bay. I work for Thom Hanks."

Grace frowned at the name.

Like the movie star?

"What friend did you see?" Mac asked. "I need you to write down their name and number."

Grace tore off a piece of paper from the small pad she carried and handed it to John with her pen. He wrote it down and slid it back to her.

"His name's Luke. We're old friends." John crossed his arms. "Met at the shop. He fishes. Hadn't seen each other in a while, so we were catching up. Listen, you're wasting your time talking to me. You have to go see Mickey Clarke."

"Why?" Grace asked. The name sounded familiar.

"Lily had a restraining order on him. No contact. She used to work for him until a month ago, and after she quit, he didn't get the hint that she wasn't interested in him. He'd show up at her new job."

"Where's that?" Mac asked.

"She worked at his club, Wild Card, as a server and bartender while taking classes to be a realtor. She graduated this summer, and she quit as soon as she sold her first home. He'd show up at her office or follow her and pretend it was a coincidence when they saw each other."

He spaced out again and looked up at Mac.

"I took her to see you guys at the department—twice—and it took a bruised arm before you granted her the no contact order," John said through his teeth. "He's a dangerous prick, and he hurt her. He'd do it again. It was him." Tears welled up in his red eyes.

"We'll be checking into Mr. Clarke," Mac said. "I told you, we'll follow up on your concerns. For now, you were the person closest to her. We need to hear from you."

"Why did you bring her flowers?" Grace asked.

"It was just something I did every once in a while," John sniffled. "She deserved more. I should have given her more."

"Were you fighting with her?"

He shook his head and pressed his lips together.

Nonverbal. Something's up with him.

"Mac," the officer from outside called down the hallway, "Chief's back."

Mac left the room without a word. He and Banning spoke in low voices down the hallway, and another female voice joined them.

"When you walked in and found her, John, what was the first thing you thought?" Grace asked.

"He did it," John said with wide eyes. "He's finally done it."

"Mickey Clarke?"

John nodded and covered his mouth with his hand, shaking his head.

He's going to go into hysterics if I don't keep him calm.

"How old are you, John?"

"Forty-one."

"And Lily?"

"Twenty-seven. Her birthday's coming up. She would have been twenty-seven this year."

"John, we need to contact Lily's parents. Do you have their number?"

He shook his head. "She doesn't talk to her parents much. I don't have a relationship with them."

"Why's that?"

"They've just never liked me," he shrugged. "The age difference, I think. Since we got engaged, her dad wasn't speaking to her anymore."

The peace offering of the vase from her mom.

"But her mom does?"

He nodded.

"Why don't they like you?" she asked.

He shrugged. "I'm too old? I'm not good enough for their daughter. I never would have been. They'll blame me."

"For her death?"

He shook his head. "For estranging them from their daughter. It's her father's fault he didn't speak to her. He hurt her so bad because of that…" He stared past her.

"John?"

"I'm sorry."

"That's alright," Grace said. "We'll get their number. Is there anyone else you can think of who'd want to hurt Lily?"

"No one. Everyone loves her."

"Anyone else who has keys to your home?"

He shook his head.

Would Lily have let Mickey Clarke in after she'd just been granted a no contact order against him?

Grace stood from her chair, passing him a tissue from the box on the marble island.

"Did you wear a coat when you left?" she asked, staring at the tattoos on his forearms as he took it.

"Yeah," he said, frowning.

"When did you take it off?" she asked.

When did you have time to think about taking off your coat?

She walked around the marble island and stood on the other side. Banning, Mac, and the officer entered the kitchen.

"Just after he got here," he nodded to Mac.

"You're going to have to stay somewhere else for a while," Mac said. "Do you have anywhere you can stay?"

"I'll get a hotel room."

Mac nodded. "Officer Malone will escort you to your room to pack a few things and answer any questions he's able to. When you know where you're staying, this is my number. Please contact me and let me know."

Mac handed him his card, and John stood from the table and took it. He was tall, and as she stared up at him, she couldn't believe he was over forty.

With a girlfriend in her twenties.

Officer Malone followed John out of the room and up the staircase just off the hallway.

Banning shook his head. "This is the first body this year. I want you *both* on this, and use Malone when you can too, alright?"

Mac nodded. "When Lockwood gets back to me with her findings, I'll let you know."

"You'll notify the parents now, then?" Banning asked.

Mac nodded. "There's someone else I want to question tonight, too."

"You've got a busy night ahead," Banning said, nodding to Grace.

Banning turned back down the hallway, and Mac followed him. A woman in a dark blue coat stood beside a man photographing the scene and nodded to Mac.

Chief M.E. had been stitched in yellow writing on the back of her jacket.

"I need that report ASAP," Mac said.

The woman nodded.

"I'm Detective Inspector Grace Sheppard."

"Raven Lockwood," she replied, nodding. "Chief M.E."

"Nice to meet you," Grace said, then followed Mac out the front door.

Still trying to keep up.

"You get the parents' address?" he asked.

"No," she said. "I asked him, but he didn't have their number, so I'll look—"

"Don't bother. I already have it."

"Then why did you ask?"

"You'd better ride with me," he said, shaking his head as they passed another officer lugging an evidence box up the driveway. "Don't want you to fall behind."

Grace rolled her eyes, and as they reached the bottom of the driveway, Banning stood in front of two reporters and a cameraman. Madigan was at the front with her phone held out in front of her.

"You coming?" Mac asked.

She caught Madigan's eye and nodded to her. She'd never thought of her as *The Press*. Just a writer for the local paper, but more often than not, Grace found the media got in the way of the cases she worked.

Grace turned and jogged to Mac's car. As soon as she got in, he started to roll away.

"I'm going to need you to pick up the pace," he said.

I'm not slow.

Am I going too slow?

"I wanted to talk to the neighbour across the way," she said.

"I've got Malone on it."

He sees things in black and white. He wants facts.

"I've heard of Mickey Clarke," she said.

"Yeah?"

"He owns Wild Card, and he's one of the owners of Salty Rocks too. He's a rough guy."

Once she'd gotten close to her contact, Leah, she'd also caught the eye of her boyfriend Conrad Burke's best friend, Nick Hill. She'd been instructed to get closer with him, and they started dating, hoping the more intimate relationship would get her closer to Burke and any intel on the drugs they'd been moving.

Salty Rocks had been their group's favourite club, and Grace suspected the owners were involved in other unsavory business too.

"Any priors?" Mac asked.

"Nope. Nothing they could catch him with. John Talbot?"

"He was arrested and sent to juvie as a teen for possession with intent to distribute," he said. "After that, it's just parking tickets through his twenties. Couple months ago, he was involved in an altercation on Seventh in the city. No charges though."

"Seventh?" Grace frowned. "That's where Wild Card is. Who was he fighting with?"

"Guy didn't leave a name. Didn't have a record, I guess, but John's name was on the record."

"Think it was Mickey?" she asked.

Mac shook his head. "They'd know who he was, wouldn't they?"

Of course they would. Why did I ask that?

Mac turned up the radio, and as they merged onto the highway bridge toward Amherst, she wondered if meeting a friend was John's real reason for going into the city that night.

"We should check the café," she said as they got off the bridge and took an exit lane. "See if he was there for as long as he said he was with who he said he was with."

"Tomorrow," Mac said. "I want to see her parents and then Clarke tonight. Her parents live just outside Amherst, technically in Deerhorn County. Then we'll carry on to Wild Card and see if we can find Clarke there. If not, I want to pay him a visit at home."

Grace nodded. "I think they were fighting."

"John and Clarke?"

"John and Lily. I mean sure, men buy women flowers just because, but it was more likely they'd been fighting, it was his fault, and he was trying to make it up to her. I asked if they'd been fighting, and he shook his head, but I think he was evading the question."

"I like to work with facts," Mac said. "Not theories."

Add predictable to the list of Mac's weaknesses.

She would keep her theories to herself until they turned into something more.

If only Mac would keep his snide comments to himself, they might have a chance at working together in a cohesive manner to find out what happened to Lily.

CHAPTER FOUR

Madigan had followed far enough behind Grace that she was sure she hadn't been spotted, and once Grace went inside the house, Madigan turned down the street.

"Do you sleep next to a police scanner?" Madigan asked as she stopped her motorcycle beside the Tall Pines news van, where Thane stood talking to their photographer.

"I gotta say, Knox, I'm surprised you're here," Thane said, and the photographer hopped into the back of the truck. "I can't always keep it straight, so help refresh my memory. Are you working on your own tonight, or as my helper?"

"I'm here for my own story."

A story that will get me on the front page so my Tall Pines Elementary article can be included.

"Alright," he said, shrugging. "But tell me—how did you find out about the body?"

A body?

Murder?

"I've got my ways," she said, lifting her feet and driving on past the second house, parking just before the dead end on the short street.

She took out her cell phone and pulled the strap of her bag over her head, adjusting it across her chest.

Another patrol car parked in front of the house, and Police Chief Paul Banning stepped out.

This is big enough, Ornella. Very big.

Without any extra effort, she'd be chasing the same story as Thane, and from there, it would be a write-off to see who could tell the better story. Thane had her there, hands down.

She needed a better strategy, and as she met Thane and the cameraman on the road in front of the house, she decided to keep her enemy close.

Thane's strength was his tenacity, but his weakness was his ego. If she fed into it enough, she might find a way to beat him at his own game.

As *The Gazette's* photographer snapped shots of the house and stepped back several feet to include the ME's vehicle in the frame, Madigan turned to Thane.

"So seriously, how did you get here so fast?" she asked. "You must have some good connections."

"Maybe I do," he smirked, "but I'm not telling you."

She shrugged and smiled. "Fair enough. I bet it's because people are excited to tell you things. You're this popular news reporter, and I've never told you this because your head would be too big to fit through the front door of *The Gazette*, but you're a real celebrity around here."

Thane laughed and shook his head.

Just a little more.

"I bet you haven't had a story this good in a while. Actually, I'd like to learn from you."

He peered down at her from his peripheral. "Oh yeah?"

Does he buy it? Maybe not, but I've got him talking.

"Just let me know if I can help. What's going on in there

anyway?"

"We won't know much until Banning comes back out," he said. "They haven't brought the body out yet."

Someone's dead. Who?

"I see. What do *you think* happened?" she asked.

"I overheard the officer tell the Chief M.E. she's fresh."

"Fresh?"

"Not dead long," he said. "Now, when Banning comes to give a statement, it's important to ask the questions our readers want to know. The tough ones, like who was killed? What happened to her? Are there any suspects?"

"Couldn't it be an accident though?"

Thane shook his head and waved his pen around. "They don't make this kind of fuss over an accident. They have to at least suspect something else."

"Oooh, I see," she cooed, pretending he'd enlightened her.

Her phone rang in her hand.

Will.

"Hi, babe," she said.

"I got home, and you're not here," Will said. "Everything alright?"

"Yeah, I'm just out on a story. There's been a murder, I think, and…"

A man followed an officer out of the home, and camera lights flashed across the man's face. The first person without a uniform to come from the home.

A witness?

A suspect.

"Put your phone down and focus," Thane hissed.

This is my out.

"It's important," she hissed, holding her hand up and walking toward the end of the driveway.

"Will," she whispered, "I have to go."

"Alright, be careful."

She hung up and searched her phone for the record app as the man followed the officer down his driveway.

"Thank you, Will," she whispered under her breath, "for the excuse to lose Thane."

I'm right where I need to be.

The man stopped at the car at the bottom of the driveway, and the officer continued, ducking under the police tape and walking to his car. Madigan waited for the officer to reach the road before she crossed over the neighbour's front lawn and stayed tight against the long bushes that separated the yards, jogging toward the man.

"Sir," she said, holding her phone in front of her. "I'm with the *Tall Pines Gazette*. Are you related to the victim?"

He glanced her way over his shoulder, squinting into the bushes before fumbling with his keys and turning back to the door.

The Amherst news crew had arrived, and a small group had formed, shouting questions at the man while the officer held his arms out, keeping them back away from the tape.

"Sir, were you there when the victim died?" she asked, having heard Thane's voice ask the same question in the crowd moments before.

"Please," he said, "leave me alone."

Whoever it was, the victim meant something to him.

She heard it in his voice and remembered the news crews that hounded her after she was released from the hospital following her accident with Drew.

"I'm sorry." Madigan sighed and lowered her cell phone. "I'm sorry for your loss."

He opened the door and hesitated. "She was my fiancée," he said, turning around to face her.

Why was he telling her this? She'd hoped he'd talk to her, but now that he was, she couldn't understand why he would.

He must be in shock.

"Do you live here?" she asked, holding her cell phone out toward him again.

He nodded, looking back at the house.

With her phone in her hand, she felt silly. A pest bothering a man who'd just lost his fiancée. Or a man who'd just murdered her?

What do I need from him?

"What's your name?" she asked.

Most people liked to talk about themselves. It always led to something else.

"John Talbot. Listen, I have to go."

"John. What was her name? Please?"

"Lily," he said, staring at the ground.

He's not looking at me, so no one is noticing me. Keep looking down.

"Do you think I could talk to you sometime? Interview you for the paper?"

"I don't think it's a good idea." He shook his head and grabbed the handle inside the door before getting into the car. The tattoo on his left forearm above his watch caught her eye.

A black scorpion.

I've seen that...

He shut the door, and before he left, he turned to look at her through the window.

She stepped back, hoping to be hidden by the bush.

Do I know you?

He stared in her direction before rolling down the driveway. He pulled out onto the road, and the patrol car followed him, leaving the other officer alone on the other side of the police tape.

He hadn't given her much—just names and relations—but it was more than Thane had.

I can work with this.

John Talbot.

She'd never heard of him before.

That tattoo. It's generic but...

The light from the second-story window across the street went out, and she studied the large house with the wrap-around porch.

Maybe they're a witness.

The news group started shouting once more as Chief Banning walked down the driveway toward them. "I'll make my statement, but I'm not taking questions at this time," Banning started.

Now's my chance.

"An investigation will be launched into the death of a young woman who will not be named at this time. The circumstances are suspicious in nature, and the Tall Pines PD will be cooperating with a regional detective in this matter. That is all I can confirm at this time..."

Madigan jogged across the street while members of the news shouted questions at Banning. She strode up the pathway, climbing the stairs to the neighbour's porch and knocking twice at the storm door.

She was pushing it for time and luck, but if she didn't try, she wouldn't know. The house had an unobstructed view of John's home.

A short older woman with curly white hair opened the door and peeked out.

"Hello," Madigan said. "Pardon the disturbance. I'm not sure how much you know about what's going on across the street—"

"I think it's a murder," the woman said, opening the door wider.

"I'm Madigan Knox," she extended her hand.

"I'm Dorothy," she said, shaking her hand. "My friends call me Dot."

"Dorothy, nice to meet you. Why do you think it was a murder?"

"The medical examiner is still there," she said. "No one got taken away in the ambulance. Must have some reason to investigate."

Dorothy nodded toward the driveway. "John just left. I'm afraid it's Lily."

"How much did you see?"

"Not much," she sighed. "I normally can't fall asleep before midnight, but today I was out gardening, and I think the sun got to me. I fell asleep while watching *Jeopardy*."

"So around eight or eight thirty?"

Dorothy nodded. "I woke up to the sirens. Red and blue flashing against the living room curtains. I saw them go in, and I saw John come out just now, but Lily's—well—she's probably in there." She rested her hands on her hips.

"Did you know Lily well?"

Dorothy sighed. "We didn't talk much, but she was a nice young girl. Too young to be with him, if you ask me. I've spoken more with her than her fella. Though, there was one time I put out the recycling, and the wind blew it all over the street. No sooner did I realize, and he was out there, running around, fetching it all for me. I thanked him and asked if he'd like to come in for some coffee and cake, but he said no, just like that. Who passes up coffee and cake? Didn't surprise me. He just comes and goes."

"I love coffee and cake," Madigan said.

"Mhmm, I make a lovely spice cake. Anyhow, she's out there gardening on weekends. Beautiful garden." Dorothy smiled and leaned her weight against the door knob.

"Dorothy, before you say anymore, I want you to know I'm a reporter for the *Tall Pines Gazette*. Anything we talk about is confidential but I was hoping to get a statement from you about Lily."

Dorothy studied her, and her lip twitched. "Well, she was a nice young girl, like I said, you can quote me on that. I wonder what happened to her."

Madigan nodded.

"Do you think John could have…"

Dorothy made a face. "You never really know a person. They haven't been here for a year, even."

"Okay."

"Well," Dorothy smacked her lips together. "He makes me uneasy, I guess. Coming and going at odd hours. Never waves or smiles at me. Don't get me started on the tattoos. Please don't quote me on that, though. I'll get a lecture from my daughter."

Madigan shook her head, grinning.

What would she say about the crescent moon on my hip?

"You don't think…" Dorothy put her hand to her cheek. "You don't think someone's randomly breaking into houses, do you?"

"I doubt it was random, but you lock up, alright? If you see anything suspicious, you should call the police."

Dorothy nodded. "Thank you, dear. I think I've just read too many mysteries. I'll be fine."

"Well, it was nice to meet you, Dorothy," Madigan smiled.

"Oh, call me Dot. You know, I just remembered. I saw John leave before *Jeopardy* started. I was about to close the blinds—I hate the glare from the sun setting, but I hate keeping the curtains closed all day—so I close them every night and open them every morning. What was I saying?"

"You saw John," Madigan said, smiling.

"Right, yes. He left just before *Jeopardy* started."

"And that was at eight?"

Dot nodded. "Hope that helps you, dear."

"Thanks so much." Madigan nodded. "Have a good night."

"You too," Dot said.

Madigan started back down the driveway. She glanced over her shoulder, and Dot waved to her before starting to close the door, but she stopped, her mouth opening as she stared across the road.

The medical examiner rolled the stretcher with a body bag out the door, and another man helped her guide it toward their vehicle.

Madigan walked back to her motorcycle, and instead of going home, she made a turn for the ride to the office. Thane thought he had a head start, but Banning only gave the media a bread crumb. He'd be shocked by her new information when he read her article on the front page.

CHAPTER FIVE

"Have you done this before?" Mac asked as they parked in front of the Martin's home.

Grace nodded.

She had wanted to be the one to tell Leah's parents about her death, but her sergeant told her it was against procedure as she was suspended and under investigation. She often wondered how the Culpers reacted to the news of their daughter's death and if the officers who told them had been as sensitive and professional as possible. If they had handled it with the sensitivity Grace had each time she'd delivered the news of a death to a family.

They got out of the car and walked to the door of the bungalow together in the quiet suburb. Mac pushed the doorbell and checked his watch.

Grace knew whoever opened the door at that hour would be startled, confused, shocked, and finally dreading the words the officers came to deliver. Some stood in disbelief, although they knew the truth in their hearts.

Mac knocked, and a light came on the other side of the

door. A man with short salt-and-pepper hair opened it, standing in his robe.

"Mr. Martin?" Mac asked.

Mr. Martin nodded and opened the door a little wider. "What's going on?" he asked.

"Is Mrs. Martin in?" Mac asked.

He nodded and stepped back. "Come in. What's this about?"

As they stepped into the foyer, a light came on upstairs, and a woman with Lily's matching blonde hair came downstairs in a pink robe.

"Oh God," she said, clutching the sides of the robe together around her chest. "What's happened?"

"I don't know," Mr. Martin said, wrapping his arm around her shoulder. "Could you please tell us why you're here?"

"I'm Officer MacIntyre, and this is Detective Inspector Sheppard. We're here to inform you that your daughter, Lily Martin, was found deceased in her home tonight."

Mr. Martin looked down at Mrs. Martin, but she just stared at Mac. She shook her head and stepped into the porch light. Dark circles surrounded her small green eyes, and deep frown lines formed across her forehead.

Mr. Martin's hands dropped away from his wife's shoulders and clenched into fists. "He did it," he said. "He killed her."

Mickey Clarke. Had they known about her no contact order against him?

"Mr. Martin?" Mac asked.

"John," he said. "John Talbot. That bastard killed her. Oh, God. I told her. I told Chris…"

He stared down at his wife.

She's not saying anything. She must be in shock.

"Mr. Martin," Mac said. "Why do you think she was killed?"

"He beat her," Mr. Martin said. "He's got a terrible temper, and she came to us one time with a bruised arm. She was crying, and she said he'd kicked her out of his home. She said she was scared of him."

His wife looked up at him and grabbed his arm.

"I told her I'd protect her," Mr. Martin finished with tears in his eyes. "Chris, I'm so sorry."

Chris wrapped her arms around him and shook in his arms, wailing until he wrapped his arms around her.

It's finally sunk in for her.

"I knew this was going to happen, but she wouldn't listen to me," he said. "I couldn't just stand by and watch it happen...but I should have been there."

"We should have kept her here," Chris said. "Taken her... and then... never..."

Grace couldn't distinguish the words.

"Mr. and Mrs. Martin," Mac said. "I want to give you a moment, and then I have some questions I'd like to ask about your daughter. We want to find out what happened to her, and we're investigating the circumstances around her death. There is a chance this was accident."

Mr. Martin rubbed his wife's back, and she took deep breaths as they parted.

"Tell me," Mr. Martin said. "Just tell me what you know."

"Maybe Mrs. Martin would like to go in the other room with Detective Inspector Sheppard?" Mac asked.

Chris looked at her husband—still sobbing—her red eyes searching his face for answers. Mr. Martin nodded and squeezed her shoulders. She sniffled, trying to catch her breath.

"Just until I ask the questions," Mac said.

Chris nodded but stood still.

"Chris?" Mr. Martin said.

She looked up at him and started wailing again.

"I think," he cleared his throat, "I think I should put her to bed."

"Oh, God," she wept, reaching out for him.

Mac nodded. "We'll wait down here."

She shuffled to the stairs in her slippers as Mr. Martin led her by the arm.

"I'm very sorry for your loss, Mrs. Martin," Grace said.

As the Martins started up the steps, Grace stepped into the alcove to the living room. Other than a magazine on the seat of the Lazy-Boy, everything was organized—clean like John and Lily's place.

Mac stopped in front of a picture on the wall. Just Lily, in a cap and gown, likely graduating from high school.

"They're both convinced it was the fiancé," she said.

Mac nodded as footsteps thudded down the stairs.

Maybe we should have brought him in for more questioning.

"We need to talk to John again tomorrow," she said.

"You need to lock him up." Mr. Martin entered the living room and gestured for them to sit. He took his place on the Lazy-Boy and leaned back, gripping the arms of the chair.

"It was John," he said, muttering toward the ceiling. "He did it. He did it."

"When did it all start?" Grace asked. "When did you become worried for her?"

"When we discovered she was dating a man old enough to be her uncle," he said, scoffing. "Either of you have children?"

"I don't," Grace said. "I can't imagine what you're going through."

"You worry from the start. Her mother noticed she wasn't happy with John early on. Chris told me their first fight was a nasty one. Chris confides in me about things like that. Lily used to, anyway, until he began to isolate her."

"How?"

"She worked at a club in the city. It's how they met. He'd

be jealous of the attention she got there. Pretty normal, I thought, but he'd take it out on her. Make her feel bad for what she wore. For working there at all, but she stayed because she was putting herself through real estate school—supporting herself until she finished. She graduated this year." His smile faded as tears slid down his cheeks. "He took her away from us—before this I mean." He pressed his lips together and closed his eyes.

"I'm very sorry, Sir, but it's important we ask these questions," Mac said. "You said something about her leaving him?"

He nodded and opened his eyes. "We were shocked when she came to stay with us about two months ago. She'd graduated her realtor's exam by then. She stayed here almost a month, and then she said she was leaving. This was just a month ago. We were horrified when we heard it was to move back in with him. Couldn't understand it. I—I wouldn't speak to her after that. They were engaged, you know, and we just—we couldn't understand it. How could she not see that he was all wrong for her? He didn't really love her."

"What was Lily like?" Grace asked.

"Kind. Easy to get along with. Funny sometimes, but always curious. Ambitious. Always wanting to do her own thing. And nurturing. He took advantage of her."

He covered his face with his hands and wiped them over his closed eyes.

"We'll do our best to find who did this," she said.

"You don't have to investigate," Mr. Martin said, shaking his head. "It was John. I know it was. Chris just told me something up there I think you should know."

Lines formed across his forehead. "Before she came to stay with us, Lily had relations with someone else. That's what she and John had been fighting about. It's what made her come to stay with us. I should have made her stay…"

"Does Chris know with whom?" Mac asked.

He shook his head.

"So she'd been cheating on John. Do you know for how long?" Mac asked.

He shook his head. "Just because she stepped out on him doesn't mean she deserved how he treated her. What he did to her…" He clenched his jaw and balled his hands into fists again.

"Her arm?" Grace asked.

He nodded.

The same bruise John said Mickey Clarke had caused.

"To see your daughter like that—" He shook his head. "When someone hurts your child—when a man hurts your daughter—you want to make *him* hurt. I took Lily being home as a sign that things would get better, and I tried to help her look forward to a life without him."

"Do you have any other reason to believe John would have killed her?" Mac asked.

"They were always fighting," he said, his eyes searching the floor just in front of him. "That's what Chris has told me."

"Okay," Mac said.

"And," he said, raising his forefinger, "she'd just signed a big contract to represent a wealthy client. Maybe he wanted the bonus money for himself. That selfish sonofabitch. He never knew what he had with her. He never knew—she was so special." Tears slid down his cheeks.

Getting her money before they were married would be difficult.
Not much of a motive.

"Mr. Martin," Grace said. "Do you know anyone else who had issues with Lily? Who could have hurt her?"

He shook his head.

Mac held his card out to him. "If you have any questions, day or night, please call me. As we investigate your daughter's death, we'll notify you when we can of anything important. If you remember anything else, please let us know."

He nodded and leaned back in his chair.

"We'll show ourselves out," Mac said.

As they left, Mac shut the door behind them.

"Let's pay Mickey Clarke a visit," he said.

* * *

The music in the club made it impossible to hear what Mac said after they entered, but instead of following him and whatever plan he had but refused to tell her, Grace took the lead.

If we have to confront Mickey now, females are less threatening. Let them see me first.

They passed the booth in the V.I.P. area and Grace forced herself to focus on the case at hand instead of remembering the great times she had with Leah on the dance floor at Salty Rocks while their entourage sat in the V.I.P. area. Times when the job melted away and she let herself get caught up in the music.

In those times, she wasn't pretending to be Cheyenne Cameron, her cover identity, but she wasn't really Grace Sheppard, either.

They reached the stairs, and two large bouncers stood with their arms crossed, surveying the crowd.

She leaned in closer to Mac, smelling his subtle cologne. "I think we should wait until we have more evidence."

Mac turned to the bouncer without glancing her way. "Mickey here?" he shouted.

"Who wants to know?" one of the bouncers asked, chewing on his gum.

"Tall Pines PD." Mac revealed his badge.

One bouncer smiled and said something in the other's ear

before starting up the steps. Mac took a step forward, and the bouncer who remained held out his arm.

"This is private property," the bouncer said while smacking on his gum. "So you'll wait."

The other bouncer walked across the metal platform to a booth in the back corner of the upper level. Mac leaned in toward her. "Let me take the lead," he said.

You're not my superior.

Can I work this case alone if he's constantly against me?

Maybe he knows what he's doing.

Maybe he knows better than me.

The bouncer sped down the steps and nodded to Grace.

They climbed the stairs behind him, and voices of the people on the platform muddled together with music. People laughing and having fun. Men in deep discussion as the music became more of an echo.

"Officer MacIntyre," Mac said as he reached the booth first. "This is Detective Inspector Sheppard."

She stepped beside him and in front of two men in the booth with a young woman between them.

Mickey hadn't changed since she'd last seen him at Salty Rocks. He was a sharp dresser with a buzz cut and a stoic expression. The woman tugged on the other man's tie and giggled before giving Mac elevator eyes.

"How can I help you?" Mickey asked Grace.

They'd rather speak to me.

Maybe they underestimate me.

"Mickey Clarke? Where were you this evening?" Mac asked.

"Here," Mickey said, staring up at Mac from below his furrowed brow.

"All night?" Mac asked.

Mickey nodded.

"Can anyone corroborate that?" Mac asked.

"My business partner." Mickey nodded to his side, and the other man nodded once. "You're from Tall Pines?"

Mac nodded, and Mickey glanced over at Grace, scanning her body with his eyes.

Does he recognize me? We've never spoken. He couldn't...

"You're a long way from home," Mickey said. "What's a small-town girl like you doing in a big city like this?"

No smile on his face.

What is he thinking right now?

"You have an order of no contact out against you," Mac said. "Lily Martin filed that report."

Mickey frowned. "That was a misunderstanding." His thick, strong features became more pronounced when he frowned.

Threatening.

"When was the last time you saw Lily Martin?" Mac asked.

"Almost three months," he said. "Day before the no contact went through. Is she telling you I saw her?"

"Lily Martin was found dead in her home tonight," Mac said.

Mickey's eyes opened wide, and then he squinted up at Mac, his jaw clenched.

Mickey, you're either a great actor, or you're genuinely surprised.

"Lily's *dead?*" the other man asked.

Mac nodded. "Can anyone else say they saw you here all night?"

Mickey's chest heaved. Grace tried not to stare at him. His eyes scanned the empty table in front of him, back and forth.

"Everyone up here, I'm sure." The other man nodded and turned to Mickey. "Man, I'm sorry."

He knows there was something between them. That Mickey cared for her?

"In the report, she claims you squeezed her arm so tight, you left a bruise," Mac said. "There's evidence of it."

"I never hurt her," Mickey said, zoning out, still staring at the table.

"Is there anyone you can think of who wanted to hurt Lily?" Mac asked.

"Her boyfriend," Mickey said, looking up at Mac. "He's a piece of shit."

"We're not saying anything else without a lawyer present," the other man said, then put his arm around Mickey's shoulder and squeezed his neck. "It's for the best, Mick."

"Were you having sexual relations with Lily during her relationship with John Talbot?" Mac asked.

Mickey waved to the bouncer. "Show them out."

He's shutting down. I need more from him. He didn't ask for the lawyer—his friend did.

The bouncer nodded and took a step toward them.

The fight on seventh...

"When did you last see John?" Grace asked.

Both men stared up at her.

"He still comes in here for a drink once in a while," the other man said.

"I don't speak to that *prick*," Mickey said.

"Fair enough," Grace nodded. "I ask because he was involved in an altercation on the road in front of your establishment here. Did you know anything about that?"

Mickey frowned, his stoic look replacing any bit of expression from his face.

"Who won?" Mickey asked.

"Pardon?" Grace asked.

"Who won the fight? I hope he got the shit beat out of—"

"That's enough," the man beside him said. "Get them outta here."

"Thank you for your time," Grace said.

She started back toward the stairs before the bouncer made a move and Mac followed her.

As they left the building, her head throbbed from the music, but her heartbeat slowed down to normal.

"I'll take you back to your car," Mac said before they got into his.

She wanted to discuss Mickey's reaction with Mac, but she knew there was no use running scenarios by him. He wanted to stick to the facts, but Grace used everything she had to solve a case.

Facts weren't always as clean-cut as they seemed.

They rode back to Tall Pines in silence, and when they got to John's house, she unbuckled her seatbelt.

"Thanks," she said.

"Meet back here in the morning before we pay John a visit," Mac said.

"What time?"

"Six," he said.

She nodded and stepped out of the car.

"Hey," he called, and she bent down. "I told you that was my line of questioning."

And I told you it wasn't a good idea to go so soon.

She leaned against the car door and readjusted her jacket.

There's no point in arguing.

He didn't care what I thought.

He still won't.

"Sorry," she said.

"Why'd you do it anyway?"

"I wanted to know about the fight John was in. I think it's important."

"Next time, don't try to be a hero. They're dangerous men."

She stood and rolled her eyes.

If you read my whole undercover file, you'd have an idea of the kind of company I kept.

She walked to her car and got in, glancing at her rearview mirror. Mac waited until she started her car before turning back up the road.

I'm not a liability. I can follow direction. I'll prove it tomorrow.

I have to prove it.

CHAPTER SIX

After tipping the cold remnants from her fourth cup of coffee into her mouth, Madigan re-read everything she'd written. She had managed to dig up some more facts on the victim, Lily Martin. She found information on Lily's new career as a realtor and pictures of her on Facebook with friends and family—even a few with John.

But she couldn't find much on John Talbot. No Facebook page of his own, though Lily had posted some about him and their relationship.

As Madigan scrolled through the pictures, something about John felt familiar.

He worked at Thom's Tackle, that much she'd gleaned from Facebook, but the shop itself had no website, just an address on Google.

Thane couldn't have identified the victim or the fiancé, and being ahead of the game should have set her at ease, but she wanted to know more about Lily and John.

Why does John look so familiar?

"You're here early," Thane said as he passed her cubicle.

"I've been here all night," she mumbled.

Three-thirty in the morning. She'd made it through without nodding off.

"I suppose it takes you much more time and effort to craft some semblance of a story," Thane said, smiling. "It might do you some good to compare your story to mine on the front page, just see where you went wrong with yours since you disappeared earlier while I tried to give you a lesson in journalism."

"You're just mad I decided to go it alone," Madigan said.

"No, I think your writing needs improvement, and since we covered the same story, you can compare and note where yours was weaker. It'll help next time."

"There is no next time," Madigan said, gathering her papers.

She didn't need Thane getting any ideas from her work.

"Well, I'm off to write front page news," Thane said, his deep voice echoing through the empty office.

"The higher the horse, the farther the fall," Madigan muttered and turned back to her article.

With the quote from the chief of police, the I.D. and info on John Talbot and Lily Martin, not to mention Dot's quotes—this has to be enough.

As Cindy passed her desk on her way in, she emailed her the article for edits and a copy to Ornella to approve.

Ornella's heels clicked down the hall, and she walked straight past Madigan.

"Good morning to you, too," Madigan muttered.

Her cell buzzed. Will's name lit up the screen.

"Hi."

"Hey, babe," he said, his voice sleepy. "I woke up, and you still weren't home. Just checking on you."

"I'm at the office. It's been a long day—well, night—and I'm hoping to come home in an hour or so and cuddle up with you until you have to go in."

"Erhm," he said, the duvet cover rustling in the background. "I have to go in *now*."

"Ah, alright. Rain check for tonight then." She leaned back in her chair.

"I wanted to tell you in person, but since you weren't home," he cleared his throat, "that good news I have? I've been asked to speak at the twenty-first annual society of surgery conference next July."

"Oh, wow," Madigan sat up, rubbing at her eyes. "Congratulations, babe. That's amazing."

"I've gone every year since I started medical school, and now *I'm the one speaking*."

The excitement in his voice made her smile.

"I'm thrilled for you, babe. We've got to celebrate."

"About that. I told my mom last night, and she and my dad want to have dinner. Here. Tomorrow night."

"Oh."

The Rosenbergs had avoided her the first and only time they'd met at Will's father's retirement party, and since, he'd passed messages to her for his mother.

Mom says hi.

Mom wondered if she could have your email to send you a recipe she knows I love. She wishes you'd cook for me more.

My mom was terrified when I told her I rode your bike this weekend. She says you should trade it in for a sensible car.

That had been the last straw, and Madigan stopped pretending to be sorry for refusing each time Will asked about getting together with them.

"Babe?"

He expects me to say no, but he deserves better.

"Oooh, well, good idea," she said. "Let's do that."

"And they'd like us to invite your parents too. They've never met, and it's kind of a big deal to them."

Not again.

"I've told you, Will. They're away."

"Again? I'm sorry, I guess I forgot. Well, could you invite them and then we'll go from there?"

Sure, if you want me to reunite with my parents for the first time in almost a year at your family dinner. For them to fly in from Florida on a day's notice to meet the parents of a man they've never heard of. Why not?

She cleared her throat and leaned back in her chair, taking a deep breath.

It's not his fault I haven't told him.

He would try to understand, but with a life like his, how could he?

How could he know what it's like to be abandoned by the only parents who ever loved you—whom you loved, too?

"Will, I'm so proud of you and your accomplishments. I can't wait to show you off to my parents, but it'll have to be another time."

"I understand. I'll let my mom know. See you tonight?"

"Sounds good. Have a great day and congrats again."

"You too," he said, then hesitated. "Bye."

What else did he want to say?

"Madigan?" Cindy called from her cubicle.

Madigan pressed end and set her cell phone down before rushing over to Cindy's cubicle.

"What is it?" Madigan asked. "Is it good? Oh, no, it's bad, isn't it?"

Cindy smiled up at her. "It's the best thing you've ever written. Thane's just came in. About to read his."

Madigan nodded. "Thanks, Cin. I'm going to go see Ornella. See what she thinks."

As Madigan approached Ornella's office, muffled voices from the other side of the closed door made her hesitate.

"…will be great," Ornella said.

"Thank you," Thane said with a smile in his voice. "And thanks for the tip."

So that's how he knew about the crime scene.

"Anything for our best writer," Ornella said in a higher voice than usual.

"Okay, well, I'm sure Cindy will have it edited and back to you shortly," he said, then opened the door.

"Morning, Ornella," Madigan said. "I just wanted to see if you'd had time to read my piece?"

"Not yet. Actually, could you both sit down? I see it's in my inbox."

"Sure," Madigan said, and she and Thane took their seats.

Ornella clicked her mouse a few times. "Now you understand, if I'd known about this, I'd have put you on the story together. Had you working for Thane. Two articles? How impractical."

Madigan cocked her head to the side and stifled her grin.

If she'd known. Come on.

You didn't see me coming, and you hate me for it.

"I told Ornella I'm happy to have you tag along with me next time," Thane said as Ornella concentrated on the screen. "I told her you insisted on going it alone."

"That's right," Ornella scrolled. "Thane's story was great. As usual."

"Thank you," he nodded, winking at Madigan.

Madigan rolled her eyes and crossed her legs.

"Right," Ornella nodded. "Madigan, let's see what you've got here."

Madigan folded her hands in her lap. Ornella squinted behind her glasses, reading line after line, her head stopping a few times. Her eyes opened wide, and she peered over the screen.

"Knox, *you spoke with the victim's fiancé?*"

Madigan nodded, and Thane turned to her. "How?" he scoffed. "When?"

"When he came out of the house," Madigan said.

"You've identified the victim," Ornella's voice raised in pitch as she spoke. "Ah, you've added some flavour in here with a quote from the neighbour. *Interesting*."

"When did you speak to a neighbour?" Thane whispered.

"After I spoke to John Talbot." Madigan smiled.

Thane frowned and pulled his head back in a swift motion.

He can't believe it.

"That's the name of the vic's fiancé, Thane," Madigan said.

Ornella pursed her lips and leaned back in her chair.

"This was some good investigative work, Madigan." She nodded to her. "You've identified the victim and likely one of the suspects."

Thane's head turned back and forth between her and Ornella.

"Thank you. I'm hoping this means my story gets the front page, and I can include the article about Tall Pines Elementary?"

"Oh, we'll run your school article." Ornella nodded.

Madigan sat forward in her chair, squeezing her hands together and smiling.

"I'll let Cindy know to include it," Ornella said. "You definitely brought me something interesting that the people of Tall Pines will be eager to read—after Thane works his magic on it. I'd like Thane to take the notes from your article, apply it to his, and you'll both have your name on it."

Madigan rubbed her brow. "Seriously?"

"Furthermore, I'd like you to work on this story together. I want to know more about Lily Martin. I want to know who this John Talbot is. I want to know how she died."

"My article—" Madigan said, hesitating.

My article is better, isn't it? It has the important parts.

Is it still not good enough?

"I don't want you to focus on the writing, Knox," Ornella said. "I want you to focus on getting the story. On working together for the common good."

You want to use me to get the scoop.

"I can do that," Thane said.

"My name will be on everything?" Madigan asked.

Ornella nodded. "Of course, along with Thane's."

"And I'll be able to have just as much say on our investigation as Thane?" she asked.

"Well, yes, you're both assets to this story," Ornella said.

"Fine." Madigan stood.

She strode out of the office and stopped by Cindy's cubicle.

"She's going to run the Tall Pines Elementary piece," she said.

"Oh." Cindy clasped her hands together. "That's great. What about—"

"I don't want to talk about it," Madigan said. "I'm going to contact the lunch lady and let her know to look out for the article."

"You need sleep," Cindy noted.

"I'll see you tomorrow." She went back to her cubicle and grabbed her bag and helmet before shuffling her way to the door.

"Knox," Thane called down the hall, "congrats on *finally* making the front page."

She pushed through the front door.

"Hey, listen, I've made it seem like us working together is alright with me, but it's not ideal for me either, alright?" Thane said, following her out. "You're not exactly easy to work with."

"And you are?" She laughed.

He opened his mouth to speak, but she interrupted.

"I don't care whether you like me or not," she said.

I'm not giving this one up.

"Likewise," he said.

"How do we do this?" she asked, stopping in front of her bike.

"This afternoon, I'm going to the station to see if there's an update. Another official statement, or a press release coming out soon. Want to come?"

Does he realize I'm an asset now, too, or is he placating Ornella like I am?

She nodded. "Give me a call, alright? I'm going to get some sleep."

"Sure. Hey, and I meant it. Good work."

"Thanks," Madigan said, turning away from him to hide her grin.

Thane jogged back inside, and she turned to watch him go, wondering if there was a better chance of doing the story justice together.

I'm not going to be his lackey.

If he gets in the way of my investigation, I'll leave him in the dust again.

CHAPTER SEVEN

G race hesitated at the bottom of the driveway.
She expected to see Mac's car in front of John and Lily's home, but a man in a patrol car sat in front of the house instead. It was the man from the night before, but she'd forgotten his name.

"Hi." She waved.

He waved back.

Before she started down the path to the door, she turned around, remembering the movement of the curtains the night before, and crossed the street to make good use of her time.

The officer's already been here, but I should hear it firsthand.

The door opened, and a short woman with curly white hair stuck her head out.

"Good morning, Ma'am. I'm Detective Inspector Grace Sheppard. I'm working with the Tall Pines Police Department on the case across the street. I was wondering if you saw anything last night? Anything that could help us with our investigation?"

"I already told that officer across the street and a nice

reporter who came by last night that I fell asleep just after eight, but before then, I saw John leave across the road there."

"And you're sure about the time?"

The woman nodded. "That's when my show comes on."

"Thank you, Ma'am. Is there anything else you remember?"

"Just waking up to see the police across the street," she said, fussing with her hair.

"And your name?"

"Dorothy Hutchins."

"Thank you for your cooperation, Dorothy. If you remember anything else, here's my card."

A car rumbled down the road behind her, and Mac's car slowed in front of the house.

"Well, alright then," she said and started to shut the door.

"Ms. Hutchins?" Grace asked. "Did you ever hear any fighting from over there or see anything odd between John Talbot and Lily Martin?"

Dorothy frowned. "About a week ago, I guess, I could hear them shouting. Windows were open, and I guess they didn't know that voices carry on this quiet street. Didn't last long. I haven't seen anything else. They mostly keep to themselves. She's really dead?"

Grace nodded.

"I hope you find the person who did this."

"Were you close with Lily?"

"Not close, no, but she was a sweet girl." Dorothy fussed with her hair again. "If it was some random break-in or her boyfriend, John there—makes no difference—I don't feel safe."

"Make sure to lock up, and police detail will be there another twenty-four hours at least. We're putting every effort and resource we have toward finding out what happened to Lily." Grace nodded. "Have a good day, Ms. Hutchins."

She strode down the driveway and met Mac at the other officer's patrol car.

"He's at the Whitestone Lodge," the officer said.

"Good." Mac nodded. "We'll be on our way to see him after we finish up here. Thanks, Malone."

Malone. Right. Why didn't I remember that?

Grace followed Mac to the door.

"No signs of forced entry." Mac stepped inside. "I'm going to check the other points of entry. Would you look around the house, and we'll meet in the living room?"

Grace nodded and took the steps upstairs. Three rooms merged off the hallway: a bathroom, an office, and a bedroom.

She walked into the bedroom with a king-sized bed dressed with several throw pillows. A jewelry stand sat on the dresser, and Grace walked toward it. Some of the pieces looked like costume jewelry, but many looked like the real deal.

Lily had only made her first sale that year, and John worked at a bait and tackle shop.

Where's she getting the money for this? Gifts maybe? From her parents? Mickey?

If any was stolen, why leave the other expensive ones behind?

Grace opened Lily's nightstand. A vibrator was tucked in the corner with a jar of lotion in the middle.

A Narcotic's Anonymous bible sat alone in John's drawer.

A recovering addict?

After checking the office and bathroom without finding anything suspicious, she went back downstairs, and on the way to the kitchen, she ducked into the powder room.

She crouched, searching for traces of hair or water across the bright white tile. She knelt beside the garbage can and snapped on one of her plastic gloves, pulling out a few tissues and a Q-tip.

"Anything?" Mac asked, and she jerked away from him, startled. "Sorry."

"Upstairs is clean. No forced entry." She stood and followed him to the living room. "He's an addict. I found a Narcotics Anonymous book in his beside table."

Mac nodded. "I know the type. You think he was on something last night?"

"No, I didn't get that impression at all," Grace said as they stopped in the entryway. "He might be clean."

"Maybe. Maybe we should test him."

"Lots of expensive jewelry. They weren't here for that."

"I didn't find anything stolen," he said, stepping onto the carpet. "No glasses in here. No cigarettes. If anyone else was here, they didn't leave a visible trace."

"You see where the vase was." Grace pointed to the outline created by blood and roses. "Right by her head there, under the table. I'm interested in what the M.E. has to say about that. If someone threw it at her, I can imagine it landing so close to her head, but if they were standing close and hit her with force, and maybe dropped it…"

"There you go with your theories again." Mac shook his head. "Here's what I see. Blood ran from the back of her head and created a puddle there, but it doesn't have clear outlines on this side. She could have been moved slightly, but not much, or she could have moved herself. The point is, there was movement."

Grace nodded. "The M.E. will be able to confirm whether it was before they moved her or not."

"It's not clear whether she was hit with it, or it was thrown at her," Mac said. "But there's blood on the corner of the table, there. She hit the back of her head for sure, and she may not have seen it coming. If anything was found under her fingernails, it would help to tell us whether or not there was a struggle because everything else in here..."

"Is exactly in its place." Grace nodded.

"I want to question John some more, but I don't want him lawyering up like Mickey Clarke," Mac said.

So now you wise up.

"So we'll question him where he feels comfortable," Grace said. "And maybe no drug test?"

Mac started for the door, and she followed.

"I was thinking you could question her co-workers and friends while I talk to John," Mac said.

Grace stopped behind him.

"I'd like to be there when you talk to John again," she said, trying to think of an assertive, yet professional way to tell him it wasn't his call. "I can speak to the co-workers and friends afterward. In Amherst, we interviewed in pairs."

"Suit yourself. It would be useful to spread out and cover more ground. Two people don't need to be there to question John. Not how it's done in Tall Pines."

If I don't go, he'll try to edge me right out of this case.

"I'll meet you at Whitestone Lodge," she said as they reached the road.

"Fine," Mac said and strode to his car, waving to Malone.

Malone didn't acknowledge her.

Maybe they were talking about me while I was at Dorothy's.

Now Malone thinks he knows me too.

Grace got in her car and turned the key in the ignition as Mac drove down the street.

He's not used to working below anyone but Banning. Remember that.

She took a deep breath and started out, hoping to catch up with him and follow him to the motel.

* * *

75

Meet me at the PD in 20.

Madigan read Thane's text with Buster lying at her feet, his hairy golden tail wagging—waiting for a promised slice of apple.

After five hours of sleep, she figured her leftover tiredness would help her sleep later that night, instead of lying awake, thinking about her brother, Drew.

If only she had moved faster.

If only she had paid more attention to him.

If only she had been a better swimmer.

She put her dish in the sink and filled Buster's water bowl, rubbing his head goodbye before handing him a piece of apple and dashing out the door.

When she arrived at the department with three minutes to spare, Thane's car wasn't in the lot. As she pushed the heavy front door open, a woman glanced up at her from behind a tall counter where she stood.

"Hello, I'm here to—" She'd never been to speak to the police before.

Don't sound like a newbie.

"I'm Madigan Knox from the *Tall Pines Gazette,* and I'm here to get a statement regarding Lily Martin's death."

The woman glared at her. "You people don't talk to each other? One of your reporters was already by."

Madigan shook her head. "I think there's a mistake. What's your name?"

The woman shot her a dirty look. "Rhonda."

"Rhonda, okay. This reporter, was his name Thane Wilson?"

Rhonda checked a book on the counter.

"This tall," Madigan held her hand well above her head. "Black man in his late forties, early fifties."

Rhonda nodded. "That's him. Guess you just got scooped."

"Thanks for your help, Rhonda," Madigan quipped and marched out of the department.

So much for attempting to work together.

He was probably back at the paper, typing out the statement for the next day's news.

This is why I haven't made the front page. What did I expect? I ditched him at the crime scene. Of course he played me now.

Thane had been so by-the-book, she hadn't expected him to try to ditch her.

"I'm on my own now," she muttered as she marched to her motorcycle. The feeling liberated her and scared her at the same time.

I need to find out as much as possible before tomorrow.

If she knew where John Talbot was staying, she'd try to question him again. He seemed comfortable talking to her, although it could have been the shock of it all.

As she got into her car, she remembered the articles about him working at the bait and tackle shop on the shoreline of Bones Bay.

"Maybe he's there right now," she said, pulling out of the lot and making a right.

It would be odd to go back to work so soon after your fiancée's death—or worse—*finding* your fiancée dead, but it was the only lead she had.

As she drove along the coast, the salty air of the ocean calmed her, washing away her worries as it always did when she rode.

After parking in the small gravel lot of Thom's Tackle, she couldn't see John's car, but took a chance going inside. The handsome older man behind the counter nodded to her with a half-hearted grin as she strode toward him.

"How can I help ya, Ma'am?"

"I was actually here looking for John," she said.

The smile dropped from his face, and he straightened up.

"I'm afraid Johnny—well—he won't be in for a while. Maybe I can help you?"

"I heard what happened," she said.

"Ah, well then." His sad eyes roamed the shelves behind her until he frowned. "Then why were you coming in looking for him?"

He won't talk to a reporter. He cares for John.

"I'm a friend of Lily's—was. I was hoping to speak to him."

"Do you know Johnny?" he asked.

"No. Lily and I were friends from high school. Good friends."

"Johnny's a good man. He's—he's broken over this."

"You've spoken to him?"

"I went to see him last night. He didn't do this to Lily." He leaned against the counter. "He loved her, alright? More than anything in his whole life, so whatever the news wants to make it look like, it wasn't him."

Why is he already defending him?

"Okay." She nodded. "I guess I'm just trying to make sense of this, and she told me she was engaged. I thought maybe talking to him might help."

He nodded, and tears welled up in his eyes.

"My name's Ma—ry," she said, holding out her hand.

"Thom Hanks," he said, shaking her hand with a firm grip. "I'll save you the question. I'm older than he is, so I was Thom Hanks first. Plus, mine's spelled with an 'H' as you saw on the sign out front."

Madigan grinned and nodded, letting go of his hand. "How long have you known John for?" she asked.

"Since he was about twenty. How much did Lily tell you about him?"

Madigan shrugged. "Not much."

"They had their issues," Thom said. "All couples do, but if

you'd gotten a chance to see them together, they were the real McCoy. Love birds."

Madigan smiled. "So you knew him well before they got together."

Thom nodded. "Oh, yes, Ma'am. Doesn't feel that long. I had him working for me shortly after."

He walked out from behind the counter.

"I'd like to show ya something," he said, waving her toward the back room.

He entered the office first, and she walked in afterward. The windows offered a spectacular view of the ocean, and the walls were covered with pictures, bulletin boards, and little taped notes.

"This here's a picture of us after winning the Tall Pines Fisherman award for the biggest fish a few years back. I had that hanging in the shop for a while."

She nodded, studying John's face. His well-trimmed beard matched his thick, short hairstyle. His eyes smiled, but his lips pressed together—modest in a way.

She couldn't shake the familiar feeling.

"This is the one I wanted to show you," he said, smiling, and pointed to a picture Madigan had seen on her computer. "Our annual customer appreciation picnic just this past summer. That's me and the wife. John and Lily. He's my business partner now. Owns the shop with me."

"Oh really?"

He nodded, his eyes glazed over as he stared at the photo. "Can't believe she's gone, but you knew her. You see how happy she is with him there?"

Madigan nodded. "Do you know what school he went to? Or where he grew up?"

She glanced back at the old wooden desk at the stack of business cards piled in the corner.

Madigan took a casual step back and swiped one, tucking it into her purse.

"I couldn't tell ya where he went to school, but he grew up in Amherst," Thom said, gesturing to another photo. "This one was taken just before our first boating trip together, right after he started working here. Fish out of water he was out here, I'll tell ya that."

Madigan stepped forward and turned to the picture of Thom, his arm draped over the shoulder of the much younger man, both standing just in front of their boat by the shore. John had an eyebrow piercing, jet black hair gelled up into a Mohawk, and jeans hanging down further than any manufacturer had intended them to go.

I've seen you before. At the house on Warbler Way.

She remembered coming home from school one day with Grace, and the boy in the picture standing at the side door talking to Evette. He passed them on the driveway without a word, but she remembered his hairstyle and eyebrow piercing. He looked rough, like many of the people Eli and Evette associated with.

They each held a fishing rod in the picture, and John's scorpion tattoo faced the camera. Her knees felt weak beneath her, staring back at the face she recognized and the tattoo she'd seen in person at the same house.

A tattoo that had haunted her dreams.

A tattoo she couldn't have been sure existed—until then.

But it can't be him.

"First picture we took together, if memory serves me…"

She couldn't focus on Thom's voice or pretend to listen any longer.

"Have you met his parents?" she asked, her voice shaking.

Thom leaned against the chair behind his desk. "He doesn't talk about them much. Johnny was adopted."

A lump formed in her throat.

Her heart raced as she remembered the picture her foster mom, Evette, kept of Johnny, their son they had adopted who'd left before they took her and Grace in. Evette only ever spoke of him once. The only reason she'd studied the picture so well had been the fact that Evette hid it from everyone. Even Eli.

And secrets made her curious.

"You alright?" Thom asked. "You miss her already? I know I do. I can't even believe—"

"I—thank you for showing me," Madigan nodded and started for the door.

He followed behind her, stepping back behind the counter. "If you'd like, I can tell John you came by? Maybe leave your number so he can get in contact with you? What did you say your name was, again?"

"You said you saw him, and he wasn't doing well?" she asked, clearing her throat. "Last night?"

Thom nodded and shoved his hands in his pockets.

"Maybe I'll give it some time, then. Thanks, though."

"Alright." He nodded with a grin as she walked backwards to the door. "I'm real sorry for your loss. You take care."

"You too, Thom."

As she strode to her bike in a daze, kicking the gravel beneath her ankle boots, she wondered how she could have missed it. He looked so different, and he hadn't kept their last name, but that wasn't shocking. Madigan had taken on the name of her next adopted family, and Grace kept her given last name, having never been adopted.

Thinking of an angle that would help get a story on the front page was one thing, but it was another to be fueled by her personal curiosity, and where it led kept her heart pounding in her chest.

The dreams—they were real. That night was real.

The first summer she and Grace had lived on Warbler

Way with Eli and Evette, strange things had happened. At seven, she couldn't remember much of that first year, but she'd been afraid—always on edge—since before their first beating.

But there's more to it than that.

One night she awoke to the sound of arguing, but she couldn't make out the voices. She climbed out of the bunkbed and crept downstairs, noticing the garage door in the hallway standing wide open. Something made her run back up the steps, and there—sitting on her perch, peeking between the railing spindles—she saw a body being dragged down the hallway—by the ankles.

And the scorpion.

The dark tattoo had been on the hand or arm, or even wrist. She couldn't remember, and it had been different during each nightmare.

The body changed, too. Sometimes a man. Sometimes a woman. Sometimes a child.

But the dark tattoo was always part of it.

Madigan got back to her motorcycle, swung her leg over, but couldn't move after sitting down. The gravity of what she'd put together washed over her, weighing her down.

The man who had lived in the same house—with the same parents—had found his fiancée dead in their home.

Did he kill someone else on Warbler Way?

Only three people might know what went on in that house at the time he was there.

Eli, their foster dad, rotting in prison for his crimes of child exploitation and drug dealing. She wouldn't agree to see him if he were the last person on earth—never mind seek him out.

Evette, whom she doubted would still have contact with John after the way she acted about him and that picture, hiding it away under her nightstand beside their bed. Her contact with Madigan consisted of birthday cards they'd send each other every year, and Grace refused to have anything to do with her.

And then there was John himself, but before she tried to call him using the business card she'd swiped, there seemed to be a window of opportunity to do something she'd never had the courage to do.

Madigan drove in the direction of the city.

* * *

As the door creaked open, John leaned out from behind it, squinting into the sunlight. He took a step back into the dark room, leaving the door open. Grey bags hung under his bloodshot eyes, and he wore the same shirt as the night before after taking off the one he found Lily in to submit into evidence.

Grace walked into the room with Mac close behind. John sat on the edge of the unmade bed, and Mac sat down on one of two chairs by a small table beneath the window.

He's been crying. Or doing drugs.

She scanned the room.

If he has, he hasn't left it out.

"We've got some follow-up questions for you, John," Mac said. "I called Luke, and he confirmed you met with him last night at the coffee shop."

Oh, thanks for telling me, Mac.

John nodded. "So did you talk to Mickey?"

"Hold on there," Mac said. "There was a time discrepancy with your friend. Luke said you were only there for the length of a coffee."

"Yeah," John said. "About an hour."

"But see, you didn't give us a time. You said you met your friend Luke, then took a drive up the coast and back home.

You were gone, by your own account, for roughly three hours," Mac said. "It takes less than an hour to get to the city and then again to drive back. So you were driving up the coast for an hour?"

John nodded.

Mac stared at him. "Why?"

John shrugged. "I've asked myself that all night. If I hadn't taken the long way around Bones Bay. If I'd just come back…"

"Were you and Lily fighting?" Mac asked.

John frowned. "No, why?"

"During our investigation, we've been told you had some altercations in the past several months of your relationship," Mac said.

"Alter—what? No." John shook his head. "I've *never* hurt her."

"But you kicked her out of your home last month," Grace said.

John turned to her. "You've been talking to her parents."

"Why did you kick her out, John?" Mac asked.

John bit his lip and stared at the burgundy carpet, rubbing the stubble along his jaw. "She'd been unfaithful," he muttered.

Grace crossed her arms. "Why didn't you divulge this information last night?"

"I wasn't thinking about it. I've tried to clear it from my mind." He clenched his jaw and fists, looking up at Mac.

"Did you hurt her, John?" Mac asked.

"Never." John shook his head. "I was pissed, yeah, but I never laid a hand on her. It was a misunderstanding, though. That's how we were able to move past it. Mickey forced himself on her."

Mickey?

"He made her uncomfortable while she worked for him

and preyed on her. He didn't stop until I convinced her to get that restraining order after she came back to me crying with a bruised arm. I told you about that already."

The same bruise Lily's parents and Mickey implied were from John.

"John, you need to be straight with us," Mac said. "You should have told us last night. This information is important to catch whoever did this."

"I didn't lie," John said, sitting up straight.

Push him any further and he'll lawyer up.

"Withholding information is the same thing," Mac said. "Be straight with me. Were you fighting last night?"

"No." John stared straight at him, jaw clenched.

"John?" Grace asked, softening her voice. "You broke up with Lily because she had been unfaithful. Does that mean she willingly cheated on you with Mickey?"

"I don't think so. I think he forced himself on her."

Shifting blame helped to take the pressure off the person being questioned.

"How did you find out?" Grace asked.

He rubbed his palms along his jeans before balling them into fists.

"She told me," he said, clearing his throat. "Lily came to me after her final realtor exam about two months ago. Maybe three. She told me he was there, waiting for her with flowers when she got to her car. She'd already quit working for him at Wild Card that week. I think he felt her slipping away and wanted her back. He kissed her, and she pushed him away. That's what she told me. She got in her car, drove home to me, and told me he'd been doing shit like that for years, but that was the first time he kissed her since she was with me."

"Did you confront him?" Mac asked.

John shook his head. "I told her we were done. I didn't—I

85

couldn't believe she hadn't told me before. Never mentioned his behaviour once to me. I felt like she was hiding it. I was angry, and I wish like hell I'd have taken the time to calm down and hear her out, but I told her to leave. She took her things and moved in with her parents."

"And then she came back," Grace said.

"I swallowed my pride, and I listened. I had to. She showed me the bruise on her arm he left after following her to one of the houses she was showing. I told her I was sorry I hadn't protected her from him, and we went and tried to get an order of protection, but apparently the bruise wasn't bad enough yet, or they didn't believe her. I don't know. We came back when the bruise was purple, and she made her case again and got the order."

"Does Mickey know you knew about how he handled her?" Mac asked.

"I—I don't think so. I just wanted to get her away from that, and we made sure of it. Things were better."

"Last night you said to look into Mickey, but you didn't tell us about the infidelity," Mac started. "You can't keep things—"

"Last night I was in shock. I still am. It's real, but it's not. I feel like I could go home, and she'd be there. Like we're just starting our lives…"

"John?" Grace said.

He zoned out, staring past her. "She's gone," John muttered.

"John," Grace said louder, and he turned to her. "You were involved in an altercation outside Wild Card a couple of months ago. Why were you there and what happened?"

He squinted up at her before shaking his head and running his fingers through his hair.

"That was before Lily moved out. I went to visit her at work and some guy hit on her. It happened all the time, but this guy wanted a fight, and I'd had one too many, so I took it outside."

"Did you know him?" Grace asked.

He shook his head.

"After that, did you fight with Lily?" Mac asked.

"No." John frowned. "Why would I fight with her? It wasn't her fault some jerk didn't take no for an answer."

Lily's dad made it seem like you blamed her when other men came on to her.

"Guys flirted with her a lot when she worked there?" Grace asked.

John nodded. "She hated it more than I did, I think, if that's possible. She was a good woman. I—I didn't deserve her."

"We'll give you some time, alright?" she said.

Mac looked back at her and frowned.

John ran his fingers through his hair again and sighed.

"You have our number if anything comes up, and we'll do our best to find out what happened to her," Grace said, turning toward the door. "We'll be in touch, John."

Mac followed behind her as she opened the door. Mac closed it behind them. "What was that in there?"

"What?"

"You interrupted my rhythm," he said, stalking toward the car.

"He was going to shut us down, Mac," Grace huffed.

He shook his head. "It's not up to you to make that call."

Challenging him this early on would only further destroy any semblance of a professional relationship they could be capable of. Worse, he could report back to Chief Banning that she'd been difficult. Obstructive.

Don't rock the boat.

She got in her car and pulled out of the lot, cursing under

her breath. He pulled out from behind her, passing her before they reached the traffic light.

"Very mature," she said.

As she followed him to the department, she wondered if maybe she shouldn't just let him take the lead on this first case.

His territory, but I outrank him.

As she parked, Mac jogged inside. She wanted to lean back against her seat and throw a pity party, but instead, she got out of the car, and strode to the door.

You can do better. Don't let him see weakness.

He stood beside the coffeemaker with two other officers, laughing, before she caught his eye. He nodded to the men and strode to a small room adjacent from Chief Banning's office. She followed him and shut the door behind them.

"Tarek's running through Lily's phone records as we speak," Mac said and grabbed a dry erase marker. "So we've got John Talbot." He wrote his name and taped his picture beside it.

"Prime suspect," Grace nodded.

"Mickey Clarke," he said as he wrote the next name. "Suspect number two."

"Anyone else?"

He shook his head and took a sip of coffee. "No one else with a motive we know of."

"We should run through their records. Find what we can on them," she said.

"I'll take John, hometown boy. You take the city slicker," he said, pointing to a pile on the table. "I've already looked through his file anyway."

"Technically, John's from the city."

"Well, he's a resident of Tall Pines *now*," Mac said. "That no contact order was granted to the vic just a month ago. That's the prime motive right there."

He wrote it on the board. "Whether she was sending signals like she wanted something to happen between her and Mickey, or like John said, he came on to her and stalked her, that order must have upset him. Triggered him maybe."

"But who do you think physically assaulted her?" Grace asked. "Parents say John. John says Mickey. Mickey implies it could have been John."

"Not sure yet," Mac said. "Lily's statement says it was Mickey."

He wrote the word *bruises* under his name.

"Then why did her parents think it was John?"

"Maybe she never told her mom specifics. Maybe her mom didn't want to hear them. She was probably just happy to have Lily back home."

"Maybe," Grace said, opening the file. "Hopefully her cell records paint a better picture. When's the DNA due in?"

Mac shook his head. "Takes weeks usually, but this might come in a little sooner."

"You're serious?"

"You're not in the city anymore. Things don't get done so fast around here, but they get done *right*."

Don't take the bait.

"What would John's motive be?" she asked.

"Jealousy?" Mac wrote the word with the question mark.

"Lily didn't work at Wild Card anymore. No contact with Mickey—that we know of. She sold real estate, so maybe a male colleague from work?"

"Have you checked with them yet?" Mac asked.

She shook her head. "I'll go after I get through this."

He shrugged. "Why don't you just take it home and go over it tonight? Check out her work now."

She pressed her lips together and stared down at the table.

Let him lead.

She nodded and stood. "Yeah, might as well. I'm off, then. Call me when the records are back, alright?"

He nodded without looking up. "Tomorrow morning, we'll meet with Lockwood at the morgue."

Grace grabbed the files and tucked them under her arm. "Right," she said. "See you then."

Have it your way, Mac.

CHAPTER EIGHT

Madigan jogged up the steps to the middle house in the triplex and slipped through the first door. She'd read over the address many times and memorized it for all the birthday cards she'd sent Evette. She'd ridden by the triplex twice, trying to work up the nerve to knock on the door.

She hovered her hand over the doorbell but then took it back.

Am I crazy to be here?

She only remembered Evette speaking about John once and while Eli wasn't around. A few times she caught her sitting on her bed, holding the picture of him and stuffing it back under her nightstand when Madigan entered the room.

Had Evette lost him completely, the same as Grace? Or was it possible they still had contact too?

The building was nicer than she'd imagined both times she'd made it that far. The first time, she'd almost confronted Evette in anger, blaming her for who she had become.

She'd been failing a few of her high school classes, always suspicious of her boyfriend's whereabouts when they weren't together, and wondering how different her life might have been had she been sent to the Knox family instead of Eli and Evette from the beginning.

The second time, she longed for the way Evette always made her feel better, regardless of what she'd been through. The time she considered the worst in her life, when her brother, Drew, passed away after the boating accident.

Both times, she decided not to go for the same reason.

I was eleven the last time I saw her.

I'm no one to her anymore, and she's no one to me.

She knocked on the door and took a step back. A tapping noise came from somewhere behind the other side of the door, followed by a thud.

She's home.

Her heart beat fast in her chest as the door opened, revealing a shell of the woman Evette used to be. Her frizzy grey curls hung just over her shoulders, fried from all her perms. She wore an oversized pink house coat with a stain near the bottom hem and had a cigarette wedged between her fingers, as it always had been.

"Maddie," Evette whispered, covering her mouth. "It's really you."

She found a comfort in her voice, just as she had during her dark days on Warbler Way—when Evette happened to be home.

"Evette." She nodded.

"Well," Evette said, glancing behind the door and back at her, "come in, won't you?"

Madigan followed her into a long living room. A soap opera played across the large screen TV over the fireplace, and a bag of Cheetos sat on the living room table, along with an empty bottle of vodka and a pile of cigarette butts in a crystal ashtray.

"I'm sorry the place is such a mess," Evette said and

coughed at the end of the sentence. "I never was much of a clean freak. You know that. If I'd known you were coming..."

Madigan peered into the kitchen to the right where dirty dishes filled the sink.

It was never this bad. Then again, Eli was always over your shoulder, telling you what to do. Threatening to punish you if it wasn't just so.

This must feel like freedom.

"Please, sit," Evette said, nodding to an armchair beside the couch. "Tell me, to what do I owe the pleasure of your company?"

Madigan sat on the edge of the seat cushion and folded her hands together.

"There've been a few times I wanted to see you," Madigan said. "That I meant to come and see you."

She'd never meant to admit it, but Evette had a way of disarming her.

Evette smiled and tapped her ash into the tray, her thin fingers, covered in rings, shaking until she pulled them back toward her.

"I'm surprised," she said before going into a coughing fit.

Madigan sat forward on the chair, waiting for her to stop. "You didn't think I'd want to see you?" she asked.

"I didn't think you thought of me at all," she said. "Except for maybe bad things. Bad memories."

Madigan nodded.

"I have them too," Evette whispered. "Nightmares."

The nightmares you told me weren't real.

Madigan took a deep breath. "I'm here about John."

Evette squinted at her.

"Your adopted son."

Evette looked down at her lap, smoothing her robe over her knee and taking a puff of her cigarette.

"Have you kept in touch, Evette?"

"Just about the same as you," she sniffled and butted her ash again. "Birthday cards and memories are all that's left."

"What happened with him?" Madigan asked. "Why did he leave?"

"He was practically an adult."

"So did Eli kick him out?"

Evette frowned and set her cigarette down on the ashtray. "Who told you that?"

"Eli never spoke about him, and you hid that picture of him."

"You remember that." Evette raised her brows and nodded. "Well, I guess it was a mutual decision. Eli wanted him out, and John wanted out. Plus, you girls were coming."

"Then why didn't he keep in touch with *you*?" Madigan asked.

Evette sighed. "I don't know what you're thinking. You, Gracie, Johnny. I don't know what you think of me, but it can't be good."

She shook her head and picked up her cigarette again, puffing away at it, supporting one frail arm with the other.

It wasn't all bad with you.

"You protected me," Madigan said. "When you could. I remember that."

"Ha." Evette shook her head, blowing smoke in the opposite direction. "A lot of good that did."

Evette could have ended their suffering by calling the police or child services a thousand times, but she didn't. Maybe she didn't want to have the girls taken away, or maybe she didn't think she could make it on her own.

Whatever you did, it was based on fear.

It was the reason Madigan held out so long before getting them out. What they endured in that house never seemed as bad as it could have been if she'd been split up from Grace.

Madigan pursed her lips and sighed. "I'm just letting you

know what I think, and I don't think it was your fault—not all of it."

Tears slid down Evette's cheek, and she wiped them away, sending the ash of her cigarette drifting through the air and onto the carpet. She maintained eye contact with Madigan.

"Thank you," she whispered.

Madigan cleared her throat. "I—I guess you know where John lives now?"

She nodded. "He moved into his first house two or three years ago."

"And his last name?" Madigan asked.

Evette took another puff. "Maddie, are you wanting to meet him?"

Madigan shook her head, trying to decide how much to tell her.

"Well, what is it?" Evette asked.

"I recognized him in the paper. His fiancée was found dead in their home last night."

Evette's jaw hung slack, and she raised her brows.

Madigan nodded.

"No," she whispered. "Oh, my poor Johnny."

"I couldn't even be sure it was him, but I remembered your picture of him. He looks different now."

Evette opened her mouth to say something, but instead, puffed on her cigarette, and Madigan winced as the embers inched closer to her fingers. Evette tapped it out into the ashtray and sat further back in her seat.

"I didn't know her." Evette licked her lips. "I don't know much about his life at all."

What do you know about mine?

"Well, do they know who did it?" Evette asked.

Madigan shook her head. "I don't know much about it at all."

"I'll have to send my condolences along to him. Would that be appropriate when I never met her?"

"If you care about him, I think he'd appreciate it." Madigan nodded.

"Care about him?" Evette scoffed. "I love him. He's still my son. You're still my daughter—same as Gracie."

How? How could you still think that?

Madigan tried to hide her reaction, but Evette had seen it in her face.

"Even if you don't consider me your mom," she said and went into a coughing fit once again.

She reached for her cigarette pack and tapped one out. "Is that all you came for?" Evette asked, an edge to her voice.

The dream. I saw him.

"I remember seeing John at the house one time. I was little. You don't remember?"

"Can't say I do. I don't think he was ever there when you girls were." Evette put her cigarette in her mouth and grabbed a pink lighter from her pocket.

"You said you have nightmares."

Evette froze and took the cigarette out of her mouth.

"I do," she said, nodding. "Of Eli beating me. Beating— well beating you girls. I don't know how I stayed with him for so long, just afraid of what he might do next. In my nightmares, he's always this dark shadow. He's always lingering over me. Waiting for me to step out of line. To punish me."

Will you remember my nightmare?

"It's probably normal," Evette said, clearing her throat.

"I guess so."

Evette nodded and lit her cigarette.

"I used to dream of a body—a dead body," Madigan said, staring down at the carpet. "I don't know if you remember, but I used to dream of someone dead in the house, being dragged across the floor."

Evette blew smoke from her mouth, nodding. "You don't *still* dream about that, do you?"

Madigan looked up at her, watching a small glint of concern flash across Evette's face.

"Well, like I said, it's probably normal. You saw a lot in that house. We both did. The beatings, the emotional abuse. The bad business Eli was always a part of, dragging us into it." She shook her head. "You've got to try to let it go."

She's got to be kidding.

Madigan made a scoffing noise and moved to stand.

"I'm sorry," Evette said, and Madigan stayed in her seat. "You have to know I'm sorry."

She imagined the grief and guilt the woman lived through alone each day, and she'd always assumed she *was* sorry. Sorry for letting her husband use their foster children as drug mules and hustlers—stealing from people. Sorry she'd let him abuse them, just as he'd abused her. And sorry for the way it all ended and what she said the day they were all taken away.

"I know," Madigan whispered. "But you can't just let it go. You know that."

Evette nodded and scratched her thin arm. "You doing alright for yourself, Maddie?"

Madigan nodded.

"Good," Evette whispered and stared off in a trance.

"I'd better get going."

"If you see Grace," she said, "would you tell her, too? That I'm sorry."

She would have recommended telling her in person, but she doubted Evette would ever get the chance. Madigan nodded.

"That's a good girl." Evette smiled. "Good to see you,

Maddie. Thank you for coming to see me, if only to deliver some bad news."

Madigan walked to the door and lingered there while Evette stayed in her seat.

I'm being silly, and I've embarrassed myself over a nightmare.

"Well, then," Evette asked, "is that all?"

Some part of me wanted to see you. Needed an excuse.

Madigan nodded, unable to put her feelings into words. "Goodbye, Evette."

She waited, but Evette stared down into her lap, smoothing her robe over her knee again.

Madigan saw herself out. She hopped down the staircase, each step releasing a flood of emotions.

Evette was sorry, just as she'd known all along, but the words made it real. She had always been a sad woman, but the years hadn't been kind to her, and Madigan carried guilt over it. Like somehow it was her fault.

She was the reason they escaped from that hellhole.

The reason Eli was taken away in handcuffs the same day she and Grace were taken back into the custody of child services.

The reason Evette screamed at her, telling her what a bitch she was as Eli was shoved into the police car and child services arrived.

Two officers held Evette back as she turned her attention away from Madigan, reaching out for Eli, crying in hysterics.

On some level, Madigan thought there was a chance once Eli couldn't hurt her, Evette could be the woman she was when he wasn't around. Fun and oftentimes silly. Sweet and more attentive to her and Grace. More relaxed.

But Evette had blamed Madigan.

As the police car drove off that day, and she stopped struggling against the officers, she gave Madigan the dirtiest look, a look intended to burn through her. But abuse,

Madigan had learned since, took control of the victim in ways of pain and binding shame. With guilt and psychological warfare.

Madigan learned that after her first relationship, where she too had been abused. When Drew found out, he and his best friend, Jack, met her and her boyfriend on the way home from school and kicked him until he stopped moving.

After that, she stopped speaking to Drew for weeks, and her abusive boyfriend never spoke to her again. Drew forgave her, and she learned through her experience that it was possible to become attached to your abuser in ways no one else understood.

To want to be with them despite, and in a twisted way, because of, the pain they caused.

She was just upset that day. Lashing out. She didn't mean it.

Maybe now, I can forgive her like Drew forgave me.

As she got on her bike, she debated calling Grace to tell her what she'd discovered about John, but decided against it.

The news was meant to be told face to face, just as Evette's apology would be.

Maybe Grace can forgive her, too.

On her ride back along the coast of Bones Bay, she thought about the ever-changing nightmare of the body being moved in the house on Warbler Way.

"I saw some crazy shit," she muttered to herself, agreeing with Evette's sentiment.

Maybe it was just a dream.

But the scorpion.

The nagging feeling of something more, just under the surface, tugged at a place deep inside of her.

After parking in her driveway, she pulled the business card from Thom's Tackle from her purse.

John Talbot, Co-Owner of Thom's Tackle—the office number and his cell number typed out just below.

She took her cell phone from her purse and punched in his number.

Was it you in my nightmare, John?

What have you done?

She hovered her finger over the green call button.

CHAPTER NINE

Grace strode out of the real estate office without gaining any insight into what happened to Lily that night. In her car, she tucked Lily's colleague's statements into her file folder, counting through the files. Number six was missing. As she walked back through the department, Mac and Tarek, the tech analyst, had congregated by the coffee pot.

As she approached, Mac did a double take.

"I thought you were checking out the vic's co-workers?" Mac asked.

"She brought in the least out of the whole office; she was extremely new to the game, and no one had anything of interest to report about her. One of her colleagues last spoke to her that afternoon after she'd shown a house for her and said she seemed normal. It's a dead end."

"I see," Mac tucked his thumbs into his belt.

"Any leads from the cell records?" she asked.

That you didn't think to call me about?

Tarek turned to Mac, who nodded. "I was just telling

Mac, I finished looking through the records of the night in question and the night prior."

"Should we go back to the board?" Grace asked.

"Uh, sure," Tarek nodded, and they waited for Mac to start walking back to their room before following him.

"Okay," Tarek said. Mac grabbed a dry erase marker. "Lily Martin called John Talbot's place of work, Thom's Tackle, the night prior. No one picked up, and I doubled-checked. They were closed."

"She might have thought he stayed late," Grace muttered.

"Then we've got a call from Mrs. Christine Martin, her mother, the night prior, just after eight. They had a fifteen-minute conversation. No texts the night prior."

Mac nodded and continued to write. "And day of?"

"One text to a colleague, agreeing to show a house for them that afternoon upon request from the client. Patricia Colt texted her back with 'thanks,'" Tarek said.

Grace nodded. "She showed the client a few houses, brought the keys back to the office, and that was the last they said they'd heard from her."

"The next activity came at 8:35 p.m. An outgoing call to an unlisted number, a pay-as-you-go cell phone."

"Okay," Mac said. "Know where the phone was located at the time Lily called?"

"I've narrowed it down to one cell tower in Amherst," Tarek said and referred to his papers for the first time. "That last call lasted for less than a minute. That was the last phone communication she had."

"Where in the city?" Mac asked.

"Near the distillery district," Tarek said, handing Mac a piece of paper with a map on it. He'd outlined the area with a red circle.

"Wild Card's in that area," Grace said. "Where Mickey said he was."

"Yeah," Mac said. "But he didn't mention a call. That's a big area. The warrant for John Talbot's and Michael Clarke's records should come through soon enough, and I want you on them ASAP."

"Got it," Tarek said, then strode past Grace toward the door.

"If Mickey used a burner phone, it won't be on his actual cell records," Grace said.

Tarek nodded. "But we can see if his phone ever left that area."

"Good call," she said, nodding, before Tarek left the room.

"Have you looked through Lily's phone yet?" Grace asked.

"They're still processing it. I'm going to collect it after the coroner's tomorrow."

Grace nodded. "Yep, I'll be there. Eight tomorrow to see Lockwood?"

Mac nodded and passed her, stalking down the hallway toward the break room.

She leaned over the desk and grabbed Mickey's sixth file that had been tucked under one of John Talbot's files. Banning assigned them both the case, and there was no reason she couldn't look at John Talbot's files for herself if she wanted to.

She opened a thick file with John's name on the side and flipped through it, glancing at the door every few pages.

So why do I feel sneaky?

She stopped at the first image, a mug shot of John, age nineteen. His cold eyes betrayed his smirk, revealing a certain sadness at the time of the photo.

Arrested for possession and sent to jail for six months.

Grace herself had been a drug mule for her foster father, although she'd never been caught, and for the first year or so hadn't a clue what she was delivering.

John served his probation cleaning the area surrounding

the locks by Bones Bay. He started Narcotics Anonymous for the first time that she could see in his records at that same time. She placed the file to the side and flipped open the next. Foster care records, as well as adoption papers.

Something else we have in common, John, although I never found anyone who wanted me as their own.

"Sheppard?" Mac asked, poking his head into the room.

She jerked away from the files. "Hmm?" She looked up at him, clutching Mickey's files to her chest.

"Don't write on my board," he said in a deep voice, and she smiled. "Seriously."

"I wasn't," she called as he disappeared back around the corner, and she exhaled, shaking her head.

What have I gotten myself into?

She grabbed John's files and took them to the room across the hall with the photocopier.

I'll leave your files alone and make some of my own.

CHAPTER TEN

M adigan hit the green button, but hung up straight away.

She couldn't find the right words, and without a real introduction, John had no reason to speak with her.

As she danced around the kitchen, cooking dinner for the first time that week, she referred to the recipe book before each step. She wanted to make it up to Will for leaving her side of the bed empty the other night and thought she could use the cooking practice before the next night when his parents would come to celebrate Will's news.

She glanced at her phone.

What would I say to him?

She needed more evidence to prove her dream was real or a better way to connect with John.

Maybe Evette could make the connection?

As she danced toward the garbage can with a cutting board of carrot shavings, Buster nudged her leg.

"Hey, boy." She smiled down at him. "You like my moves?"

Buster wagged his golden-haired tail and sat between her and the garbage can.

"Ahh, I'm sorry." She turned toward his doggy bowl, brushing some shavings into it. "There ya go."

Buster's tail wagged faster as he trotted over to the other side of the bowl and chomped on the shavings.

Madigan sang along as she turned back to the counter and set a red pepper atop the cutting board, belting out the chorus and shaking her butt as she grabbed her knife. In the reflection of the kitchen window, a dark shadow moved behind her, and she jumped, turning around.

"Hey, babe," Will said, taking his wallet out of the pocket of his scrubs. "Sorry, did I scare you?"

"Yes, and I have a knife!" Madigan set it back on the counter. "You did that on purpose."

Will laughed and nodded. "I'll admit it, but I wouldn't have if I'd known about the knife."

"You know not to mess with me when I have a weapon," Madigan whispered.

He cornered her between himself and the counter.

"I know you're dangerous *without* the weapon." He leaned in close. "But I like messing with you. You're cute when you're surprised."

He kissed her lips, then her cheek, continuing across her neck.

"Oh, yeah?" She giggled, grabbing his toned arms.

Since when do I sound like a giddy schoolgirl?

She caught herself every once in a while saying and doing things she'd never have imagined. Being with someone for so long, letting them lead the way like she had with Will was unimaginable at one time in her life. Letting herself be physically vulnerable had always been easier than being emotionally vulnerable.

He pushed his forehead against hers and stared into her eyes. "God, I love you," he huffed, smiling.

A push and pull for power—their dynamic kept things

exciting, but each time she exposed herself emotionally, she felt like someone else.

She pushed his arms away from her, and he stared down at her with a confused smile.

"Everything alright?"

She nodded and turned back to the counter, avoiding the expectation of reciprocating his feelings for her, and chopped the pepper.

He kissed the back of her neck and she closed her eyes, enjoying his soft touch. "I'm going to have a shower quick," he said.

"Want company?"

He didn't.

He never asked her to shower with him after work, and she knew it. She used it as a way to make it seem like she was trying without having to follow through.

Why aren't I really trying?

"Maybe next time," he said, pulling away from her and popping a carrot stick in his mouth. "But later tonight, maybe you could show me those moves?"

Madigan laughed as he walked toward the front staircase with Buster wagging his tail close behind.

"You're sexy when you dance like that," he said. "I'd like my own private show."

"If you're lucky," she called to him.

As Will jogged up the stairs, Buster trotted back to the kitchen, watching Madigan at the counter.

"You're a good boy," she said and hummed to the music instead of singing out loud as she finished preparing the food.

While she'd lived with Evette, their regular diet consisted of take out and frozen dinners, when they remembered to feed them. After moving to her adoptive parents' home, she learned to cook from her mom. Felicity took pride in the meals she made, emphasizing that the cooks of the family brought everyone together.

Madigan realized years later that the simple idea had been the true motivation for her passion for cooking. To please the people she loved and to bring them together, even when everything else seemed to be falling apart. To keep them together, even when she wasn't sure it was possible after Drew's death. It worked for a short while, until her mom and dad retired early to Florida for three quarters of the year.

Every year.

"Babe," Will called to her as he entered the kitchen from the foyer. "I'm off tomorrow, so make me a list of whatever you need for dinner tomorrow night, and I'll grab it, okay?"

She nodded and kissed him as he walked by. Each time he did something nice for her, she felt even more out of place.

"Thanks," she muttered under her breath.

He went to the iPod station and changed the music to a jazz song she couldn't recognize.

"Babe," she said, "I was listening to that."

"Oh, sorry," he turned to her. "But I thought this song would be fun."

She cocked her head to the side as he waltzed over and took her hands in his. "To dance to," he said, smiling, and spun her around.

"You're so cheesy," she laughed and let him lead her around the kitchen.

"You make me want to dance." He pulled her in close. "I can't help it. I still want a private show after dinner though."

After dinner, she had a drink date with Grace.

"Ah, Will, I can't," she said, letting go of his hands. "I forgot, I'm meeting Grace at Roy's for a drink."

His hands dropped to his sides, and his smile faded.

I should invite him to come. I should want to invite him to come.

"It's just for a little while. I'll be back before eleven."

He nodded and rounded the counter to the other side as she dropped the pasta into the boiling water. "I was hoping to have you to myself tonight."

"I know." She turned around, the invitation to him on the tip of her tongue, but she stopped.

I need to talk to Grace in private about John.

"But," she said, smiling and gesturing to the stove, "hopefully this dinner makes up for it."

He smiled, but it wasn't real.

Say something. Get mad at me.

"So how was work?" he asked.

She sighed and stirred the pasta. "Alright."

Why can't you just get mad at me, and then we can get over it instead of letting it fester?

He sat at the kitchen table and rested his head on his hands. She couldn't stand to see him mope around.

"Actually," she said, setting the spoon down. "I got the front page."

"What?" He held both hands out. "That's great!"

"Well, I'm sharing it with Thane, but it's a step in the right direction, I guess."

He rounded the counter and lifted her up, giving her a peck on the lips before setting her down again. "Your hard work's finally paying off. I'm sure you'll get the cover all by yourself. So what's the story?"

"A woman was found dead in her home."

"Oh, I heard about that," he said and smiled. "That was you? See, your story's got everyone talking."

"She was a realtor here in town. Her fiancé is probably a suspect."

"Wow," he said, shaking his head and setting the table.

"They say it's always the husband. It's an odd saying, because obviously it's not always true, but it had to come from somewhere."

As he continued on, she thought about John.

Maybe he's more messed up than I am, living in that house for so long.

After dinner, Will insisted on cleaning up, and Madigan headed out to Roy's.

On the ride down the coast, the motorcycle's engine drowned out the crashing waves along the rocky shoreline. The sun had almost set as she pulled into the lot and drove around the whole thing twice before she found a space.

As she entered Roy's, the amber light fixtures glowed in the darkness, illuminating the bar, and tiny red candle holders gave a romantic, cozy glow to the booths around the perimeter. Billiard balls clicked together behind the bar, and between the loud chatter and laughter that filled the room, it felt like coming home. It had been a second home when she worked there as she attended college, until she got the job at the paper.

Roy's howl rang out above it all, and he smiled, nodding to her as she reached the bar.

"There's my favourite lady," he chuckled. "What'll ya have? The usual? It's on the house, Knox!"

Madigan nodded. "You're in a great mood."

She turned to one of the old regulars beside her. "Billy, can you guess why?"

"I've heard all about it," Billy groaned.

Roy chuckled with his back to them while mixing her a Jack and Coke.

"I want to meet this woman," another patron called from the other side of the bar.

"You won't catch her in here with the likes of all you

assholes," Roy hollered, laughing as he added four cherries to Madigan's drink.

"Shut up." The patron laughed.

"Can you believe it, Billy?" Roy asked as he handed her the drink. "I'm dating a sober woman."

"For the tenth time, Roy," Billy sighed. "I don't care if she drinks or not. So'long's I get mine!"

Madigan took a sip of the drink, the fizzy carbonation tickling her nose. As she waved to a regular across the bar, just past him, Jack Holden took his shot at the pool table.

As he stepped back, he looked straight at her, like he felt her presence. Madigan nodded toward him, and he handed a friend his cue before shuffling through the crowd toward the bar.

Toward her.

"She texted me over lunch," Roy said.

Madigan smiled and nodded to him, pretending to be deep in conversation.

"Did she tell you you owed me this drink?" Madigan took a sip, and the carbonation bit at the back of her throat.

"She didn't have to." Roy winked at her. "I know how to treat a lady. I'm seeing Cindy tomorrow for lunch."

"Great, Roy." She nodded, feeling Jack's presence behind her. "Oh, and cut it out with the swearing around her, alright?"

Jack's pine-scented cologne wafted around her. "Madigan," he said, nodding.

He slipped into the space between her and Billy, his leg brushing against hers.

He'd taken the time to style his short, shiny, dark hair, and instead of one of his old firehouse t-shirts she always saw him in, he'd opted for a fitted white dress shirt and dark jeans.

His biceps are huge.

Or are those his triceps?

Is he on a date?

I shouldn't feel jealous, but I'll be disappointed if he's with someone.

"Jack." She smiled. "How are you?"

"Doing good, thanks," he said, turning toward the bar and scanning the bottles of alcohol.

"Out for a good time?" Madigan asked.

He looked at her and grinned. "Huh?"

"If you're out for a good time," she said, "I suggest Jaeger or my personal favourite shot, tequila."

"I think beer's more my speed tonight." He grinned. "Another pitcher of Canadian, Roy."

Roy nodded and turned away, leaving them there together. Alone—even in a crowded room.

"So what about you?" Jack asked. "Are you here for a good time tonight?"

"I'm having a drink with Grace." She smiled.

He frowned and leaned in closer.

He can't hear me over the crowd.

"I'm having a drink with Grace," she said louder, and he nodded. "She should be here soon. I'm surprised actually. She's never late."

His cologne overwhelmed her in a way she would never admit, in a way that made her want to lean in closer.

"I could sit with you until she comes," he said, his lips almost brushing her ear.

I need space.

"No," she waved him off, and he took a step back. "That's fine. You know I can take care of myself."

His gaze fell, and she knew he was thinking about Drew. Drew had been her protector since the moment they met, a year before they became siblings legally.

Jack Holden had been Drew's best friend since birth.

They rarely went anywhere or did anything without the other and grew up across the street from each other.

The Knoxes and Holdens had been the best of friends.

Jack took Drew's death hard, just like Madigan had, but they'd only grieved together until the day after the funeral service, when Madigan made the mistake of kissing Jack.

She'd mistaken his kindness and sympathy for a real attraction, having had a crush on him since she'd arrived at the Knoxes' home. He had pulled away just after their lips touched, telling her in no uncertain terms that he was sorry before leaving the funeral parlor.

She remembered his shocked expression and the embarrassment she'd felt for months afterward, but the feelings of grief and guilt made the moment of embarrassment between them feel inconsequential, and she supposed it had for Jack too, because in all the years after the accident, every once in a while he'd check on her. It was a duty that had been passed on from her brother to his best friend without words, merely by an unspoken bond of brotherhood.

She had taken care of herself before she'd met Drew, and since, but while they were siblings, she'd never felt more safe. He had made sure she would never let another man abuse her again, first because of him, and after, because of Jack.

"Are you here with anyone?" she shouted, keeping her distance.

"I'm just here with the guys," he said. "Why?"

She smiled and shook her head. "Nothing—you just—you look like you're on a date."

"I do?" He laughed, tilting his head to the side and pressing his lips together, shrugging while rubbing the stubble on his chin.

She took a sip of her drink as Roy worked his way back over with Jack's beer.

"You know I'm here if you ever…" Jack said, the smell of beer on his breath.

Madigan nodded as Roy set his pitcher down on the bar in front of them.

Before he could say goodbye, she stood from her stool, saving them an awkward moment.

"Have a good one," she shouted and grabbed her drink, shuffling through the crowd to the patio door.

She carried her drink around the large wrap-around patio that faced the ocean and spotted Grace sitting at a small table, watching the waves crash in toward them beneath the royal blue sky.

She's sad.

Madigan knew, instinctually, as if they had been sisters by blood. As if they were twins with a special intuition that kept them in tune to each other's feelings.

"Hey," Madigan said, sitting down on the chair across from her. "I didn't know you were here already."

Grace pulled her blazer closed over her chest and smiled. "I love taking in this view."

"I know," Madigan said and took a sip of her drink. "I saw Jack inside."

Grace raised her brows and turned to her. "Really?"

"Yep," Madigan sighed. "Awkward as ever."

"I'm sure he's forgotten about it. You should, too." Grace brought her wine glass to her lips and sipped the mahogany liquid.

"Tough day?"

"You could say that," Grace said. "How about you?"

"I got the front page. Well, sharing it with Thane, but still…"

"Yes." Grace set her glass down. "You broke the news about my case."

Madigan nodded.

"Listen, it's important to find out what really went on while assuring the town we're doing everything possible to keep them safe," Grace said, leaning forward in her chair. "So I'd appreciate it if you could run your info past me before publishing it. In the future."

Madigan cocked her head to the side.

"Just for this case," Grace said.

"I know you have a job to do, Grace, but so do I. This is big for me."

"It's not just a job. This is my career. It means a lot to me," Grace said. "I'd like to make a good first impression here."

Madigan wanted to argue that she had a career too, equally important, but before she spoke the words, she knew she'd be lying.

She tried her best, but she didn't take the job with the paper even half as seriously as Grace did hers. Grace had been through several schools and programs to become a special detective. She'd come so far, but whatever happened while she was undercover had nearly drowned her—the waves still sucking her in, and she needed to keep afloat.

That's all she's trying to do, and I have to help her.

"Alright, but I can only control myself. Thane's a shark, and when he smells blood—"

"That's all I ask." Grace held her hand up and leaned back in her chair. "Thanks."

Madigan nodded. There wasn't a good way to bring up what she'd discovered about John, so she took a big gulp of her cold drink to prepare. It burned her throat, and she smacked her lips together, kick-starting her confession.

"I found something out today," Madigan said. "Something that connects us to your case."

Grace pursed her lips and frowned. "What do you mean?"

"When I saw John Talbot, Lily's fiancé, outside the house last night, he looked familiar."

Grace frowned even more, revealing a few tiny lines across her forehead on her otherwise wrinkle-free face.

"I did some digging," Madigan said.

"Of course you did."

"And it turns out, John is Johnny. Eli and Evette's kid. They adopted him, unlike us, but still."

Grace's eyes opened wide, and she stared past Madigan.

"I know. It was hard to believe at first for me too, but I checked it out. I went to his employer's place and spoke with him. I saw a picture there, and he looked just like he did in the photo Evette kept hidden in her drawer."

"I never saw it," Grace said, shaking her head.

"Then I—I went to see Evette."

Grace furrowed her brow. "You *what?*"

"I had to know for sure before bringing it to you." Madigan pulled a piece of hair away from her face and tucked it behind her ear, safe from the wind.

Grace stared at her. "I can't believe it."

Grace could be disappointed in her all she wanted, and she could think what she wanted about Madigan's motives to see Evette, but the fact was, they knew a suspect. Lived in the same house he did. Were raised by the same people he was.

"She confirmed it's him. She doesn't keep in contact with him either except birthday cards."

"Like she does with you." Grace folded her arms over her chest.

"And you," Madigan said, "before you changed your address and didn't tell her."

"I don't want her cards. I don't want anything to do with her."

"Well, it doesn't change the facts about John."

Grace took a sip of wine and swirled it around in her glass. Madigan pictured her mind moving in much the same way.

"Don't believe me?" Madigan asked.

"I've seen his records. I haven't had time to study them, yet. It makes sense, but it doesn't make him anything to us. He's not our brother."

"Our past is connected though," Madigan said. "There's no denying it."

Grace tilted her head back. "What am I supposed to do with this?"

She's not asking me. She's talking to herself.

"Hey, we won't say anything. I'm not telling anyone. I don't want the people at the paper finding out. Or Will. No one needs to know."

"My boss does," Grace said. "And my partner."

"Do you think John knows about *us*?"

Grace pressed her lips together and shook her head.

Madigan thought she might have seen a glimmer of recognition in John's eyes the night before in his driveway. If Evette had ever mentioned them, it wouldn't have been enough, but if he'd come back like she remembered, he might have seen them. Known their names.

If he knew about them, maybe he'd agree to meet with her.

"You sure?" Madigan asked. "You've talked with him. He didn't seem to know you? Your name?"

"No, and I want to keep it that way."

* * *

Grace had always known one's past could haunt them.

It followed her, taunting her, and taking away any moments of happiness in her personal life, but as her connection with John sank in, it had the potential to end any chance of rebuilding her life in Tall Pines.

"Anyway," Madigan said, "I just had to tell you. I—I don't

know what it means for your case. I'm still trying to figure out what it means for us. In general."

"Nothing, Madigan." She grabbed the handrail that divided them from the rocky coast below. "It's not going to affect us at all because it's in the past."

Madigan rubbed her forehead and cleared her throat. "Do you remember that nightmare I used to have? About the body being dragged across the hall on Warbler Way? There's a chance it was him, Grace. I think it was John."

"But it was just a nightmare."

"That's what Evette told me, and you started telling me the same thing when I'd wake up and climb down into your bed, but it came from somewhere, and he has a tattoo like the one in my dream. The scorpion."

"You never told me that."

"Well, I hadn't put it together until I saw that picture at Thom's Tackle. If he killed Lily—"

"Madigan," she turned to her sister, "I don't want you getting any more involved in this. I've got it handled. It doesn't mean anything."

She tried to convince herself as much as Madigan, but because of their similarities, she knew neither would drop it.

Drop the conversation, then.

"Is that the reason you invited me here?" Grace asked.

"Well, I had to tell you in person, but I also wanted to spend some time with you."

She studied her sister, her long highlighted hair blowing in the wind, hiding a disappointed look on her fair face.

Grace gave her a small smile and sighed. "Me too. I was wondering if you'd be bringing Will along. I'd like to get to know him."

"He has to work early." Madigan cleared her throat. "And besides, I wanted it to be just us. Like old times."

Doesn't explain why he couldn't share a quick drink with us.

Madigan twisted one of the cherry stems from her drink around her finger.

"Is everything alright with you two?" Grace asked.

Madigan had walked on eggshells with her since she'd been back to town, but if she ever hoped to get back to the place they once were, it had to be give and take. Madigan had to be herself again too.

"Will's perfect as usual, and I'm so, so far from it. As usual."

Grace sipped from her wine glass and rolled her eyes as she swallowed. "Madigan, you never give yourself enough credit."

"Will's like this dream guy. He's—he's *your* kind of guy."

Grace shook her head. "I don't have a kind of guy. I haven't thought about a guy in a long time."

She had to pretend to like the last man who paid her attention while undercover. Pretend to have chosen of her own volition.

They told her that eventually, it might feel normal. Get easier.

It didn't—especially not when she had no choice but to shoot him.

"Well, maybe you should be open to it." Madigan shrugged and sipped on her drink.

"Back to *you*," Grace said. "You're not getting away so easily."

"He's just so—he's a surgeon for crying out loud. I'm a local news entertainment reporter who—" She stopped and took a drink, shaking her head. "He gives medical lectures at fancy conferences. I lecture Buster about waking me up in the middle of the night to be let out. He's written medical articles. I write articles for the local paper. He's successful, even-tempered, reliable. And *he* wants to be with *me*. It's pathetic."

"You're not pathetic. Will loves you. You yourself claim he's brilliant. He has a good head on his shoulders, and he's chosen to be with you. Do you want to be with him?"

"I do," Madigan said, resting her drink against her chest, covering the A and M in Pearl Jam. "You're right, I have to get over it. Sometimes I wish he was more passionate. More emotional."

"You can't change him, Mads. You know that."

Madigan tossed the rest of her drink back. "I'm all vented out. How about you?"

Madigan had been open and honest, and she felt the need to reciprocate, but not about the dark things. She couldn't open Pandora's Box.

"My new partner's kind of a jerk." Grace sighed.

"How so?"

"He doesn't want to work with me, for starters. I think he's heard rumors about me, and just like every one else, he believes what he hears."

"What has he heard?" Madigan asked.

Grace shook her head. "Hell if I know, but it makes this case harder than it needs to be. I don't feed into it. I keep hoping maybe once he sees how I operate, he'll get a better understanding of who I really am."

A man at the railing by the corner post caught her eye. He kept looking her over, puffing on his cigarette. Dread washed over her as she fought to concentrate on Madigan.

"…but I'm sure it'll get better," she said.

The man pushed himself off the railing and sauntered toward them.

She didn't know many people in town, and no one should recognize her. If they did, they were from the city. Maybe from her time undercover.

"We should go," Grace whispered to her.

If her cover had been blown, despite the reassurance that

her mistake had been contained, someone could want revenge.

Madigan gave her a confused look as the man stopped at their table.

"Ladies." He smiled and focused on Grace. "I was wondering if I could buy you both your next drink?"

Grace stared up at him, but the man only smiled, swaying back and forth from side to side, waiting for someone to speak.

Grace exhaled and shook her head. "No, thank you."

"Thanks for the offer." Madigan smiled up at him with her big blue eyes, set off with thicker black eyeliner that reminded Grace of the way she'd done her make up undercover as Cheyenne. "But I'm taken."

He held his hands up and flicked the butt of his cigarette over the railing.

"Had to try." He grinned and backed away from them.

"You alright?" Madigan asked.

Grace nodded and fixed her hair.

"Grace, tell me what you're thinking."

"Sometimes, I feel like someone from the past is looking for me. Someone from my undercover op."

Madigan frowned. "I thought they were all in jail or…"

Dead.

"The ones who had any power are, yes." Grace leaned in closer. "But I met a lot of people during that time, and if anyone knew who I really was…"

"You're safe, Grace." Madigan leaned over close to the table. "You put the bad guys away, and you moved here. No one knows you here. It's a clean start."

My past always catches up with me.

"Madigan, you know better than most that there's no such thing as a fresh start."

Madigan pursed her lips. "I'm starting to wish I'd taken him up on that drink."

"Me too," Grace sighed. "I know I'm just paranoid sometimes, but it's part of the job."

"It must be exhausting."

"Sometimes. I try to focus on moving forward, though."

"Me too. You're right. Let's get another drink. It's on me."

"I think I'm good for the night. I have an early start ahead and files to go over."

Madigan nodded, and Grace recognized the disappointment in her eyes. "How about you come over tomorrow night?" Grace asked.

"I can't. I have the family dinner from hell."

"Ah yes." Grace laughed. "I'm sure it'll be better than you think." She stood and tugged at the bottom of her blazer.

"Maybe," Madigan said, standing with her glass in hand. "I'm not holding my breath, though. I'm going to bring these inside for Roy. I'll text you if I learn anything else, alright?"

Grace nodded and handed her the wine glass. "Thank you. Sounds good."

Madigan disappeared through the door into the noisy bar. She took the steps down off the deck toward the path to the parking lot and wondered if John was having a drink of his own.

She knew he had more in common with her than she thought—an advantage that could help her understanding of him as a suspect.

The roses. Just like Eli gave to Evette after a fight.

If Banning kept her on the case, she'd make the connection an asset. Even if he did, her connection to John would be another strike against her in Mac's eyes. Another reason she wasn't fit for the job.

Still, truth was the best policy.

Nothing good has ever come from a lie.

CHAPTER ELEVEN

Raven Lockwood stood at the counter, staring down at her clipboard. Grace knocked at the window of the steel door, and she waved her in with a polite smile.

"Grace Sheppard. We met the other night."

"Raven Lockwood," she said, leading Grace over to Lily's body, taking long strides as her voluptuous curves swayed back and forth. "I remember you because it's not often there's a new face in town. Especially not with the Tall Pines PD."

Grace cleared her throat and folded her hands together in front of her, glancing at the covered body of Lily Martin.

"How do you like it here?" Raven asked.

"It's a beautiful town," Grace said.

"Charming, right?" Raven smiled. "If it hasn't yet, it'll grow on you. I've been here all my life, and once people come to visit, they usually stay."

"Is that so?" Grace said.

"Don't get me wrong. It has its downsides. Everybody knows everyone else's business like any small town. There's a bit of ignorance here, too, but I'm proud to call it home.

Visible minorities like us are generally met with tolerance at the very least. What's your background?"

It had been a long time since anyone had asked.

"I actually don't know. I'm told my dad was white and my mom was aboriginal," Grace said. "How about yourself?"

"Dad's grandparents were from Sudan before they came here. Mom's Caucasian, and her parents' side traces back to England." Lockwood smiled and tossed her thick dark braid over her shoulder. "Have you had any bad experiences here regarding your race? Being mixed?"

"In Tall Pines? No." Grace shook her head. "But I haven't been here long."

Amherst was another story.

Lockwood nodded. "You do plan on staying, right?"

The steel door opened, and Mac strutted into the room in a dark suit.

"Mac, you clean up nice," Raven smiled. "For me?"

He laughed and shook his head. "Always for you. I also happen to have a meeting later on."

"Ah, with the lawyers?" she asked.

He nodded. "You didn't start without me, did ya?"

Lawyers. Personal or professional?

"Of course not," Raven smiled. "Just getting to know Grace a bit. Let's begin."

They stood around the slab, and Lockwood pulled the sheet down, revealing Lily's grey face and dull blonde hair, chunks of which had kept their orange tinge from soaking in blood.

"I'll begin with the obvious," she said. "Blunt force trauma to the back of the head leaving a triangular laceration deep enough to mark the skull. That was the COD."

"Instant?" Mac asked.

"Not long after," she said. "The laceration is one point

three inches deep, right against the skull, as I said. No further causes contributed to her death."

Mac nodded. "With a cut that deep, it seems like our suspect had to be close to create that kind of mark. In your opinion, could it have been caused by a vase, or would the edge of the table be more plausible?"

Lockwood grabbed a photo from the file on the tray beside them and held it under the light.

"The marks line up exactly with the corner of the table," she said, pointing to the corner stained in blood. "Stomach contents included spaghetti, tomato sauce, and bread. No materials found under her fingernails or in her mouth; however, through a rape kit, I was able to produce a sample to send for testing along with the underwear she was wearing."

"Good," Mac said. "What else?"

"No broken bones, current or previous, and a few small bruises on her knees and forearms. Aside from a papercut, she's clean."

"Tox?" Grace asked.

Raven stared down at Lily. "The tox screening showed a .07 blood alcohol level. Other than that, she was clean."

"Anything else you feel worth noting?" Mac asked.

Raven pursed her lips and shook her head.

"In regards to the COD," Grace said, "where exactly is the head wound?"

Raven grabbed a file and handed it to Grace. "That's my copy. I have yours to go. First page."

Mac stepped over and stood over Grace's shoulder as she flipped the page.

"See where I've made the mark? That's an exact replicate."

Grace nodded. "Right on the very back of her head. So she wasn't turning around. The bruises, were they recent?"

"Some." She pulled the sheet down all the way, "One on

each knee were recent, but the marks and bruises on her forearm in the shape of finger prints have almost healed. I've documented them all."

Mac nodded. "Thanks for meeting with us, Raven."

"Of course," she said, covering Lily back up. "Any questions, please don't hesitate to call."

Lockwood held the file out to Grace, but Mac swiped it away from her and tucked it under his arm.

"Have a good one." Mac nodded and started for the door.

"Take care." Grace nodded to Raven, and she nodded back, leaning closer.

"Don't let him do that," Raven whispered. "Us women have to stick together, and you can't let him walk over you like that."

Grace's cheeks emanated heat, and she hesitated before following Mac out of the building where he held the front door open for her.

"Thanks," she nodded as she stepped by him. "So the only way this was an accident is if she was holding the vase, then slipped and dropped it, because the glass was beneath her too. It broke before she hit her head against the corner of the table, and then she bled out."

"What could she have tripped on?" Mac asked.

"I don't—"

"I've checked the pictures. There was nothing there to trip on. Why would she have picked up the vase? Doesn't make sense."

"You think someone else touched the vase? Threw it? Broke it?" Grace asked.

"Or she moved it," Mac said, stopping as they reached the side lot. "Listen, I don't want to speculate on this until we can get to the crime scene and go over it with what we know. How many times do I have to tell you? I don't work on theories. I want the facts."

Mac sighed and rubbed the back of his neck, shaking his head. "Just meet me at the crime scene, alright?" he said.

Grace nodded, and they parted ways. Being passive wasn't getting her any further with Mac. No matter what she said or did, it wasn't right.

So what? I just shut up? Let him embarrass and belittle me to gain his respect?

She followed his car out of the lot before he sped up on the street.

He doesn't even want me near him while we're driving. He can't stand me.

Maybe he thinks I don't belong here, but this is my case too.

Raven Lockwood is right. It's just as much mine, if not more.

She stopped just after the traffic light turned yellow and let him speed through the intersection.

Then act like it, Grace.

CHAPTER TWELVE

Madigan clicked the bookmarked link to the previous year's fishing competition and read the article headline from the *Tall Pines Gazette*.

Thom Hanks and John Talbot win Biggest Catch, Tall Pines 2016.

She skimmed through the article, but found no new information to be gleaned. She clicked the next article she'd saved, an event held at Thom's Tackle. Even less information that time, but a related article led to a link she hadn't noticed before.

It was coverage of a charity event held by Thom Hanks to raise money for the Big Brothers and Sisters program in Tall Pines. She saw the same picture from Thom's office of Thom and his wife with their arms wrapped around each other, and Thom's arm around John, while John held the hand of Lily Martin.

All four had huge smiles and seemed close.

John Talbot was an easy man to track, but he'd only existed for the past decade. Before then, Madigan couldn't find his last name or any articles or websites that mentioned him.

Grace has access to background checks. She must already have information from his time at Eli and Evette's. Time served, if any. His whereabouts during that year after he left and we moved in.

The year someone dragged a body through the hallway on Warbler Way.

She typed in the year she and Grace had turned seven along with Eli and Evette's last name, Thornberry.

No results.

Her cell phone rang, and she answered it. Paul from the business section shot her a dirty look from the cubicle across the way.

"Hello?"

"Hey, babe," Will said. "Listen, I'm on my way into an emergency surgery. I'll be out by 2:30, 3:00 at the latest, but I was wondering if you could pick up those groceries for tonight?"

Madigan shrunk down in her seat. "Yeah, of course."

"Thanks, babe," he said. "Gotta go."

"Bye," she said, pulling the phone away from her ear, but he'd already hung up.

Great.

She caught Paul looking at her again.

"This isn't a library," she said. "We don't have to be quiet." She shook her head, glancing back at the screen.

Did you take their last name when you were adopted, John? Or did you keep the last name you were born with?

"That's cute," Thane said from behind her, and she sat up rigid in her seat. "You're trying to find a lead, aren't you?"

She ignored him and minimized the internet tab.

One last piece of information to check out before grocery shopping for the dreaded dinner. Paul from the business section had unwittingly given her the idea.

The newspaper's archives for the year in question had yet to be transferred online, including unpublished articles and research the reporter at the time may have done on any missing persons. Tall Pines Library kept the archives, no doubt collecting dust, but if there were any leads, she'd find them there.

"Not talking to me now?" Thane smirked. "Real professional, Knox."

Madigan swiveled around in her chair. "And it was so professional of you to have lied about the police department."

Thane shrugged. "You know what they say about the early worm. Anyhow, how'd you like the front page today?"

His interview with Chief Banning that he'd tricked her out of had made front page, and she assumed Ornella hadn't even questioned him when she learned the article had been his alone.

Madigan picked up her side bag and threw it over her shoulder, grabbing her helmet from the floor under her desk. He stepped in front of her, his chest puffed out and his arms crossed in front of it.

"You don't want to work together?" She raised her brow. "That suits me just fine—but stay out of my way."

She pushed past him and strutted down the hallway to the front door, feeling his eyes burning into her until she left the building.

On the way to the library, she passed the on-ramp for the highway to the city. There was one person who could tell her John's prior last name, something Thane didn't have, and all it would take was a quick visit.

This time, I won't let her avoid the question.

She made a U-turn and merged into the right lane and onto the highway. The whole way there, she blasted music on the radio, trying to settle her nerves.

When she arrived, she found a parking spot a long way

down the road. As she drifted into it, a man jogged to the stairs of the triplex and looked up and down the street.

John?

Madigan took off her sunglasses and squinted in his direction. He jogged up the front steps, looking both ways again before entering the building.

John. What are you doing here?

She turned the radio off and rested her hands on the handlebars.

She had planned to pretend it was a regular visit, just because she wanted to see her.

If I go up there now, I'll need a plan.

She searched the street—almost positive he didn't have police detail following him.

No one knows you're here but me.

Half an hour passed, and each time someone exited the other doors of the triplex, her heart beat hard in her chest.

Maybe I should go in. Have Evette make the introduction.

Her cell phone buzzed beside her. A text from Will.

Babe, could you pick up chardonnay? The kind my mom likes. Two bottles.

She had two hours to get back to town, pick up the groceries, wine, and prep dinner before his parents arrived.

This dinner is important to Will.

I should go.

I'll regret it.

Maybe just five minutes.

Five minutes turned into another half an hour, yet she couldn't make a move to start the bike again or get off.

Now or never. Don't chicken out.

Drew had repeated those words so often over the course of the seven years she knew him, she'd parroted them back to him when he needed an extra ounce of courage.

Despite the fact he'd never told her, she knew he didn't think she was a chicken.

At times, when she opened up to him or their parents about the years previous to her adoption into the family, she'd catch a pitying stare from all three of them, but Drew had always tried to hide his.

He somehow knew that pitying stares upset her more than retelling the difficult parts of her past did.

He knew what she'd been through, and a time or two, he told her he thought she was brave. Once he uttered those words, she never wanted to live up to them more.

As Madigan climbed the steps, she tried to keep her composure.

I've been thinking about old times, she rehearsed, as she reached Evette's first door.

I've been thinking about old times, and I want to be close again. I want to get to know John.

As she reached the second door, it creaked open, and John stood on the other side, staring. A flicker of recognition filled his puffy bloodshot eyes, and Madigan stopped in front of him.

"You're Madigan," he said.

"Hello, John."

CHAPTER THIRTEEN

"Has John been back here?" Mac asked Officer Malone in the patrol car out front.

"Nope. Only people to come in and out of this road are the other two neighbours. This is what happens when people want their privacy," Malone said. "You wanna be alone. Fine, but no one'll hear ya scream out here."

Mac rubbed his forehead and stood up tall beside Grace.

Malone doesn't mince words.

"That'll be all, then." Mac tapped the top of his patrol car before Malone started his engine.

As he drove off, they started up the steps toward the front door, and Mac's keys jingled as he searched for the right one.

"Listen," he said, staring down at the keys. "Sorry about back there."

Grace frowned, not knowing what to say.

He stuck the key in the keyhole and paused.

"I had a meeting with my ex this morning at her lawyer's office in the city," he said without looking at Grace. "She wants more child support."

"Oh."

"Which is ridiculous," he looked up at Grace, "because she was having an affair with some guy at her work. I think she's living with him now. Can't prove it, though. So she's going to get the money." He shook his head and twisted the key, opening the door for Grace.

"Sorry to hear that. Why don't you know where she lives?"

"She's probably nervous that I'll pay her boyfriend a visit," he said, shaking his head. "I wouldn't waste my time. This whole split has shown me a different side of her. We meet at a drop off point to drop our daughter off and pick her up."

You didn't answer when Mr. Martin asked if we had kids.

He separates his personal and professional life well.

"That must be tough."

"Yep," he said, clearing his throat.

They walked to the living room entrance and stared down at the bloodstain on the carpet and the rose petals that had turned a dusty rose colour, going on brown.

"Alright," Mac said. "Friday night. No rain. John comes home late from work with flowers."

"Lily puts them in that vase, and then puts them where?" Grace asked, taking out her notebook. "If she herself moved them, it could have been an accident, but if they were put here from the start, that rules out the possibility she broke it."

Where were the flowers?

"Right," she said. "Let's say she put them in the middle of that table, okay? For the purpose of our re-enactment. We'll ask John soon."

Mac nodded. "They eat spaghetti, bread, and drink a bit of wine. John leaves soon after, just before eight."

"Dorothy, the neighbour across the street, confirms that," Grace said.

"Lily cleans up the kitchen," Mac turned in that direction,

"then she calls someone. She knows John is gone to Amherst. Knows he'll be gone at least two hours."

"So maybe she invites them over? No signs of forced entry."

"So they come over," Mac turned back to the door. "She lets them in. They talk? Have sex? Argue? They end up here."

"If they fought, there's not much sign of struggle. Nothing under her fingernails. Nothing out of place or damaged in here, except the vase."

Mac nodded and stepped into the living room. "So does she pick up the vase, drop it, trip over her own feet, fall back and smack her head?"

"Or does someone else pick up the vase, smash it, and then push her over?" Grace asked.

"To hit her head like that, she had to be standing here, facing the front window. If someone pushed her, they wouldn't have grabbed her from behind. There's no room with the table and how she fell. She'd have been watching them."

Grace nodded. "She'd have looked her killer in the eye."

"If the call was insignificant, which I don't think it was," Mac said. "There's a possibility John came home late, they fought, and he pushed her over by accident. If he put those bruises on her arm, he's certainly capable of doing that much."

"So he scrambled. As she bled out, he thought about calling for an ambulance, but he knew he'd look guilty?"

"Maybe," Mac said. "I want to know what prints were on that vase. If any had been wiped away. I just don't see how she could have tripped at that angle. There's nothing to trip on."

"It doesn't make sense why she'd be moving the vase. Maybe she had it in the kitchen and moved it to the living room, but with the time of death closer to eleven than ten, I don't see why she'd have waited that long to do it." Grace scanned the room. "So can we rule out the possibility it was an accident and treat this as a murder investigation?"

"If John tells us the vase was in the living room from the beginning," Mac said, nodding. "I think we have to treat it as a murder."

As they locked the door, the neighbour, Dorothy, waved to them from her garden. They both waved back before walking to their cars.

"Meet back at the station to check out Lily's cell?" Mac asked.

Grace nodded before they parted ways.

Back at the department, Mac made a beeline for the coffee, and Grace continued down the hallway.

"Hey," Mac called. "Don't touch anything 'til I get there."

Grace didn't bother looking back, but by his lighter tone, she guessed he was smiling. Instead of going to their room where the evidence had been dropped off, she turned right and knocked at Chief Banning's office door.

She had to let him know about Madigan's discovery before she went any further in the case.

I should have come right here, right away this morning.

Why didn't I?

"Come in," he called.

Because this truth could take me off the case.

She opened the door, and he looked up from his papers. "Ah, Grace," he smiled.

"I was hoping I could talk to you for a second about the Lily Martin case."

He nodded, dropping his pen on the paper in front of him, and gestured to the seat across the desk.

"What about the case?" Mac asked as he bustled in with his foam coffee cup and sat in the chair next to her before she could.

I guess you might as well be here.

"There's been a development I need to discuss with you," Grace said. "Through research into one of our suspects, John Talbot, I've found a connection that might be of some concern to you."

"This is the first I'm hearing of this," Mac said to Banning, frowning.

"Chief, I discovered John was adopted by the same foster parents I had during the early part of my childhood, and while we were never at the household at the same time, and I'd never met him or heard of him, it loosely connects me to the case," she said. She felt Mac staring at her, and she couldn't read the Chief's expression. "Of course, I understand if you have concerns with this connection, and so I wanted to bring it to your attention—"

"I don't." Banning pushed his chair back from the desk and folded his hands in his lap.

"You don't have concerns?" Mac asked. "Well, I do. I'm concerned you didn't come to me and let me know."

"It's the first time I've been back here since discovering this information, and I'm following procedure by bringing it to the Chief first."

Mac laughed and leaned back in his chair. "Following procedure. You. That's a good one."

Chief Banning shot Mac a look, and he stopped laughing and continued fidgeting in his seat.

"I appreciate your candor regarding this recent development, Grace, but I don't see how it affects the case. You did not know him previously, correct?"

Grace nodded. "I just found out about him now."

"And are you still in touch with that foster family?" he asked.

"Not since I left them at age eleven," she said.

He nodded. "I don't see the issue, then."

"The issue," Mac said, standing, "is that even if she's telling the truth, she could still have some bias toward the suspect, not to mention the issues with taking this case to the DA while connections can be formed. What if the media gets ahold of this? How could we prosecute if John Talbot is the killer, while the person collecting evidence, is what? His sister?"

"He's not my brother," Grace said. "We do not have any relation, only a shared home at separate times."

"I'll speak with the DA, but as I said, I can't see this being an issue," Banning said. "If it is, Mac, she's already been on the case. Already been at the crime scene, questioned the suspects, had access to the evidence…"

"And everything would be thrown out in a court," Mac said.

"Don't get ahead of yourself," Banning said. "And both of you—not a word to anyone. I'll clear this up with the DA and get back to you. Until then, keep working."

"Banning," Mac said. "What if the connection is discovered before then?"

"I hardly see it as a connection," Banning shrugged. "In a small town like this, aren't we all connected in some way? We'll deal with it if it comes up. Back to work."

"Thank you, Chief," Grace said, and stood.

She walked past Mac out of the office. Mac and Banning exchanged words, but she didn't catch what they said.

Why does a clear conscience feel less than clear?

She pulled out the small folder of John's files she'd photocopied and sat down.

She needed the one thing missing from John: a motive.

Was it the cheating with Mickey? No, they made up.

Did she cheat again? Maybe.

Or was it a simple accident? Less likely, but possible.

"You know something?" Mac asked, stomping into the

room. "You're *worse* than I'd heard. Didn't think it was possible."

Many of the cruel things her colleagues at different levels in law enforcement said behind her back had gotten back to her when others threw it in her face. She'd heard much worse than anything Mac had said, and she promised herself she'd let it roll off her back. Keep the past far away from her future.

Grace stared up at him. "I'd like to focus on the case at hand."

"No. No excuses or distractions. Why didn't you tell me first?"

"It's procedure—"

"I don't want to hear that bullshit. We've been together all morning, which means you knew since then at least. Who knows? Maybe you saw him and recognized him."

"I didn't."

"And you didn't say a word to me."

"Honestly, I didn't think I had to. Banning doesn't seem to think it's a big deal, so why make a fuss over nothing?"

"Banning's checking into it, and you'll be off this case by the end of the week. I guarantee it."

Kicked off her first case back. Another dark mark to add to her file.

Grace sighed and closed the file. "Is this business or personal?"

"I know what you did in the city."

"This feels personal. You're so angry, and for a man who doesn't believe in theories and hearsay, you sure gobbled up whatever gossip you heard about me."

His brow rose. She'd caught him.

"They got their intel on you from the reports. Straight from your sergeant's mouth."

"It's still gossip," she said. "If you're going to judge me so much on my past—which by the way, you only *think* you know—instead of getting to know me for yourself, we can't work together."

"No," he said, "we can't."

He stared down at her, sneering.

Are you trying to intimidate me?

"This is my turf," he said.

And the next piece of information I need is from the cell phone.

She stood and grabbed her purse and the photocopied files before strutting past him. Her heels clicked down the hallway, and the door slammed behind her.

She turned the corner and approached Tarek. "I'm looking for Lily Martin's cell phone that's been processed, sent over from evidence," she said.

He nodded toward a box on the back counter. She opened the box and unzipped the bagged cell phone. She turned the phone on and the screen lit up. Footsteps slapped against the tiled floor behind her.

"Mac doesn't like anyone touching his—"

"I'm Detective Inspector Grace Sheppard," she said, extending her hand. "I don't think we've been properly introduced."

"I'm Tarek," he said. "Tech analyst."

"I'm on the Lily Martin case as well, as you know."

"I know, but Mac—"

I won't let him treat me like that.

"Mac needs to learn how to play well with others." Grace smiled.

Tarek grinned and shrugged. "It's on you then."

"Yes, it is. Nice to meet you, Tarek."

She turned back to the phone, and as he walked away, she tapped the messages. She scrolled thro ugh the ones marked "John." The last text she received from him was at 6:30 the night before she died.

Hey baby, I'll be a little late for dinner.

Lily hadn't replied.

Grace read through the past texts.

How's work?

Congrats on the sale, baby.

I'll be late again.

John, where are you? You said you'd be back before midnight.

Pizza or Chinese?

Thom's wife's retirement party is next month. What should we get her?

Something for her garden.

Great idea, baby.

Nothing out of the ordinary, so Grace scrolled back as far as she could through their text history.

Congratulations, Baby! That's great news. How are we going to celebrate your promotion to partner?

How about dinner out tonight?

Sounds good, I'm thinking I've got dessert covered.

Lily had sent a risqué photo of herself in lingerie.

She's beautiful, Grace thought.

You're beautiful, you know that? How did I get so lucky?

The rest of the texts ranged from the mundane to racy, and at worst, impatient, as John seemed to be home late a lot.

Where were you, John?

Footsteps slapped against the tile behind her, and she turned around. Mac rested his hands on his hips, standing before her with pursed lips.

He expects me to be the shrinking flower I've been since I got here, but it's gotten me nowhere.

"Since we aren't working together anymore, you can have this when I'm finished with it," Grace said.

Mac opened his mouth, but she continued, "Or, we can look at it together."

He shook his head and walked away. Before he reached

the door he pointed to Tarek. "You coulda given me a heads up," he said.

Tarek raised both hands and laughed. "Sorry, Mac."

"Bring it to me when she's done," Mac said.

Grace turned back to the phone and clicked on other texts.

Messages to her mom's cell phone let her know she was alright and to stop worrying. She could feel the love her mom had through her worried messages and remembered being like Lily, just wanting space from her final foster parents.

The last number Lily called that night sat at the top of her call history list, and Grace wrote it down. Tarek told them it had been a burner phone, but Grace thought once she had more information, she could give it a call herself. Or a text.

As she left the department for the day, she thought about the chaos she and Mac working independently would cause.

She wanted to go back and ask John more questions, but their connection was more than she'd let on, even to herself. She was nervous to speak to him, knowing where he'd lived. Who his foster parents were and what they'd been capable of. What they'd made her and Madigan do.

She wondered what John had been made to do as she reached her car and debated paying him a visit. Instead, she took a page from her sister's playbook. It had gotten her more answers so far.

She drove in the direction of Bones Bay, hoping John's employer knew how late he had been working, and moreover, where he'd gone afterwards all those nights he was late getting home.

CHAPTER FOURTEEN

"I'm surprised to see you again so soon," Evette said.

John opened the door all the way and stepped to the side. Evette smiled up at her from the same seat on the couch, and Madigan took the seat she had the day before. John closed the door and stood facing it.

"Please, help yourself to a drink," Evette said. "Still like room-temperature water?"

Madigan pressed her lips together and shook her head with a small smile.

"See, I remember everything," Evette said, the smile fading from her lips as she picked up the butt of her cigarette. "I could have guessed it was just a phase."

"She's a reporter," John said, striding into the living room and standing by Evette. "She's the one who ambushed me, quite literally, that night."

"Oh," Evette said, her mouth remaining open.

"I'm sorry about that," Madigan said. "I honestly didn't know who you were, and I was just doing my job."

"Is that why you're here?" John asked, and Evette stared at her with the same skeptical look.

"I've been thinking about old times," Madigan said, glancing at the clock.

Fifteen more minutes. Then I'll be home in time to start dinner.

"So have we," Evette said, nodding. "We were just catching up."

John walked around the coffee table and sat on the other end of Evette's couch.

"How long's it been since you two saw each other?" Madigan asked.

John opened his mouth.

"Oh," Evette said, "must be a while now."

John shot her a look but kept his mouth shut.

"I thought you only sent him cards—like me," Madigan said.

"Well, we've seen each other from time to time. Right, Johnny?"

He nodded and rested his hands in his lap.

Why did she lie to me?

"I'm really am sorry for your loss, John," Madigan said.

"Thanks," he muttered. His long sleeves hid his tattoo, and she willed him to roll them up like they'd been the night she first saw the scorpion.

"It's terrible," Evette said, fussing with her rings. "Just terrible. I was just telling John if he needs me to help organize the funeral services at all—"

"I told you," John said. "Her parents will be doing that after they're finished with her body. They won't let me have any part of it, I'm sure, and since we were only engaged..."

Tears welled up in his eyes, and he licked his lips before clearing his throat.

"It's just as well they're taking care of it, Johnny. You're grieving right now," Evette said, grabbing a cigarette out of her pack. A taller pile than the day before sat in the ashtray.

"I'm sure if you speak to them," Madigan said. "Or maybe

write them a letter to let them know how much Lily means—meant to you—"

"Why are you here?" John lifted his head. "Really, is this for a story?"

"I didn't know you'd be here. To my knowledge, you didn't even visit each other."

"We do, Maddie. I just—I didn't want to say too much yesterday." Evette lit her cigarette, taking a puff before waving the smoke away.

"Why?"

"I'm protective of him." Evette shrugged, like she couldn't help it. "I'm his mom. I'd feel the same if, God forbid, you should ever go through something like this. Losing a loved one."

Madigan clenched her jaw and sat back, recoiling from the sting and memory of Drew drifting down the river away from her.

"Seriously," John asked, "why are you here?"

I came to find out your last name, but having you here might be even better.

"John," Evette said, barely finishing his name before a coughing fit came on.

Gain his trust. His weakness is the loss of Lily. His strength is his skepticism.

"I lost someone, too," Madigan said. "It was almost ten years ago, but I'm still not over it, so I don't suppose you'll be in that time, John, I'm sorry to say."

John stared at her, his eyes a deeper red than when she'd arrived.

"I was going to tell you," Madigan said, turning to Evette. "The day after it happened, I was going to come here and tell you. I wanted you to comfort me. Make it better somehow, like you used to when things were bad. Really bad. They'd never been that bad."

Drew's head disappeared under the water and never came up. The harder she tried to swim, the further away from him she felt.

They both stared at her.

Remember why you're here.

"I came to admit something," Madigan said. "I've kept all the cards you sent me. Ever since I was eleven."

"I've kept yours too," Evette said.

"Me too," John muttered.

Evette stood and rubbed her temple with her index finger. "I've got vertigo worse than ever. It takes me a minute after I stand up to get my footing. Patience for me?"

Madigan nodded and checked the time again.

Eight minutes.

She disappeared down the hallway, and Madigan sat in an awkward silence with John until a thump came from down the hall.

"You alright, Ma?" John called.

"Fine," Evette called back.

"I never knew much about you and your sister," John said. "Not back then. She's told me a bit about you since, though."

Madigan nodded. "She kept a picture of you. You looked familiar."

"Ah. Listen, I'm sorry about your loss. Who was it, if you don't mind me asking?"

"My brother. Best brother in the whole world."

John pressed his lips together and stared down at his lap as Evette shuffled her way into the living room with a shoebox in each hand. Evette set them on the table and coughed as she bent over, opening one. She took out one of the cards and handed it to Madigan.

"This is the most recent, and all the way to the back is from when—when you left."

Madigan opened the card and pretended to read it, although she still remembered picking it out. Choosing a card with the proper wording always took longer than she liked, but it was important to express her feelings and be true to herself. To their relationship.

Evette had seemed to do the same.

While each of Madigan's cards ended only with her first name, Evette always included the word love.

Evette handed John a card. "That's the first one you ever sent me back. After you left."

John lifted one leg over the other, resting his ankle against it as he opened the card.

He's relaxing. Good.

"Evette, could I have that glass of water now?" Madigan asked with a smile.

"O'course," Evette said, shuffling her way into the kitchen.

"I came when I was seven, to Eli and Evette's," Madigan said. "Left when I was eleven. How about you?"

"They adopted me at birth. You didn't know?"

Madigan shook her head and lowered her voice. "She didn't really talk about you. Especially not in front of Eli."

He nodded. "No, I guess she wouldn't."

"I took my adoptive family's name." Madigan leaned forward, still whispering. "I was never more proud than to share my brother's last name."

He nodded. "I kept my birth name. Briar. Only thing I have from my parents, and they insisted it not be changed."

Madigan nodded and leaned back. "More than I have. Why did you change it?"

"I wanted to start over," he said, pursing his lips afterward.

"I know what that's like." Madigan stared at her hands in her lap, avoiding his gaze.

"It's nice that you get it. I don't know anyone else who was adopted, or fostered, I mean," John said.

"Me either. Just my sister."

"Grace," John said.

"Madigan," Evette said, stopping just in front of her with the glass in her frail hand. "I love you and Gracie. And Johnny. You know that?"

Madigan nodded, although she hadn't known that for sure back then. She'd since discovered what real love was.

Evette handed her the glass. "But I tried, and I'm still trying."

She picked her cigarette back up from the tray and took a puff before sitting back down, coughing until she got comfortable.

Madigan glanced at the clock.

Time to go.

"Madigan," Evette said and leaned over her lap. "You kept the cards, and I'm glad for that, but why didn't you come to me that day? When you needed me? I'd have been there for you. What happened?"

"The day my brother died," Madigan said.

Evette looked around the room and tilted her head back, wiping at her eyes. "So much loss," she huffed. "I'm so sorry for both of you."

"It felt like we'd grown too distant, Evette. It's hard to explain, I guess."

"But you still wanted to come here," Evette said.

Madigan nodded.

"It's natural," Evette said, before taking another puff. "Just like Johnny."

Madigan gave John a half-hearted smile, and he returned one.

"We have a connection," Evette said. "A bond that time and distance just can't break. I even share one with Gracie, whether she'll ever admit it or not."

Madigan shrugged.

"I don't understand that girl," Evette said.

Madigan frowned.

"What?" Evette asked. "I know it was difficult, but she must know I tried. I did my best, and I just don't think she can appreciate that."

"It's complicated," Madigan said.

"Still sticking up for her?" Evette raised her brow.

"Evette—" Madigan started.

"You don't think I was a good mother either," Evette said, crossing her arm over her lap. "Just say it."

"You're not going to put that on me," Madigan said, standing from her chair.

"No," Evette said, her voice quivering. "I'm not. You're a grown woman. You make your own choices. You understand consequences now too. It was my fault. All of it was my fault, and what I said to you the day the police came—"

She pressed her lips together.

"Ma," John said, reaching for her hand.

Madigan opened her mouth, but Evette held up her hand. "I'll *never* forgive myself," Evette hissed. "You were just a child —and you saved us. You ended it."

Madigan's shoulders drooped, and she grabbed both arms of her chair.

She's admitting she was wrong. That I did the right thing.

She doesn't hold it against me anymore.

Evette shook her head. "I know I made mistakes, but now I'm all alone. Johnny's all I have left. When you came yesterday, I was shocked, but it was the best thing to happen to me in a long time. You've always been a ray of sunshine, Maddie."

Madigan stood in front of her, speechless.

"I'm glad you came to see her," John said, grabbing Evette's hand. "I'm glad I got to meet you. Officially. There was something about you…"

Madigan nodded and caught the clock from her peripheral.

Ten minutes late.

"I should go." Madigan grabbed a pen from her bag. "I'm leaving you my number, okay?"

Evette nodded. "Whatever you think of me, and whether or not you decide you want to see me again, when you walk out that door, you hold your head up high, my girl."

Madigan wrote her number on the newspaper on the coffee table, wishing she could show Evette that same tenderness John did.

Finally, just let it go. Forgive her.

"Good bye, John. Evette, you can call me, alright?"

Evette released an exaggerated sigh and nodded, smiling up at her.

"I forgive you," Madigan whispered before slipping out the first door.

A weight lifted off her chest as she trotted down the front stairs, repeating one word over and over.

"Briar."

It would help with her search for the paper, and for truth about what really happened that night.

A nightmare or reality—she had to know.

CHAPTER FIFTEEN

Grace entered the shop to hearty laughter and two men standing by the front counter.

"You tell your son to bring him here next time," the tall man with salt and pepper hair said before turning to her. "Hello, there. Fine day we're having."

Grace nodded. "Great weather."

"Great weather for fishing," the other man said and nodded to her with a wink. "So, I'm off."

"Good luck!" The man nodded and waved as the other passed her, staring at her chest.

Covered or uncovered. Doesn't matter to the ones who view women as less than.

"How can I help you?" The older man asked as he walked back behind the counter.

"I'm Detective Inspector Grace Sheppard," she said, and he winced. "I'm investigating Lily Martin's death. I'd like to speak to the owner, Thom Hanks."

"That'd be me," he nodded and rested his hands on the counter in front of him.

"I'm here regarding specifics about John Talbot's

employment here," she said. "Were you working with him the night of the nineteenth?"

Thom shook his head. "He closed up that night."

"Okay, when was the last time you saw John?"

"Morning of the nineteenth."

"How did he seem?"

Thom shrugged.

Grace waited instead of making any suggestions for him. People always told you more when it was in their own words, when you forced them to break the silence.

"He went about his work as usual," Thom said.

Didn't answer my question.

"Did he seem like his normal self?"

Her cell phone vibrated in her pocket, but she stared at him.

"He was working hard; I know that much. We're just finishing the busy season here, and there's lots of preparations ahead, so he's been busy."

"Mr. Hanks, how would you describe John's demeanor that morning?"

"A little stressed maybe." Thom shrugged again. "I told you, he's got lots of work ahead of him."

"I need to know his work hours for the past month."

"Well, he's not just an employee," Thom said. "I made him partner of this place. As such, he makes his own hours. There's no clock in or out here."

So the times he was late were his choice.

"What can you tell me about the past month, Mr. Hanks? Was John here a lot?"

"Oh yes, he sure was. He's here more often than I am, now. That was the point of making him partner—so I could work retirement hours."

"Mornings or afternoons?" she asked.

"Both. John's a great worker. He didn't always have a

great work ethic, but it developed over those first few years here as his passion for fishing grew. He's here all the time, before and after close too."

"Do you have security cameras here?"

"You're not from here, are ya?" Thom laughed. "This isn't the type of place that needs protection, Ms. Sheppard. No need for that sort of thing here."

But they do now.

"What can you tell me about John?"

"He's a great man. This loss has hit him hard. He loved Lily with all his heart—more than anything in the world—I guarantee it."

"John has a history of criminal activity and drug use."

Thom pressed his lips together and shifted his weight from one foot to the other. "Well, he's not on drugs and hasn't been since I became his sponsor. Didn't relapse once. Not once."

He seems sure of it.

"What do you know of John's past?"

Her cell phone vibrated again, and she took it out of her pocket.

Madigan's name lit up the screen, and she read the part of her text that showed up on the home screen.

I'll be at the dinner from hell but...

Grace shoved it back in her pocket. "I'm sorry, go on."

"I know he's a different man now than he was back then. Raised by people who adopted him—the father sounds like a nightmare—and went it alone when he was of age. Hooked on drugs since he was a teen, he said, but he didn't blame anyone but himself. We got him clean, and he's been sober for well over a decade now. Has to be closer to two."

"Did he tell you much about his family?"

"John doesn't like to talk about it. Just here and there he's said some things, a lot of it I forget, but one thing he said struck me. He said good people do bad things, and bad people do good things, but what makes a person good isn't their intentions. It's their actions. He said that's how he changed. He'd always had good intentions, but he realized his actions didn't match up. He said he wanted to make up for his past. To start new and be the man he always wished he was. He became that man, Detective. He didn't do anything to Lily."

"What did you know of John's relationship with Lily?"

"Had its ups and downs like any relationship." He shook his head. "I'm sorry. I just can't believe I'm talking in past tense, here. They had a bright future. They supported each other's dreams, and now—"

Now Lily didn't have a future.

Lily was dead.

So was Leah.

"I understand it's difficult to think about." Grace bowed her head, thinking of all the things Leah would miss out on.

"Do you?" Thom asked, and she peered up at him.

"I do. It's a dark void where a bright light used to be."

Thom grimaced and nodded. "Yeah, it is. Lily was beautiful. She supported John here, and he supported her with her career. He's a loyal man."

"And Lily?"

"I won't speak ill of the dead," he said.

"This is an investigation into her death, and since it's my job to figure out what happened, I appreciate your full cooperation."

"There was infidelity," he muttered. "I guess it was a one-time thing. A big mistake on her part. They split for a little while there, and John was a mess, but he took her back."

"Did she come asking for forgiveness?"

"I don't know." He shook his head. "I don't know the details. She was back in his life...our lives, and things just kept getting better—that's all I know. They seemed better than ever."

"I appreciate you speaking with me," she said. "If you remember anything else, please give me a call."

He nodded and took her card. "Say, have you taken over the case?"

"How do you mean?"

"Well Mac was already in here and asked me questions, but I see you've got a bigger title."

Grace shook her head. "It's my case too."

Thom nodded once before Grace turned and walked out the door.

Thom seemed to be hiding something, and with such loyalty to his friend and business partner, she couldn't blame him, but she needed to figure out why he wouldn't give a straight answer about John's state of mind and mood that morning.

Stressed.

Not a good sign.

She grabbed her cell phone and opened Madigan's texts to find two, the one she partly read, and an earlier one she missed.

I met John. He knows who we are. Call me when you get this.

I'll be at the dinner from hell, but that's not until seven. Call me before then, please. You need to hear this. Don't be mad at me.

At ten to seven, Grace hoped Madigan would answer as she hit the call button.

Why did you meet with John? Looking for trouble again?

* * *

The doorbell rang just before Madigan's cell phone vibrated on the counter, playing a Foo Fighter's song.

"*That's* your ring tone?" Will asked, stirring pasta.

Madigan stopped chopping peppers and stared up at Will. *He's judgy because he's stressed.*

"I wanted something different than the standard chimes," Madigan said, wiping her hands on a towel. "It's Grace."

"Can it wait?" Will asked.

She'd already disappointed him by arriving home at the same time he had after picking up all the groceries and alcohol. She told him the store check-out lines had been through the door instead of why she'd really gotten hung up.

She bit her lip as the doorbell and her cell rang again. "I think it's important," she whispered.

"I'll get the door, then; you get the phone," Will said and started for the foyer.

Madigan picked up the phone as Will left the room. She'd promised him he'd have her full attention, and she was already breaking it.

She set the phone down without answering and rushed to his side. He opened the door, and his mom and dad stood on the stoop, both dressed for the country club.

His dad held a black box with gold lines around the middle, no doubt his fancy cigars to celebrate Will's latest accomplishment. His mom held out a bottle of champagne, much more expensive than the one Madigan had bought on a whim, and she took it.

"Thanks, Maureen." Madigan smiled. "Come on in."

Will wrapped his arm around her, and they backed up as his parents came in.

"Thank you for having us." Maureen wrapped her arms around Will, pulling him away from Madigan. "We're just so proud of you."

"Thanks, Mom," Will said, and his dad gave him a pat on the back.

"Can I get you both a drink?" Madigan asked. "Chardonnay, Maureen?"

"Oh, I think I'll have a scotch," his dad said, nodding and smiling at her. "Maureen loves vodka martinis. Think you could whip her up one with a twist?"

I guess I spent sixty dollars on her favourite wine for no reason.

"Sure," Madigan said. "Coming right up."

Will kissed her cheek before she scurried off to the kitchen and ushered his parents down the hall toward the living room at the back of the house. She picked up her cell phone, hitting Grace's number.

"Madigan," Grace answered. "Why did you meet with him? What did you find?"

"I went back to Evette's, and please reserve your judgment for later," Madigan said, taking glasses from the cupboard. "John was there. I watched him go in, and he was there for, like, an hour before I—I went in too."

"You stayed and watched for that long?"

"I wanted to know what's going on, so yeah," Madigan said, peering down the hallway. "I went there originally to figure out John's other last name. I know you already know, but you're not allowed to tell me that stuff, so I found out on my own. It's Briar. He told me."

Madigan waited for her to say something as she poured two shot glasses of scotch, second-guessing her pour.

"Grace, you still there?"

"Yeah."

"Okay, so I think I've developed some kind of rapport with him. He seems wrecked over Lily's death, but it could be a show. He could be nervous about being a suspect too. I don't know. Point is, Evette lied about how often she saw him."

"She lies, and you're surprised?"

"Well, I thought it was weird, but it seems like she just wanted to protect their relationship. Could be, though, that she didn't want to be involved. Questioned. You know how skittish she gets around police."

Madigan poured some vodka into the martini glass, and laughter came from the living room as she set the bottle down.

"Grace?"

She's mad I'm interfering.

"Yeah, I'm here."

"So maybe she knows more. Maybe you should question her."

I'll leave it at that. I don't want her upset with me.

Madigan grabbed a lemon from the fridge and set it on the counter in front of her, staring at it.

"Okay, first of all, we can't believe everything Evette says, alright, so wh—"

"I know," Madigan sighed. "Listen, regardless, I had to tell you."

"You can't tell anyone, okay? Don't interview her for the newspaper. Don't tell Will, and I don't want you going back to Evette's without me."

"Without you?" Madigan frowned. "So we're going together?"

"I'll be right back," Will said, his voice echoing down the hallway to the kitchen.

"I haven't decided y—"

"How do you make a lemon twist?" Madigan whispered.

"What?"

"Never mind, I gotta go." Madigan grabbed a knife from the drawer. "I'll call you tomorrow." She pressed end and set the phone down before Will strode into the kitchen.

"Everything okay in here?" he asked, smiling.

"Yeah," she said, tucking her hair behind her ear. "A martini with a twist is with a lemon twist, right?"

Will nodded.

"How the heck do you do that?"

"I thought you were a bartender." Will laughed and rested his hands on her shoulders.

"I was. For years," she said. "No one at Roy's ever ordered a martini with a twist."

"Babe, you just had to ask for help," he said. "I don't care that you don't know how to do it. I'll teach you."

Madigan smiled and nodded. He took the knife from her hand and put it back in the drawer, taking out a peeler instead. She pretended to pay attention to him with the lemon, but all she could think about was the fact that Grace was open to visiting Evette. Even to question her.

A huge, unexpected leap. One she wasn't sure Grace was ready for.

But they'd be together.

Her chest filled with butterflies as Will set the perfect twist of lemon peel on the edge of the martini glass and handed it to her before grabbing the glasses of scotch and leading the way down the hall.

"Think you could call them Mr. and Mrs. Rosenberg?" he whispered over his shoulder. "I don't think they're comfortable with a first name basis yet."

"Oh-kay," Madigan said.

She'd called them that when they first met, but it felt too formal for their second meeting.

Did his mom say something to him?

"Mr. and Mrs. Rosenberg," Madigan said, clearing her throat as they entered the room, and handed Maureen her drink. "I'm sorry that took a moment longer than expected."

They exchanged pleasantries until Madigan felt their judging eyes on her, and the pressure became too much. She had chosen a pair of jeans without any rips and a plain black knitted sweater for the occasion, but she still felt underdressed. Maureen's quick glares at her outfit made her squirm.

I'm not dressed up enough.

Or maybe I'm not skinny enough for her.

"I forgot the veggie plate," Madigan said. "Be right back."

As she rushed back to the kitchen, she turned on the extra lights beneath the cupboards to compensate for the lack of light through the windows. The shadows of the trees in the front yard danced in front of the navy blue sky, and Madigan wished she were somewhere else.

She poured herself a shot of tequila and downed it before she summoned up the courage to go back into the living room. She picked up the veggie plate as Will met her in the alcove.

"Babe?"

She stared at him and gulped.

"Relax. Everything's going to be fine." He smiled down at her.

She admired his confidence in most situations, and it eased her nerves as he took the tray and winked at her.

"I've got this," she told him, and he nodded before disappearing down the hallway with the tray.

And she did feel better, because she had an excuse to hide away in the kitchen to finish preparing the dinner, away from the small talk and judgment, an excuse for a break to be herself for just a little while before breaking bread with the Rosenbergs.

CHAPTER SIXTEEN

The call from Chief Banning came in between calls to and from Madigan.

He let her know that the DA saw no reason she shouldn't proceed with the case. He told her he'd be calling Mac to let him know, and he hoped they'd stay on the same page to find the culprit and do their part in bringing the victim and her family some justice.

Grace thanked him for calling, but the weight that had lifted off her chest after his call was dropped back down on her again after speaking with Madigan.

The last thing she needed was to have more personal involvement in the case, but Evette seemed to have the answers she was looking for.

Exactly like she used to.

Not long after being placed in their care, Grace saw the duo of Evette and Eli as good cop, bad cop. Eli always played the bad cop, but as terrible as he was, he was true to himself through and through. Grace knew what to expect from him, at least.

Evette had been different.

Her honeyed voice and tight hugs that comforted them sent mixed messages when paired with her enabling ways with Eli and the times she'd lose her temper when left alone with them for too long.

Evette had been fighting for survival when Grace entered their house, and she did so by any means necessary, even if it meant throwing them under the bus, giving them up to the bad cop, or leaving them with him when she couldn't deal with it.

Even if it meant that sometimes, whether Madigan wanted to admit it to herself or not, there was no cop worse than Evette.

Grace took out a box of leftover Chinese food from the fridge, grabbed her fork and a glass of wine before moving to the living room and settling in on the couch.

As she ate, she spread Mickey and John's files across the table and poured over each of them, settling them each back in their folder when she was done.

John Talbot hadn't been in trouble with the law or had so much as a parking ticket, while John Briar, the teenager, had several run-ins with the law. He'd been in trouble for many of the same things Madigan had before moving in with the Knoxes: vandalism. Drug possession. Drug selling.

Everything Eli had put them up to, and when Grace refused to do something, Madigan did it for the both of them.

To save them from the beatings.

On her birthday, when Evette had taken them to the fair in Tall Pines, she'd been sure their expedition wouldn't be discovered by Eli. He'd forbidden them from going anywhere, and Evette took a chance by taking them anyway.

Running away from her would have been scary, but Evette would have been compromised had she told Eli they left her when they weren't supposed to be at the fair in the first place.

Grace could never have worked up the nerve to run away to the shore if it hadn't been for Madigan. She'd never have gotten out of the house on Warbler Way if it hadn't been for Madigan either. But Madigan hadn't been with her in the city while she was undercover, and day by day, she gained confidence in herself.

Confidence that was destroyed the night Leah died.

Grace walked into her bedroom with her glass of wine and pulled out the worn binder from beneath her bed. She sat on the edge and flipped it open, setting her glass on the nightstand.

Conrad Burke, Drug King of Amherst, and those accompanying him to check on the incoming drug load had been locked up straight away, denied bail at their first hearing before the judge, and sentenced to twenty-five years for the drug-related crimes they committed, as well the murder charge for ordering a hit on Leah.

Nick and Parish, Conrad's lackeys sent to kill Leah, would have been sent to jail too, if Grace hadn't killed them, but not before they killed Leah.

Too late.

If Evette had answers and could speak to John's state of mind in a way that correlated with what Thom Hanks said, it would be worth a visit.

Follow all the leads, no matter how small.

She'd never imagined she'd be seeing Evette again. Talking to her.

I'll keep it professional.

As she tucked the binder under her bed once again, she promised herself that no matter what she found, she would report it to Banning—regardless of the impact it might have on her career.

By the book, Grace. Follow the rules.

Her cell phone rang, and she frowned down at the number.

* * *

Madigan's cell phone buzzed against her hip for the second time since she sat to eat with the Rosenbergs, but she couldn't disappoint Will by excusing herself to check it.

"Will, could you please pass the potatoes?" Maureen asked.

The bowl of potatoes sat right in front of Madigan, and she picked them up before Will put his fork down, handing them to his mom.

"Oh," Maureen said, sounding disappointed. "Well, thank you, Madigan. So this conference you're asked to speak at, dear. How long have you been going?"

"Close to a decade now." Will smiled and took a sip of his scotch.

His dad clinked scotch glasses with Will. "I'm so proud of you."

"Thanks, Dad." Will nodded and stared at his plate.

"He's blushing," Maureen laughed.

"*Mom*," Will said, shaking his head, "you know, I'm not the only one with good news tonight."

No. Don't do it.

Madigan shook her head in minute movements, hoping he'd catch the signal to stop.

"Is she being modest, Will?" his dad asked.

"As usual," Will wiped his mouth with his napkin. "Go on. Tell them what just happened."

Madigan clenched her jaw and wished she taken a second shot of tequila to deal with this embarrassing moment of attention. "It's nothing," she muttered.

Nothing compared to being a keynote speaker at a medical conference.

"I'd love to hear it," Maureen said, smiling.

"Madigan got her story on the front page yesterday morning," Will said.

"The one about that girl found murdered in her home?" his mom asked, eyebrows raised.

"It's an ongoing investigation, actually," Madigan said, "and they don't know what happened yet."

"Well that's great news, hmm?" Will's dad said before sipping his scotch. "You're moving on up."

"It's actually a shared article with a colleague of mine," Madigan said, tucking her hair behind her ear and clearing her throat as her cell phone buzzed once again.

"Ah," Maureen said, before taking a sip of her martini. "This twist is…cute."

Trying to belittle me, again.

Madigan smiled. "Your son made it, actually."

"It's still great news," Will said, nodding.

"Pretty soon, she'll be working for the *Amherst Times*, hmm?" Will's dad set his empty scotch glass down. "Do you aspire to move on to the city news?"

"I'm sure she could be working there right now if she wanted to," Will said.

Lie. Does he even know it's a lie?

"Well, I'm sure one has to go to college for such a position with the *Amherst Times*, don't they?" Maureen asked.

"Mom." Will finished chewing before continuing. "I told you, Madigan graduated the journalism program from Tall Pines College."

"Oh, that's right." Maureen smiled and nodded to her. "The *community college*. Well then, you should apply for a position in the city. I'm sure there are many more opportunities for front page news."

And what top-notch university did you go to, Maureen? Did you get a job with your degree, or just a husband?

"Yeah, maybe," Madigan nodded, her fingers grazing over the phone in her pocket.

Get me out of here.

"Mr. Rosenberg, can I get you another drink?"

"No, no." He held his palm over his glass. "No more for me. I'll be driving. Say, my partner's brother-in-law is the chief editor for the *Amherst Times*. Maybe I could put a good word in for you?"

"Oh—" Madigan started.

"That's a great idea." Will nodded, and Madigan sat back in her seat.

"Of course," Maureen said, "they might need more credentials than someone who's only made the front page of her local paper *once*."

"*Mom*," Will said.

"I'm just saying," Maureen said, holding her hands up in front of her. "Maybe a bit more experience would do you some good, Madigan. Couldn't hurt to pad the resume. Unless, of course, you don't plan on working after having children. Might not be worth it, then."

Madigan almost choked on her broccoli.

"No plans for children," Madigan said after swallowing. "I'm just going to get myself another drink. Would anyone—"

"No children?" Maureen placed her hand over the center of her chest and glared at Will. "She can't be serious."

Madigan started to stand, but Will grabbed her hand and held it tightly.

"Maybe we should move on to dessert?" Will asked.

"That sounds great," Madigan said. "Right after your mom tells me why it's any of her business whether I want kids or not."

"Ha," Maureen laughed. "I want grandchildren, Madigan.

I know my son wants children, too. You're...who he has chosen to be with. That's why it's my business."

"We haven't discussed that, yet," Will said. "That's a conversation for Madigan and me."

"Of course," Maureen said, rubbing his shoulder. "I'd have thought you'd already discussed something *so important.*"

"Dessert sounds great." Will's dad nodded to Madigan.

She stood from the table and marched to the kitchen, rolling her eyes and pulling her cell phone from her pocket. One missed call from an unknown number and another two from work.

Maybe something happened with the case.

She hit the word Work on the screen and leaned against the counter.

"Hello, Madigan?" Ornella said.

"Hi, Ornella. What's going on?"

"I tried to call you earlier, but you didn't answer."

"I'm sorry," Madigan whispered. "I was having dinner with my boyfriend's parents."

"Alright. An important piece of information has come to my attention and has forced my hand. I'm afraid since you've been keeping your personal connection to one of the suspects in the investigation into Lily Martin's death, and other pertinent information to the case from *The Gazette*, I have no choice but to let you go."

Madigan's chest heaved as she steadied herself against the counter.

"Would you be this upset if Thane had used his personal connections?" Madigan shook her head. "Thane can do no wrong in your eyes. How did you find out?"

"About your foster connection to John Talbot?" Ornella folded her hands on the desk in front of her. "Let's just say I have employees here who are *true professionals* and know how to find crucial information and the importance of sharing it with the company."

Thane.

"This doesn't make any sense," Madigan said.

I never belonged at the paper.

I'm not a true professional.

I'm nothing.

She took shallow breaths, pressing the phone to her ear.

"Madigan, your actual writing is average at best. You put your own personal gains above telling the truth, which is what we're about here at this paper. It's what professional journalists do."

"I thought you were about selling papers, Ornella," Madigan spat.

Madigan remembered her confrontation with Thane the day before, and the search information she must have left on her computer before she left the office with him standing by the cubicle.

"My employees remember their journalistic integrity—"

"Journalistic integrity—ha."

"You always make it personal."

Madigan opened her mouth to argue, but she was right.

She wanted to work on stories that meant something to her. To the community. To find the truth and let it be known. To inform her community. To hold people accountable for what they'd done. To make things better and make a difference.

As long as the paper employed her, they'd stand in her way of each of those objectives. Her own writing abilities would stand in her way.

I'm not good enough.

Who did I think I was?

"Best of luck on your *future endeavors*, Madigan," Ornella said, and Madigan could tell she was smiling. "Cindy will bring you any personal belongings you may have left here, if you'd like to call her and arrange that."

Madigan shook her head.

Not even allowed back in the building.

Maureen's heels clicked across the tile and stopped just before they reached her. Madigan pressed the end button and set her phone on the counter.

What now?

"If I said something that upset you, I apologize." Maureen pressed her lips together and folded her hands in front of her. Will and his dad rounded the corner.

She knew what she'd done, and pretending she didn't was probably just one more way she acted her way through life, but Madigan wanted her gone. She wanted them all gone and wished they hadn't come in the first place.

Will's shoulders hung forward, and his straight face hurt her to see.

He's disappointed.

Just keep it together a bit longer—for him.

Madigan nodded. "Thank you."

"Thank you for dinner." Maureen hugged her, tapping her back as Will came to her side, smiling.

It's okay. It's okay.

"We'll be skipping dessert to get home before the storm," Maureen said.

A storm? The dark sky seems calm, but any excuse for them to leave is a good one.

"I'm glad you're both alright," Will's dad said and put his arm around Madigan as she parted ways with Maureen. He pressed the itchy wool from her sweater against her skin, and she found the urge to scratch it.

"Son," his dad said, shaking his hand, "we're proud of you, and I have every confidence that you'll do great at the conference. You're a smart young man, and we trust you'll do right in this world."

However fake they seemed at times, their love for Will was real.

Their awkward, stiff love.

Maybe I'm jealous?

"Thanks, Dad," Will said and showed them to the door. "Have a safe drive home."

"Come by tomorrow after work," Maureen said. "I've got delicious apple pie waiting for you."

Nope. Not jealous. Irritated by their facades and judgments.

And I tried to be someone I'm not to please them.

"I'll see what I can do," Will laughed, and he waved as his parents walked down the driveway.

"Wow," Madigan whispered.

They stepped back inside and shut the door.

"You don't have to say I told you so," Will said. "I'm sorry. I shouldn't have pushed to have my parents here."

Madigan shook her head, and he wrapped both arms around her, rubbing the itchy wool against her skin once more.

"Talk to me," he said. "Tell me what you're thinking."

"I'm thinking you shouldn't feel bad to want to invite your parents over, but I shouldn't have been attacked like that."

"Attacked?" he asked, pulling away with a grin on his face.

"Okay," Madigan said, sighing, "maybe that's dramatic, but I'm not here for her to make me feel this small and stick her nose in my business. I mean, kids? We haven't been together a year."

The smile faded from Will's face, and he took a step back.

"Listen, my mom was rude. You know how she can be. I should have listened to you—but this isn't how it's always going to be, you know."

Madigan sighed, wondering what a life filled with Maureen's judgments and arguments over family dinners would be like.

"I don't want to find out," Madigan said, shaking her head.

"Babe," he said.

He never calls me that with his parents around.

"Once my mom realizes we're together for the long term, I'm sure things will be better. They'll be amazing, actually."

"I wish I could be as optimistic as you are."

Will frowned. "You normally are."

She shook her head and shrugged, recalling Ornella's words.

I'm a bad writer.

I always make it personal.

I'm not good enough.

"I'm just not having a good night," Madigan said, pulling her sweater over her head, leaving her tank top on and freeing herself of the frustrating itch.

"Is it true?" Will asked. "You don't want kids?"

"Not anytime soon. Can we not—"

"Hold on," he said, pulling her in closer. "I'm not attacking you, alright? It was already brought up, and *it's almost been a year*, babe. I know things with your folks might be complicated, and I know your past with adoption and foster homes might factor into your decision about children, but I think you'll change your mind."

"There's a lot you *don't know* about me and my life." Madigan pulled away from him. "My relationship with my parents isn't just complicated. They—they blame me for what happened to Drew. Not directly, but I was the only one with him at the time, and I think they wish I'd done something. That I could have—"

Tears welled up in her eyes and spilled down her cheeks. Will wrapped his arms around her.

"I wish I could have saved him too," she cried.

"I'm sorry," he whispered in her ear. "I'm so sorry. I had no idea."

"That's my fault," she whispered. "I just wasn't ready to share that yet. It's hard."

She tried to catch her breath and let herself relax in his arms. "It's hard to even admit it to myself."

"Okay," he said, "that's—I understand, and you have to know, it wasn't your fault. That was an accident. You couldn't do anything about it."

Madigan nodded, wiping the tears from her eyes as he bent down and kissed her cheek.

"I didn't mean to push you, okay? Now that I know, I won't mention your parents unless you want to talk about it, alright?"

She nodded again, and her shoulders drooped. Drained and exhausted, as her cell phone rang, she remembered the unknown number.

What now?

Cindy's name flashed across the screen.

"Leave it," Will said. "Let's go to bed and cuddle up, alright? I'll give you a nice massage."

She held his hand as they walked back to the kitchen.

"I'll clean this up and meet you up there, okay? Hey, dinner tasted amazing."

"You're the best," Madigan whispered and walked back to the stairs as her cell buzzed in her hand again.

A voicemail. She pushed the button and pressed the phone to her ear.

"Madigan, Ornella just called to tell me—well, that she let you go, and I'm so sorry. She told me you'll be calling about your things. I won't—"

Mumbling in the background distracted her.

"Sorry," Cindy said. "There's a fire at John Talbot's house. I have to make some calls. Talk soon, alright? Call me anytime."

A fire.

Madigan hung up and turned back to Will.

"Work?" he asked, defeated.

Kind of.

She nodded. "I'm sorry your night was spoiled."

Will shook his head and followed her to the front door where she grabbed her keys.

"Do you have to go?" he asked, and she bit her lip. "I guess that's a yes."

"Sorry, this is big."

"Sure," he muttered, nodding.

"I'll make it up to you," she said, but as the words left her mouth, she knew that's what she'd been promising for the last half of their relationship.

"Sure," Will said again and turned away, walking back toward the kitchen with his head hung down. It wasn't like him to not at least fake a smile to make her feel better.

Will or the other?

That's the choice she had to keep making, and she rarely chose him.

Tonight...

She swayed in the doorway, feeling each second slip by and the fire growing in John's home.

What if John's still inside?

She grabbed her jacket and swung the door shut behind her, rushing down the steps toward her bike.

Tonight would be the same—her own solemn escape into the unknown.

CHAPTER SEVENTEEN

"Fire at John Talbot's house," Banning said. "I'm on my way now."

"Fire?" Grace asked, standing beside her bed.

"I told Mac to call you," Banning said, mumbling to himself. "Just get out there."

"Yes, sir."

Grace hung up and scrambled to her feet, grabbing her jacket and slipping her cell phone into her pocket before strapping on her holster.

Of course Mac wouldn't call.

As she pulled onto the main road, smoke swilled up into the sky above John's neighbourhood.

John, where are you? Please don't be inside.

A fire usually meant someone was sending a warning, or there was something someone wanted to destroy.

Did you set the fire, John?

Maybe someone's got something to hide from the night Lily died.

As Grace turned down his street, a fire truck sat several meters away from John and Lily's on their neighbour

Dorothy's side of the road. The local news van had a reporter getting ready to go live, no doubt, and Mac stood out front with Chief Banning, speaking to Madigan and another man beside her.

Even Madigan knew before me.

As Grace got out of the car, she glanced over at the neighbour's home.

Have you seen anything, Dorothy?

"That's all we've got," Banning told Madigan and the other man. "Please leave room for the firefighters to do their job."

Banning stepped away from them and turned to Grace.

"What do we know so far?" she whispered.

"Someone driving past the street called it in," he said.

Mac stepped beside them. "John was apparently in the city and then out for a drive again." His gruff voice sounded even more coarse than usual. Tired.

"No alibi?" Grace asked.

"We've got Malone on him now back at the motel," Banning said. "After you speak to the neighbours, I want you talking to him."

Grace nodded. "From now on, he needs a tail on him at all times."

Banning nodded. "Done."

Mac stepped aside and started for the police tape.

"Stick with him." Banning nodded toward Mac. "His bark's worse than his bite, okay?"

Grace nodded and stared at the flames.

"Shouldn't be too long before it's out," Banning said.

Grace stepped back while staring up at the flames. She turned toward the police tape, and Madigan stood on the other side, waiting for her, while Mac had already jogged across the street.

"Grace," Madigan said as Grace ducked under the tape

and lowered her voice. "Have you told them about what I said? About Evette maybe knowing something?"

Grace shook her head and kept walking down the boulevard. "Not a word, alright? Not until we see her."

Madigan stopped and reached for her arm, but Grace kept going.

"Listen, *I have work to do*," Grace said. "If you find out anything, text me before you put it in an article, alright? Call you in the a.m."

I shouldn't have snipped at her.

It's not her fault she was here before me.

She left Madigan behind as she crossed the street and caught up with Mac as he stopped in front of Dorothy's front door. He knocked and waited.

"Her car's not out front," Grace said.

"Was it the other day?" Mac asked.

I don't remember. Damnit.

Why didn't I pay attention to that?

Mac turned around and strode down her pathway as Grace followed.

"Thanks for calling me," Grace huffed as she caught up with him.

"We're not working together anymore," Mac said.

"Actually, Banning said I'm still on the case. Got the go-ahead from the DA, and I think it's in the best interest of the case to pool our resources."

Mac let out a short burst of laughter. "You saying you need my help?"

"I'm saying we should put our differences aside for the sake of the case," she said. "We're questioning people twice; you've kept things from me—"

"If I believed you'd be a help to me," Mac said without looking over at her, "maybe I'd agree, but I'm not here to carry your weight."

"This is ridiculous," Grace said, walking double time to keep up with him.

Mac turned up the driveway to the other neighbour's house, and she followed him. The couple hadn't seen or heard anything unusual, and until the fire truck showed up, they had been asleep, unaware of the fire. As they walked back down the driveway, Grace stood in front of him, stopping him.

He's acting like a petulant child. Someone has to take the high road.

"Before we go to see John," she said, "I want you to know I went to see his employer turned partner today."

Mac frowned. "Why?"

"If I knew you'd already been there, maybe I wouldn't have. He said John's been sober—he's his NA sponsor too—but he also wasn't up front or open about John's state of mind the morning of Lily's death."

Mac scratched his chin and glanced down the street at the fire. "I didn't get that impression. He didn't have any new info when I asked."

Maybe you didn't ask the right questions.

Grace shrugged, trying to bite back her opinion.

"The friend John met up with that night, Luke?" he said. "His alibi? He's got several drug-related arrests on his record."

"So if John's clean, why is he hanging around him?"

"I didn't think much of it except poor taste in friends," Mac said. "I want to follow up on the guy. See if they have any mutual friends with similar backgrounds."

"And listen, I have a lead I want to work on. It could give us some solid evidence before we speak to him."

"Maybe we let him sweat it out," Mac said, shoving his hands in his pockets. "He's got Malone watching him. He's not going anywhere. He's gotta know about the fire too."

If we wait, he could have time to form a false alibi.

"You want to talk to him in the morning instead of tonight?" Grace asked. "Why?"

"I think he's scared of something. He's hiding something, don't you think?"

She nodded.

Thom too.

"Together," Grace said. "We go to see him in the morning, *together.*"

"Yeah." Mac turned away from her. "Fine. Eight. We'll get the story on the vase too. Where Lily put it and all that."

He started walking away from her, back down the street, and she searched for Madigan. Her motorcycle was still parked in the same spot, and she saw her sister's back, not far off, talking to someone behind the fire truck.

Madigan had parked between John's house and his only other neighbour's property on Dorothy's side of the road. A team of firefighters worked to extinguish the burning fire, and she spotted Jack, Drew's closest friend, by the wheel of the hose straight away.

Two cars were parked outside the house, one police and one unmarked, along with the local news van.

The first time it doesn't matter, I make it here before Thane.

Madigan jogged toward the house where two officers unrolled a new line of police tape closer to the road.

Paul Banning, Chief of Police, stood speaking with one of the firefighters in front of the flames, and not even the reporter and cameraman had approached him yet.

Where's Grace?

Thane's station wagon pulled up by the curb behind

Madigan's bike. When he saw Madigan, he did a double take, and Madigan laughed to herself.

He can't believe I'm here first.

It'd be funnier if I hadn't just been fired.

"Knox," he said. "What are you doing here?"

"What does it matter to you anymore?"

"I heard you were just fired," he said, rubbing his chin.

"News travels fast," Madigan sighed.

"Does when I'm around," Thane said. "Seriously, why are you here?"

"I want to know what's happening. I wanted to make sure no one was in there, and, well, I guess you know about my personal connection to the case."

"Yeah," he said, taking out his notepad. "Ornella wants me to look into that more."

Madigan pressed her lips together and nodded. "I'm sure she does."

"I don't think it was fair how it all happened." He pursed his lips and stared past her at the fire, its bright orange lights reflected in his eyes.

"Wonder where John Talbot is tonight?" he asked.

Not inside. If he were in there, they'd all be scrambling.

Maybe he thinks I know where John is.

Chief Banning and Officer MacIntyre walked toward them.

"No official statement yet," Chief Banning said. "But there's another truck on the way. Fire's under control for now."

"Is there anyone inside?" Madigan asked.

"We can't confirm or deny that right now," Chief Banning said, and Officer MacIntyre whispered something to him as Grace stepped beside him.

She's just getting here now?

I should have called to let her know.

As Grace pulled the Chief aside, Madigan walked away from the gathering group of news outlets down the line. No lights on at Dot's place.

Wonder if she saw anything.

She caught Jack staring down at her from the firetruck. She nodded to him, but he turned his attention back to the fire.

Great. He thinks I'm so awkward.

Officer Mac jogged past her, and Grace followed further behind.

"Grace," Madigan said as Grace ducked under the tape and lowered her voice. "Have you told them about what I said? About Evette?"

Grace shook her head and kept walking down the boulevard. "Not a word, alright? Not until we see her."

She'll know if John was in there.

She reached out to her. "Listen, *I have work to do.* If you find anything else out, text me before you put it in an article, alright? Call you in the a.m."

No more worries about what I do or don't know, Grace.

I'm unemployed now.

Grace crossed the street and caught up with Mac and stopped in front of Dorothy's house.

I have to talk to Dot.

They stood at the door and looked up at the house before striding down the driveway toward the other neighbour's house.

Guess she's not home.

When she turned around, the Amherst City news reporter was in front of the camera, as composed as ever.

I'm not like them. I'm not a professional.

"So," Thane said, stepping beside her. "What do you bet whoever set this fire killed Lily Martin?"

Madigan rolled her eyes. "I'm not placing a bet about a dead woman."

"Sorry about your luck, Knox," Thane said, taking out a cigarette. "For what it's worth, you almost gave me a run for my money this week."

Madigan pressed her lips together and folded her arms in front of her. Thane shrugged and took a puff of his cigarette before walking back across the street as the last of the fire smouldered and grey smoke lingered around the property.

Her cell vibrated against her side, and she took it out. It was the unidentified number from earlier that day.

"Hello?"

Please don't be a bill collector. I don't have the patience.

"Madigan?" a voice said.

"Yes." An ache swirled in her stomach. "John?"

"Yeah, it's me," he said. "I'm at the Whitestone Lodge. Are you at my house?"

"Yeah."

"How bad?" he asked.

"It's bad." She huffed. "I'm glad you're not inside. No one was telling me anything."

"I didn't do it," he said. "I was with Evette for a while and then took the long drive back to the lodge here. I'm sorry for calling you, but I just needed to know how it was over there."

"Why don't you come? Speak to the police. To Grace?"

"They'll be coming to see me soon," he said. "Could you keep this talk between us? Please?"

He sounds desperate.

"I don't know."

I have to tell Grace.

"I'm sorry to burden you with this," he said. "I just thought you'd be there for the paper. I'm sorry I called. Take care, alright?"

He's reaching out for help.

"John?" she said, pressing the phone to her ear. "I'm glad you called."

"You are?"

"Yeah, like I said. I was worried. So don't feel bad for calling, okay?"

"Yeah," he said, with warmth to his voice she'd only heard when he spoke to Evette. "Okay."

"Okay, bye."

"Bye."

She pressed end and walked back toward the small group gathered by the police tape, searching for Grace.

Jack caught her eye, climbing down from the truck. "Madigan," he called to her, and she walked toward him. "How are you?"

"Good." She nodded. "You?"

"Busy," he sighed. "The other truck's taking care of what's left of it, but I've got to go in and..."

"And?" She smiled as he froze.

"And I forgot. I'm speaking to Madigan Knox, reporter for the *Tall Pines Gazette*."

Madigan grinned. "You're speaking to a friend. Off the record."

"I saw your article on the front page," he said.

"Oh, yeah?" She tucked her hair behind her ear.

"Congrats." Jack smiled, putting on his hard hat.

"Thanks. It's no big deal."

Jack shrugged. "Isn't that an accomplishment? To make front page news?"

"I guess."

A few lines formed across his forehead as he stared down at her. "You sure you're good?"

She nodded. "I'd be even better if you could tell me something about the fire. Strictly off-record."

"You know I can't say anything," he said, pressing his lips

together afterward, but smiling with his eyes. "I don't really know anything yet anyway, except no one was inside. I'm going in to see if we can determine cause."

"Ah," Madigan nodded.

They stood in silence for a moment.

"Still riding Drew's bike," he said, nodding past her.

She turned and caught Grace walking toward her bike from her peripheral.

"Yeah. I've gotta go."

"Me too." Jack nodded. "You take care."

"You too." Madigan turned and walked toward Grace. "So?"

Do I tell her John called?

Like he said, she'll find out everything they talked about later anyway.

"So," Grace said, putting her hands on her hips. "We're going to Evette's. Tonight."

CHAPTER EIGHTEEN

The smooth ride across the highway would have given Grace time to think if Madigan could keep her mouth shut.

"If John's childhood was anything like ours, we know more about him than we thought," Madigan said, and Grace glanced at her for a second before returning her attention to the road. "If he's closer with Evette, maybe their connection will help you with the case?"

She had thought of the same scenario and many others like it, but she couldn't help but wonder if John had turned out the way people would assume an abused, manipulated, and neglected child would.

Growing up, although Eli controlled the drugs, Evette did them too. Maybe she even had favourites that Eli would bring in just for her, but she didn't tell the police that when they were caught.

Finding their file was one of the first things Grace did once she had access to them.

The day Eli was arrested on charges of possession, dealing, child endangerment, child abuse, and evading the law, Madigan faced some of her own minor charges after dealing to a local teen who'd sell the pills at his high school. Grace had been there too, but she'd had a funny feeling as they rode their bikes to meet with the teen that summer day. She told Madigan, and instead of Madigan accusing her of being a worrywart, or cautioning her of the trouble they'd be in when they got home if they didn't make the deal, she told Grace to wait in the bushes with their bikes as she met with their contact.

Grace stayed out of sight as Madigan made the deal, and when the police car drove past the park, Grace shouted to Madigan—tried to warn her it was time to leave by whistling as Eli had taught them—but Madigan couldn't hear her.

The police came after her, and instead of stopping or running back to Grace and their bikes, she took one look at Grace and ran the other way. The police caught her after a longer chase through the neighbourhood than they had admitted in the report, and when they found her, she wouldn't talk. Wouldn't say where she was from or how she had the drugs. The police found their foster parents' address in her file from their records, and before they called, a female officer found the bruising on her arms and backside.

Later, Madigan told Grace she hated the woman for noticing the abuse and loved her at the same time. She'd been brought to tears when she finally told Grace about it. She hated the officer because of the trouble she'd get into when, yet again, the police and child services didn't find enough to back up any claims of abuse or neglect from neighbours or teachers. When Eli would know she got caught on a deal because he'd believe she ratted him out, and the punishment would be far worse than anything she'd ever dealt with.

But she also loved the officer because she was the only one who made her feel safe besides Grace. Who promised her that she and Grace wouldn't be hurt by them again if she just told the truth about the abuse, neglect, and drugs. And she was the only person to follow through.

That day, the police brought them back to their foster home to collect their things as Eli was being cuffed and taken away, and Evette screamed her head off. She'd told them so many times how she protected them. How if it were up to her, they'd be safe together without Eli.

And yet that day, as he was taken, she spat the cruellest, most vile words at Madigan. Grace couldn't remember her exact words, but she doubted Madigan could forget them.

"Maybe Evette could have John come over and..." Madigan continued, but Grace tuned her out.

But Madigan went back to see her—after all these years.

Had the ugly scars of the past worn away, or had she found a way to hide them? Deny them in favour of the possibility that the lies Evette told them were true? That she was the good cop and Eli, the bad?

"... I don't know if that's an option. Grace?"

Do you want to believe her so badly that you can't see the truth?

"Grace?" Madigan repeated.

"Yeah?" Grace said.

"I said, I guess you just want it to be us and Evette this time," Madigan said. "I didn't know if involving John was an option at this point or—"

"Just us and Evette," Grace said, sighing. "I'd say you should call to make sure she's home, but I don't want to give her the heads up."

"I don't even have her number," Madigan said. "She's got mine though."

Why am I not shocked?

"I need you to let me do the talking, alright?" Grace asked. "You're here to facilitate the meeting and corroborate what you told me earlier this evening if she tries to deny what she said or change her story at all from what she told you. That she didn't see John. That she had minimal communication with him."

"Alright," Madigan said. "Are you nervous? To see her again?"

"No."

But her heart beat fast.

This is something else. Not fear. Not nerves.

"I was," Madigan said. They got off the highway and merged with city traffic. "I honestly never thought I'd see her again. I just thought it'd be birthday cards until she passed away, and that's how I'd know she was gone."

Grace clenched her jaw, hearing the sadness in her sister's voice.

"Have you ever checked up on Eli?" Madigan asked as thunder rolled through the sky.

"Here comes the rain they needed earlier for the house," Grace said, looking up at the dark sky.

"Grace?" Madigan said, and she could tell Grace was staring at her.

"Yeah. I do. To make sure he's not getting out."

Her answer must have satisfied Madigan because she didn't speak again until she pointed to a triplex on their right.

"She's in the middle one."

Grace parked down the road a little. Rain pattered against the windshield as they sat in silence.

Madigan nodded. "Let's get going."

Grace followed her upstairs and waited as she pressed the button.

"Who's there?" a raspy voice came from the other side of the door.

Grace wouldn't have been able to identify it, and it threw her off.

"It's Madigan. And Grace."

"Come in," Evette said, and the lock clicked out of place.

There, that sounds like her.

Dread washed over Grace.

What if John's the killer?

What if Evette becomes part of the investigation?

What if she knows?

What if...

Madigan walked inside without hesitation, as if walking into her own house.

She's happy to be here—happy that I'm here.

Madigan closed the door, and they came face to face with Evette. Her frizzy curls hung on her shoulders, and she couldn't remember Evette having all those wrinkles around her mouth. Black mascara was smudged under her lids, and she blinked her red eyes up at Grace.

Grace nodded as Evette stared.

"I know it's late," Madigan said.

"I knew you'd be back," Evette said. "But I never thought *you'd* come."

The house reeked of cigarette smoke, just like on Warbler Way, and Grace took shallow breaths.

"I'm here on police business," Grace said.

Evette nodded and squinted one of her disapproving looks at Madigan. Madigan walked past her and sat down on an armchair in the small living room.

Good. Don't let her get to you.

"I need to ask you some questions about John Talbot. What's your relation to him?"

"He's my son," Evette said, sticking out her chin.

Does she still consider us her daughters?

No, because John was adopted and we weren't.

Just focus on the case, Grace.

"And how often are you in contact with him?" Grace asked.

Evette stared at Madigan, as if willing her to send a signal of how much Grace knew.

She's not your puppet anymore.

"How often are you in contact with John?" she repeated.

Evette took a cigarette out of her package. "We speak monthly—not every week—not usually."

"How often do you see him?"

Evette lit her cigarette and took a puff. "I don't know, Gracie. Maybe once a month?"

Don't say my name like that.

She swallowed hard and took a deep breath, washing the nickname from focus.

"Where were you the day before Lily Martin was found dead?" Grace asked. She glanced at Madigan, who stared at Evette.

"You can cut straight to the chase. I saw Johnny the day before. He told me he was getting out."

"Of?" Grace asked before she could go on.

Madigan frowned, staring at Evette.

She doesn't know, either.

"Of his involvement with some bad men," Evette said, butting her ash into the ashtray. "He told me he'd been done with it for a while, like a month, but they wouldn't let him go. That the next night, he'd be done with them for good."

Some bad men.

"Drug dealers?" Grace asked.

Evette opened her eyes wide and shrugged.

I don't buy the act. Never have.

Grace shifted her weight from one foot to the other.

"When was the next time you spoke with him?"

"He came here today." Evette puffed on her cigarette, and white clouds escaped her mouth. "He didn't bother to call after what happened to Lily. He just *showed up*."

"And this upset you?" Grace asked.

"Of course. I was worried about him. When he told me he was going to make it clear he was done with whoever these people are, I told him to call me the minute it was over. To let me know he was alright. I—I didn't think things would go as smoothly as they did, but he's out. He told me today."

She doesn't give a shit about Lily.

"What did he say about Lily?"

"Oh, he's crushed," Evette said. "Absolutely devastated. Madigan saw. He doesn't see a future for himself anymore. He doesn't understand that life goes on—that it *will* go on."

Madigan frowned at Evette.

What an odd choice of words.

"I told him not to worry about the police. That they'd know he didn't do it and find who did." Evette gestured to Grace. "I couldn't have imagined I was speaking about you. You've really made something of yourself."

"Do you believe there is any relation to John making a break from these people and Lily's death?"

Evette raised her brows. "So it *was* murder."

"I said death, Evette. Not murder." Grace shoved her hands in her pockets. "So you've gotten yourself tangled up with a dealer again."

Grace threw the bait out, hoping she'd guessed right about John's acquaintances.

Evette squinted at her. "John's *not* a dealer. He's out."

Bingo.

"What do you know about them?" Grace asked.

Evette tapped her ash out into an empty tray and sniffled.

"Just that he was mixed up in something that wasn't his fault, and he smartened up, got out, and they wouldn't leave him alone, I guess." Evette scratched her arm and played with the many rings on her fingers. "Calling him, I guess."

Grace took in her surroundings. It reminded her of the house on Warbler Way and her desperation to escape.

This is bigger. More hollow.

"I'll need you to come down to the station and make a statement," Grace said.

"Haven't I just made one?" Evette asked, twisting her thick silver ring around her skinny finger. "No? Then let me make it clear. John hasn't dealt in a long time. He got out. He didn't kill Lily. There. There's your statement."

"Where were you on the night Lily was found dead?"

"I was here having dinner. Then I went to the store down the street to buy a lotto ticket and some ice cream. Came back home and watched the women's network the rest of the night. All alone."

"Right."

"But please, let's be real. You know *I* didn't kill Lily," Evette said. "You know I couldn't kill anyone."

Grace didn't put that past anyone anymore.

"And if I search your place, Evette? Will I find anything that shouldn't be here?"

Evette cocked her head to the side. "Drugs? I don't know *where* you got that idea."

"Uh huh." Grace let out a huff of laughter. "Let's go, Madigan."

"So that's it?" Evette asked after Madigan stood. "You never would have seen me again if it weren't for *this*?"

Grace stopped at the door and turned back to her.

No. A thousand times no.

But she couldn't say it.

Maybe it was seeing how Evette had aged and having some sympathy for her physical condition and the loneliness she must have felt every day in her pale grey hell she called home.

The demons she, too, had to live with.

She'd never even raised a hand to them, but she'd let Eli beat them countless times.

"Do you hate me that much?" Evette asked.

Grace's eyes opened wide, and her shocked expression matched Madigan's. Evette had never been a confrontational person. Tears had pooled in Evette's droopy lids. Evette swallowed hard without taking her eyes off Grace.

"No," Grace said with a sigh. "I don't hate you. I don't even think about you. You're not a part of my life."

"You'll *always* be a part of mine," Evette said, her voice faltering at the end as she wiped away a tear that wasn't even there.

Grace turned away, back to the door. She used those fake tears to manipulate them so often, the only reaction she had was disgust at the familiar feeling.

Why aren't you coming to the door, Madigan?

"You're here now," Evette said, clearing her throat. "Regardless of the reason, I have to tell you I'm sorry."

Grace rolled her eyes and glanced back as Madigan stared at Evette with sympathy in her eyes.

Oh, come on.

"I bet you are," Grace said. "Let's go."

Madigan walked slowly across the living room, staring at the carpet until she reached Grace's side.

"I never thought I'd get to see my two girls together," Evette said, and when Grace looked back, Evette was crying. "You're both beautiful, you know that?"

"Evette—" Madigan whispered.

"God, I'm so sorry for what happened. What I let happen." Evette's hand shook as she set her cigarette in the ashtray. "You have to know that I'm sorry. I don't expect your forgiveness, but you deserve to know that if I could go back, I'd do it all over."

"There's a lot I'd do differently." Grace set her hand on the doorknob. "We were children, and you took advantage of us. We were used and abused. You might not have hit us, but you neglected us. I've moved on. I—I hope for your sake, you can too."

Madigan squeezed her arm with pleading eyes, and Grace nodded to her. It was the most compassion she could muster, but she couldn't leave Evette crying like she was. Madigan grabbed a tissue and handed it to Evette.

"Thank you." Evette sniffled and dabbed at her dry cheeks. "I don't sleep at night—not most nights. The ones I do, I have nightmares about the past, just like Maddie. I don't doubt you do too."

Grace turned to Madigan, who stared at the floor.

What have you told her?

The dream about the body and the tattoo, again?

"I'm not looking for sympathy." Evette covered her mouth as she coughed. "I'm alone in this life, save for what relationship I have left with Johnny. He's a *good man*. He came from the same place you two did, and he's made it out. Finally, he's made a life for himself that has nothing to do with the one he had with me. He's not judged by his past anymore. You both must know how good that feels. Can you let him have that too?"

Is that what she thinks I feel? Good?

Grace shook her head. "You don't just get to forget who you were before you start fresh. It stays with you. I live with it. So does Madigan. John must, too. We're never free from our pasts, Evette. You of all people…"

Evette stared up at her with big glassy eyes. "I'm so sorry," she whispered. "I'm sorry."

Madigan nodded, and Grace twisted the knob.

"Take care, Evette," Madigan said as Grace stepped out the door.

Madigan closed the door behind them, and after rushing down the stairs and through the rain to the car, Grace wiped the rain and tears from her cheeks. She'd never expected to get an apology, and she hadn't thought she needed one, but a heavy feeling lifted from her chest.

She pitied Evette, and the words she spoke made her realize she'd held on to her past as tightly as Evette had, but she hadn't done anything wrong. Not back then, at least.

Evette had something to be sorry about, but Grace didn't.

"You alright?" Madigan asked.

Grace nodded and started the car.

"Maybe you've been right all along." Grace sighed and checked her rearview mirror. "Maybe it's better to forgive and let go."

Madigan nodded. "Doesn't mean I forget."

"I know." Grace sighed again, finally able to breathe. "She looked awful—and that cough!"

"I know."

"Did you tell her about the nightmare again?"

Madigan nodded. "I had to. She still says it didn't happen. Maybe I should let it go, like you say."

With her confirmed story and more of a connection than she'd like, but not enough to mess with the case, Grace felt confident about what she had to bring to the table, as Mac had said.

You're lying, John.

To whom?

CHAPTER NINETEEN

As Grace dropped Madigan off at her bike that night, she promised to message her right away should anything official happen that she could put in an article for *The Gazette*. It didn't feel right to burden her and dampen the mood with the fact she'd been fired, so Madigan went along with it.

When she woke, Will had already left for work, but he'd also left a note on the kitchen table.

Come home tonight. I want to talk.

A pit in her stomach ached from the time she read his words until she started out on her bike for the library. She'd been sidetracked once before, but no matter what she told Grace, she couldn't let it go. The nightmare was real to her, and if the evidence said otherwise, she'd be happy to admit to Grace she'd been wrong.

After arriving, her favourite librarian, Mallory, showed her to the *Amherst Times* archives, and she found the year she and Grace moved in to Warbler Way. She started from the first of the year and checked each paper. Hundreds of missing men, women, and children.

I have to narrow this down.

She found *The Gazette's* old archives and went through those, paying particular attention to the fall.

It felt like autumn in my dream.

It was cold and damp.

After each article in August, she began with September and got a week in before it skipped a date.

The paper for September eighth is missing.

"Mallory?" Madigan approached the front desk. "Do you have copies of the articles?"

"No, why?" Mallory asked.

"There's an article for *The Gazette* missing," Madigan said.

"You've got to be kidding me," Mallory said, pulling herself closer to the desk on her rolling chair. "Reader's aren't allowed to check those out. Someone would have had to steal it. Maybe it's just misplaced? When from?"

"The mid-eighties. No back-ups then?"

"Everything's on the computer system starting in the nineties," she said. "This just missed it, huh? Okay, there's one person who might be able to help. Arthur Cooper. He and his wife have collected the town paper every day since they married in nineteen seventy-two. She was a hoarder, and it was mostly her doing. Since she passed away, Arthur stopped collecting them, but he kept all of the ones they already had. Can't bear to let them go."

"Could I have his address?"

"Let me call him for you."

Mallory made the call and set up a meeting that afternoon.

As Madigan arrived at Arthur's bungalow, he sat on the front porch with a mug in his hand, waiting.

"Mr. Cooper," she called as she swung her leg over the bike. "I'm Madigan."

He nodded. "That bike there. That a Sportster?"

Madigan took off her helmet and nodded.

"I remember those. They came out just after I quit riding."

"You rode?" Madigan raised her brow.

"Sure did. Wife wouldn't let me after the grandkids were born. I think she just didn't want it taking up room in the garage where more of her *things* could go. Had to sell my Harley."

"That's a shame," Madigan said as she stepped up onto the porch. "Well thank you for seeing me so soon."

"Mallory told me the date of the article you're looking for, and I took it upon myself to get it for ya. If you searched for it, you'd be searching when it got dark. It's a mess, but as Colleen said, it's an organized mess."

"Thank you, Mr. Cooper." Madigan smiled.

"Call me Arthur." He swiped the article from the table and handed it to her. "You mind if you stay here to read it?"

She pressed her lips together and shook her head.

"I know it's silly, but I just can't even let one of them damn articles go."

"Has anyone been here asking to see any of them? This one in particular?"

"Not that one," he said, sipping his coffee. "More recent ones, sure. They don't want to bother fetching one at the library. It's a shame really—"

Madigan nodded, and he gestured for her to sit beside him as he spoke, but she focused on the article.

Amherst resident, Valerie Hall, Missing

Valerie Hall, twenty-three, last seen by her parents in Tall Pines Friday night, reported missing early this morning by her fiancé, Joe Harris.

Hall and Harris reside in Amherst, in the old factory district, where Hall works at a department store. When she didn't show up for her shift this past Saturday, her manager tried to get in touch with her, but to no avail.

"If anyone has seen or heard from Valerie, please let us know," her parents told news outlets at eight this morning, while her fiancé gave his own plea.

"Please, Valerie, if you're listening—come home. Just let her come home," Harris begged as he stared into the camera.

If you have any information on Valerie Hall, please contact Amherst police...

"Arthur," she said, looking up from the paper. "Do you have the next few days following this one?"

"We've got 'em all," he said, standing. "I shouldn't say we, I guess, but—"

Madigan shook her head. "You should say whatever feels right to you. They're still her articles—in a way."

He grinned and nodded. "Yeah, they are. Back in a flash." He hobbled over to the door and left her on the porch with the article.

This has to be why the paper was stolen.

By the time Arthur came back out, she'd reread the article at least five times and stared at her picture.

Is she the dead body in my nightmare? I don't recognize her.

He walked over with ease and handed her the papers before sitting down again.

The next issue's front page included a story about the town's oldest resident, Ida Collier. Madigan flipped through the pages, but no mention of Valerie or any missing woman had been made.

The next issue had something different on the cover, and as she flipped through, she stopped when she recognized a name.

Joe Harris cleared of all suspicion in case of missing city woman

The city police have cleared Joe Harris' name from their suspect list in regards to twenty-three-year-old Valerie Hall. Harris, twenty-five, had been away on business the week of her disappearance, arriving home on Saturday to find her missing.

After speaking with Hall's parents and contacting police, no missing persons case could be opened until this past Monday, following procedure.

Joe Harris has been cleared as a suspect.

When asked how he's holding up, Harris said, "Now that I'm cleared of any suspicion or wrong-doing, the city police can put all their attention on finding Valerie. On bringing her back home to me."

Valerie Hall's parents are no longer talking to the media amid rumors surrounding her disappearance circulating, and as many as thirty sightings with no leads reported to the PD.

"This is a hard time for all of us," Harris said at his residence on Warbler Way.

What? He lived on our street?

"I hope the Halls' privacy can be respected at this time," Harris continued. "If anyone has any leads, instead of contacting them directly, please contact the police."

Her heart beat fast as she read over the article, taking her cell phone from her purse.

"I'm just going to take some pictures," she muttered and started snapping pictures of both articles.

"Sure, sure. Seems you found what you were looking for."

Madigan nodded. "Missing woman."

"I was looking at that while I waited for you. It brought back some memories. Did you know her?"

Madigan shook her head, searching the next few papers, but no mention of Valerie or her family was made.

"Did they ever find her?"

"Not that I know of. O'course, I could be wrong. That was a while ago, but I don't think I ever heard she was found."

"Do you remember anything else about it?"

"Sketchy neighbourhood," he said, nodding. "Her parents

live in that mansion just off Pekoe Place, that subdivision before the road to the lighthouse. Have since before their daughter went missing."

"You know them?"

"I know of them. I guess everybody does because of their daughter. I remember people fussing over the fact that the Halls had money, but their daughter and her guy there lived in a dump."

It was *bad.*

"I appreciate your help, Arthur," she said, setting the papers on the table between them.

"Sure thing. If you ever need to reference a paper, you know where to come."

"Thanks Arthur," she said, walking back to her bike. "I will."

"Hey, maybe you'd let me take that thing out for a spin sometime."

She smiled and nodded as her cell phone buzzed in her hand and Will's name popped up.

Could you be home for dinner?

She checked her watch. Just after three. She'd lost track of time looking through the articles.

I'll see you then, she texted back and shoved the cell phone in her pocket.

Not home. Not yet.

CHAPTER TWENTY

G race pulled up to Mac's condo at six, and he strode out the doors before she put the car in park. His patrol car had been pulled off the lot for a check up, and he'd texted her asking to ride to John's together.

As he slid into the vehicle, his fresh cologne wafted toward her.

"So?" he asked.

No thanks for the pick up?

"I might have enough to hold him," Grace said.

Mac's eyes lit up, and he nodded.

"Good, because I found some things, but they're not enough. What've you got?"

"The foster mother that John and I shared? She was able to let me know that John was dealing drugs. She didn't tell me who they're from—just that he was dealing—but he wanted out. Apparently, he got out, but they continually contacted him. He was going to tell them it was over the night of Lily's death."

They wouldn't let him leave, but how? Had they threatened

him? Kept calling? There had to be a reason he went back to cut ties again.

"Huh," Mac huffed.

The sound you make when you're impressed but can't swallow your pride enough to say so?

"Anyway, John lied to us. He said he went to meet his friend and then for a drive up the coast when he came back from the city, but according to Evette, he went to end things with whoever his supplier was that night. Could it have been the friend? Luke?"

Mac shook his head. "He's got a sordid past at best, but he's not our guy. Not too sharp. Not intimidating, either."

"How do you know for sure?"

"Well, I've known there's a gap of time missing." Mac turned to her. "John says he was out for a drive, but if he was going to end it with these people, say it *was* Luke who he met at the café, he wouldn't just casually take the long way home to get back to Lily. He'd want to get home to her. The people would be dangerous, and he'd want to make sure Lily was safe. Besides, he and Luke could have corroborated their stories and said they were there for over an hour and then John went right home. Tarek says no calls went to or from John and Luke after John left home."

So we received John's records, and you didn't tell me?

"When did you get John's records?" she asked.

"Yesterday, after *you left* the PD."

Pick your battles.

"So it's probable—he went somewhere else then," she said. "To see whoever wouldn't leave him alone, *if* we believe Evette's story. How do you want to play this?"

"John could have set the fire. He told the officer he was at his mom's and then came right back. He could have gone by the house and covered up evidence, or even drugs by burning the place down. He was out all day and didn't get back to the motel until 9:30. Malone knows not to leave him, now."

Grace nodded. "Right, but the fire could have been set by his supplier. By whoever he pissed off by trying to get out. They could have killed Lily to punish him or send a message. Set the fire to destroy any evidence left behind."

"So let's get the answers we need from him," Mac said. "We're going to see what he knows. I'll call Banning about the details on the way and see if it's enough to hold him if he lied to us. For now, let's get to the lodge. I want to surprise him."

Grace drove out of the entry as Mac made the call.

Where did you go last night, John?

Were you still at Evette's?

"Banning says he'll see what he can do about a warrant, but John has to admit he lied to us about where he was," Mac said. "My car should be ready before lunch. Wanna drop me off at the station after this?"

"Sure, but I don't mind driving today."

"I've got a meeting with my ex, actually," Mac said, turning to the window.

"Ah."

"She knows how much I make," he said, shaking his head.

"How many children?"

"Just one. Listen, I'm going to call Malone. Let him know we're coming."

"Sure."

Speaking about his ex and child revealed a sad and vulnerable side to Mac, evoking more contemplation than anger. The last time he'd opened up, she'd surprised him by keeping her connection with the suspect from him.

He has the guts to be transparent with me about something so personal. He probably just needs someone to vent to.

He's not warming up to me.

He's just sad and lonely.

But she liked that side of him.

I won't break his trust again.

By the time they reached the motel, John's detail stood outside his car waiting for them.

"Hasn't been out since last night?" Mac asked before shutting his door.

The officer shook his head, and they spoke as Grace took her cell phone out of the car. She dialed the PD and asked for Evette's number, having them redirect the call to her.

Evette's line rang several times.

"Hello?" she asked.

"Evette, it's Grace. I'm calling about John. Was he over there yesterday?"

"Yes, he came to visit before you two did," Evette said.

"How long did he stay?"

"Oh, I don't know," Evette said, dragging out the words. "It was dark out."

"Evette, do you know what time he left?"

"Could have been nine just as easy as it could have been ten."

Grace rolled her eyes and shook her head.

She knows about the fire. She'll cover for him, regardless.

"That's all. Have a good day," Grace said.

"You too, Gracie."

Grace brought the phone away from her ear, rolling her eyes again.

I hate that name.

She caught up with Mac and told him about the call. He waved for Malone to follow them to John's room.

"We might make an arrest here," Mac told him. "If I knock on the door from inside, alright? Might take a while."

Malone nodded and stepped to the side, out of the way. Grace knocked on the door, and John peeked out from behind the curtains before unlatching the lock and letting them in. He sat on the chair by the small table beside his well-made bed.

He hasn't slept.

"Have you found anything yet?" John asked. "Why my house got torched? It's a cover-up, isn't it? Whoever killed—whoever did this—they want to make sure you don't find anything on them."

"Where were you last night, John?" Mac asked.

"I told the guy outside," he said. "I went to see my mom in the city, and then I came back here. I don't know when the fire started because I wasn't the one who set it, but I was back here around nine thirty."

Mac rubbed his smooth chin, and she noticed the stubble John had grown, close to forming a beard.

Mac pulled out the chair, gesturing for Grace to sit down.

"Special Detective Sheppard here found out some very interesting details involving your case," he said and nodded to Grace as she sat.

He's really letting me take the lead.

"Involving you, specifically," Grace said. "John, you haven't been straight with us, which can only lead me to believe that you don't want us to find out who killed your fiancée."

John shook his head and stared up at Mac wide-eyed. "No. I want you to find who did this."

"Then why are you lying?" Grace asked and folded her hands in front of her on the table.

John pinched his lips with his thumb and index finger, his eyes darting from the windows back to Mac and Grace.

"If there's someone else we should be considering that you haven't suggested—" Grace started.

John shook his head.

"No?" Mac asked.

"Then maybe someone you *have* suggested," Grace said, remembering the night he spoke about Mickey.

John stared down at the table, shaking his head.

"John?" Grace whispered. "Whatever you're afraid of, if you're honest, we can help you."

She remembered saying something similar to Leah the night she was killed.

You don't have to be afraid. I'm here for you. I promise.

Grace shook the thought away and made eye contact with John.

"I spoke to Evette," she whispered.

He raised his brow and leaned back in his chair, his foot tapping the floor in a nervous jitter. "Madigan told you we met?" John asked. "That I know who you are?"

Grace glanced up at Mac, and he nodded for her to continue.

"She did. Evette told me you two see each other more often than she led on to my sister."

John tapped the tip of his finger against the table, chewing at his tongue or cheek.

"John?" Mac asked, his voice booming, and a look of fear flashed in John's eyes as he flinched.

John shook his head, tilting it down, and stared at Grace from just beneath his brow. "I didn't kill Lily. I didn't—"

"You were caught up in something bad, John," Grace said. "Evette told us."

He squinted at her and stared without moving an inch.

"Told us you were going to end it for good with your dealer the night Lily died," Grace said. "Who were you working with?"

John shook his head.

"Who?" Grace asked.

He opened his mouth, and she was sure he'd ask for a lawyer until he shut it again.

Don't push too far.

"John, I'm going to need an answer," Mac said.

"Evette's lying," John said, turning to Grace. "You know how she is, and it's not her fault. I think she does it for attention. I'm not even mad at her, honestly, because she just doesn't think about anyone but herself sometimes."

Grace stared into his eyes and he sighed. "Most of the time," he conceded.

It's true.

"Why would she tell Grace that? Why would she make something like that up?"

"I don't know," John said, running his fingers through his hair and grabbing at the ends. "I don't know why she does half the shit she does, but I know in the end she doesn't mean harm. Grace, you know her. You know how she is."

"Why would she say *that* though?" Grace asked.

He sat up straight. "When Lily and I first started dating, I still hung out with some of my friends from the past. Lily never wanted to be in the same room with them, and she didn't understand why I'd want to be friends with these people. I had this rule. Bros before—well—I always promised myself I wouldn't let anyone tell me who I could or couldn't be friends with. Most of 'em are harmless."

"Dealers?" Grace asked.

"Some," John said. "Some had been to juvie, and we met that way. A couple just partied too hard. Thom, my business partner, he was always after me, just like Lily, to leave them in my past. He said it wasn't healthy as a sober person to associate with people who still use. After the restraining order against Mickey, we both agreed to leave the past behind us, and that included my friends. I told Evette I was meeting Luke. That Lily had a problem with some of my friends, and it might be the last time I saw him because we were going down separate paths in life. Maybe she got mixed up, or maybe she just took it and ran with it assuming the friend I was meeting with was into the same shit I used to be. Luke's not a bad guy—at all—but I had to respect Lily's wishes."

She turned to Mac, remembering he'd said Luke wasn't their guy.

"Like I said," John leaned back in his chair, "Evette exaggerates sometimes. I'm used to dealing with it, but at the very least, she's confused."

Grace rubbed her lips together and nodded to Mac.

"John," he said, "we've got police detail on you at all times."

"Good," John said straight away. "Then you'll know I haven't done anything. All I want to do is bring whoever killed Lily to justice."

"That night," Grace said. "You brought her flowers."

He nodded, and his eyes lit up.

"What?" Grace asked.

"Lily and I weren't fighting. I know it's what Eli used to do for my mom, but you've got the wrong idea. She was looking forward to us finally moving forward with our lives."

He rolled up his sleeves, revealing the scorpion tattoo on his forearm along with a few other designs.

"When you brought her the flowers, she put them in the vase straight away?" Grace asked.

"I think so," he said, staring off past her. "She smelled them first. She always closed her eyes and took a deep sniff. Then she thanked me, and I went upstairs to shower before dinner."

"When you came downstairs, where were the flowers?" Grace asked.

He frowned. "I don't know."

"Not in the kitchen?" Mac asked.

John opened his eyes wide and sat up in his chair.

He shook his head. "They were in the living room. I saw them when I left. The vase. Did they hit her with the vase?"

"We can't talk about that right now," Grace said. "You're sure they were in the living room when you left?"

He nodded. "On the table. Then, it was broken…"

He stared off past her, no doubt remembering the crime scene.

"John," Grace said. "Did you move anything when you found her?"

"No." He looked up at Mac. "I already told you. I touched her arm. It was cold. I felt for a pulse. That was it."

He winced before his Adam's apple bobbed in his throat.

Grace stood and exchanged a look with Mac.

It was murder.

"Let's go," Mac said.

Grace nodded and followed him to the door. "We'll be in touch, John."

He didn't look up at them—only stared past her—maybe remembering the moment he saw Lily's dead body, whether he'd caused it or not.

Mac nodded to the officer as they passed him, and when they got into her car, Mac turned to her.

"Do you believe him?" he asked. "His story about his friends and your—his mom lying?"

"Everything he said about Evette is true. She is a liar, and she looks out for herself first. I mean, it could have easily been confusion, but I don't know. I can't say for sure. Thom didn't mention anything about John's friends, but maybe I can follow up and see if that part's true."

Mac nodded. "He hasn't lawyered up."

"I know, and we have to keep it that way."

"He could be playing us." Mac leaned his arm on the armrest. "He could be lying and just enjoying the fact we haven't figured it out yet."

"But it was murder. Accidental or not," Grace said. "And talking to him can help."

After pulling into the department parking lot, Mac grabbed his door handle. "I'm off to get my car," he said.

"Good luck with your meeting."

"Meet you back at the precinct at five. Fire chief's coming in to give us the results from their fire investigation."

Grace nodded before he got out and shut the door behind him.

John knows she's a liar, but he doesn't hold it against her.

He keeps her in his life. Maybe because she adopted him. She's his mom.

Maybe because he doesn't hold a grudge like me.

Some of her anger toward Evette melted away the night before.

Maybe I'm just not as compassionate as John and Madigan.

She clenched her jaw and texted Madigan.

How's it going? Let's get together soon.

A familiar, envious feeling arose inside her when she compared her shortcomings to Madigan's strengths, but instead of breeding contempt, it moved her to be more like her sister. To have more compassion and sympathy for others. To be a better person.

As she entered the department, Mr. and Mrs. Martin stood from the bench by the front desk.

"Detective Sheppard?" Mr. Martin asked.

"Are you arresting him?" Mrs. Martin asked with bloodshot eyes glaring at her. "John? He set fire to his own house, for God's sake. He's getting rid of the evidence."

"He killed her," Mr. Martin shouted.

"Mr. and Mrs. Martin," Grace spoke in a calm voice. "We haven't arrested anyone for Lily's death yet, and this has just been deemed a murder investigation."

"When?" Mr. Martin asked.

Mrs. Martin's eyes opened wide.

Why did I tell them like that?

She must have thought it could have been an accident.

I'd hope for an accident too, over murder.

"We just made the development this morning," she said.

The truth would be out in the papers the next day, regardless. She'd give Madigan the story as she promised once she spoke to Mac.

"I was about to call you to let you know. I can't tell you any more as of yet."

"I'd say that's a big advancement." Mr. Martin shook his head. "What'd he do? What did he do to our Lily?"

Mrs. Martin wrapped her arm through his and seemed to pull him back.

Holding him back from attacking me?

"For now, as I said, I can't say much more. We are checking out the leads we have, and when we know something concrete, we'll let you know, alright? You came here for a reason. Can I help you in any way?"

"We came to figure out why John hasn't been held accountable," Mr. Martin said. "We think she was going to leave him again, so he killed her."

Mrs. Martin nodded with tears in her eyes. "It was only a matter of time, I know it."

"But Mr. Martin," Grace said, "John was the one who left Lily, even by your own admission."

"But he begged for her to come back," Mr. Martin said. "So he could abuse her some more. She didn't want to be with him. She cheated on him with someone else, and even after he left, he couldn't stay gone. He had to come back. Had to ruin her."

"And you still don't know who she cheated with?" Grace asked.

Maybe it's better that way.

"No," Mrs. Martin shook her head. "But if she loved John, she wouldn't have cheated on him. It's him, Detective Sheppard. He killed our—" She choked on the last words, and Mr. Martin pulled her tight against his side.

"I suggest you do your job and find out how," he said and led his wife away.

As they left, Grace stood in the middle of the foyer, watching them.

I'm not at my best.

Maybe Mac could have made more progress without me.

Maybe I can't help anyone anymore.

"You alright?" Rhonda asked at the front desk.

Grace nodded. "Just need some sleep, I think."

On the way home, she willed her cell phone to buzz with a reply from Madigan, but by the time she'd crawled into bed, she just wanted to shut out the world and wake up ready to do whatever it took to find Lily's killer.

To prove to herself and everyone else that she could.

CHAPTER TWENTY ONE

Madigan parked her bike on the road above the rocky shoreline. Across from the Hall's mansion, the sun touched the horizon.

Mr. Hall had invited her in under her guise as the daughter of an old friend of his daughter's. She followed him into the large front foyer with a large marble staircase, everything painted or tiled in a cream tone.

Clean, and yet less bright than it should have been. Curtains covered each of the windows.

Mr. Hall led her to the living room.

"Please have a seat," he said. "What's your mom's name? Maybe I know her?"

"Maureen," she said without it registering she'd used Will's mom's name until the words came out. "She passed away just recently."

"I'm sorry for your loss," he said, bowing his head before sitting in the armchair across from hers.

Expensive furniture decorated yet another cream coloured room, and she noticed family photos on the mantel above the grand fireplace before turning her attention back to Mr. Hall.

"My mom was close with Valerie, and she was heartbroken when she went missing. We moved a few years after it happened, and she never knew what happened to her friend. She'd talk about it a lot, and, well, I guess I'm here hoping she came back?"

He folded his hands in his lap and cleared his throat, shaking his head.

"I'm sorry," she whispered.

"Her case went cold the week she went missing as far as I'm concerned. City cops seemed to have—more pressing matters to deal with than—"

He cleared his throat again, and she avoided eye contact in an effort to give him some dignity.

"I only came because she hoped that one day I'd know Valerie. I was too young back then to remember her."

"She was beautiful," Mr. Hall said. "Her leaving broke her mother's heart. She rarely leaves the house. I guess—well—it's been a deep loss to anyone who knew her. Especially Joe."

"Her fiancé, right?"

He nodded. "Joe held out hope longer than the rest of us."

"You said her *leaving*. You think she left on her own?"

He looked behind him toward the alcove of the foyer and leaned in closer.

"She was seeing someone behind his back. None of us wanted to believe it, but one of her friends said she swore she saw Val with someone else. God, even saying her name…"

Tears welled up in his eyes, and he took his glasses off, setting them on the mahogany table between them.

"Word spread, and some people got to thinking she left with him. Nobody knew who he was. Joe never bought into it. Didn't want to believe it, I guess. Neither did we, but some things of hers were missing when Joe got home from his work trip that Saturday morning. That, paired with her friend's account, and the police gave up."

"No one saw her leave?" she asked.

He nodded. "The next door neighbour. That's the other thing. When she left the house, she had her purse and her bag. It was all confusing, though, because she never used her bank cards. Never withdrew money, and she had some. We gave her a weekly allowance. Kept giving it to her for the next year, just hoping…"

He pressed his lips together and shook his head. "Well, I don't think I can talk about it anymore, but I appreciate you coming by to check and—and your mom was right. I wish you could've known her."

He stood up, and she stood after him.

"Thank you for your time, Mr. Hall. May I ask one last question? My mom never told me where she lived exactly, but I think it was close to us."

"Warbler Way," he said, shaking his head. "She and Joe, they refused to take our money to get a proper place before their wedding. Wouldn't take money for the wedding either, so they ended up in that dump. That's what makes me think —you never know what kind of person might've seen her walking alone…"

Madigan walked toward the fireplace.

"Did your mom have any pictures of them?" he asked.

She shook her head. "Couldn't afford a camera."

"I'm very sorry to speak about the area like that if that's where you're from," he said.

"It's alright. It *was* a bad neighbourhood."

"I'm glad you got out," he said, following her. "There's Valerie and Joe."

"She is beautiful." Madigan nodded.

"I tried to put these away once, but her mother wouldn't

let me. She had them all back up when I came home from work."

Madigan leaned in and noticed how close Valerie and Joe seemed. She sat on his lap with her arms around his neck, and he kissed her hand, a hand wearing a ring similar to one of Evette's.

"I'm talking too much," Mr. Hall sighed and walked away. "Maureen?"

The same ring as Evette's.

"I'm sorry," she said, following him to the foyer. "I won't bother you anymore."

"Not a bother at all," he said. "I like hearing how Valerie touched others' lives. The rumors left a murky nature surrounding her disappearance, and I just wish she'd be remembered for who she really was. Who we knew she was."

"Are you still in touch with Joe?"

Mr. Hall opened the door, and a flood of golden-rose light filled the room. The colour made his sallow face come to life.

"He checks on us now and then, but he has his own life. Still in the city. He loved her. Without a doubt, he still does," he said.

Madigan stopped in the doorway. "Did Valerie ever mention anyone named Eli, or Evette, or John?" she asked.

He pursed his lips, and his moustache twitched.

"Eli," he said. "I think that was the next-door neighbour who saw her leave Friday morning. She was coming to see us. It was a good visit. We were the last to see her."

Right next door.

"Thank you for your time," she said. "I appreciate you talking to me."

"I'm glad I could give you closure," he said as she stepped outside. "I only wish someone could give us some. I guess I like to think Valerie's still out there. In love with the man she left it all behind for. That's better than…"

He folded his arms over his chest.

"I hope you get closure too," Madigan said, nodding to him before turning back toward the sunset and starting down the driveway.

You will. We both will.

After getting back on her bike and buckling her helmet, she rode down the coast, wishing she knew for sure whether the ring on Valerie's finger had been the same as Evette's.

What are the chances it's a coincidence?

Slim.

Am I imagining it too? Exaggerating it to fit my own narrative?

I have to make sure they're the same.

Riding into their subdivision, she couldn't avoid the talk with Will anymore.

I don't think I should be with him, but I don't want to lose him, either.

I'm selfish.

What if I'm wrong?

If I stay, I'll always feel like this. Less than. Waiting for his disappointment in me to trump his love for me. For his frustration to grow into something insurmountable. Waiting for him to not love me at all anymore.

She parked her bike and jogged up their driveway, as if a few seconds of hustling could make up for her lateness.

I can't even focus on what to do about Will.

I can't focus on anything but my nightmare—looking evermore like reality.

"Will doesn't deserve this," she muttered to herself, taking off her helmet and shaking out her hair.

Her chest already ached for him.

For the man who'd been there for her when she felt most alone.

For the man who loved her unconditionally.

For the man she wished would stay—except they never did.

Nothing good remains.

Even if things never changed, and he always loved me unconditionally, could I truly be happy?

By the time she unlocked the door, she had her answer.

CHAPTER TWENTY TWO

G race flipped the final page of the file over before slipping the binder back beneath her bed. Every few nights, she had skimmed over the words that became familiar. Each time, her heart broke for Leah and ached with grief and guilt.

I have to read it. I can't allow myself to forget what I did.

Her phone rang, and she picked it up without looking at the caller ID.

"Sheppard."

"My meeting ran late," Mac said, the hum of his car engine in the background. "Be at your place in ten."

He's picking me up?

When she got in the car, she made a point not to question him about why he came to get her, but after parking at the department, he spoke up.

"I didn't want to owe you," he said.

"What?"

He got out of the car, and she followed him to the door. "You picked me up; now I've picked you up," he said. "We're even."

"Alright." She laughed.

He led her into their room where Jack Holden sat waiting with a foam cup in his hand.

"You guys actually drink the coffee here?" Jack said without turning around.

"Today's wasn't the best," Mac said, laughing. "It's gotta be better than the shit you boys drink at the fire station."

As they walked around the table, Jack sat up straight, making eye contact with her.

"Jack." She nodded with a smile.

"Grace." He grinned. "I thought I saw you at the fire. You're on this case?"

She nodded. "Transferred to Deerhorn County."

Though she had never been to the other three small neighbouring towns, Grace had been put in charge of investigations in all four towns that made up Deerhorn County.

"How do you two know each other?" Mac asked.

"Well, Grace's sister was also my best friend's sister," Jack said.

"Sounds...complicated." Mac sat down, and Grace took the seat between them.

"Not really." Grace smiled. "Good to see you. I thought we were meeting the fire chief?"

"So did Greg, but while he was waiting to meet you guys, he got a call about a fire at Tall Pines Elementary. Not a big one, but they think one of the kids set it after school got out, and they need to make sure they find out who. So, you're stuck with me." Jack grinned, but it faded fast. "We were pretty sure of the cause of the fire at John Talbot's place before it was even out, but we had to perform a thorough investigation, and I did so myself. That's why the Chief asked me to come and present my report."

"Don't keep us in suspense," Mac said.

"The gas stove." Jack cleared his throat. "This was foul play, but whoever did it didn't want to get caught. There was a pan with oil on the stove, as if someone was going to cook on it."

Mac nodded. "Any evidence of who did it?"

Jack shook his head. "The whole main floor is burnt up. You couldn't find prints in there if you tried, and the top floor is not good either. We can tell you, whoever did it broke in. One of the window panes by the back door in the kitchen had been broken. The rest were still intact. They probably hoped the door would be destroyed by the fire to hide the break-in, but it burnt right off the hinges and landed just outside."

"Can you tell us anything else?" Grace asked.

"The fire started at about eight p.m.," Jack said. "It wasn't reported until it was pretty far along. Any other small details, such as damages, are in the report. Now, we did find something unusual."

He pulled a metal lockbox up onto the table in front of him and pulled out a plastic bag with a hand gun.

"Found this under the floorboard in the kitchen," Jack said. "It wasn't in this bag. It wasn't inside anything. It was brought in for processing along with this box. This was on the kitchen table—what was left of it, anyway."

"There wasn't anything on the kitchen table when we left," Mac said. "Or on the stove."

"It seems as though it was left for us to find," Jack said. "Well, us or you. This box obviously wouldn't be damaged by the fire. The lock was simple and easy to break, but we haven't opened it. Banning told me to give it to you." He slid the box over to Mac.

Mac frowned and pulled on gloves from his pocket. Grace did the same. She walked around the table, leaning over his shoulder.

Several four by six pictures wrapped together by an elastic band sat in the middle with a small piece of white paper on top with three words.

JOHN IS GUILTY.

Mac took the note off and set it on the table beside the box as he unwrapped the elastic.

John wouldn't have left this.

The first picture of Mac and Grace leaving the police station, taken from a distance, made her squint hard.

Someone's been following us.

It had to be taken the morning after Lily was found dead. She wore the same clothes she had that day.

Mac set it down, revealing the next picture of just Grace, getting into her car in the department lot. Goosebumps covered her arms, and her breaths grew short.

The next, a picture of Mac entering his condo building, was taken from across the road.

Then there was a picture of Grace sitting alone on the deck at Roy's, looking out at the waves, taken from somewhere below her on the beach.

The next was of her and Madigan talking at the table, taken from the same point of view.

They know who Madigan is. That she matters to me.

Focus on the case.

She took a deep breath.

Calm down and focus. Stay professional.

Why are they sending us this?

Grace took the picture from Mac. Her hands shook as she studied it. Every detail important. Their glasses empty. In deep conversation.

The man was about to approach us and offer to buy us drinks.

She squinted at the left corner of the picture, but the man wasn't there.

Had he left, or was he not there yet?

Was he taking the picture?

"Grace?"

Jack's voice echoed around her, but she couldn't take her eyes off the picture.

"Grace?" Mac asked, still staring at the final picture in his hand.

She leaned over his shoulder once more. Most of the pictures focused in on a date: the day of the fire.

A newspaper, held up in front of the camera.

Just above the paper, John entered a building at dusk.

Grace took the photo from Mac and held it closer. Part of the sign had been cut off at the top of the picture, but enough of the letters had been included.

"That's Wild Card," she muttered.

John's a liar. A good one.

I shouldn't be surprised.

We were taught to be.

Mac stood. "Jack, thanks very much for your help."

Grace stood, and Jack shook both their hands.

"Grace, could I speak to you in the hall for a sec?" Jack asked.

Grace nodded and set the picture down before following Jack into the hallway. He stopped just outside the door.

"It's good to see you," Jack said.

"Yeah, you too. You've grown up," Grace said, trying to smile. "I barely recognized you, but you were at John's place."

"You've changed too. From what I remember, you used to be more—well—less like Madigan."

"You think we're more alike now?"

He nodded. "It's hard to explain, but that's a good segue into what I wanted to ask you about. Is she alright?"

Grace smiled up at him.

He's kept his promise, all these years. Still trying to look after her for Drew.

227

"She's fine," Grace said.

Except if someone's watching me, they might be watching her too.

He nodded, his features seeming to relax. "Last night, we spoke, and she just seemed—off."

Grace walked backwards toward the room. "You could give her a call sometime. She'd probably like that."

"Things have changed a lot since Drew's death. Things are more difficult for everyone, and we're not kids in the same neighbourhood anymore. We've lost touch a bit."

"Well, I appreciate you looking out."

Jack waved before turning around. "Take care, and good luck with the case."

Grace stepped back inside as Mac stood over the photos, looking up at her with lines across his forehead and clenched fists.

"John lied," she said.

"He'll answer our questions this time," Mac said.

CHAPTER TWENTY THREE

Madigan set her keys in the bowl by the front door and locked it behind her. "Buster?" she called.

Where is that dog?

"Will?" she called and took her jacket off, leaving it by the door. She took a few steps to the kitchen and stood in the doorway, leaning in.

Nothing.

She walked down the hallway to the living room, and the light by the sliding door glowed through the glass. She pulled it open and stuck her head out.

"Buster? Will?"

"We're out here," Will called.

Seconds later, Buster bounded around the hedge toward her, and she bent to scratch his head.

"Wish me luck," she whispered and stood.

Her favourite lantern illuminated the portion of the patio table where Will sat with a drink of scotch in his hand.

He never drinks much and not scotch unless he's with his dad.

This is bad.

"It's nice and quiet out here," he said, gesturing for her to take the seat beside him. "Join me?"

She sat down, and Buster flopped down at her feet, staring up at her.

She stole glances at Will, avoiding eye contact by feigning interest in the hedges surrounding the yard. Her heart thudded hard in her chest, making it difficult to concentrate.

"How was your day?" he asked.

She sighed.

"That bad?"

"I'd rather not get into it. I know we need to talk," she said, licking her lips with a dry tongue. "I'd rather just get it over with."

"Alright." He set his glass on the table. "Lately, you've seemed kind of distant. I guess it's been a month now."

Since Grace came. It's been since then, but you won't say it. You won't blame her.

Madigan folded her arms over her chest. "I'm sorry."

"I know," he sighed. "I know. I didn't even want to bring it up again, but after last night with my parents—"

"I know. It was worse than I thought it'd be."

"It didn't make things easier," he said and sat forward in his chair.

Here it comes. I've never been this close to someone breaking up with me.

She opened her mouth, eager to break up with him before he could crush her, but his light eyes stared back at her with the glow of the lantern in his irises, and she couldn't put out the light within him.

He doesn't deserve a broken heart, either.

"Do you love me, Madigan?"

She swallowed hard.

Yes. I do.

She could think it and feel it, but she couldn't utter the words. She hadn't been able to since she fell for him.

It won't do me any good to confess it now.

"It's just I say it, and then you don't," he said and held up his hand. "I know, I know. You've had a past most couldn't understand, and I don't claim to, but I know you've been hurt. I know your trust has been broken. I already know what I need to do, but I want to know. Don't I deserve that?"

She nodded. "I love you, Will," she whispered with tears in her eyes. "You're one of the best things to ever happen to me, and I've blown it. I do it every time, so I'm not surprised, but you don't deserve it. You—out of everyone—don't deserve this."

He scratched his head. His chest heaved, and he stood from his chair.

"I was trying to say that I'm sorry, Will," she said, clenching the armrests of her chair. "You deserve someone more stable. More present."

He searched the area around them, seeming to ignore her pleas.

"Will, you know what we need to do, and so do I."

"Ah," he said, lifting the lantern off the table and grabbing a small remote.

He pressed a button, and tiny string lights glowed in the bushes, woven through the hedges surrounding them.

"Will," she said, looking up at him, "what is this?"

He bent down, and her heart dropped as he rested one knee against the patio.

"Will," she hissed, shaking her head and grabbing at his arms. "You're not doing this."

"Babe, I know you're scared of commitment, and I was too, before I met you," he said, grabbing her hand.

She stood and used his hand to pull him to his feet.

"Babe—" he started.

"Will," she whispered with tears in her eyes, face to face with the man she loved.

But not enough.

"I can't do this," she said, and his grin faded. "You can't do this."

"I don't understand," he said, his brows pushed closer together. "Why?"

"It just doesn't feel all the way right," she said, sighing.

It makes even less sense saying it out loud.

"But you love me. And I love you. You know that. Madigan, I want to marry you. I've wanted to since the moment we met. You brought something to life in me. Something I didn't know was there. I told my parents right away. They knew I was going to do this, and that's why my mom got so upset."

"I can't." Her whole body shook in the cool night air.

I can't be with Will and be thinking the way I do about Jack whenever he's around.

"I don't understand."

"I can't explain it more than it—it just doesn't feel right," she said.

He let go of her hand and let it drop to his side.

"Will."

She clenched her cold hands into fists, already missing the heat that radiated from him.

"You don't want this," he said. "You don't want me?"

"I thought I did." She folded her arms over her chest and hugged herself, eager to ease her jitters.

He shook his head and rubbed the back of his neck, looking around the yard.

He doesn't understand because we don't feel the same way.
He cares more.

"I'm not trying to confuse you, or hurt you. It's the last thing I want. It's just not fair to you. You're this freakin' brain surgeon. This man with it *all*. The house. The career. The doting parents. The bright future. I don't fit into that, Will."

"Stop. Stop that right now. I knew you felt that way, but I tried to make you see. I tried to make you feel like you're worthy. It's a victim mentality, Madigan."

"Maybe." She shrugged her shoulders.

Tears spilled down her cheeks. The painstaking reality of the end twisted in her stomach.

"We just don't belong together."

He stepped away from her. "Why can't you just accept love?"

She shook her head, crying.

I want to.

"You know none of it matters, right? None of what you said matters. I've worked hard for my career, but it's taxing. I've bought a house, a car, but these are things. Just things. You can't hold it against me that I have parents and that they love me."

She winced, and he stepped toward her.

"I'm sorry," he said, trying to reach out to her. "You know I didn't mean it like that."

"I know." She pressed her arms against her abdomen.

I feel sick.

Maybe I've made the wrong decision.

"But don't you get it?" Will raised his voice. "I'll never have a love like yours. I'll never find someone I want more than you."

He knelt on one knee, his eyes searching hers.

"So tell me you don't deserve this life, and I'll prove to you that you do. Tell me you love me, but you're just scared, and I promise I won't let you get hurt. I'll protect you. Tell me anything, Madigan, anything, and I'll be here for you, but if you don't want me to—just say it."

Her heart felt like it was ripping apart in her chest with each word he spoke. Each kind gesture she felt she didn't deserve. But in the end—it wasn't about whether or not she deserved him.

I'm sacrificing what could be for a feeling I'm chasing.

A great love for a love that is unrequited.

She opened her mouth to speak—to tell him she didn't want him—but she couldn't force herself to say it. Putting the onus on herself had been easier.

It's my fault after all.

"Be straight with me," he said, grabbing for her hand, and she let him take it, "because I need to know. I can't force you to do anything. I need to know that you still want to be with me, and then I can—I can be what you need."

You can't.

I have to let him go.

"I'm what you want right now, but I'll never be what you need, Will." She took a deep breath and shook her head as tears stung her eyes, letting go of his hand. "And I wanted you to be the one so bad, but you're not." She blinked down at his crestfallen face through her tears.

He broke eye contact with her and stood. He turned away, stalking up the path and wiping at his face. Buster stood, staring at him as he rounded the hedge, disappearing behind it.

She burst into tears and bent down, hugging Buster tightly. "What have I done?" she cried, feeling hollow all at once.

A rumble came from the front of the house—Will's car starting.

He's leaving.

She gathered her energy to stand and wipe the tears from

her eyes as she started up the path and the engine grumbled further away.

Buster followed behind her as she stepped back inside and ran upstairs, pulling out her suitcase she'd had since she was eleven, and packing her favourite clothes into it. Buster watched with a concerned look on his face.

"I'm okay."

The words were as hollow as she felt, but it was what Grace would tell her.

She grabbed a few of her things from the bedroom and bathroom before zipping up her suitcase and carrying it downstairs again.

I should write him a note. Tell him where I've gone.

But we're not together anymore, and I don't have to let anyone know where I've gone, or why.

She pulled her jacket on and grabbed her keys.

That should be a relief.

Before opening the door, her stomach twisted, and she ran to the bathroom, falling to her knees in front of the toilet.

After being sick twice, she washed out her mouth and splashed cold water over her face. Buster stared up at her as she opened the door.

I can't take you on my bike.

She reached into her pocket and pulled out her last lifeline, hitting Grace's number.

She's all I've got left, and you, Buster. I wouldn't leave you.

The phone rang and rang until her voicemail picked up. Madigan hung up and stared down at the contacts in her phone.

Her mom and dad were out of the country.

She kept Drew's number—although his phone was long gone—she couldn't bring herself to delete it.

Cindy from work wasn't close enough to her, and Mary,

her old co-worker from Roy's, would spread the gossip around town.

She tried Grace again to no avail.

One number left besides Will's.

She hit the button and tried to clear her throat as her phone rang.

CHAPTER TWENTY FOUR

With each minute that passed on their drive to Whitestone Lodge, the sky turned a darker shade of blue, until they arrived beneath a dark autumn sky.

"Whoever sent those pictures knows we're coming to see John," Grace said.

Mac parked beside the officer on duty, a man she didn't recognize.

"He lied to us, and it's enough for an arrest," Mac said. "I told Banning to get me the warrant."

"Whoever left that box wants the attention on John. If we bring him in, he'll lawyer up. We won't get to talk to him."

Mac shook his head. "I should have trusted my instincts the last time we were here."

"Okay, he lied, but we don't know the story until we talk to him."

"Sounds like you're sticking up for him," Mac said before stepping out of the car.

He had a quick word with the officer before catching up with her on the way to John's room.

"Hey," she said, touching his arm. "I'm just as upset as you about those pictures. More, maybe. Somebody's threatening us—playing with us, even—but I won't let any personal feelings cloud my judgment. It's important we stay focused on the facts, like you said, Mac."

His chest heaved before he knocked on the door. John opened it, and they walked in, closing it behind them. Mac had his cell phone clutched in his fist.

Waiting for the arrest warrant to come through.

"I'm done playing games," Mac said. "You were at Wild Card yesterday. Why?"

John stared up at him and started to shake his head.

"I'm done with the bullshit," Mac hollered and took a step toward John.

John tilted his head back, puffing out his chest.

"Hey," Grace said. "Just the truth, John. That's all we'll hear at this point, or you're on your own."

John bowed his head and shook it.

Any more lies, and it's over for you.

"Mickey Clarke," John muttered. "The sonofabitch has taken everything that matters to me."

"You met with him." Mac stared him down.

"He told me to come. Told me if I didn't, I'd go down for Lily's murder."

Mickey knew he'd be there. Maybe he set him up. Took the picture.

"Did he say he killed Lily?" Mac asked.

John shook his head. "Didn't deny it either."

"Then why?"

"He wanted me to stay quiet," John said, sitting down at the round table. "Not to say anything to you guys."

"What aren't you supposed to tell us?" Grace asked and glanced up at Mac. "About the drugs?"

John's eyes opened wide again, like he couldn't believe Evette had sold him out.

"Yeah." He rested his forearms on the table, and she couldn't help but stare at his tattoos. "He owns the club, and he's in charge of the dealings that go on in there."

"You both worked for him. You *and* Lily?" Mac asked. "Before or after Lily did?"

"Before," he said. "It's how we met. I was in there. I saw her. That was it. We were together ever since."

"And you kept working for him," Grace said, "even after your girlfriend took out a no contact order against him?"

He shook his head. "I'd been trying to get out since then. I didn't know what was going on between Mickey and Lily. She never told me because she—she didn't know what I did, but she knew Mickey and I were connected, and she didn't want to make trouble for me. She was afraid Mickey would make it look like they were having something on the side, you know? Like she initiated it."

"Did he?"

He nodded, snickering. "I told her she was being silly. That I believed her, and I did, but now I know. Now he's threatened me and Evette and threatened to turn it around on me like he did with her. I know why she didn't tell me until he hurt her. She was scared."

"Evette?" Grace asked.

"He said he'd kill her if I said anything to you guys."

"Do you deal straight with Mickey?" Mac asked.

John shook his head. "I deal with his lackey, Blaze."

"Blaze?" Mac asked. "Real name?"

"I don't know," John said.

"So, tell us what really happened that day," Grace said. "If you lie or leave anything out—we can't help you."

He exhaled and leaned in over the table. "Lily and I had been fighting for a week before. I told her what I was into and that I'd tried to get out, but I couldn't. I kept getting calls from Blaze. She thought I'd relapsed. That I was still using, but I wasn't. I've been sober for a long time. She threatened to leave me this time. She said she wouldn't marry a dealer. I promised her I was getting out no matter what. I brought her flowers that night to show her how much I loved her."

I knew it.

Just like your dad.

"I told her what I was going to do, and she seemed nervous, but happy. I saw hope in her eyes." He swallowed hard.

"So you went to Wild Card the night Lily died," Mac said.

John nodded. "I met with Blaze and told him I was done for good. He told me I'd regret it, but I told them to go fuck themselves."

"And you *didn't think they might come after Lily*?" Grace asked.

"I went to meet Luke, like I told you, and asked him to keep his ear to the ground for me. He hangs with Blaze sometimes, and he goes to Wild Card a lot."

"A customer of yours too, no doubt." Mac leaned against the back of Grace's chair. "What happened?"

"I came back to Tall Pines and got home around eleven, just like I said. I found Lily, just lying there with the flowers."

"And you thought it was Mickey?" Mac asked.

John shook his head. "I wasn't gone that long. Three hours—tops. I don't understand how he could've been at the club, to my place and back, but he was the only one with anything against her, the no contact order, and me."

"Oh, *and you?*" Mac said, taking a step closer to him. "You told them to go fuck themselves, and you didn't expect retaliation? Didn't think they might take something close to you away?"

The pictures of us. Of me and Madigan.

It's a threat.

A threat if we don't prosecute John.

"No," John said. "Not at the time, no. I was just happy. I was free, and I was going to tell her we were free…"

"John," Grace said, "why didn't you tell us when I asked about what Evette said? What if we could have caught him by now?"

"Then you would have already." John rested his head in his hands. "And I did tell you. I told you it was him."

Mac pounded his fist on the table, and John jerked back. "You wanted to save your own ass," Mac shouted.

He thinks John should have protected Lily.

He should have.

John pressed his lips together and shook his head. "Wouldn't have made a difference."

"How can you think that?" Mac asked. "Are you honestly that stupid?"

He's letting his own feelings interfere.

"You'll never get him," John said, shaking his head. "Mickey Clarke is *untouchable*."

"You're a coward," Mac said before striding to the door.

"I didn't know this would happen," he said. "I was screwed if I stayed working for him and screwed if I left. You have to believe me. You have to keep Evette safe. They'll be after her if they think I talked. If he thinks you're on to him in anyway. I lost Lily. I can't lose my mom too."

Grace stared down at him.

"Please," John said.

Grace nodded and followed Mac outside.

"I'm staying here all night if I have to," Mac muttered as he stalked to the patrol car. "I'm waiting for the warrant to come in and arresting him myself for obstruction of justice."

It's not going to help.

"Mac," she said, but he didn't turn around. "Mickey must have sent those pictures to incriminate him. He wants him locked away."

"I'll have Officer Vila drop you off at home," he said before studying his phone.

If he's here left to his own devices, he'll put John away without thinking about the big picture. Without realizing this is exactly what the person who left us the pictures wanted.

"I'm staying too," she said.

Mac turned around, glancing up from his phone with a frown. "Fine," he muttered and turned back around.

I need to convince him John could be an asset—and I need to get protection for Evette.

CHAPTER TWENTY FIVE

Jack parked by the curb, and Madigan locked the front door to Will's home behind her. She raced down the stairs with Buster and over to his car.

"Hey," he said as he rolled down his window. "Talking to two sisters in one day. I'm a lucky guy."

"Hey," she said without any energy behind her voice. "You saw Grace?"

"Yeah, at work. About the fire. You alright?"

She nodded. "Could you take Buster to Grace's place? I texted you the address. I'll follow behind you on my bike."

He nodded, and she opened the back door and patted the seat before Buster jumped inside. With his tail wagging, he stepped over the center console and into the passenger's seat.

"Hey, Buster," Madigan said. "Back here."

"Naw, it's alright." Jack smiled. "You can ride up front with me."

Buster panted with delight, sticking his head out the window. The sight of Jack and Buster's silhouettes would have been enough to make her laugh, never mind smile, but as she sat behind them at the traffic light, she couldn't get her mind off Will.

Where did he go? Is he alone?

I shouldn't have come out and said it.

What else could I have done?

When they arrived at Grace's, a crescent moon resembling her tattoo sat high in the sky, shining down on them. Madigan parked her bike in the driveway behind Grace's car and strode toward Jack's car, eager to get inside to Grace's room and bury her head in her pillow.

Maybe she's sleeping.

She opened the door, and Buster jumped down, still wagging his tail and panting hard. A Tragically Hip song played on the radio, and the old, familiar lyrics threatened to strip away her brave façade before she slammed the door shut.

"That guy's the best company." Jack laughed through the cracked passenger window. "Doesn't try to change the radio station. Doesn't talk much. Doesn't ask questions."

Madigan nodded, stepping closer to the door, but she couldn't force a smile.

"But I do," he said. "Could you please just tell me you're alright?"

"Mhmm, thanks for the ride, Jack."

He nodded. "You know I'm here for you no matter what. It's no trouble."

I'm your obligation because of Drew.

That's all I'll ever be to you, isn't it?

She had allowed his kindness and sympathy to lull her into a false sense of security once before, letting down her walls and imagining an attraction from him that had only been wishful thinking.

She wouldn't let it happen again.

"I appreciate this," Madigan said, taking a step back.

"Madigan?" he called through the small gap in the window.

She bent down a bit to make eye contact with him.

"He didn't hurt you, did he?" he asked.

She shook her head.

Other way around.

"I had to ask—" he started.

She turned around before her tears slid down her cheeks and pulled her suitcase up to the front door. She bent over and picked up the fourth rock from the flowerpot, and felt around in the darkness for the spare key, finding it and sliding it into the keyhole.

As she opened the door, she turned around, and Jack sat in his car, waiting to see her in. She nodded to him and stepped inside, closing the door behind Buster.

"Hey, Buster, stay," she whispered, and he wagged his tail, standing in one spot but sniffing the air all around him.

She felt her way through the dark entryway to the end table, flicking on the lamp and setting the key down. The motion detector light in the backyard flashed on, and she walked to the door with Buster beside her. She opened the door and stuck her head outside, and Buster let out a few gruff barks.

"Grace?" she whispered.

No movement on the patio or anywhere out back.

"I'd let you out, Buster, but from the sound of that growl, there's probably a rabbit back there or something," she said, closing the door and locking it.

She kicked off her boots and set them by her suitcase at the front door, and by the time she flopped down on the couch, the back porch light had turned off again. Buster lay down in front of the couch below her, and she ran her hand over his back as she propped her head up on the hard decorative pillow.

"See, Buster? It's alright," she whispered.

He stood up and walked into the kitchen again.

"Buster," she whispered.

If he barks, he'll wake Grace for sure.

She didn't need to be bombarded with her drama after a long shift at work, and maybe it would seem better in the morning. Be easier to talk about.

Buster sat by the back door, staring out into the darkness. She closed her eyes and fought the thoughts that flooded her mind.

He's better off without you.

You did him a favor.

The look on his face when I told him we don't belong together wrecked me.

I messed up.

Buster's bark made her open her eyes again, and she stared at the bright light in the backyard.

"What's out there, boy?" she whispered.

Buster scratched at the door, and she sat up on the couch as he barked again.

"Shh, you'll wake Auntie Grace," she whispered.

She picked herself up off the couch and tip-toed toward him.

The light turned off again, and Buster let out a deep growl.

* * *

"No can do, Mac," Banning said.

Mac pressed the phone closer to his ear, and the rest of Banning's words came out too muddled to understand, but they were enough.

"He lied," Mac said. "We got him on that. Listen—no."

"Could I speak to him?" Grace asked.

Mac frowned but handed her the cell phone.

"Chief Banning, this is Grace. I gather you know about the threats Mickey Clarke's men have made against John?"

"He filled me in."

"Could we get police detail on his mother, Evette's, home? I can send you the address."

"We have it, and that's fine. I'll have someone on it 'round the clock."

"Thank you for taking it seriously," Grace said, having already prepared a rebuttal if he had said no.

"Well, I don't thank you," Mac leaned over and shouted toward the phone. "You get no thanks from me, or the Martins, or the people of Tall Pines if we let this guy go."

She could hear Banning sigh on the other line.

"Tell him to get me more," Banning said. "I could do it if we had more on it. Listen, tell him the DNA results'll be in tomorrow. On my word."

"I hear him," Mac grumbled.

"He hears you," Grace repeated.

"Alright, get me something that sticks," Banning said before the line went dead.

Grace passed the cell phone back to Mac. "About time the DNA comes in," she said.

"I told you, it usually takes weeks. He's pulling strings to calm me down."

"He knows you well, then."

"And I know him." Mac turned to her. "He's got ulterior motives. He wants this case dealt with. Bad."

"His reputation?"

"Something like that," Mac mumbled and shoved his cell in his pocket. "Listen, you were right. We can get more out of him if we appear neutral to him, but I won't be played."

He's admitting I'm right.

She stifled a grin. "I get it."

"And I don't know that it was him," he continued, "but I know he was unaccounted for when the fire started. Those pictures. We didn't have detail on him when they were taken, am I right?"

She nodded.

"So it could have been him, trying to throw us off his scent," Mac said. "Or it could be whoever killed Lily."

"Mickey?"

"If he threatened John, or had his men do it, I think it's more to do with his drug op than Lily's murder. Could be both, though. We need to put pressure on him."

"Make him realize he's being watched?" she asked. "I don't think that's a good idea. I've known someone like him. He sent his thugs to do his dirty work, and they were disposable to him. These men are protected."

Mac nodded and leaned back in his seat.

"They took a picture of my apartment," he said, his jaw clenched. "My daughter, she visits me there. Whoever did this isn't getting away with it. I don't care what it takes."

"I know how you feel—well—I don't have kids, but they took a picture with my sister in it. I'm angry. I won't let anyone threaten her."

"I think the job is part of what split my ex and I up. Aside from the affair she had." He huffed out a chuckle and shook his head.

It still stings him.

"She knows how I put my life on the line every day, and for a long time, it's been different. It's Tall Pines. It's supposed to be a cozy, quiet little coastal town, and for a long time, it was, but the crime rate has risen. I work overtime a lot. There was an incident last year where I pulled over a city slicker for a DD offence, and he pulled a gun on me."

"What?"

"Some rich kid. His dad works for the government. He

got off easy, but I didn't. My wife—" He stopped and looked over at her. "I'll just say she finally had an excuse to leave and take Kenzie with her."

He turned his head toward his window and stared out at the lot for a while.

"I'm sorry, but is your daughter's name MacKenzie?" Grace asked, and he turned to her. "MacKenzie MacIntyre?"

She grinned, and he smirked. "No. Her name's Kensington, after the place her mom and I met. It's in Toronto."

"Ah," Grace nodded. "Because it'd be weird if you named her after you."

"What? No, it wouldn't."

"A little vain." She smirked.

He pursed his lips, holding back from smiling with teeth before turning away again.

"I love her more than anyone knows. Even her mother, I guess. When they threaten me at my home, it's a threat to her too."

"I know."

"Your foster sister. Did you meet in that foster home? With Evette?"

"Yeah."

"Any other family besides your foster sister?"

"Not like her. My last foster parents were good. They helped me a lot, but there wasn't much of a bond between us. They didn't adopt me like Madigan's parents did after we left Warbler Way. Madigan is my *sister* though. No other word before it and no other person like it."

"We're going to catch whoever killed Lily," he said. "And whoever took those pictures and left them for us? They'll pay too. You don't mess with family."

* * *

Madigan tugged on Buster's collar, pulling him away from the sliding door and back toward the living room.

"That's the last thing I need right now," Madigan hissed, remembering the last time he got sprayed by a skunk. "We'll go out later."

A hollow clunk came from the bathroom, and Buster turned toward it, tugging even harder against her.

"No," she said. "Look, you've woken her."

She pulled him back to the living room and sat on the couch with his collar still in hand.

How much should I tell her tonight? It's late. I'll just apologize for waking her and...

A creak echoed down the hallway. Buster lunged forward, and she lost her grip on his collar.

"Okay," she sighed.

Don't know how happy she'll be to see you.

Buster's bark raised the hairs on her neck. She took a step toward the hallway, and heavy steps thudded toward her.

A figure dressed in black with a ski mask emerged from the shadows.

Madigan ran for the kitchen, trying to create distance. To arm herself.

He's got something. A weapon.

She reached for a knife in the butcher block as two hands grabbed her shoulders and yanked her backwards.

Her hip collided with the cold tile and throbbed with pain. She used her arm to prop herself up, turning as Buster jumped on the man. He kicked Buster, sending him tumbling to the ground with a whimper and sliding across the tile.

"Buster!" she screamed.

He got back on all fours, taking another run at the man. He turned to him with the long, black thing in his hand.

Madigan scrambled to her hands and knees as the man raised the weapon above his head, preoccupied by

Buster. Every fiber in her being wanted to run, but she fought the dull ache at her side, pushing herself off the ground.

You're not touching him.

A deep anger boiled inside her as she pushed herself to her feet and lunged at the man in one solid motion, wrapping her arms around his neck.

He stumbled sideways, and she closed her eyes as he lost his footing. Something heavy crashed against the tile.

He dropped his weapon.

He landed on top of her, and she cried out in pain. An extra weight added to the pile as Buster jumped on him.

"Fuck," the man hollered.

Did he bite you? Yes, Buster. Yes.

She scrambled to get out from beneath them before the man's weight lifted, and she gasped for breath, inhaling her first full one.

Lights flooded the living room.

Headlights.

Someone's here. Someone else is coming.

They're going to kill me.

* * *

As Mac turned down Rosebank Drive, his headlights reflected off something in her driveway.

Is that Madigan's bike?

Mac parked the car just behind the bike, and a small shadow popped up in her front window.

Buster?

She grabbed her files from the seat. "Thanks for the drive," she said.

"That yours?" Mac nodded to the bike.

"My sister's. See you in the morning."

Mac nodded as she opened the door and got out of the car.

She walked up the L-shaped walkway toward the front door, where Buster barked at the window.

What's Madigan doing here?

She opened the door and dropped her bag with the files as Madigan pulled herself off the floor.

Something's wrong.

"What's going on?" Grace asked, unable to articulate how she felt.

Something's wrong.

Madigan turned to her with tears running down her cheeks.

"A man—" she said. "Someone broke in, and he ran. When you came, he ran out the back."

She gasped for breath and reached her arms out. "Buster," she cried.

He ran to her side, and she knelt, wrapping her arms around him.

"He's gone?" Grace asked.

Madigan nodded.

Grace turned around. "Stay there."

She waved her arms at Mac, who hadn't left the driveway, and he stepped out of the car.

"Someone broke in. They attacked my sister. They just left around back," she hollered.

"I'm going," he called. "You stay with her! I'll call you."

She nodded and ran back into the house, locking the front door behind her and taking out her gun. She went from room to room, clearing it before reaching the open bathroom window, locking it.

She locked the back door, and after clearing all points of entry, she holstered her gun and returned to Madigan and Buster.

"Did he hurt you?" Grace asked.

"Just my hip," Madigan said. "I'm fine."

"You're okay," she said.

It wasn't a question.

It never had been.

Not after any beatings.

Not after Drew passed away.

Not now.

"You're okay," Grace repeated as her phone rang, and Madigan sniffled back her tears.

"Go," Grace said, standing up and pressing the phone to her ear.

"Didn't leave by the road that I saw. I'm going to the beach on foot," Mac said, tires screeching in the background.

"What did he look like?" Grace asked Madigan and put her on speakerphone.

"Taller than me. Ah—average build," she said, catching her voice in her throat. "All black. Ski mask. That's all I saw. That's all I saw."

"You're sure it was a man?" Grace asked.

"I just knew." Madigan nodded. "Then he shouted. I think Buster bit him, and he shouted."

Grace nodded. "Did you get that?"

"Got it," Mac said. "Call Banning. I want units going around here."

"On it," Grace said.

"Is she—" Mac started.

"He left something in the kitchen," Madigan said, wiping her eyes with the back of her hands. "On the floor."

Grace walked over and found the crowbar, half hidden under the table.

"A crowbar," Grace muttered.

"Is your sister okay?" Mac asked.

"She's fine," Grace said. "Thank you."

She ended the call and dialed Banning, passing the information on to him. He promised to send out all available units, and after Grace hung up, she led Madigan to the couch with Buster by her side.

"I'm going to make you some tea," Grace said, gliding into the kitchen.

She needs me calm. Be calm.

She poured water into the kettle and set it on the stove, turning on the gas.

Buster lay on Madigan's feet, and she bent over, rubbing his head.

Whoever took the photos took it further. It had to be the same person.

"Hey," Grace said. "Chamomile or green?"

Get back to normal, Madigan. Come back to me.

Madigan made eye contact with her.

"Chamomile or green?" Grace repeated.

"Chamomile," Madigan said.

There you are.

"Good, coming up," Grace said.

She wanted to call Mac and get an update. She wanted to stay busy because without anything to do, Madigan would be her focus, and looking into her hurt face just made her want to be out there looking for whoever did it too.

She brought Madigan her hot mug and held it out to her instead of setting it on the table.

Take it. Feel the warmth.

Madigan took the mug. "Thank you."

Grace sat beside her and rubbed her back.

"I thought you were home. Your car was in the driveway. Buster knew something was up. He saw him outside. I wasn't paying attention."

"That's not your fault. I'm sorry I wasn't here."

"I'm glad." She turned to Grace. "But I'm glad you came."

Grace nodded and sat back on the couch.

"He came down the hall and then after me. Buster tried to stop him, but he kicked him. That bastard *kicked* him," her voice broke as she rubbed Buster's head once more. "He was going to hit him with the crowbar, but I jumped on him, and he fell on me, and then he got up. Because you came."

Madigan set her mug down and turned to Grace.

"You need to drink your—" Grace started.

"Just hug me," Madigan said. "Will ya?"

Grace wrapped her arms around Madigan and squeezed her back tightly.

She needs this. Why do I always try to control things?

"He didn't do anything else to hurt you?" Grace asked.

He didn't. You would have said. I would have seen something. Please tell me.

"He didn't," Madigan said. "My side will be bruised and maybe Buster's too, but it could have been so much worse. I should get Buster checked out."

Madigan pulled away from her. "Is someone after you?"

Grace sighed. "Drink your tea."

Madigan must have known not to argue with her because she picked up her mug and took a sip.

She doesn't need to know everything. Not yet.

"The case I'm working," Grace said. "There's always a chance someone won't like what I'm digging up. Whoever killed Lily—we might be getting close."

Madigan nodded. "Too close for them."

A knock at the door made Madigan jump. Mac peered in through the front bay window, with three units parked on the road behind.

She opened the door. "Come in."

He bowed his head and stepped inside.

"We still have two units looking, but nothing yet," Mac said before peering behind her.

"This is my sister, Madigan. This is Officer MacIntyre."

Madigan nodded. "I know who you are. I worked for the *Tall Pines Gazette*. You're their favourite interviewee."

Worked?

"I'm sorry this happened," Mac said. "We're doing everything we can to find him."

"I appreciate it," Madigan said. "I heard his voice. I could probably ID him that way."

"Okay then." Mac nodded to her before turning back to Grace. "I'm headed back out."

"Thank you," Grace mouthed to him as she followed him out the door.

He nodded. "Call if anything comes up."

"I will."

"Listen," he said, lowering his voice. "Whoever was in there was after you. To hurt you, scare you, or worse."

Grace swallowed hard and bowed her head.

Someone's after me. I know it's true, but I was thinking about Madigan.

My only concern is Madigan.

"Hey," Mac said, touching her arm, and she lifted her head to meet his gaze. "We're going to get the prick who did this, and until then, your sister's going to be safe."

Grace nodded and stepped back through the door, letting his hand fall away from her arm. She locked the door, and he walked down the path and driveway, speaking to the guys before getting in his car. Another left after him, but one stayed on the road.

He has someone watching out for us.

She returned to the couch and curled up beside Madigan.

"Good boy," Grace whispered and scratched Buster behind the ears before slipping off her shoes. "Did you and Will get into a fight or something? Is that why you came?"

Madigan lay on her back, and Grace pulled her legs up onto her lap by her ankles, one by one.

"Will and I aren't together anymore," Madigan said. "I don't want to talk about it."

"What? Why?" Grace asked.

Madigan shook her head and stared at the ceiling.

She had a few boyfriends since her late teens, and none of them lasted too long. Her high school sweetheart seemed hopeful for a future, but before he left for college, she broke it off without even attempting to maintain the relationship.

Too hard, she'd said.

No point.

"It's not like that this time," Madigan sighed. "Although, I get why you'd think that."

"So what is it? You can tell me."

"You've been dealing with a lot, and you don't need this drama on your plate too," Madigan whispered as Buster curled up at her end of the couch.

"If it matters to you, it matters to me. I'll never be too busy for you. I know you went through a lot, but I don't want you shutting down on me."

"Like you do to me," Madigan mumbled.

"That's different," Grace said. "I was undercover."

"Yeah, but I couldn't see you. We barely talked for almost a year."

"I know," Grace sighed. "I wish I could have."

No I don't. I wouldn't want her anywhere near those druggies and derelicts. Wouldn't even want her to know about it all.

It's my fault she was attacked tonight.

This is on me.

"Do you?" Madigan asked.

"I wish I could have been there for you," Grace said. "But no. I guess I'm glad I didn't get you involved in the shit I had to deal with."

"Because I couldn't have dealt with it?"

"No." Grace pulled her hair back in a ponytail. "Because you shouldn't have to. I mean, I could have called more, but I wouldn't have been able to tell you about my day. Oh hey, Sis, I had to babysit a bunch of meth heads last night and pretend I was high too. Or if I'd come to visit and you had to see how much weight I'd lost because I wasn't eating or sleeping well. Or hey, what if I'd invited you over to my apartment where my boyfriend dealt drugs, and the druggies would have to try before they buy? Had you sit on the couch on the other side of me while—"

"While what?"

Grace shook her head.

"Tell me."

"While my cover's only true friend cried most nights about her boyfriend beating her. About him coming home and raping her when she didn't want it. Having to listen to her without being able to do anything about it because she was *my* in, and her boyfriend was the guy we were there for. To take him down. We needed her. I needed her more than she needed help. That's what I was trained to think."

Tears burned in her eyes as Madigan lifted her feet off Grace's lap and sat up in the middle of the couch.

"I imagined worse," Madigan said.

"It was," Grace spat back.

Madigan turned to her and bent her knee up close to her chest. "Tell me," she whispered.

Grace shook her head as tears fell down her cheeks. Madigan grabbed her hand, and although Grace fought to pull it away, Madigan overpowered her, lacing their fingers together.

"I couldn't be there for you then," Madigan said. "But I'm here for you now. I always will be if you'll let me. And even when you won't."

Grace swallowed hard and smiled, turning to her. "I don't want to get into it after what happened to you tonight."

"You know you like when I tell you stories after something hard happens?" Madigan asked. "This could be like that, only for me."

"I know," Grace whispered. "It's too hard."

"We made it through our first four years as sisters. From seven 'til eleven, we lived through everything Eli did. Everything he made us do, and I don't know if I could have without you and you without me. And now tonight."

She squeezed Grace's hand. "Tell me what happened," Madigan said. "I'm here now."

Grace exhaled and took a deep breath, hoping this wasn't the one thing that could break it all down.

Don't hate me.

"You can tell me anything," Madigan said as if reading her mind.

Grace nodded and let go of her hand.

"A shipment was scheduled to come in. Biggest one yet, and the one we were going to nail Conrad and the rest of them with, along with his partner overseas. The week before this, when Leah tipped me off, she told me because she found out she was pregnant, and she wanted to get out. She thought I had no clue what the boys were really into, and she told me because she was scared to bring a child up around that. After she told me that, I didn't need her for information anymore, but my captain told me she had to stay. He didn't want to send up any flags with Conrad. It had to be business as usual."

"I told her to avoid him. To stay away or else he could beat her and she'd lose the baby, but to wait until after the shipment when things had settled down. I told her I'd help keep her safe and get her away from it all if she just waited. She agreed, and I didn't see her for three days after that, but when I spoke to her, she'd changed her mind. Conrad had been in good spirits, bought her presents, and reaffirmed his love for her. She wanted to stay. I kept my mouth shut, but I'd made up my mind. I knew when I was done, I was getting her out.

"The night before the shipment was due, we all went out for drinks to celebrate Nick's birthday, and probably the shipment on its way, but they didn't know I knew about that. It was a good night. No one was sloppy for once, probably because Conrad threatened that it was an important time, and if anyone dropped the ball, they were dead. We parted ways that night, and Leah seemed so happy.

"The next morning, she came to see me in tears. She told Conrad about the baby, and he told her to get an abortion. She didn't know what to do, but she was scared all over again, and I told her that would be her life if she stayed with him. I told her she had to do what was best for her and the baby. She asked for my help one final time, and I'm trained to say no. I'm trained to keep the job my top priority. But I said yes, Madigan," Grace said, turning to her. "I promised her I'd keep her safe."

"I'd have done the same thing," Madigan said.

Grace nodded.

I know you would have.

"I told her she wasn't going back to him, and he wouldn't have missed her that day anyway. She packed some things; I gave her some money, and I was going to drive her to the bus station just after dinner, but she had stomach pains. Bad ones. I told her she was going to the hospital first, so that's where we went. We waited for hours, and even though I was supposed to have come back in to debrief after finishing my undercover work, I stayed with her. Conrad called her just before eight. Wanted to make sure she was home when he returned, and she told him she would be. She got a clean bill of health, and the doctor told her a little bit of bleeding was normal, so we left. Before we arrived at the station, she realized she left her passport in her bedroom armoire. I told her she could get a new one—to leave it—but she told me she wanted to go and live with her stepsister in the United States. To raise the baby there, because Conrad wouldn't find her. So I took her back."

"But they'd all be at the drop-off for the shipment, right? And then arrested?"

Madigan nodded. "They were, except Conrad sent two of his guys after her. One was my—well—he wasn't my boyfriend, but he wanted to be. Maybe I let him think he was."

"He didn't know she was leaving."

"No, but he had a sense she wouldn't go for the abortion. He wanted to make sure she didn't have his baby. That's the only thing that makes sense. We went back to the house, and no cars were there, so I waited in the driveway while she went in to make sure no one came. They were already in there though. Leah was smart. She got out, and she was running to the car when one of them shot her in the back. I was out of the car by that time, and I covered her, taking out the other guy. Nick hid in the bushes as I dragged her back to the car, and when I dragged her inside, he crept up on the other side and shot through the glass. The bullet went right through the glass—killing Leah. I shot him, point blank."

Madigan wrapped her arms around her, pulling her back to reality and out of the nightmare she'd survived.

"She's dead because I couldn't protect her," Grace said. "I was given orders, and I ignored them."

"But you were just trying to help her. To save her life. How can you be in trouble for that?"

Grace shook her head. "Unless you're in law enforcement, I guess it's hard to understand. It could have been a lot worse for me. They could have stripped me of my badge and gun. They could have dishonorably discharged me from the force. Being demoted to a smaller, quieter territory was a gift I guess. One I'm supposed to be thankful for, and I guess in a way I am, because I can work my way back."

"Yeah." Madigan pulled away and rubbed her back. "And you will. You're a hero to me, though. You always will be."

Grace pressed her lips together. Her old colleagues hadn't forgotten her disloyalty, and no one who heard her name or read her file soon would.

"So that's been tough," Grace said, letting out a huff that resembled laughter, and let go of Madigan's hand. "But the guilt I have over Leah's death..."

She shook her head and closed her eyes, imagining her friend's smile. Picturing her face as she ran toward the car while shots rang out into the night air. Her eyes and how they opened wide when the bullet entered her back.

"If she were here, she'd know you tried. Maybe she still does on the other side. If there is one, she knows what you were up against."

"She knows I used her," Grace shook her head. "If it wasn't for me—"

"Hey, you don't know what would have happened," Madigan said. "If she's up there in heaven, she knows you chose her over the job in the end. She knows you cared for her, in life and death. You risked your life and job for her, Grace. What other sacrifice could you have made?"

Grace rubbed at her eyes and ran her fingers through her hair as she tilted her head back.

"I've run through all the scenarios with the therapist. There's no right answer. There's no good answer."

"Wouldn't Leah want you to live a full life?" Madigan asked. "I do."

"I'm trying. I'm clawing my way back, Madigan."

THE GIRLS ACROSS THE BAY

"I know." Madigan nodded. "I wouldn't expect any less from you, but you don't have to do it alone."

Madigan reached behind Grace and picked a strand of hair from her ponytail, picking it up and letting it fall, swishing the whole thing back and forth, sending tingles down Grace's spine.

All the tension in her body washed away, and she shook from the leftover adrenaline.

It's out, and she still loves me.

She turned to Madigan, smiling. "I appreciate that. You know same goes for me, so spill."

"Compared to yours, mine's nothing," Madigan said.

Grace cocked her head to the side and smiled. "Well, thanks. I'm good for something at least, even if it's just to make you feel less shitty."

"Oh, I still feel pretty shitty," Madigan sighed. "Will tried to propose, and I broke up with him."

"Ouch," Grace said, squinting through the secondhand awkwardness she felt for her sister.

"Yep." Madigan tugged at a loose thread on her shirt. "Might be the most damage I've done yet. He's not the only one hurting right now, either. If it was the right decision, I shouldn't be feeling like this right now."

"How do you feel?"

"Heartbroken."

Grace shrugged. "Maybe you would. You really cared about him. I know that."

"How?"

Grace smiled. "You care about everyone you're close with, but you—you went against your nature for him."

"So what, is it in my nature to be alone?"

"I don't know, Mads. You're great on your own, but in a relationship, something changes. You get that look in your eye like a caged animal. Like you're in a place you shouldn't be, and you can't get out, but you put yourself there in the first place."

"I know," Madigan sighed. "I like feeling wanted. Who doesn't?"

"Was that it with Will?"

"No. He treated me better than any man in my life ever has, except Drew—and Jack, I guess."

"You miss that." Grace nodded and patted her just above the knee. "I know."

"And Will saw something in me. He had confidence in me like you do—but he doesn't know what I've been through."

"Because you don't open up," Grace said, sitting forward on the couch.

"Speak for yourself." Madigan nudged her upper arm.

"I'm trying," Grace said and stood, stretching her legs.

Tears slid down Madigan's cheeks.

"Hey," Grace said. "It'll get better, okay?"

Madigan shook her head. "It's not that."

"What happened tonight?"

Madigan shook her head and stared up at her. "I thought I was losing you."

"I came back here, and I'm with you now."

"Yeah, but you're always somewhere else up here." Madigan tapped her temple with her finger. "You wouldn't let me in."

Grace rubbed her forehead, wishing there was a better way to describe how difficult it had been.

Madigan wiped her tears away and curled her legs up underneath her. "Don't do that again, alright?" she whispered.

Grace nodded. "I saw you called on the way back. I'm sorry I couldn't answer. That I wasn't here sooner."

"I know what you're working on is important," Madigan said. "Was it something about John?"

Releasing her secret had bonded them even closer, and although she couldn't give any details, she felt the need to tell her about John as it pertained to Evette.

Better to find out from me.

"The people John's involved with?" Grace said, and Madigan nodded. "They threatened his life and Evette's if he cooperated with us."

"What?" Madigan sat up straight.

"Yeah, I know," Grace said. "Listen, I'll fill you in in the morning. I'll tell you the version for your article first, and then I'll tell you what nobody can know yet, alright? I just need some sleep."

She waited to see if Madigan would correct her about her job after talking about it in past tense with Mac.

Madigan nodded. "Okay."

Maybe tomorrow, then.

"You can come sleep in the bed with me like we used to," Grace said, but Madigan shook her head. "Alright. Help yourself to whatever you need. If Mac calls, I'll let you know."

"Thanks for listening," she whispered.

By the time Grace wrapped herself up under the covers in her bed, she had overcome the urge to look at the binder beneath her bed.

I can't do it anymore.

Leah had a fighting spirit that reminded her of Madigan since they met. Leah always treated Grace like a younger sister, even though they were about the same age. She'd taken her under her wing and welcomed her to a life of abuse, drugs, and manipulation. A life Grace already knew too well, but she'd still learned so much from her.

Not just how to survive, but how to live with passion.

Madigan's support helped more than she would know. She could almost picture Leah saying the same things with more attitude and a sharper edge.

Wouldn't Leah want you to live a full life? I do.

"I can't if I keep reliving it," Grace whispered into the dark bedroom. "I can't move forward if I look back, but I don't want to let it happen again."

Grace took a deep breath and exhaled.

If I can't let it go, I have to let it make me stronger.

Better.

For Madigan.

She leaned against her headboard, her gun on her bedside table in her peripheral vision.

You don't mess with family.

CHAPTER TWENTY SIX

"I'm having a security system installed tomorrow," Grace said as she entered the kitchen. A tight bun set off her high cheek bones and dewy complexion.

She looks lighter.

Better.

Madigan rubbed Buster's head and poured another coffee.

"Buster's a security system," Madigan said. "If I'd listened."

"Speaking of, will you and Buster be staying?"

Madigan passed her the mug of coffee and walked to the sliding door, letting Buster out back.

"Mads, it's fine if you need to stay here. You know you're always welcome."

"I know," Madigan sighed. "I would get my own place but —I lost my job at the paper."

Grace pressed her lips together and joined her at the sliding door, watching Buster sniff around the yard.

"I had a feeling," Grace said. "For how long?"

"Couple of days. I've thought about trying to get my job

back more than once since, but my heart's just not in it. I'll get a job and be out of your hair soon, alright?"

"You can stay as long as you want," Grace said, opening the sliding door. "Come on."

She stepped outside into the early glow of the morning sun peeking just above the horizon. Madigan held the door handle, willing herself to step outside.

That's where he was. Lurking. Just waiting to get in.

Grace sat down on her patio in her Muskoka chair overlooking the gorgeous view, the breeze blowing through her hair as she sipped her coffee.

She looks peaceful.

She won't say anything, but she knows.

She knows this is hard for me.

"Will you be home tomorrow for the security team, or should I make sure I can be home in the morning?" Grace asked without turning to look at her.

"I can be here," Madigan said, taking a step out and feeling the breeze against her face.

That feels nice. I can do this.

She closed the door behind her and sat in the chair next to Grace. Buster trotted to her side as she scanned the back garden, squinting toward the treeline to her right.

Why can I feel safe in the kitchen where it happened, but not out here?

"Great," Grace said. "A unit will be outside the house until then, so don't mind them. I have to go in a little bit. You'll be okay."

Madigan nodded. "I've got this guy." She rubbed Buster's rump, and he wagged his tail.

"Will you be staying here all day? Or any plans?"

"Cut to the chase," Madigan said. "You don't want me going out, do you?"

Grace smiled before hiding it with her mug.

"Well, I've got to look for a new job. And there are a few other things on my to-do list."

"Such as?"

Do I tell her about Valerie? She'd probably be as curious as I am.

"Did you know our next door neighbour on Warbler Way went missing the first year we lived there?"

Grace frowned. "No, I didn't."

"I know you're going to tell me to give it up, but I looked into missing girls around the time I had my nightmare, or whatever it was, and she was a young woman next door with a fiancé and parents living in Tall Pines. You know the mansion before the road to the lighthouse? That's where they've lived ever since."

"And you think she could be the dead body you saw?" Grace asked.

And you think it's ridiculous.

"I saw a picture of Valerie wearing a ring that looks like the one Evette wears."

"Looks the same or *is* the same ring?" Grace asked. "And which one? She wears so many."

"A big silver one. I'm going to check it out. And Eli was the last one to see Valerie besides her parents the day she went missing."

"They lived next door?" she asked. "I don't remember them."

"He must have moved out soon after. It was a single mom with a teen daughter there, right?"

"It was," Grace said. "I know you're going through a lot. Are you sure you shouldn't take a break and just relax a bit?"

Madigan sipped her coffee, letting it warm her tongue and throat as she swallowed. "I think it's worth looking into."

"If you think so."

"Yeah?" Madigan turned to her, smiling.

"Maybe it'll help you finally put the whole thing to rest," Grace said. "I know you're under a lot of stress right now, and maybe it's a good thing to keep busy—until you get something—you know?"

She thinks this is just busy work.

"You think what I told you is a coincidence?"

"It could be. You're not sure about the ring, right?" Grace stood. "I'm going to work now, but I want you to text me every hour on the hour until I see you again."

"You're kidding," Madigan said, squinting up at her.

Grace shook her head.

"Is there something you're not telling me about last night?"

"I can't say much about the investigation, but I've told you what I think. Someone is disgruntled and thinks we're getting close to something. Maybe that's why the fire was set."

"You don't think it was John, do you?"

Grace stared down at her. "We have a unit watching out for Evette now too. We don't know who's doing it, but we're trying to protect people with a connection to this case as best we can. I'm sorry for what happened last night—"

"Stop saying that like it's your fault," Madigan said.

"I'm just saying, we need to stay alert, okay? So you'll text me?"

You won't be able to focus on the case otherwise.

"I will."

"Good." Grace walked to the sliding door. "I'll see you for dinner, okay? If plans change, I'll let you know."

After she left, Madigan pulled herself together and went on her laptop, searching Joe Harris and Amherst.

You moved, Joe. Where to?

Just one recent link matched. A profile on LinkedIn.

Joe Harris. Telecommunication Sales Manager of EdgeCorp.

"Still in the city," she muttered. "But where?"

She typed the phone number on his profile into her cell and hit send.

"Hello," an older man's voice said.

How old is he?

"Hi, Joe," she said with a smile. "This call may seem like it's coming out of the blue, but I'm with the *Tall Pines Gazette* and we're doing some follow-up stories from decades ago. Things the town might still be wondering about. I came upon the articles regarding your missing fiancée. I was hoping to get an update from you?"

Joe laughed on the other line. "Oh, *now* you wanna to do a feature? That's funny."

Two stories in the paper. Only one front page. I'd be upset too.

"Sir, with all due respect, I believe this story has been on the minds of the residents of Tall Pines to this day."

An exaggeration.

"You weren't around back then, were ya?" he asked.

"No."

"Whaddaya wanna know?"

"Well, to begin with, were there any developments on her case that weren't covered by the media? Anything that happened right after or since?"

"Lot's happened, but nothing that's helped," he said, slurring. "Her parents' lives were ruined. My life was ruined."

"May I ask, what do you think happened to Valerie?"

"I think her parents and friends were right, and I just didn't want to lisssten," he said. "I think she was seeing someone else."

"So you think she left?"

"I didn't say that. Valerie would've never *just left*. Never. She loved me. I loved her."

"So what do you think happened?"

"I'll tell you what happened," he said, raising his voice.

"Our next door neighbour John killed her. That's off the record—fer now."

Madigan's eyes opened wide, and the hairs on her neck raised. Goosebumps spread over her arms, and the tingling lingered as he went on. "Valerie was younger than me. It was a pretty big difference to other people, but not to us. It made more sense to other people why she went behind my back to see John. He's younger. What they call a *bad boy*."

Is he drunk?

"What makes you think it was your neighbour?" Madigan asked. "I thought no one knew who she supposedly ran off with?"

"They didn't. I didn't want to believe it. I still don't. I never told anyone about my suspicions because he dis'peared too. That is until recently. You're a reporter, s'you know him as John Talbot. Ring a bell?"

"Yes."

"He's currently under investigation for the murder of his fiancée. Seeing a pattern?"

"If you want this off the record, does that mean you haven't told the police your suspicions?"

"They don't listen. They didn't do a damn thing more than what they said was their duty back then, and they won't now. But he did it. He killed Valerie, and now he's killed again."

"Mr. Harris," she said. "I won't print this, but I—I wonder why you're telling me?"

"Because in this article you're writing, I want to make damn sure you're getting it right. Valerie didn't run off with some guy. It's what everyone thinks since her friend saw her and some guy out. In public. Holding hands. She wasn't some whore. I want what you write to reflect the truth. If you're setting things straight, then her name should be cleared. Valerie was a beautiful person, and she loved me. She's my soulmate, and she didn't leave of her own free will. You quote me on that."

"I will."

"You covering the case of John Talbot personally?" he asked.

"I have," she said.

"Have you ever spoken to him?" he asked. "In person?"

"Yes, sir."

"Then you've looked the devil in the eyes," he said.

I looked a broken man in the eyes. That's for sure.

Madigan shivered and rubbed her lips with her fingers.

"He was the lowest of the low. Whole family was. Arrested in the years that followed. Had their other foster kids taken away from 'em, rightfully so."

"The family," Madigan said. "They must have known where John went."

"If they did, they wouldn't say. Bunch'a low lifes."

"Don't you want it to be known? If he did it?"

"*I know,*" he said, "and that's enough. We're finished here."

"The number I've called you with is my cell," she said. "The story won't be printed until the end of the month. If you think of anything else, please don't hesitate to call."

He hung up before she ended her sentence.

If Valerie was seeing John, how did Evette end up with her ring?

If it was her ring.

Joe doesn't have any proof.

He must have witnessed something to be so sure.

Madigan texted Grace, letting her know she was alive, before tucking her phone into her bag at the front door. As she slipped on her boots, the officer in the unit out front got out of the car and looked around the neighbourhood, stretching his legs.

"Buster, you'll be safe until I'm back," she said, kissing him on the forehead. "Good boy."

She grabbed her helmet and waved to the officer before getting on her bike.

Evette could be wearing Valerie's ring.

She was her neighbour when Valerie went missing.

She rolled out of the driveway and down the street, headed for Amherst to get some answers.

CHAPTER TWENTY SEVEN

G race checked her phone and opened the latest text from Madigan.

Still alive. Send cake.

As they passed the lighthouse on the way to the highway, Grace thought about the family of the missing woman. How Madigan must have spoken to them and what they might have said.

A woman disappearing next door might be more than a coincidence, but without a real connection to this case, I can't go there. Not right now.

"I spoke to Evette on the phone this morning," Mac said.

"You did? Why?"

"She asked about the unit in front of her triplex," he said, placing both hands on the steering wheel. "Quite the woman."

"You have no idea," Grace huffed. "Was she upset, or?"

"She thinks she's being watched. Which makes me wonder if she's got something to hide or feel guilty about."

"Oh, plenty. Whether it's tied to this case or not, I don't

know. Last time I talked to her, it seemed liked she'd protect John no matter what, so unless we catch her in a lie…"

"Like mother, like son." Mac twisted the radio volume down. "How long were you with her?"

Grace rolled her eyes. "Don't pretend you haven't already looked it up."

"Alright." He nodded. "That's fair."

"It was four *long* years," Grace sighed.

"Well, I did look into it, and I'm sorry for whatever went on there."

Grace stared out her window, telling herself the same thing she always did when she reflected back on that time in her life.

I wouldn't change a thing because I gained a sister for life.

It was true. She'd go through the beatings and sneaking around dangerous neighbourhoods, meeting dangerous people all over again to have found Madigan.

"Your sister okay?" Mac asked.

She nodded as they drove onto the bridge. "She's shaken up, but who wouldn't be? I'm having a security system installed tomorrow so we can get that unit you put out front of my house back on the street again. So thanks for that."

"Oh, yep. Okay, good," Mac said, fumbling over his words. "I just—you know what we're doing here, right?"

"Putting pressure on Mickey?" she asked. "Yeah."

If he left the pictures in John's house before burning it down or attacked Madigan in her home, police presence—specifically theirs—at Wild Card, might push him even further.

"If he gets a sense we're on to him about something, he could go after John too," Mac said.

"We have everyone protected. I won't be intimidated."

Mac nodded. "You're a tough one. I guess you've had to be since, well, your childhood."

"My foster father went away the day we were taken on child endangerment and abuse charges, drug dealing and possession charges, and Evette came away clean. He bullied us for so long, it's all I knew. It'll never happen again."

"In the file, it says he beat Evette, too."

Grace nodded.

He did beat her, but the file only stated what Madigan had reported that day when she'd been caught selling drugs at the high school park. All the things Eli had done to them. To Evette.

"She's not innocent," Grace muttered. "The file doesn't tell you some of the most important things."

They pulled up to an empty spot across the street and down from the club.

"Hey," Grace said. "I want to thank you for last night."

"Oh." Mac waved her off.

Don't push your luck, Grace.

She shrugged. "Just glad you were there."

A knock came from beside her, and she turned to see Bruno Colette, her old supervising sergeant. She rolled down the window.

"Who's this?" Mac asked.

"Sarge," Grace said. "What are you—"

"Leave," Bruno said. "Now. Go back to policing your small town where we put you, and stay out of the big city."

"Hey, who are—" Mac started.

"She'll tell you," he said, shooting her a dirty look. "This is our turf. Just get out of here and leave Mickey Clarke out of your investigation."

How did he know?

Grace turned to Mac. "He's my old supervisor. When I was undercover."

Mac nodded to him. "This has become a murder investigation."

"Not anymore," Bruno said, staring straight at her. "Take it up with Banning. I don't want to see you here again."

"Yeah, I'll do that," Mac said, his voice deeper than usual.

"You better. Sheppard here doesn't like to follow orders, but I'm sure you've heard that by now, *and some*." Bruno chuckled and pushed himself off the car, shaking his head. "Pretty thing, but she's a liability. Good luck with her."

As she turned to Mac with hot cheeks, he already had his phone pressed to his ear, and Bruno smacked the trunk of the car with an open palm before disappearing down the street.

"Banning, yeah," Mac said and paused. "You did? Yeah, I hear you. Fine." He pressed end and chucked the phone into the center console between them.

"So?" Grace asked.

"Mickey's involved in worse things than a murder investigation, apparently," he said, rubbing the stubble across his chin. "He's being investigated by more than just the police here."

How is it possible Bruno's still making it difficult for me to do my job, without having any authority over me?

"I would have known," Grace said, shaking her head. "Banning—"

"Banning didn't know until they called him just now while that asshat was out here trying to scare us off," Mac said, turning the key in the ignition and gripping the wheel with white knuckles. "You made quite the impression on him."

He nodded to the van that pulled out of its spot into the street with Bruno in the passenger's seat, giving them a dirty look again.

"You read the file when I went undercover," Grace said, turning to him. "I guess everyone has read it." Her cheeks burned, and she released her clutched fists.

"Yeah, but like you said," Mac turned to her, "the file doesn't always tell you the most important things."

He's taking my side.

Grace exhaled, letting herself lean back against her seat. "No, it doesn't."

"If we can't look into Mickey anymore," Mac said, "we'll go back and wait for the DNA. If his is in there, Banning said he'd get us a warrant."

"Even after *that?*" Grace gestured to the street.

Mac drove without a word.

Maybe John's right.

Maybe Mickey Clarke is untouchable.

CHAPTER TWENTY EIGHT

Evette opened the door with a cigarette between her smiling lips. She stared up at Madigan and took the cigarette out, puffing white clouds into the air above her head, her smile disappearing.

"You're back."

"I am." Madigan nodded and tried not to inhale too much, choking back a cough. "Can I come in?"

"Oh, sure," she said, walking back to the couch with her hand gliding along the wall. "I thought you were one of them. Did you see my security detail out there?"

"I did. I'm glad you'll be safe."

Evette grinned as she sat down and puffed at her cigarette as soon as she caught her breath.

Should I come right out and ask about Valerie?

Why not?

"Do you remember our next-door neighbours?" Madigan asked. "The couple?"

Evette side-eyed her. "I'm surprised you do. You were so small."

"Did you see them much?" Madigan asked. "Keep in touch?"

"Well, no, why?"

"The newspaper's doing a feature on cold cases," Madigan said.

Same lie as I told Joe Harris. Keeping them straight is an ugly artform.

"Oh?"

"Apparently the young woman went missing."

"Oh, yes," Evette said. "I remember that. So sad. Creepy really."

"Why?"

"You know the neighbourhood. I worried for you girls. Who knows which unsavory neighbour could have been a pedophile? Or a kidnapper? You know? Anytime something like that happens, it makes you think."

Yet, for the next four years our of childhood, you rarely knew where we were.

"What do *you think* happened to her?"

"Oh, I don't know," she said. "It's so odd you brought that up."

Madigan shrugged. "It's quite a coincidence."

"Hmm," Evette hummed and tapped out the ashes of her cigarette into the ashtray. "So tell me, how did you and John get along here the other day?"

She got over that pretty quick. Just like Lily's death.

Her sister's words came to mind: *Evette only cares about Evette.*

"Good." Madigan nodded.

"He's a real softie when it comes down to it," Evette said. "Only the people who take time to get to know him see that."

"Right." Madigan tried to catch a glimpse of her ring, but she waved her hands in the air as she spoke. "He seems nice."

She fidgeted with her rings, and Madigan couldn't help but stare at the one she came for.

No distinct markings.

"Where did you get that ring?" she asked. "The silver one. The thick one."

Evette held her hand up close to her face. "Oh, I'm not sure. Maybe as a gift from Eli."

Thick and curved.

Same as in the picture of Valerie and Joe.

"I don't remember where I got half of these," she said.

Madigan noticed she still wore her wedding ring.

Does she still love Eli? After everything? After all this time? None of my business.

"So John," Evette said and puffed at her cigarette, "I told you, he's a real sweetheart. The more time you spend…"

"What happened to make John leave? He told me he stayed away for a while until well after Eli was put away."

Evette squinted at her. "I think some things are better left in the past."

"If you'd like for John and I to get to know each other more, I think you should tell me what happened." Madigan sat up straight. "Unless there's something you're hiding from me?"

"You're suspicious of him? Still?"

Madigan gave her a blank stare.

I am, but I can't let you think I am.

"He and Eli didn't get along," Evette said. "Never did. I think Eli thought he was taking his place. That's why it was different with you girls. I was never jealous like Eli was of the attention we gave you kids."

"Okay, but why did he leave for so long?"

"He and Eli got into a big fight a while before you girls came. John would stay at a friend's place most nights out of the week since then. He came back when he knew it was only me home, and he'd try to get me to leave Eli."

"So he *was* there that time I remember. The first year we were there?"

Evette shrugged. "I guess. It's difficult to remember exactly when he left. He drifted, really. Drifted right out of our lives. He told me he couch-hopped, or surfed or whatever, and then for a little while, he was homeless. By the time Eli was sent away, I hadn't heard from him in at least two years. Almost three. Then he came by the house again, looking like a man. A new man. I was shocked, but I was so happy to see him safe and well. He got me out of that dilapidated house and into this nice one."

With his drug money.

How could she still afford this place? All her nice things?

He must have stopped giving you money when he left his dealer.

That's why you didn't care for Lily.

"So you never met Lily?" Madigan asked.

"Oh, let's not talk about her." Evette waved her off. "Tell me about you. What's going on in your life?"

That's the first time she's asked since I came to see her.

"It's going," Madigan nodded.

Even that's a lie.

She puffed at her cigarette and spoke as the smoke drifted out. "You're not happy," she said before a coughing fit came on.

I somehow managed to keep busy long enough to get Will off my mind for a few hours, and she brings it up again.

Her cell phone rang, and Grace's name flashed on the screen.

"What's that music?" Evette asked, scrunching up her nose.

"One minute," Madigan whispered and pressed the phone to her ear. "Sorry. I forgot."

"I figured," Grace said. "It's alright. I'm just back at the station. Should be home for dinner. Where are you?"

She'll give me grief if she knows I'm here.

"Dinner sounds good," Madigan said. "Talk to you then, okay?"

"Alright…"

Madigan pressed end and sat up. "I've got to get going."

"Alright, well, feel free to stop by any time you're in the city. I love seeing you, you know that. Maybe you, John, and me could get together sometime soon?" Her face lit up as she waited to read Madigan's face.

Madigan smiled. "I'll be in touch."

"Great," Evette said.

"Don't get up," Madigan, striding toward the door. "Have a good day, and keep an eye out, okay? The police will watch you here, but when you're out…"

"I love it when you worry about me," Evette said. "Isn't that *awful*? But it's true. You be careful too."

Madigan nodded with a smile and closed the door behind her.

She knows things are bad with me, and I didn't even have to tell her.

She always read me so well.

As she went down the steps to the front door, she wondered if John would have the same story as Evette about why he left.

The rings look the same, but maybe I'll pay you a visit, John.

Joe Harris thinks you're the devil, but you're the only chance I have of finding out more about Valerie at this point. No way to tell if the rings are one in the same.

She took out her phone as she reached her bike, scrolling past John's name, and hit Will's.

I have to try.

Leaving Will without closure weighed heavily on her

heart, and each time she thought of him hurting alone, she felt sympathy pains.

But I don't feel guilty about doing my own thing anymore.

No more excuses for living my life the way I want to.

Without an answer, she hung up and searched through her call log, hitting John's number.

"Madigan?" he asked.

"Hey, John, I was wondering if we could meet up?"

"I can't really leave the lodge. Could you come here? Whitestone Lodge."

Even better. Police protection.

"Great," she said. "Be there in an hour."

CHAPTER TWENTY NINE

G race ended her call with Madigan and clasped her cell in her hand as she walked into the station.

She's hiding something.

She's doing something she knows I wouldn't like.

Mac greeted her with a cup of coffee. He led her to their room with a file folder tucked under his arm.

"The results? Did you look?" Grace asked.

He shook his head and opened the door for her.

"Listen," he said, walking to the dry erase board with all of their findings and information. "How your old Sarge spoke to you back there was uncalled for. He's a prick."

She pressed her lips together and sat at the table.

"I spoke to you the same way when I know better. I'm sorry."

"It's fine." She shrugged.

I've never been apologized to at work.

It feels weird.

"I've never had a partner, alright, so when you came, I looked you up. Did my research. I didn't like what I read and heard," he said. "Trusting someone with your life, I mean, you've done it before, right? You want to have some faith in the person."

She nodded, remembering her first and only other partner as an officer with her own beat in Amherst.

"Listen, the file looks bad." Grace took a sip of coffee. "It was a bad situation, and I was at fault for a lot of it. I own it, but it was never my intention. I'm trying to move on from that, though, and right now, this is the most important thing I can spend my time worrying about."

He nodded and grabbed a marker before opening the file with the DNA results.

"Okay, regarding the vase," he said. "The only prints on it were Lily's and Christina Martin's. Her mom."

He wrote their names on the board. "Okay, so it was a present from her mom," he said, referring back to the file.

A peace offering.

"Lily's blood was the only other thing found on the glass. No other bodily fluids."

"Okay, not a surprise there," she said.

"In regards to the rape kit that was used, there wasn't evidence of force, but she had sexual intercourse that day. The sperm belongs to—"

He flipped the page and stared up at Grace.

"Michael Clarke."

"Mickey," she whispered under her breath. "He was with her that day."

Mac wrote it on the board under Mickey's photo.

"Still, it says it wasn't rape," he said, turning back to her. "Might not be enough to prove bad intent."

"What do you mean? This is *big*. The last call Lily made pinged off the cell tower right by his club, probably asking him to come over. Trying to help John out of his mess, maybe, or maybe things between them weren't as John knew, because, come on Mac, Mickey's DNA *inside* her? He was there. He was with her. She let him in."

"Doesn't mean he was there, Grace," Mac said. "Doesn't even mean he saw her that night. Could have been in the morning, or afternoon, or anytime before John came home for dinner. We can't place Mickey there that night after John left. He has an alibi."

"But the call she made— "

"Could have been to anyone in that area. His prints weren't on the vase."

"He wore gloves, then," Grace said.

"Maybe," Mac sighed. "Listen, I don't like this any more than you, but until we have crucial evidence that without a doubt means Mickey murdered Lily, we can't touch him. It's just something we can add to the evidence that he had an intimate relationship with her. They had a relationship in the past at least. Maybe she never broke it off with him?"

"So what, we're hoping he'll confess...just come in and give himself up?" Grace sighed and rubbed her eyes. "Who do you think left the marks on Lily's arm?"

"Could have been John, like her parents say." Mac took a seat beside her at the head of the table. "Could have been Mickey, like John and the reports say. Could have been someone else entirely. We're not getting anywhere playing a guessing game."

"We're considering other suspects?"

"I want to look into John more," Mac said. "He's ours for the questioning, thanks to your level head and, you know, the fact we can't arrest him yet. He's not going anywhere."

"John." Grace tapped her pen against the desk. "If he knew Mickey and Lily had been intimate that day or night..."

"Right, a motive," Mac said. "He could be making up the bit about the drugs Mickey had him running. Evette's the only one who corroborates his story. She could be working

EMERALD O'BRIEN

with him, or he lied to her. Could be trying to frame Mickey. No signs of rape that Lockwood could see, so we have to move forward believing it was consensual."

Grace sighed and shook her head, remembering her time with Leah.

"Sad as it is, Mac, women have sex for more reasons than just because they want to," she said. "Could have been a means to an end. A way to help John get out. An agreement or arrangement. A way to avoid being killed."

"Okay, okay. But the photos in John's house. They were left for us. If John left them there, he could have wanted us to see the photo of him going into Wild Card. To set up his whole story."

"But he was being watched while my house was broken into and my sister was attacked."

"He could have had someone do it," Mac said. "Mickey and John. One of 'em is going down. Listen, I don't like working on theories, so let's use the evidence, even the circumstantial, and create a case against each of them. Maybe it'll sort things out. Get it ready to present to the DA. "

"I thought you'd never ask," Grace said, standing and grabbing the marker from the table.

"Ah."

"What?" Grace smirked. "I thought we were good now?"

"No one writes on my board but me," he said and swiped the marker from her hand.

She rolled her eyes and sat back down as her cell vibrated in her pocket.

"News?" he asked.

She opened Madigan's text.

Still alive. Where's my cake?

CHAPTER THIRTY

That should buy me an hour with John.

Madigan tucked her phone into her pocket and walked past several doors to room eight.

"Excuse me," an officer said, climbing out of his car. "I'm sorry, but you can't go in there. He's not accepting visitors at this time."

She stopped and turned around, facing the officer.

"He invited me over. My name's Madigan Knox, and I'm actually under police protection as well. I'm Detective Inspector Grace Sheppard's sister."

"I understand that, ma'am," he said, "but I'll have to call this in and make sure—"

"She's my sister," John said from behind her.

She turned around. He stood in the open doorway, his clothes wrinkled and his hair a mess.

"Sir, you'll need to step back inside now," he said.

"It'll just be a quick visit," Madigan said. "I promise. In and out."

"I'm not going in until she comes in too," John said.

The officer sighed and glanced around the lot, before

nodding. "Fine," he called. "Get inside. I'm still calling this in though."

"Fine by me," Madigan said and followed John into his room.

He closed the door behind her and gestured for her to sit at the table. "I'm going crazy in here."

"Doesn't smell so great in here," she said, taking a seat.

"They haven't even let the maid in." John took the seat across from her and turned it around, sitting backwards. "So are you here because of the case?"

"I just wanted to pay you a visit. Now that we've met, I wanted to get to know you. It's a bad time, I know, but you're not busy. I know that."

He stared at her, his eyes narrowing. "You're lying."

She craned her head back. "What?"

"I know you're lying," he said. "Your tell is that—"

"I talk too much," she finished. "I know. Grace told me that, but I thought the only person I had to watch myself around was her."

"So you keep things from her?"

Madigan folded her hands in front of her and stared at them.

"She doesn't know you're here, does she?"

"No."

"She will soon," he sighed. "So don't waste time. Why did you really come?"

"I've had this question I've wanted answered since I was little."

He swallowed hard. "Okay."

"Evette kept that picture of you hidden. She never spoke of you. I saw you once; I know I did. Why did you leave?"

"It's complicated," he said, shaking his head.

"Is it really, though? Maybe to someone who didn't share

the same childhood home, but, I think, out of anyone, I have the best chance of understanding."

He cleared his throat. "I guess you do, but it wasn't the beatings. It wasn't the manipulation or making me sell drugs —do drugs—he never made you do them, did he?"

She shook her head. "We'd get contact high. That's it."

He nodded. "Well, it wasn't any of that. Eli was my future."

Madigan propped her head up with her hand. "What do you mean?"

"I lived in that house since I was a baby. Eli and Evette are the only real parents I've ever known. They raised me, and as much as Evette tried to make it different, I was becoming Eli. It started at around ten. I noticed it even then. How I'd treat other kids at school. How I'd treat Evette sometimes. That's what really got me."

He leaned his arms on the table, revealing his scorpion tattoo. "I'd treat her like shit, and she'd let me. Forgive me or not even think I needed forgiveness. She was so conditioned by Eli that she just accepted it."

Madigan nodded, and light faded from the room as the sun hid behind the clouds. She glanced at the tattoo.

I can't be sure about the tattoo, or the ring, or anything.

Why can't I remember?

"I didn't want to be like him, but it was part of me," he said. "I think it still is."

She frowned. "But you got out."

"They're still in my head. If you think he's not in yours, you're lying to yourself."

"I wasn't there as long as you were."

He leaned back in his chair. "Ever get your way by lying?"

"Yeah, but everyone—"

"More than the average person. Pretend to be someone else to manipulate people into giving you what you want?"

She sat still, staring at him.

He knows me more than I'd like to admit.

I won't admit it.

"Tell yourself you're garbage? Not good enough? Never will be? Who'd want you?"

What else do you know about me?

Things I don't know about myself?

"Ever punish yourself?" he asked. "Left before someone had a chance to leave you?"

"That's enough," she said, sitting up and pushing her chair away from the table.

"He's still got his claws deep into us, Madigan. Grace too. We're adults, for Christ's sake. We create our own destiny. We take responsibility for our actions, and yet they're not entirely ours, are they? We're the sum of our parts. Our experiences. He's part of us. So is Evette, and what we experienced there, no kid should ever go through."

Madigan blinked hard, trying to keep her tears away.

"You're right," he said. "I did get out. I went and stayed with friends. Lived on the street a while after that, and then I found a shelter in Amherst. I found Thom Hanks, and I found hope. He reminded me why I left. Because I wanted to be like him—not Eli—and I made that choice."

"I did too," Madigan said. "Well, not the same, but I made the choice to get out of there."

He nodded. "But the shitstorm follows us everywhere. I made a better life for myself. I became more like Thom than Eli. I found the love of my life, and she's gone. When I found her, time stopped. I was nothing without her. When the police got there, I was more Eli than Thom. I was a suspect. I was a criminal. Everything from my past has come back to haunt me. If it hasn't happened to you already, it will. You can't prepare for a thing like this."

"You don't have to be Thom *or* Eli," she whispered.

"You're John. The man Lily fell in love with. You can still be that man."

He shook his head, and tears fell down his cheeks.

"I've lost myself," he muttered. "I'm a monster, Madigan. I always have been. Always will be and I was foolish to think I'd change."

He stood from his chair and dragged his fingers through his hair, pacing back and forth from the bathroom to the door.

"The roses," he said over and over. "Grace is right."

"What are you talking about?"

"I've become my father," he said, stopping in front of her.

Why would he be saying that?

"John, I don't understand." She took a step toward him. "You didn't kill Lily, right?"

He stared down at her with his clenched jaw.

"John? Did you hurt Lily like Eli hurt Evette? Is that why you think you're like him?"

He stared past her, his eyes flickering slightly to the left or right every few seconds.

Did he black out? Does he not know?

"Maybe what I did was worse," he muttered.

He's on the verge of something. He's talking. I have to ask him.

Her hands shook, and she wanted to create a distance between them, but it wasn't right. It felt right to be there. To be present to witness his truth.

"To Lily?" she asked and swallowed hard before opening her mouth, willing the courage to say her name. "Or Valerie?"

His eyes opened wide as the door swung open, letting the glow of the setting sun inside, and disarming the spell she had on him.

Or he has on me.

The officer marched into the room.

"You need to leave now," the officer said. "You don't have permission to be here."

"Okay, okay." She nodded and grabbed her bag.

John went to her side and wrapped his hand around her arm, leaning close to her face. She stared into his eyes piercing through hers.

"Don't say a word," he whispered, his voice shaking.

"Hey," the officer said, stepping toward them. "That's enough."

"Please," he said, shaking his head.

She shook her arm loose and walked past the officer, out to her bike as her phone buzzed in her bag again.

"I had to see him," Madigan said.

He was about to confess something.

"You couldn't have asked me first?" Grace said.

I lost my chance at the truth.

"I didn't know I had to." Madigan grabbed her helmet. "See you at dinner."

She hung up, tossed the cell in her bag, and got on her bike.

He didn't deny it.

He didn't deny either of them, but I didn't accuse him.

Is he scared because I caught him or because he doesn't know himself?

As she rode back to Grace's, she wondered if John was still thinking about her too. If he knew he'd gotten most of it right when he held a mirror up to her to show her who she really was.

I'm a sum of all parts, but they're not held together right.

I'm broken.

So is he.

Don't say a word.

He wants to keep something a secret, but what?

CHAPTER THIRTY ONE

G race waved to the officer out front before unlocking her front door and walking inside.

The smell of garlic and tomatoes wafted toward her, and her mouth watered.

Madigan's chili.

She locked the door behind her and found Madigan in the kitchen, pulling a spoon from the drawer. She dipped it into the pot and pulled out a heaping spoonful, using her hand to shield the floor from any drops, then walking over to Grace.

Grace blew on the spoon and took a bite. Hot chili warmed her mouth and spices bit at her tongue—the sweet and savoury flavors bringing back memories of nights she had been invited to stay over at the Knoxes' when Madigan volunteered to cook the family dinner.

Grace kept a straight face as she licked the corner of her mouth and Madigan waited for her reaction.

"Like it?" Madigan asked.

"Are you trying to make up for today?" Grace asked.

"That and thanking you for letting me stay," Madigan said.

"It's delicious, as always." Grace sighed and moved past her sister and toward her room, avoiding the goofy grin on Madigan's face

After changing and showering, she re-entered the kitchen with chili in bowls on the table and a basket of crusty garlic bread between them. Madigan washed her hands and waved at Buster to go settle down in the living room.

"There are no new leads on the break-in," Grace said.

"I figured," Madigan said.

"We have two units on it asking if anyone in the area saw someone fleeing last night," Grace said. "How was it being here alone?"

"I wasn't here much," she said. "But I was okay. I—I kept that knife within reach while I was cooking."

Her cheeks flushed, and she avoided eye contact, taking a seat at the table.

"Mads, I get it," Grace said. "You want to protect yourself. We should get you into some self defense classes."

Madigan shrugged. "Not really my style. I thought with my experience fighting off bullies in school I might have been stronger. Been able to defend myself better. Turns out I'm better at distracting myself after the fact and keeping busy. I think we both share that habit."

"We do. When someone comes at you who's bigger than you, you need to have the skills to get the upper hand," Grace said, sitting down across from her. "Think about the classes."

Madigan nodded and grabbed a piece of bread as Grace folded her napkin in her lap.

"This chili is amazing, as usual, and I'm happy to have you here," Grace said, "but we have to talk about today."

"Actually, I have a lot to tell you," Madigan said. "I should have told you about going to see John, but you would have stopped me."

Grace shook her head. "You don't think things through."

"I do the best I can with what I've got," Madigan said, grabbing her spoon. "Grace, there's more to the Valerie story than anyone knows. I did some digging at the library, and the newspaper article about Valerie's disappearance was missing."

Grace frowned. "Really?"

"So I went to see a nice man, Arthur, because he's got articles from way back when, and when I read it, I found out she had a fiancé at the time. It also said they were from our neighbourhood, so I went to see her dad, like I told you. He told me they lived on our street, next door."

"Right."

"I saw a picture of Valerie with a ring that's *the same as Evette's*," she said. "I saw it in person today. asked Evette about it, and she said Eli might have given it to her."

"They could have had the same ring," Grace said.

"I also called Valerie's fiancé, Joe Harris," Madigan said, ignoring her. "He's still upset about her disappearance and the rumors that surrounded it. A friend of hers saw her out with another man and word spread. They assumed she left with him, but Joe's sure she didn't."

"Why?"

"The usual reasons. She loved him. Even if she was cheating, she wouldn't have left him. But then he told me he thinks she was seeing John behind his back."

"Why does he think it was John?" Grace asked. "Did he see something?"

"He didn't say that," Madigan replied. "He said John was a bad person. That he did bad things and that people suspected Valerie was cheating with someone closer to her own age, and John would have been. I mean, I think he was drunk, but you know what they say. A drunk person's words…"

Grace ate a spoonful of chili and shrugged. "Are a sober person's thoughts. Yes, I know. It's a lot to consider."

Her fiancé is sure it's John, but not much proof.

With evidence stacking up, she couldn't ignore the possibility that John had done something violent in the past.

"The tattoo and the body I saw that night. The woman next door having an affair. The ring *someone* gave to Evette, and he left, Grace. John left around the time Valerie went missing. Joe tried to track him down during that time but he couldn't, so I asked Evette. She said Eli and John were at odds, and he left because of it. John said he had to get out for obvious reasons. He said he didn't want to turn into Eli."

"Okay, as I said, there's a lot to consider here. Could be a coincidence, or maybe something more." She took a sip of her drink to extinguish some of the heat from her chili. "I just need you to stay away from John. Until we sort this through with Lily."

Madigan stirred her bowl of chili.

She's thinking about it.

"Do you still think he could have killed Lily?" Madigan asked.

Maybe she needs to take my orders more seriously.

"He's still a suspect," Grace said. "I consider him dangerous."

"Do you think he could have killed Valerie?" Madigan asked, setting her spoon down. "Don't you think there's a good chance it wasn't a nightmare I had, but that I witnessed something?"

"John killing Valerie?" Grace asked. "In that house with all of us in it? Eli or Evette or both would have known."

Madigan tucked her hair behind her ear. "Maybe they did."

"There's not a motive. Why would John have killed Valerie?"

"Maybe she wouldn't leave her fiancé for him? Do you think you might find a chance to speak to Joe Harris? Question him about it some more?"

Grace took a sip of her drink.

I should anyway, but maybe I can work it to my advantage.

"He didn't tell me why he suspected John, but maybe he'd tell you," Madigan said. "If John killed before, there's a better chance he's done it again. Or…"

"You think it's possible it wasn't John?" Grace asked.

"I believe he loved Lily. My visit with him, he was incredibly stressed. He was hard on himself, just like we are, and he blames himself for Lily's death."

"He does?"

"It seems like he thinks he could have prevented it somehow," Madigan said.

By not ending things with Mickey.

She sees the look on my face. She knows she's right.

"Or maybe he…" Madigan set her spoon down. "Maybe that's what he meant."

"What?"

"I think he thinks it's his fault because bad things always happen to him. He said his past caught up with him. He says it'll happen for us too."

Or he's making you think one thing, while covering for what he did to Lily in a jealous rage.

Grace took another sip of her drink to hide her expression.

"What do I know, right?" Madigan asked, pushing her bowl away from her and leaning back in her chair.

She wants help with her investigation. Bad.

"It's just I have a lot going on right now," Grace said. "We're under a lot of pressure to solve this case and bring the person who killed Lily to justice, and I need to focus. Can you please promise me you won't see John again?"

"Do you think he'd hurt me?" Madigan frowned.

"You know I can't talk about it much, but I'm looking out for your best interests. If we can clear John as a suspect, then you can move forward with your own investigation, alright, and I'll help."

Madigan folded her arms over her chest and stared down at the table.

I hate manipulating my own sister, but I have to keep her safe.

"Promise me you'll stay away from him, and I promise I'll talk to Joe Harris. Maybe not tomorrow, but as soon as I can. Alright?"

"Fine," Madigan said and picked up her spoon again. "I just need to know."

"I know." Grace poured them each a glass of wine. "There are so many obstacles and challenges in this investigation, and I'm doing my best, but I feel like we aren't getting anywhere. It's the politics of the business, and it's followed me all the way to Tall Pines."

"Any way around it?" Madigan asked.

"I'm not as resourceful as you," Grace said, smirking. "I can't be, really. I have to follow the rules." She smoothed her napkin in her lap.

If I break the rules, I could lose everything again.

"Generally speaking," Madigan said, "a white lie can go a long way. Make someone think you know more than you do, maybe."

"Hmm," Grace hummed, sipping her wine.

Madigan's face filled with concern.

"What is it?"

"Nothing." Madigan shook her head. "Have you noticed John's weakness?"

"Right now, it's that he's the suspect of his fiancée's murder investigation, and he's isolated."

Madigan nodded. "That, and he is protective of people, and that gives him a blind spot. I'm the same sometimes."

Grace nodded. "Like he admits that realistically Evette lies and manipulates, but he still defends her. Makes sure she's protected."

And he didn't say a word about his dealings with Mickey to protect himself and Evette after he was threatened. If he was threatened.

"He seemed a bit protective of me," Madigan said. "He admitted Eli forced him to take drugs and asked if he'd done that to us. He was relieved when I told him no. It's not that he can't tell when people are lying. It's that he looks past it if he cares about them."

Grace nodded.

Like if he knew Lily was still cheating on him with Mickey, but didn't want to admit it to himself.

"And his strength?" Madigan asked.

"He's a pretty good liar himself," Grace said. "But his strength is his weakness. Protecting those he cares about and having a blind spot because of it."

"Maybe you can use that to your advantage? Maybe talking to Joe and learning about another perspective someone has of John might help."

"Thanks," Grace said, raising her glass. "You make a pretty good detective."

They clinked their glasses together and drank.

Madigan's cell phone vibrated in the living room. She left the table, and Grace finished off her bowl of chili as Madigan came back into the kitchen.

"What's up?" Grace asked.

"It's Will," she said, typing something into her phone.

"Wow, finally answering you back."

"He wants to talk tomorrow. I told him to meet me here in the morning. I'm here anyway for the security installation."

"You going to be alright talking to him?"

"I think so," Madigan sighed.

"Miss him?"

"Only when I'm by myself, in quiet moments. I've been busy, but there've been a few moments where my heart aches. Seriously, my chest aches, and there's an emptiness. It's hard to describe."

"Sounds like heartbreak. Do you think there's a chance you'd get back together?"

Madigan shrugged, and Grace stood from the table with her wine glass. "I'm headed to bed to read, alright?"

"Sure," Madigan said.

"Thanks for dinner. And remember your promise. I'll get on Valerie's case as soon as possible. You're right. Who knows? I might find something that helps."

Madigan's eyes smiled back at her before she turned the corner down the hallway.

She would be a good detective. If she could be.

Madigan's short criminal record from childhood and her less than average grades held her back in a lot of ways, but she'd made the first few breaks in the case before Grace could.

My old Sarge and Mac think I'm tough to work with, but they'd have another thing coming working with Madigan.

CHAPTER THIRTY TWO

As Will parked in the driveway, the security team had almost finished their installations. She took Buster out front, and he ran to Will. He bent over and scratched him behind the ears as Madigan closed the distance between them.

"Hey," she said.

"What's going on here?"

"Oh, just updating the security system."

"Should I be worried?" he asked.

He cares about me more than most people have in my whole life, and I'm just going to let this go?

Am I crazy?

"No." She smiled. "Not to worry. All's well here. How about with you?"

He scratched the back of his neck as one of the installation techs walked by, waiting until he reached their van before speaking.

"It's been lonely," he said, standing up, and Buster returned to her side. "Truthfully, it's taken a lot of time to let things sink in. I still don't entirely understand anything except for the fact that you don't want to be with me."

I don't either.

"Is it someone else?" he asked. "Just be honest. I can take it. I'd rather—"

"No," she said, but Jack came to mind.

There was an awkward chemistry between them—a mix of his protective nature and his past rejection of her. She couldn't ignore the butterflies in her stomach when she saw him after all the years they had known each other— something that had already faded between her and Will.

So maybe there is someone else.

Someone who cares, but not the same way, so it doesn't matter.

"I didn't think so," he said. "I know you're loyal, and I never wanted to question it, but you weren't around much, and you know, my mind wanders to all possibilities."

"It's already hurt me, what's happened between us," she said. "There's no way I could do that to you."

"That makes it easier to take, I guess, but I'll regret it if I don't admit that at this point, there's nothing you could say or do that would make me love you any less."

She bit her lip and stared at the ground. "I wish things were different," she muttered.

"Tell me why."

She shook her head. "It's not something I can explain in a practical way. I can't quantify it in any way that would make you feel better."

He nodded. "I like my facts and data."

"I know," she said. "I'm sorry. You're an amazing man. You live an amazing life. I just don't belong in it, and I'm not putting myself down. It's just not who I am."

He knows it, too.

"I love you," Madigan said. "It's easier to say now than it

was before because this is the way I love you. As a person. As someone who means so much to me."

"You're not making this easier," he said.

"I still hope one day we can be in each other's lives," she said. "But if not, I just know I'll miss you. I already do."

He bent down to hug her, and Buster jumped up on them. They stumbled away from each other smiling.

"Stay out of trouble," he said, walking backwards toward his car. "And hey, don't lose my number."

"Same," she said before he turned around and got into his car.

He was willing to spend his life with me, even if I'd cheated.

She shook her head and walked back toward the house as he drove away.

I couldn't, I don't think.

Turn a blind eye for the one you love.

She thought about her conversation with Grace the night before. John's weakness and strength in one. She pulled her cell from her pocket and hit Grace's name before typing.

If Lily was with someone else, John might have known. That could be John's motive. Maybe he tried to cover it up to protect her reputation after he killed her?

She hit send.

Joe Harris had heard the rumors of Valerie seeing another man, and the investigation into Valerie's disappearance might have been cut short because of them. Despite that, he still loved her. Never thought she'd leave.

But if Valerie felt the same butterflies for John, or anyone else, the way I do for Jack, she might leave a man as good as people said Joe was.

Or maybe she stayed?

Maybe she trusted the wrong man—but which one?

* * *

Grace read the text from Madigan as she blotted the corners of her mouth with her napkin.

"What's up?" Mac asked, stealing a French fry from her plate.

"Dry erase board is yours; fries are mine," Grace said, pulling her plate closer and shoving her cell in her pocket. "I think we should talk to John again."

"Don't you think we've exhausted all our leads?" Mac asked, wiping his fingers with the napkin.

"I want to try one more thing. I think we should tell him about Mickey's DNA."

Mac frowned. "I don't know."

"I think we need to convey that Mickey and Lily had a relationship, regardless of what the truth is, and we'll see if he knew."

Something Madigan would do.

Mac shrugged as Terry approached them with the coffee pot.

"More?" Terry asked.

Mac looked at her, and she shook her head.

"We can't take both suspects to the DA," she said. "We need something that points to one over the other."

"Just the cheque please, Terry" Mac said. "Looks like we're getting back at 'er."

On the way over, she checked another text from Madigan, letting her know the security installation was complete.

"My house is secure," she said.

"Good, you can worry less about your sister, then."

She stared at him and knew he felt her eyes on him.

"You don't know Madigan. Plus, can you tell me you'll worry less about your daughter just because she's not visiting until this is over?"

He clenched his jaw and pursed his lips.

"I hit a nerve," she said. "I'm sorry."

"It's not that. My ex might get full custody."

"What, why?"

"I'm gone a lot. This threat doesn't help right now, either. They say I'd have visitation every other weekend, but my lawyer says we should keep fighting. I'm going to, but—"

"But?"

"Maybe she'd be safer if she was with her mom full time," he said. "Shuttling her back and forth from house to house isn't what I wanted for her, and this job…"

"Mac, take it from the girl who had a house but no home as a child," she said, "all that matters to a kid is that they have people who love them. Who take good care of them. Who make them feel wanted."

He nodded as they pulled into the lot.

"They did a number on you guys, didn't they? Your foster parents. You turned out alright—"

"Well, *thanks*," she said, nudging his shoulder.

"Your sister too, I'm guessing. But look at John."

"If Lily were still alive, it seems like you'd be saying the same thing about him as you are us. He cleaned himself up. Had support. Someone he loved."

"This is going to crush him if he doesn't already know," Mac said. "But if he does, he'll know the truth is out if he was trying to cover it up."

She nodded. "Let me take the lead."

He raised his brow and grinned. "I can do that."

They knocked on John's door, and he answered looking worse than ever. "Now's not a good time," he mumbled.

"We have some information you might want to hear," Grace said.

He lifted his chin. "Oh."

"Can we come in?" she asked.

He stepped aside and stood by the TV stand as they closed the door and walked in.

He's on edge.

"What did you find?" he asked, his voice raised at the end.

"Want to sit down?" Grace asked.

He shook his head. "Can you just tell me?"

"Fine," Grace said.

Don't give him time to prepare. Make him answer.

"Did you know about Lily and Mickey?"

He frowned, and his shoulders drooped. "What do you mean?" he asked. "I've told you everything I know."

"They were seeing each other," Grace said.

"I wouldn't call it that," John said, his brows still furrowed. "Not after she told me he came on to her but the feelings weren't returned. That he intimidated her. Threatened her. Abused her."

"Did you know they were still seeing each other?" Grace asked.

"Not after the no contact order."

Grace pressed her lips together.

"What?" he asked.

"They were still seeing each other *behind your back*," Grace said. "Or at least that's what they thought. But you knew, didn't you?"

He shook his head, the same frown on his face, but his hands clenched into fists as she spoke again.

"She broke her promise," Grace said.

A white lie, maybe. Like Madigan suggested.

Maybe not.

"You promised her you were leaving your old life behind, and she promised you the same after she had been granted that no contact order," Grace said. "But when you found out about her and Mickey, you kicked her out. You knew when she worked at Wild Card she received all kinds of male attention. You were jealous. You just didn't know it was Mickey, and when you did, you saw red."

"I—I didn't know she was being forced," he said.

"Mickey's semen was found inside Lily the night she was killed."

He froze. "No," he said. "She wouldn't."

"Wouldn't she, John?" Grace asked. "She and Mickey couldn't leave each other alone. She called him over after you left. We have the records."

She called someone, but who?

Another white lie.

"W-why haven't you arrested him?" John asked.

"Because you knew she was seeing him behind your back," Grace said, raising her voice. "And when you arrived home, you knew he'd been there. Somehow you knew, and you fought with her. You fought and you killed her."

"No," he shouted, shaking his head. "No."

He can't believe it.

He stumbled to the bed, taking a seat on the edge of it and gripping the blanket.

"You'd been fighting, John," Mac said. "She was mad at you and sought comfort in his arms on your bed. She wanted you away from Mickey so you wouldn't find out about them."

John shook his head, frantically looking around the floor.

"Admit it, John," Grace said. "You knew they were together."

"No," John said. "She was upset with me, but she wouldn't…"

He didn't know.

He stood from the bed and walked to the bedside table.

"John?" Grace said. "What are you doing?"

He opened the drawer, and they drew their guns.

"John," she called, "stop now."

He pulled out a small black box and turned around, his eyes open wide in fright at the guns pointing at him.

"Whoa," he said, pointing to the box. "This is her ring. Her engagement ring."

They lowered their guns as tears dripped from his chin to the floor.

"I knew she was mad, but she took her ring off," he cried, shaking the box. "This was on her nightstand."

Grace frowned and shook her head.

She was wearing her engagement ring.

"Maybe she didn't think I'd follow through," he cried. "Maybe she was ready to leave me, I don't know, but how could she…"

His voice faltered, and he dropped down to the bed again, crying and shaking. A sick feeling washed over Grace.

He didn't know. I took it too far.

"You're lying," he said through his cries. "She didn't sleep with him. Oh, God, no. You're lying."

"She was wearing her ring," she said, her own voice shaking. "She had her engagement ring on when I saw her in the living room."

John looked up at her and gasped for breath.

"But it's—" He looked down at the box and opened it. "It's right here."

He stared at the ring and frowned, taking it out of the box and holding it closer to his face.

"This isn't her ring," he said.

Grace approached him with caution and took it from his fingers. Mac stood over her shoulder as she studied it.

Always mine. Always yours.

She turned to Mac. "Is this from him?"

"Did you get your ring at the same place where the box came from?" Mac asked.

"In the city." John nodded. "That's why I thought—"

"We need to contact the jeweller," Mac said, taking the box from John's hand. "Now."

He walked to the door and Grace followed.

"If Mickey purchased it, it could be under his name and the inscription will tie it to him." Grace placed the ring back in the box. "Prove he saw her that day if that's when he bought it. Give him a motive if she refused him. Get someone on it."

Mac nodded and left the room.

"She was still wearing my ring," John muttered to himself. "She chose me."

That's Mickey's motive to kill.

If they had sex in the bed, the DNA will be gone—burned—but if he proposed, and she refused to put it on, they could have fought. He could have seen the flowers from John and went into a blind rage, smashing them and knocking Lily over. Killing her by accident or on purpose.

"He killed her because she chose me," John muttered, squeezing his fists tightly, opening them, and balling them again.

He wants to hurt Mickey.

Kill him.

"John?" Grace said, and he shook out of his daze, staring up at her. "You need to stay here, alright? Don't leave. No one comes or goes, alright?"

His rubbed his fingers over his blotchy red face.

"I need you to tell me you understand. You'll be stopped by any means necessary if you try to leave."

"Yeah, I get it," he said on exhale.

"Good," Grace said, opening the door. "This might all be over soon, John."

Maybe thanks to a few little white lies.

She closed the door behind her and waved Malone over.

"I want another officer here, alright?" she said, and he nodded. "No one comes, and he doesn't go anywhere."

Malone nodded as Mac approached with his cell clutched in his hand.

"He bought the ring the day Lily died," Mac said.

"In his own name?" Grace asked.

"That's right. We've got our evidence. Motive. John really didn't know. We've got our guy."

"If it was an accident, I guess I can let it slide," Grace said, "but if Mickey planned on hurting her—killing her—if she refused his proposal, why would he buy the ring in his name?"

"Crime of passion," Mac said. "He didn't know it would be evidence pointing to him. He wanted to marry her, not kill her."

"Looks like that changed quick," Grace said. "Let's get to the DA now and present our case."

CHAPTER THIRTY THREE

M adigan's cell phone vibrated against the kitchen table as she searched the classified section of the paper for jobs.

Maybe I could ask Roy for a job bartending again for a while?

Is that embarrassing? Going back to the job I left for a career?

I need the money, and the tips were a bonus.

Evette's name flashed across the screen.

Maybe she needs help.

"Hello?" Madigan answered.

"There you are. I've been trying to get ahold of John since this morning, and he hasn't answered or returned my calls. Last time we spoke was yesterday around noon when he told me he'd seen you."

"Oh."

"I'm worried about him and—" She went into a coughing fit, and Madigan leaned back in her chair. "It's not like him. Have you spoken to him since?"

"I saw him yesterday afternoon."

"After you left here?"

"Mhmm."

"Oh," she paused. "Well, why didn't you invite John over here? We could have all—"

"He said he couldn't leave the lodge," Madigan said.

"I just want to make sure nothing's happened to him."

"Maybe I could call him?"

Evette coughed again and cleared her throat. "Well, if you think he'll answer *you*, go straight ahead, but he isn't answering his phone. I'm telling you."

Madigan cocked her head to the side. "Well, I don't know. I'm just trying to put your mind at ease."

Evette breathed a heavy sigh into the phone.

"Evette?" Madigan asked.

"It's just not like him," Evette said in a soft voice. "Yes. Call him."

"Alright."

"And call me right back, okay?"

"Yes," Madigan said. "Bye."

She hung up and scrolled through her phone for John's number.

It's like being the go-between in a dysfunctional family.

She hovered her thumb over John's name.

After yesterday, he probably won't answer me, either.

She hit his name and waited as the line rang.

"Madigan?" John said.

"Hi."

"I didn't think you'd want to talk to me again after…"

"What happened with you?" she asked. "I brought up Valerie, and you told me not to say anything. I don't understand."

"I can't talk about it over the phone. I need you to come here."

"I can't," she said. "You know I'm not allowed. The officer will never let me in."

"No, I mean come by the back of the motel. Don't ride all the way. No noises. You need to come get me."

"*Get you?* John, you're scaring me. I can't come there, and you can't leave. Could you please just tell me what happened with Valerie? And Lily?"

The drawn out silence between them sent goosebumps across her arms.

"John?" she whispered.

"I'll tell you what I know if you come. Be here by six, okay? I'll meet you out back. You're the only person I have left. The only one I know won't screw me over or try to hurt me."

But will you hurt me?

"John…"

"I know you don't trust me," he said. "That's good. I wish there was something I could say or do right now, but I need you to just come. You'll understand what you want to know if you come."

I promised Grace.

"Evette's worried for you. She says you haven't answered her calls."

"Will you call her and tell her I'm okay? That I'm just tired."

"Of course," she said.

"And that I love her."

That sounds like goodbye.

"I will, but I can't come to meet you."

"Madigan. Don't you want the truth?"

Yes.

"Don't you want to put it all to rest?" he asked. "I do. I have something I need to do."

He's using my weakness against me.
And it's working.
But I promised Grace.

"Why can't you tell me now?" Madigan asked.

"Because I might not be alive after Mickey gets arrested for Lily's murder."

He thinks someone's coming to kill him.

"Who's going to hurt you?"

The person who attacked her? The reason they had police watching all of them?

"I'm not going to wait here to die," he said.

"John, the police are there, and I can call Grace and—"

"Don't call anyone. It wasn't a nightmare."

"My dream," she muttered and stood up, walking to the back door. "How do you know about my dream?"

Evette must have told him.

She stared out into the dark backyard where her attacker hid the previous night.

"It was *my* nightmare," John said. "I lived it. Will you help me make this right? Please, Madigan. For you. For everyone involved. Time's up."

It was real. He pulled a dead body through the hallway to the garage.

It was Valerie.

And I'm the only thing that stands between the truth and a lifetime of no one knowing what happened to her.

"I'll see you at six," she said and hung up.

Grey clouds swept in front of the bright moon hanging high over the ocean. The wind blew through the trees, shaking the last of the crisp leaves off their branches.

"Time's up," she whispered.

CHAPTER THIRTY FOUR

As they exited the highway bridge, Grace couldn't help but wonder if sharing the news from the DA with the Martins would get their hopes up.

"You've been quiet," Mac said. "This is *good* news."

"I guess. They could still decide it's not enough, or not important enough."

Mickey Clarke is untouchable.

John's words whispered in the dark corners of her mind.

"They deserve to get an update," Mac said. "It's the first real news we have for them."

"We can't get into details with them though. I feel like they'll still think it's John."

"Well, I think we should tell them about the no contact order Lily took out against Mickey after she and John got back together. That he supported her through that," he said. "They should know that as far as we're concerned, the bruise they thought was from John was from Mickey."

Grace stared out the window, watching dark grey clouds roll in from the North, over all of Deerhorn County.

"It makes sense about burning the house too," he said.

"Burning away evidence. And the lock box with photos. I'm sure Mickey had one of his goons follow us."

And even if we arrest him, he could send more to punish us.

"Grace, you okay? We're almost there."

She nodded and pulled the visor down, fussing with her hair as he turned into their subdivision.

Nothing's going to bring Lily back.

Unless her killer is brought to justice, the Martins will have no semblance of peace.

They knocked on the front door, and Mr. Martin answered.

"Come in," he said, gesturing toward the living room. "Please, don't worry about your shoes."

He's in a good mood.

He thinks we've made an arrest.

As they entered the room, Mrs. Martin poked her head out from the kitchen. "Tea or coffee?" she called.

"Nothing for us, Ma'am," Grace said, feeling Mac's eyes looking down at her before they took a seat side by side on the couch.

Mrs. Martin scurried in and sat down in the nicer armchair beside her husband.

"So," Mr. Martin said. "You've got news?"

Mrs. Martin's foot tapped against the carpet as she clenched the sides of the armchair, digging her fingers into the material.

She's anxious.

Nervous maybe?

"Please," she said. "Tell us you've made an arrest."

Mac cleared his throat. "Well, not yet, but we just presented our case to the DA, and he has to talk to some people. We're here to let you know he said we've got a strong case."

"Well, why haven't you arrested John yet?" Mr. Martin asked.

"Sir," Grace said, "we don't want to get your hopes up. These things can take time, but through our investigation, we found details that incriminate a man named Michael Clarke."

Mrs. Martin frowned and looked to her husband, but he kept his eyes on them.

"Who?" he asked, raising his voice.

"I've never heard of him," Mrs. Martin said. "What about John Talbot?"

"We have good reason to believe your daughter had an altercation with the suspect in question the night of her death," Mac said. "At the beginning of the investigation, John let us know Lily had taken out a restraining order against Michael Clarke, a no contact order, to be exact."

"She never told *me*," Mrs. Martin said. "Those bruises, they were from John."

"Not according to legal documents filed," Grace said.

"According to your daughter, Clarke had been harassing and intimidating her before and during her break up with John Talbot," Mac said.

"Lily was living under our roof," Mr. Martin said. "We would have known. John never told us any of that. He's lying—"

"When would he have told us?" Mrs. Martin asked, looking down in her lap.

She's disappointed.

"Well, Lily would have," Mr. Martin said.

"What did he do to her?" Mrs. Martin whispered. "This Michael Clarke?"

"He left the bruise on her arm," Grace said.

Mrs. Martin turned white as a ghost. Tears welled up in Mr. Martin's eyes.

They finally realize there's a chance John is innocent. A good chance.

"We can't discuss all the details," Mac said, "but you deserve to know that a decision could be made as early as today, or it could be a bit."

"But why would she let us think John left that mark?" Mrs. Martin asked, her voice trembling.

"She didn't *let us think it,*" Mr. Martin said in a stern voice. "We assumed."

He blames himself.

He cleared his throat. "Is there anything else you can tell us?"

Mac opened his mouth to speak, but Mrs. Martin turned to her husband. "She would have told me," she said. "We talked. She—she would have said it was someone else."

"We'll discuss this later, Chris," Mr. Martin said, struggling to stand.

"Take your ti—" Mac started.

"She told us Lily should leave him," Mrs. Martin said. "That he was dangerous."

"Who told you that?" Grace asked.

"That's enough, Chris," Mr. Martin said.

Tears fell down her cheeks as she looked up at him. "She said he'd hurt our baby," she cried.

"I'd like you to leave," Mr. Martin said, speaking over his wife, looking from Mac to Grace. "Now."

Mac stood, but Grace edged forward in her seat. "Who told you that?" she asked.

"John's m-mother," she cried. "She called us the night Lily died and—"

Evette.

"Enough," Mr. Martin shouted. "I said get out, and I meant it. Leave me to take care of her."

Mrs. Martin buried her face in her hands.

If Evette called and told them John would hurt Lily, maybe they went over to try to get her to leave him the night she died.

"When was the last time you saw your daughter?" Grace asked.

"Sheppard," Mac said. "Come on. We've been asked to leave."

"Mrs. Martin?" Grace said.

"I can't, Norman," she said. "Oh, Lily, I'm sorry. What else was I supposed to do?"

Her husband went to her and kneeled at her side. "It's going to be okay, Chris, I promise."

She shook her head and rocked back and forth.

Grace and Mac exchanged looks, and Mac stepped just behind Mr. Martin.

"Mrs. Martin," Grace said. "Why did you keep the fact that John's mom called you that night from us?"

Mrs. Martin stared at her husband, shaking her head, and he clasped both of her hands between his, shaking his head.

"An innocent man can't go to prison for this," she cried, looking from her husband to Grace and Mac. "I went to get her that night right after his mother c-c-called. I went to bring her back h-home."

She started hyperventilating, and her husband rubbed her arm, hanging his head.

She was there. They've lied to us this whole time.

Because it was them.

Grace turned to Mac, and he stared back at her, wide-eyed.

"Lily," Mrs. Martin screamed as tears flew from between her eyes and cheeks. "Oh, my girl. I'm so sorry. I'm soh-hoh —oh God."

Mr. Martin lifted his head and rose to his feet with the help of the armchair.

"It was me," he said. "It was an accident."

323

"No," Mrs. Martin cried. "No, Norman."

Was it him or her?

"Chris, that's enough," he said in a stern voice, his face redder by the second. "I went to bring her back, to save her from him, and I tried to physically pull her along but she slipped out of my hands and she..."

His voice shook, and he closed his eyes, while behind him, Mrs. Martin covered her mouth, her whole body shaking.

"She fell back and hit her head on the table," he said, nodding once. "It was me. Arrest *me.*"

It was her. He's covering for her.

Everything he just said sounded rehearsed.

"Norman," she cried, reaching for him, but he pushed her hands away and stepped forward.

"Mr. Martin," Mac said. "You are under arrest for the death of Lily Martin. You have the right to remain silent. Anything you say can and will be used against you in the court of law."

He read him his Miranda rights and led him to the front door, and Mrs. Martin ran up behind him, wrapping her arms around him.

"I'm sorry," she cried.

It was an accident. It had to be, and yet they had tried to frame John.

Chris grabbed at her husband's arms, and Grace rested her hand on her shoulder.

"Mrs. Martin," Grace said. "Please let go of him."

"I love you, Chris," Mr. Martin said, and she let go as Mac led him from the house to their car.

Mrs. Martin covered her mouth with her shaking hand and watched Mac take him away.

"What have I done?" she repeated over and over with

shaky breath. "This was because of John. This never would have happened if it weren't for him. She'd still be here…"

She believed it.

They weren't pretending.

They really think if it weren't for him, she'd be alive.

Or it's what they told themselves to stay sane after Lily was accidentally killed.

Mrs. Martin turned to Grace. "We were just trying to protect her," she whimpered.

You have no idea what your lies have done.

What they've cost other people.

"Mrs. Martin," she said, swallowing hard before resting her hand on her shoulder, "please come with me."

CHAPTER THIRTY FIVE

Madigan parked her bike in the field behind the back lot of the hotel and walked through the tall brush and weeds until she could make out the lights of Whitestone Lodge lot as they came on. She checked her phone and noticed a text from Grace.

Good news. Call me when you can.

She received it as she walked through the field.

I've still got some time before she wonders.

The cool night breeze smelled of burnt leaves, and a swirl of fear and excitement danced in her stomach.

I've still got time to back out.

Her cell vibrated in her hand, and she jumped.

John.

Maybe he's backing out.

Maybe I should back out.

"Hello?"

"I can't get out. There's an officer in the lot watching my front door, and another one does laps around the building. It doesn't even take him a minute to drive around the whole thing. I need time to climb out the bathroom window."

"What are you going to do?"

"I need a distraction," he said.

Me.

"This was a mistake," she said, ready to hang up.

"Please. It's not a mistake. You're helping me because it's helping you and the families involved."

He knows that's not the only reason I'm helping him.

There's another part of this I can't put into words—or I don't want to.

"How do I know you won't hurt me?" she asked.

"Because I know now," he said. "I'm not him. I'm not Eli."

She swayed from one foot to the other. "How?"

"Lily chose me. She chose the man I've become, and I want to be that man for her even—even though she's gone."

Madigan sighed and started walking along the edge of the field toward the front of the building.

How can I make a distraction?

"You'll help me?" he asked.

She paused, looking around the field, scanning the back of the building.

"Madigan, I think we're more alike than you know. I know you want to help people, but you're like me. You like the thrill of the unknown. You feed off of it."

That's the other part.

She took a deep breath of the autumn air, sending flutters through her lungs.

"When I give the signal, run behind the lodge to the back field," she said. "I'll meet you there."

"What's the signal?" he asked.

A parking lot for the building next door backed up onto the lodge.

I'll give them something to check out.

"Madigan? What's the signal?"

"You'll know," she said and hung up.

* * *

While Mac finished booking Mr. Martin, Grace returned to their room at the station and studied the dry erase board.

Still so many things that don't make sense.

The Martins could have set the house on fire, but it's unlikely they left a box full of photos.

It doesn't fit the narrative here.

Mickey threatening John to stay quiet makes sense, but after news breaks that Mr. Martin has been arrested, maybe they'll let John be.

That's when we'll take police protection off of him.

She picked up her phone and texted Madigan.

Good news. Call me when you get this.

She set the phone down and stared at Lily's picture.

"What were you doing with Mickey? Placating him? Entertaining the idea of being with him? Were you afraid of him?"

He left you alive.

That means something and nothing at all if he hurt you.

I'm sorry, Lily.

"John and Mickey set up the dominoes, and Evette tapped the first one into motion," she said. "Your own mother…"

What's Madigan going to think of Evette?

She's already distrusting.

Grace opened her purse and took out the piece of paper Madigan gave her with Joe Harris' phone number.

"Time to follow through on my promise," she said, dialing his number while turning one of the note pads on the table toward her.

"Hello?"

"Mr. Harris?" she asked.

"Yes."

"This is Detective Inspector Grace Sheppard. Tall Pines PD." She grabbed a pen and tapped her paper, waiting for a response. "I'm calling in regards to the investigation of the disappearance of your fiancée, Valerie."

"What do you want from me?"

"I'm sorry to disturb you, Mr. Harris, but I'm following up on the cold case, and I have a few questions. I was wondering if there is any new information you have in regards to the disappearance?"

"Valerie's dead," he said, defeated. "You people didn't do yer job, and she's dead."

"How do you know that, sir?"

"Because she wouldn't have run away with anyone else. She wouldn't have left her parents, and she wouldn't have left me. She'd have used her debit card. Sent a message. Written. Anything. But she hasn't because she's dead."

"And who do you think killed her?"

"The guy you're investigating 'cause he's done it again," he said. "John Talbot, or whatever he goes by now. He killed Valerie, and he killed Lily too."

"Mr. Harris, why do you think that?"

"Because he got away with it the first time," he sighed. "Didn't you read the reports? They made her out to be some flimsy floozy, gone like the wind. Like some whore. Like I'm some douche who couldn't satisfy her."

"Sir—"

He's drunk. Great.

"Then he came back like a bloody ghost," he said. "I's in a bar one night downtown, and there he was. John fuckin' Johnny, lookin' different but the same sorry piece'a'shit, sitting at the table with a pretty blonde girl. Smilin' at her.

Laughing with her. Manipulating her like he did my Valerie. So I went right up to him, an' know what he did? He ran, 'tective. The sorry fucker ran out onto the street, and I chased him. He wasn't getting away with it again. I got a few good punches in there too."

Joe Harris chuckled, and something slammed in the background.

The fight at Wild Card outside on the street on John's record.

"Pigs pulled me off—I'm sorry, 'tective—*officers* pulled me off, an' know what he did?"

Grace waited.

"Absolutely nothing. He's a dealer, y'know that? Drugs and, oh shit, God knows. He's a prick. He couldn't shake no legs or step to my face cause he's a coward. He got my Valerie when I was away. Picks on women he thinks he can overpower. Gets 'em alone. Fights he can win, but if I hadda minute, just a moment alone with him again…"

Something cracked and popped in the background.

Another can of beer opened.

"Mr. Harris, do you have any hard evidence or reason to think it was John?" she asked.

"Hard evidence," he mumbled, laughing. "Don't need any."

"Alright, well thank you for your time, Mr. Harris."

"You nail that fucker," he said. "Lily was a good girl, that one."

"You knew her?" she asked.

"Ayuh," he said, hiccupping. "I tried to warn her. Found out she's workin' showin' homes so I booked an appointment of my own. She was smart. Didn't want to talk to a drunken stranger."

"You followed her?"

"I followed you too," he laughed, caught in a fit. He tried to speak, but kept laughing. "I sent you twits those pictures in a pretty little package. I handed you the win, and you still haven't got 'em. He have you under his spell, too?"

"You set the fire," she said, grabbing the paper, standing from her chair and rushing out the door into the hallway.

"I sure's hell did," he said. "Aren'tcha gonna thank me, 'tective?"

"Why?" she asked and put him on mute, handing the paper to Tarek at his desk. "Find me his address and get two units there, now."

"...but if you won't," Joe Harris said, "I will."

She took him off mute.

"Mr. Harris, I understand your concern about John, but we need evidence to make an arrest, and you admitted, you don't have any against John."

Mac walked up beside her, and she put Joe on mute again.

"It's Joe Harris," she said. "He started the fire and left us the pictures. The note."

"Who?" Mac asked.

"Oh," Joe said, "don't you worry, Missy. I got *all* the proof I need right here."

"He's going to go after John if we don't get units to wherever he is right now," she said.

"I'll go to his house," Mac said.

"I'm coming," she mouthed and took him off mute again. "I'd like to meet with you. Where are you, Mr. Harris?"

He laughed.

"Keep him on the phone," Mac mouthed. "I'm going."

Her shoulders fell, and she nodded.

"Oh you want to talk, *now*? Why does *everybody* want to talk *now*?" he shouted.

Mac pointed at the phone, and she pressed mute.

"Tarek's going to trace the call," he said.

"Burned his house down so he can burn in the fire like the devil he is—" Joe shouted on the line.

"Be careful," Grace told Mac, and he nodded before tapping a nearby officer on the shoulder.

Grace took the phone off mute.

Remember your training.

Keep him talking.

Everything depends on you.

CHAPTER THIRTY SIX

Madigan walked behind the first row of cars, around the side of the building, just out of sight of the lodge. "I'll have to use the sidewalk to get back," she muttered to herself before smacking her hands on the hood of the first car in the neighbouring lot. She continued on to the next, looking around the parking lot.

No one watching.

She pushed the car and yanked at the handle to open the door.

Nothing.

Third time's a charm.

She did the same to the next car.

Nothing.

Maybe it's a sign I shouldn't be here.

She turned around and bumped into the next car, parked too close, and the alarm bleeped over and over. She covered her ears and darted out from between the cars, running to the sidewalk before walking at a normal pace.

The police car drove down the Whitestone Lodge lot toward the street and straight at her.

Make them think it's something bad.

Someone else.

"Hey," she waved at the officer and pointed to the lot she came from. "Someone's trying to break in."

"We've got a possible threat." The officer spoke into his speaker as he drove out onto the street and back up into the neighbouring lot.

Madigan kept walking down the sidewalk past the lodge and made a break for it. She rounded the corner, and John ran toward the field at the same time.

She pushed herself, her heart racing as John ran into the dark field and she sprinted after him. Gasping for breath, she caught up to him as he slowed down, and she passed him.

"Come on," she panted.

Her heart beat hard in her chest and through her ears. The smell of smoky leaves sent flutters through her lungs each time she gasped for breath.

He feels the same way.

They jogged to the edge of the field and found her bike parked where she left it.

She put her helmet on, swung her leg over, and John did the same.

He's ridden before.

"Let's go," he said.

"Where?"

"The fairgrounds," he shouted over the bleeping car alarm. "Come on."

Her heart raced as she started the engine.

I should tell Grace.

I need to tell Grace where we're going.

"Let's go," he shouted.

She pushed the choke knob in all the way before driving the bike through the dirt, kicking dust up behind the spinning wheels and merging onto the road.

The fairgrounds in the fall.

An open empty field that will be dark by the time we get there.

At the next light, she made a right turn, down toward the water.

I need to let Grace know where I am.

I have no way to do that until we get there.

* * *

"I wasn't around back then," Grace said, sitting. Tarek hooked her cell up to a tracking device. "But I'm looking at the case now, and I want to help. I want to do better, Mr. Harris."

I can do better.

Grace opened the PD database and searched Valerie's name. Her case came up as the only result.

"Shouldn't be too hard," Joe laughed. "Y'know it's too late though, right? You had yer chances."

I have to keep him talking.

I have to be more personable. Like Madigan.

"Why, Joe?" she asked. "Can I call you Joe?"

"Fine," he said.

"Why is it too late?"

"Cause she's dead," he sputtered. "And John's gotta pay."

She opened the case online and scanned the initial report and information. Nothing she could have worked with at the time either.

"Joe," she said. "In the initial report of her disappearance, you never mentioned John."

His heavy breathing made her pause.

"Was that because you didn't know it was him back then?"

"I didn't even know he lived there," Joe said. "I don't think he did, you know that? But after the news came out about Valerie seeing somebody, neighbours started to talk about the hot guy 'usta live next door. How they bet it was him. How they'd seen her over there."

Grace checked the date, and Tarek made a phone call, speaking in a hushed voice beside her.

This was after we moved in.

I never saw another woman in our house except druggies.

I've never seen Valerie, or I don't remember her.

"How did the rumor start, Joe?" she asked, and Tarek tapped her arm, pointing to the screen.

A red dot blinked across the street from the Lodge. She turned to Tarek.

"I sent them the location," he mouthed.

"One of her friends, I guess," Joe sighed. "One of her stupid friends who couldn't keep her mouth shut."

Grace searched through the statements given by Joe, family, and finally the last statement given by a friend.

"Hello?" he said.

"You don't think this friend should have told the police what they saw?" Grace asked, reading the statement as she spoke.

"I was at the fair this summer, and I saw Valerie there with this guy."

"Did you recognize him?"

"No. I just know it wasn't her fiancé. I waved to Valerie, and I think she saw me but pretended not to, you know? Like she was embarrassed she'd been caught with him."

"O'course she should have told the police," he said. "Lotta good that did, though. After that she shoulda kept quiet out of respect for Valerie and her family. And me."

"Right," Grace said.

"What did the man look like?"

"I didn't get a good look. Brown hair, maybe, but I think he was wearing a hat. Plaid shirt and jeans. This was weeks ago."

"Anything else you noticed?"

"No."

"Okay, thank you."

"She was carrying a big pink bunny."

"So. You gonna arrest him?" Joe asked, and Tarek tapped her shoulder again, holding up his landline phone.

They had a big pink bunny in their room the night after the fair when Evette took them. When Eli thought they'd stayed home.

Eli put it there, hadn't he?

"Mac," Tarek mouthed. "He wants to talk to you."

Or did John?

An engine hummed in the background and she pressed her cell phone to her ear.

"Hold on, Joe," she said, grabbing the other phone. "Joe?"

The line went dead.

"Mac?" She set her phone down. "I lost him."

"So did we," he said. "Officers are checking in on John, now."

"He can't be far," she said.

Grace's heart raced as a heavy feeling in her gut hit her hard, and she picked up her phone.

"You have to find Joe, Mac," she said, pressing Madigan's number. "Hold on, okay?"

She hit call and pressed the phone to her ear. It rang and rang.

"Pick up," she hissed. "Pick up the phone."

The call went to voicemail.

"Mac?" she asked, picking up the phone. "I think my sister might be in trouble."

"John's gone," Mac said.

Her breath caught in her throat.

Madigan.

CHAPTER THIRTY SEVEN

Madigan drove through the front entrance to the fairgrounds, and John pointed to the left. She drove through the crisp leaves on the ground toward another opening in the trees. Toward the path she and Grace took that eventually led to the rocky coast.

John pointed to the right and tapped her shoulder. She turned right, and he patted her shoulder again. She stopped in front of thick trees forming a barrier around the fairgrounds. A metal fence had been set up just before them each year.

John got off the bike, and she grabbed her cell from her pocket and hit Grace's name.

Fair, was all she could type.

John reached toward her, and she hit send before he swiped the phone from her hand.

"You have to trust me, Madigan," he said. "We don't have much time."

I should have called her before, but then she'd have stopped me.
Maybe she should have stopped me.
Come on, Grace. Get here.

He tucked her cell phone into his pocket, and she took off her helmet, gripping it tightly in her fist.

I can hit him with it if I need to.

John turned and marched past the treeline into the forest.

"Come on," he said. "I'll tell you as we walk."

She kept her helmet in her hand and followed him into the forest. He glanced over his shoulder before continuing ahead.

"Everything I told you about Eli is true," he said. "I left because I didn't want to become him. Abusive. Manipulative. I didn't want his life. I don't know where I got the confidence, but somehow, I thought I could do better."

"You did," she said, scrambling to catch up.

"Eli told me not to come back once you two got there, but it was Evette who made me promise to stay away. At the time, I thought she didn't want someone like me near you two. I was—pretty bad at that point. I understand that now, but I was angry then. Now I know it's because she didn't want me to be like Eli either."

He stopped by a large fallen tree, and she caught up right behind him before he turned left.

I have to leave a trail.

She took off her necklace and hung it on a branch while John navigated the rocky terrain.

She'll see it. She has to see it.

He stopped on the other side and turned back, waiting for her. She ambled down the slope and joined him.

"But I was mad at Evette," he said. "Eli asked me back to help with odd jobs. Score some easy cash. It was all I knew at the time, so I did it. It kept me off the streets for months."

"Why didn't we see you there?"

"I came by late when you were both asleep. One night, late, I got a call from Eli that changed my life."

He stopped by a tree to catch his breath.

Or to find the way?

"He told me he needed my help and to come over right away," John said and turned to Madigan. "I was high out of my mind, but I didn't know where my next fix was coming from, so I went."

He swallowed hard and leaned against the tree.

"When I got there..."

He leaned over, and she wanted to reach out to touch his arm. Comfort him.

He grabbed me before in his room, and he'll do it again.

"John?" She gripped her helmet strap tightly.

He looked up at her. "Everything I'm about to say is true, and I'm not proud of it, but you need to know. You, and your sister. Valerie's family. Evette. If I don't make it, please tell her I love her."

"I will," she muttered. "John, what happened that night?"

"Something that haunts me. Something I'd never have been able to live with if it weren't for Thom. And Lily." A tear slid down his cheek, and he wiped it away. "They didn't know, but they made it better. Easier sometimes."

"John, please, you need to tell me what happened!"

He grabbed her hand and squeezed it tightly, pulling her close and staring deep into her eyes.

"You shouldn't have come."

* * *

Grace ran to her car as her cell phone buzzed, flashing Madigan's name across the screen.

The fair

"The fairgrounds," she whispered, sending shivers down her spine. "He's taken her there."

He brought the bunny. The fair has meaning to him somehow.

343

She got in her car and called Madigan's number as she ripped out of the parking lot.

No answer.

Something happened that night of the fair with him and Valerie.

Her cell rang, and she pushed the button and pressed it to her ear. "Mac, John has Madigan," she gasped. "They're at the fairgrounds."

"I'm twenty minutes away," he said.

"I'm ten," she said, pushing the gas pedal to the floor. "Seven. Send back up."

"Do you think Joe saw them leave and followed them?" Mac asked. "I'm sorry to ask you that, but—"

"I think so."

"John's car's at the lodge," Mac said.

"Then they took Madigan's bike. There's a chance they lost Joe on the way. He couldn't have known where they were going."

"Did you track her phone?"

"She sent me a message," Grace said, her heartbeat throbbing in her ears. "I can't let anything happen to her."

"We won't. I'm on my way. Sending back up now. I'll meet you there. She knows you'll come for her."

She let the words sink in and took a deep breath.

"See you there," Mac said and hung up.

She tore down the next street, watching for someone in a truck. She imagined Joe would drive a truck. She reached the entrance of the fairgrounds and drove through, making a wide turn, looking for any vehicles and Madigan's bike.

Her bike.

Parked by a dense tree line. She stopped short of it and took out her gun as she jumped out of the car.

No other vehicles.

344

She aimed her gun, looking through the trees and starting just ahead of the bike.

Calm your breathing.

Focus on where you're going.

Listen closely.

She exhaled, watching her hot breath escape her mouth, and crossed over into the woods.

* * *

"We're almost there," John said, pulling her along.

"John," Madigan said, trying to twist her hand away from him.

"I have to show you," he said.

She felt the weight of the helmet in her hand.

"Let go of me," Madigan said, and John stared down at her hand. "Please."

Or I'll knock you out.

He let go, staring off past her, as if in a trance. She turned around where only trees surrounded them.

"Here," he said, pointing just past Madigan at the ground. "This is where I buried her."

She stared down at the ground.

"Valerie?" she asked, her voice shaking as he walked past her, staring down at the same spot.

He turned back around toward her, his eyes open wide. She stepped away from the spot he gave all his attention to.

"Step away from her, John," Grace said.

Madigan turned around, and Grace had the gun pointed at John, waving her over.

"Madigan, come here," she said.

"I didn't kill her," John said. Madigan took a step back toward Grace. "I didn't kill Lily."

"I know," Grace called to him.

Madigan felt for Grace's hand behind her, and Grace pulled her behind her back.

"We're all leaving now," Grace called to him, hot clouds of breath expelling from her mouth.

"I don't think he's armed," Madigan whispered, shivering behind her.

"I told Madigan I'd show her the truth," he said. "You'll see too once you dig her up."

"John, it's not safe to be out here," Grace said. "I want to protect you too."

John frowned.

"Joe Harris, Valerie's fiancé," she said. "He's convinced you did it, and he's after you."

John hung his head and turned around, staring down at the dirt.

"Go back to my car," Grace whispered.

I have to see this through.

"When I got to the house that night," John said, "a woman was lying in a pool of blood in the kitchen, and Eli sat at the kitchen table beside her with a gun in front of him. I realized it was the next-door neighbour when I got into the kitchen."

His voice trembled as he turned back toward them.

"Evette was out that night, and you girls were in bed. There was a thunderstorm. I remember be-because…" He wiped his eyes, shaking his head. "Eli told me she'd come over and threatened to report them to child services. That she wanted to take you girls right then and there, and that she tried to go upstairs, but he stopped her. There was a fight in the kitchen, and when he got his gun, he shot her in the hallway before she could go upstairs."

My nightmare was real.

"You dragged her to the garage," Madigan said. "I saw you and—you saw me too."

THE GIRLS ACROSS THE BAY

He nodded, his fists clenched into tight balls. "I didn't tell Eli," he said. "I know what he would have done."

He tried to protect me.

"Thank you," Madigan said, and he nodded.

"I had no one," John said. "Eli told me if I didn't help clean up his mess, he'd pin it on me."

* * *

"I'm sorry, John," Grace said, still keeping Madigan behind her. "Did you love her?"

John frowned and shook his head. "I didn't know her. I buried a woman I didn't even know, but I know her now. She haunts me. I just want to be free."

The fair.

The pink bunny.

It was Eli who was seeing Valerie behind Evette's back.

It was a lovers' quarrel one night while Evette was out that ended in murder.

"I was scared, more than I'd ever been in my life, and you both know that's saying something," John said. "I knew he could do it—frame me. I was high, and scared, and I didn't want Evette to know. I didn't want her involved, so I told him I'd take care of the body if he cleaned up. Like it was my idea."

John choked out a low laugh. "God, he did that well, didn't he? Made us think we were doing something because we wanted to, or that we thought of."

Grace nodded and noticed from her peripheral Madigan nodding too.

"I brought Valerie out here," he said. "Where Eli told me to. He doesn't know exactly where to this day, but he knows my DNA could be found on her. You know where his can be found? On a gun I've hidden in my home."

The gun under the floor boards.

"I took it after you sent him to prison," John said, taking a step toward them. "You'll see my prints, but his too. It was the only leverage I had on him."

"I have more proof," Grace said.

Madigan stepped up beside her.

"You do?" John asked.

"Eli was seeing Valerie behind Evette's back," Grace said. "I have proof of it. There was a witness. He had something that belongs to me now."

The pink bunny had been used to cuddle with as they waited for the other's beating to be finished. A source of comfort, she'd kept it in her room in her next house and the closet in her current home.

"I know he was with her," Grace said. "He lied to you to get you to help him. To make you think he'd been defending himself or us."

"I have proof too," Madigan said. "Eli gave Evette Valerie's ring. It's the same ring I saw in a picture of Valerie."

"You'll testify against him?" John asked.

They nodded, and he stepped closer, but Grace kept her gun up.

No chances.

He frowned down at it.

"We have to get out of here," Grace said. "Will you come with us?"

"You believe me?" he asked, taking another step forward.

"Yes," Grace said, pushing Madigan back.

Keep the distance.

He turned to Madigan and took another step.

"Yes, I promise, I believe you," she said. "I promise—"

John's eyes lit up at the same moment a loud crack rang through the air. Grace turned around where a man with a hunting rifle stood, aiming his gun at them.

At John.

She aimed her gun at him, ready to take him down.

"Put the gun down, now," Grace hollered.

"John," Madigan screamed, and the warmth of her sister left her side.

The man with the rifle shifted to the right, and his hand flinched.

Grace squeezed the trigger.

He collapsed, and the gun fell out of his hands as he hit the ground, grabbing at his arm. Bushes rustled where flashlights shone through, casting stick shadows across the man's face.

Joe Harris.

Mac slid down a hill and kicked the gun away from Joe while Malone and another officer grabbed him.

Grace turned around where Madigan knelt over John, a puddle of blood pooling around where he lay upon the cold grave of Valerie Hall.

CHAPTER THIRTY EIGHT

L ight poured into the room as Evette opened the blinds. "He needs light." She coughed, turning back toward them. "He needs to feel the warmth of the sun on his skin."

Madigan grabbed Evette's cool hand and took her purse for her before helping her into the uncomfortable chair she'd sat in before Evette had arrived.

Evette coughed, then she leaned to the side closest to John's bed. Tubes ran in and out of his body, and the constant humming and beeping of the machines keeping him alive filled their own silence in the room.

Don't stop breathing.

"You should have called me sooner," Evette said.

Grace gave Madigan a look before pushing herself off the wall. "I'm going to see when the doctor will be by this morning."

Madigan nodded.

"So," Evette sighed. "Grace told me what I needed to know *then*, but now you have to tell me why."

"Valerie Hall, your next-door neighbour that went missing?" Madigan said. "Her fiancé was convinced John was having an affair with her. He came back to get revenge after all these years."

She turned to John and shook her head. "That doesn't make sense, and why would he leave police protection?"

Madigan stared at John, his chest rising and falling, just like a normal chest.

Almost like a normal chest.

"Maddie?" Evette said. "Did you hear me? You were with him?"

Madigan nodded.

There was nothing I could do.

Just like Drew.

But she'll think...

"You stayed with him?"

"Yes," Madigan said, and Evette grabbed her hand, holding it tightly. A tinge of calm came over her before Evette let her hand go.

"Thank you," she whispered.

How does she know? How does she know I did my best without having to ask me more questions?

How does she know, but my own parents don't?

Grace walked back into the room and passed water bottles to Madigan and Evette.

"Thank you, Gracie," Evette said, taking the bottle. "Now that you're both here, will you tell me what happened?"

Madigan exchanged a look of sympathy with Grace, and she nodded her permission.

"Okay," Madigan said, "but first, John wanted you to know he loves you, okay? He did what he did because he loves you."

Evette frowned and looked from Madigan to Grace.

* * *

"Back when we moved in," Grace said, "maybe before, too, Eli was having an affair with the woman next door. Valerie."

Evette looked up at Grace, frowning and shaking her head after the words sank in.

She doesn't deserve this. Not now with her son on life support.

"There's proof," Grace said. "The night of the fair? When we went for my birthday, and we ran off? He was there with her."

Tears filled Evette's eyes and streamed down her cheeks. "Eli was a lot of things, but," she choked out, "I don't believe you."

"The pink bunny he brought us?" Grace asked. "He won it for Valerie first. I don't know if maybe she wanted him to give it to us, or if he insisted..."

Evette's chin jutted out as she frowned, cocking her head to the side.

"He killed her, Evette," Madigan said. "One night while you were out, she came over, and he killed her. He called John and told him if he didn't help him get rid of her body, he'd frame him for her murder."

Evette's mouth hung agape, and she covered it with her hand and wide eyes staring up at both of them, looking from one sister to the other.

"He gave you her ring," Madigan said. "The silver one I asked you about."

Evette held her hand up in front of her face and stared at it.

Like John stared at the engagement ring.

She can't believe it.

She's in shock.

"He made John t-take care of it?" Evette asked, shaking her head and looking over at him on the bed.

This is what real heartbreak looks like.

353

"My Johnny," she whispered, wiping at her glistening cheeks.

Real tears.

Grace had seen the same ones once before, and she pressed her lips together, stealing a glance at Madigan, who teared up as well.

Madigan was right.

The night of the fair when Evette had found them, she was really crying.

Grace's heart thudded faster.

Crying about what? Us?

No.

She never cried for us.

Through the beatings and the lies and manipulation.

Never for us.

* * *

Evette stood from her chair and grabbed John's hand. Madigan wiped her hot cheeks with the backs of her hands and couldn't help but stare at John.

Will he ever get to know what happened to Lily?

"My son," Evette whispered. "I'm so sorry you had to clean up Eli's mess. You always had to clean up his messes..."

"Evette?" Grace said. "Why don't you take that ring off now?"

"Oh," Evette said, staring down at it, sniffling and coughing. "They won't slide over my knuckles anymore, Gracie. I've tried."

Madigan wiped her cheek and walked to the other side of John's bed.

"He told me he knows you tried to protect him from Eli," she said. "That you didn't really send him away."

Evette held back a whimper and nodded. "No one knows

what that man's capable of more than us—than me—but this…" Evette whispered.

"We thought it was a nightmare Madigan had," Grace said. "But it was real. She saw it."

Evette turned around toward Grace.

"Saw what?" Evette asked.

"She saw *everything* that night." Grace nodded to her and gave her a calm and knowing look.

A look that asked, right?

"I did," Madigan said.

"Oh, Maddie," Evette's voice trembled as she turned toward her.

Madigan opened her mouth to speak, but Grace spoke first.

"Tell her who really killed Valerie," Grace said, looking at Madigan.

Is she talking to me?

Evette shook her head and turned to Madigan, but she couldn't quite meet her gaze.

"You," Madigan said.

Madigan's stomach felt like it was flipping, and her knees shook beneath her weight.

Evette shook her head and let go of John's hand.

"Madigan saw the whole thing," Grace said, "but she thought it was a dream. You told her it was a nightmare."

"It was," Evette said, reaching out for the wall as she bent over coughing, walking toward her purse.

The coughing. Her loneliness. The apologies.

Everything she used to garner sympathy.

She used me.

Madigan nodded. "I'm awake now, Evette."

"You didn't take us to the fair because it was my birthday," Grace said. "It was our little secret because you took us on a stakeout to find out who Eli was screwing."

She caught him.

She knew.

"You were heartbroken at first," Grace said. "But then you were angry, weren't you? You saw it was the girl next door, and you couldn't take it anymore, so you killed her. Eli found out, and he told you to leave, didn't he?"

Evette grabbed her purse and wasted no time starting for the door, step by step as she coughed.

"You both knew John would clean up the mess to protect Eli, but especially you." Grace walked toward the door and closed it, standing in front of it. "You used him, just like you used us. You killed Valerie Hall."

She shot her.

"I kept my family together," Evette seethed, turning to Madigan. "*You* tore it apart!"

Just like that, she reverted back to her eleven-year-old self, standing in front of the house as Eli was taken away and Evette blaming her.

"You're the one who tore a family apart," Grace said in the same cool voice. "You called Lily's parents to warn them about your own son. You made that call, and they went over to save her, but there was an accident, and she ended up dead. You didn't even care, did you?"

"Except that John wasn't going to give you any extra drug money anymore," Madigan said.

Rage bubbled inside of her.

"We were *never* a family," Madigan sneered. "Never. Not a good family and not even a dysfunctional one."

Evette pointed to her with her shaky frail finger adorned with Valerie's ring.

She took it for herself off Valerie's cold, dead body.

"You ungrateful little bitch," Evette spat.

"You're under arrest," Grace said, opening the door and waving to the officer outside. "Cuff her."

She pointed to Evette, and the officer walked around her, taking his handcuffs out.

"Nobody's cleaning up after you anymore," Grace said as she sat in the chair. "Take her to the station and get her in a cell, please. I'll be there soon."

The officer nodded; the cuffs clicked on one after the other, and Evette sneered at her.

Madigan held John's hand in hers as the officer led Evette to the door. "I'll be sure to tell him everything when he wakes up," Madigan called to her.

Evette turned her head away and shuffled out of the room with the officer.

Tears ran down Madigan's cheeks as she stared down at John.

I'm so sorry.

Grace's arms wrapped around her before she knew it.

"You're fine," Grace said.

"I'm not right now," Madigan whispered.

"I know," Grace said, hugging her tightly. "But you always will be."

EPILOGUE

Grace strode down the rocky footpath and onto the beach where Madigan sat on their rock with her legs tucked up by her chest.

When she sits like that, she still looks like she did when we were little, the tough kid who protected me, made me feel brave and never stopped.

The wind whipped her hair across her face, and as if feeling Grace's presence, Madigan turned her head. Grace waved, and Madigan waved back. She navigated her way over the smaller rocks, and Madigan reached down to help her.

Grace grabbed her cool hand and climbed onto the rock, taking a seat beside her and crossing her legs. They sat in silence, letting the breeze sweep through their hair, breathing in the salty air.

She's worried about John.

His physical therapy began in November, which meant not only was he getting better, but he would be fit for trial the following spring.

"Have you been to see him today?" Grace asked.

Madigan nodded.

"I'd like to go with you one time," Grace said. "After the trials."

Madigan nodded, but her stoic expression remained.

Between wrapping up Lily Martin's case and Valerie Hall's cold case, Grace had decided to keep her distance from John. She would be called to stand trial as a witness and official for both cases, and Mac's fears that her personal connections to each case might muddy the waters in court had become her fears too.

She told herself she had enough to worry about without developing a personal relationship with John, but it hadn't stopped Madigan from seeing him at least once a week for the past two months since he'd been in the hospital recovering from his gunshot wound.

"He's still trying to piece together what went on with Mickey and Lily that night," Madigan said. "He asks me my opinion on these scenarios he cooks up. He spends too much time alone. He has too much time to think."

"Did you tell him about Evette yet?" Grace asked.

They both knew he'd find out the general details of her arrest in the newspapers and on the local TV stations, but they agreed Madigan should wait until he asked to provide the specifics.

Madigan nodded. "He usually tries to convince me she couldn't have—wouldn't have done that to him. Or to Valerie. This morning, he looked at me, and I knew he knew."

"Just like that?"

"He was shaking," Madigan said. "Just like I was."

"You and John had a lot in common when it came to her. It's good that you can be there for each other."

Madigan nodded and turned to face her. "You think he's a bad person, don't you?" she asked. "Because he buried Valerie and covered it up for all that time."

Grace shook her head.

Madigan stared at her, and then as if convinced, she let her shoulders droop.

"I want to get to know him," Grace said. "I just need time."

"Of course."

Waves crashed against the rocks beneath them, and a cool mist sprayed Grace's face.

"Madigan," she said. "What's up? I know there's something else."

Madigan licked her lips.

"I can't help but think about what would have happened if I'd called you when I should have. If I'd never gone to see John and help him get away from the lodge."

"You don't know what would have happened, and you can't torture yourself over it," Grace said. "Trust me—it doesn't help."

Madigan pulled her hair over her shoulder, and Grace rubbed her back in small circles.

"I should have trusted you," Madigan muttered just loud enough to hear over the crashing waves.

"I could say the same," Grace said and pulled her hand away.

If I'd listened to her instincts about Joe Harris, it could have come together sooner.

Maybe no one would have gotten hurt.

Madigan turned to her. "You followed through on your promise to me," she said. "I'm the one who went behind your back."

"We can't go back," Grace said.

"I know." Madigan sighed. "I just wish we knew for sure who broke into your home and attacked me."

John had been under watch at the time, and Joe Harris seemed confused when questioned about the break-in. Neither had any bite marks from Buster, and no other suspects had been considered, but Grace had a suspicion she kept to herself.

Mickey might have sent someone to threaten me or kill me.

Mac volunteered to take a deeper look into the investigation into Mickey Clarke, but no one talked—a rare occurrence between officers of the law.

Mickey Clarke might really be untouchable, but if I find out he sent someone to hurt me and my sister, I'll make him pay.

"You know I won't stop looking," Grace said.

"I know." Madigan sat up and crossed her legs under her as Grace had. "I heard that Lily's mom plead guilty too."

It finally leaked.

"I guess her guilty conscience got the best of her when her husband was ready to take the fall alone," Grace said.

"She did the right thing. They both deserve to pay for what they put John through. For what they did to Lily."

Grace recalled the night she and Mac went to their home to deliver the news about Lily the Martins already knew.

Mrs. Martin was devastated, just as she should have been, and Mr. Martin was angry.

I wish there was something I should have noticed sooner, besides Chris's prints on the vase she gave her daughter, which they ultimately fought over, sending Lily falling back and hitting her head against the table.

"I believe it was an accident," Grace said.

"John forgives them."

"You sound surprised."

Madigan stared out over the water. "They have to live with their demons like we all do."

"But we don't have to do it alone," Grace said.

Madigan nodded. "I saw that picture you have framed in your bedroom now when I borrowed your top the other day. That's Leah, right?"

"Yeah. Having her there reminds me of the good times. Of the good I was trying to do. That I still have left to do."

She had thrown the binder away the day Evette was arrested.

The past is never what it seems. Not even our own memories accurately process everything we've been through.

Time and other experiences warp the facts.

Secrets and lies distort whatever truth we thought we knew to begin with, but each experience leaves us with a feeling. Some complex—feelings at odds with each other—but they're the way we truly remember things.

I want the feeling Leah has left to be one of love and friendship. One of hope and inspiration.

I'll never forget those things, and I'll keep trying to help those who need it in her memory.

Madigan draped her arm across Grace's back, grabbing hold of her shoulder. Grace smiled and did the same with her arm.

"So—what's next?" Grace asked.

* * *

"I'd say we should go for a drink," Madigan said, "but I don't want to go to work earlier than I have to."

She had barely finished asking Roy for her job as bartender back when he welcomed her with open arms. The job had changed since she'd held the position in college, or rather she had changed.

Bartending in her thirties was a whole different experience, but it wasn't the only job she had. During her night shifts at the bar, she mulled over her case.

After visiting John for the first time since he awoke from his induced coma, his roommate at the hospital overheard them talking about what they had been through over the week before he'd been shot.

After John had bragged about her behind her back about the way she put things together, the roommate had asked if she'd look into his past for him. He too, had been adopted, but his wish had always been to find his birth parents. After coming close to death with a bad case of pneumonia, he decided it was important enough to hire someone to do the digging for him.

Before Madigan agreed to help, she conferred with Grace, who to her surprise, encouraged her to not only investigate, but to look into becoming a private investigator. She still considered the latter, but took the roommate's case seriously.

"We could just go home and have one," Grace said. "I'll drive you to work after."

Madigan smiled and nodded.

"You know I ran into Will the other day at the hospital?"

"Really?" Grace opened her eyes wide and grinned. "Awkward or nice?"

"Still weird." Madigan smiled. "But it doesn't hurt anymore. Seems like he'll move on soon if he hasn't already. You should see the attention he gets from the nurses."

"I believe it. I think you made the right choice too."

It's hard to give up on love, whether it's meant for you or not.

She still missed Will from time to time, but as weeks turned into months, she realized it wasn't so much Will she missed but the way he treated her.

The way it felt to be wanted and loved.

That's why John and I were so blinded by Evette.

She'd been mad at herself since that day in the hospital room for giving her trust to someone who had hurt her in the past, who had done so much damage to so many. Who had never truly been there for her, but she'd made herself believe it was enough. That it was all she was worth.

"You think she'll ever admit to what she did?" Madigan asked.

Grace turned to her.

You know who I'm talking about. I refuse to say her name anymore—to give that woman any more of my energy.

"No," Grace said and sighed. "But we know the truth."

Madigan nodded.

Good enough?

Maybe it had to be.

"You had her number all along," Madigan said. "I was so stupid."

"Nope, I won't let you say that about yourself. You just didn't want to see the truth. Seeing her again after all those years, I didn't really want to either if it makes you feel any better?"

Sometimes it's more difficult to see the good in people than the bad.

It used to be easier for me, but not anymore.

We'd gaze out our window on Warbler Way, wishing that one day we'd be here.

Here we are.

"Things were supposed to be better here," Madigan muttered. "Why did we think our lives would be so much better across the bay?"

The offshore breeze tousled their hair, sending shivers down her spine. Grace licked her lips and shook her head, shoving her hands into her coat pockets.

"I'm cold, too," Madigan said. "Let's go home."

Grace pulled her hand out of her pocket and along with it came the matching necklace Madigan had hung on the tree that night. She took Madigan's hand and dropped it into her palm, squeezing her hand closed tightly around it.

We'll always find each other.

ACKNOWLEDGMENTS

Thank you to my formatter and dear friend, Jade Eby, and my cover designer, Amy Queau of Q Design, for the exceptional visual components of this novel. To Roxane Leblanc, for your proofreading and insights, I thank you. To Mountains Wanted Publishing for your exceptional editing and second pair of eyes, I'm so grateful for your help.

I have an immense amount of appreciation for my beta-readers: Jade Eby and Kim Catanzarite. Your opinions and insights are invaluable. Thank you for challenging and supporting me during this process. You've each been a catalyst for my growth as a writer through this story. I feel fortunate and proud to have worked with you both.

To Shawna Gavas, Heather McGurk, and J.C. Hannigan, for your input on special components of this novel when I needed it most, thank you.

Thank you to my early readers for joining my team and your interest in Madigan and Grace's story.

To my colleagues in the book community for "getting me". Thank you for your support, encouragement, and sharing your knowledge with me. I'm proud to call you my friends.

For the continued support of my family, friends, and husband. I am forever grateful and I love you all.

Each and every person in my life who has supported me and my writing career hold a special place in my heart.

Thank you to my true-blue readers and my reader group on Facebook for sticking with me, for your curiosity, and for your company on this journey. From the bottom of my heart, I'm honored to share this experience with you.

ABOUT THE AUTHOR

Emerald O'Brien was born and raised just east of Toronto, Ontario. She graduated from her Television Broadcasting and Communications Media program at Mohawk College in Hamilton, Ontario.

As the author of unpredictable stories packed with suspense, Emerald enjoys connecting with her passionate readers.

When she is not reading or writing, Emerald can be found with family and friends. Watching movies with her husband and snuggling with their two beagles is one of her favourite ways to spend an evening at home.

To find out more, visit Emerald on her website: http://emeraldobrien.com

If you enjoyed Emerald's work, please share your experience by leaving a review where you purchased the story.

Subscribe to her newsletter for a free ebook, exclusive content, and information about current and upcoming works: http://www.emeraldobrien.com/your-free-ebook/

ALSO BY EMERALD

Don't miss these suspenseful and unpredictable reads:

The Duet

Darkness Follows

Shadows Remain

• • •

The Avery Hart Trilogy

Lies Come True (Book One)

Bare Your Bones (Book Two)

Every Last Mark (Book Three)

The Complete Avery Hart Trilogy

• • •

Standalone

Closer

• • •

The Knox and Sheppard Mysteries

The Girls Across the Bay (Book One)

Book 2 coming in 2018

ABOUT THE AUTHOR

Emerald O'Brien was born and raised just east of Toronto, Ontario. She graduated from her Television Broadcasting and Communications Media program at Mohawk College in Hamilton, Ontario. As the author of unpredictable stories packed with suspense, Emerald enjoys connecting with her readers who are passionate about joining characters as they solve mysteries and take exciting adventures between the pages of great books.

When she is not reading or writing, Emerald can be found with family and friends. Watching movies with her husband and their two beagles is one of her favourite ways to spend an evening at home.

To find out more, visit Emerald on her website:
http://emeraldobrien.com

If you enjoyed Emerald's work, please share your experience by leaving a review where you purchased the story.

Made in the USA
Middletown, DE
21 July 2020